DANE BROWN

FROM DOLLAR$ TO SENS⬚
DANE BROWN

EDIFYING SEEDS PUBLICATIONS
1942 N 5th Street, Harrisburg, PA 17110, USA
Copyright ©2017 by Dane Brown
ISBN-13: 978-0692796979
ISBN-10: 0692796975
Cover Design by Mitanni Media

PUBLISHER'S NOTE:

FROM DOLLAR$ TO SENSE
DANE BROWN

Dedications

I would like to dedicate this book to the beautiful souls of my Great Grandmother Fanny G. Buck and my Grandmother Elizabeth Thompson. The two women who instilled morals, principles, integrity, and values in me that I live and die by 'til this day. I would also like to dedicate this book to my two cousins Darryl *"D-Boy"* Evans Jr. and Warren *"Beez"* Beasley (The realest to ever lace up a pair of Gucci shoes). May they rest in peace. And most importantly I'd like to dedicate this book to my son Dane Brown Jr., who made a man out of a savage. I love you more than this world could define.

FROM DOLLAR$ TO SENS❓

The Prologue

The Makings of a Storm

"Love is the most powerful and compelling beauty in all the world. But when it feels betrayed, its wonder, hopes and dreams fade into darkness of existence. How wonderful it is to love and be loved. Yet how sad it is to lose the light of the heart. If love comes to be truthful and upright, you shall see beauty that is a wonder and a wonder that is the heart of life."

-Rahman Shadi

1984

Standing there looking ecstatically at the item in her hands, Ashley almost dropped the home pregnancy test in the toilet from excitement as she pictured having a beautiful child and family with the love of her life, Tanell.

Walking from the bathroom towards their room, she was wearing only his navy-blue Nike t-shirt. She entered the room, Tanell was laid across the bed in his plaid boxer briefs.

"Boo I got a surprise for you," said Ashley, unable to contain her excitement. Still concealing the pregnancy test behind her back while walking in a seductive manner towards Tanell.

"And what would that be sexy?" Tanell responded. While turning over onto his back he noticed her seductive walk and juicy bare thighs. His only thought was that hopefully the surprise had something to do with some good love making. Little did he know how close he was to the truth.

"Boo I'm pregnant," Ashley said as she straddled him.

"Yeah?!" He exclaimed and questioned simultaneously. Tanell was genuinely surprised as he stared at the positive sign on the home pregnancy test she was waving in his face excitedly.

"You happy boo?"

"Of course," he quickly answered, relieving himself of the initial shock as he removed the pregnancy test from her hands, placing it on the small dresser beside the bed.

"Ash you know I love you more than anything."

"I love you so much too," she responded in a hushed tone as he then lifted his T-shirt from over her head and commenced to laying wet kisses from the nape of her neck down to her shoulders and chest then to her succulent breasts. Continuous

foreplay ensued between the two of them which led to a session of passionate lovemaking.

Tanell and Ashley both collapsed onto the bed afterward as she recovered from spasms and he from a loss of breath, thanks to the best love making either one of them had ever experienced in their lives. They fell asleep cuddled in each other's arms.

Tanell awoke at approximately 4 am. As always, he was being prematurely awakened by an episode of reoccurring nightmares stemming from his troubled past. He laid on his back staring at the ceiling in silence. His eyes were oblivious to the décor above him, they were focused intently inwardly on memories that troubled him. As he glanced to his left, and noticed the aura of peace surrounding Ashley, he was reminded of the news she had just given him and he reflected on what it meant for their future.

Tanell had fallen deeply in love with Ashley although he had not been looking for, nor did he have any intentions on finding love when he moved to Harrisburg, Pennsylvania from his hometown of Baltimore, Maryland. The only reason he had moved to Harrisburg was an investigation he was facing for numerous crimes in his hometown. He found himself in Pennsylvania's capital city with a simple plan to get money the best way he knew how…by any means necessary!

Yet after he was there a little over two months, one day he walked into the record store on 7th street in the uptown plaza to buy the new *Slick*

Rick Record. That's when he first laid eyes on her.
In Tanell's imaginative mind, Ashley resembled a
young version of Pam Grier in her prime, without
the edge of Foxy Brown. Standing at 5 foot 6 inches
in her voluptuous frame. Ashley had been wearing a
form fitting blue denim skirt, a red and white striped
form fitting Phillies baseball jersey with the top two
buttons unbuttoned showing off her cleavage. She
wore her hair in that era's eighty styled bouffant
hairdo with a bang in the front. Donning big gold
door-knocker, horse shoe shaped earrings in her
ears, she appeared to be Urban Royalty.

Acting as if he was really paying attention to
the array of records in the store, Tanell secretly
observed her. Paying special attention to her
demeanor and attitude towards customers. He
noticed that even though you could tell she was
hood, she had an innocence that intrigued him.

"Wa 'sup sis," spoke Tanell to Ashley as he
approached the counter where she stood behind a
cash register.

"Nothing, can I help you with anything?"
she replied nonchalantly, looking up from the
Donald Goines book she was reading.

*"Yeah I'm looking to buy these two albums
here and I could use some help in getting to know
you so your name and number would be a good
start,"* Tanell responded smoothly, a sly smirk
resting in the corner of his lips.

*"The two albums come to eighteen dollars
altogether but sorry I can't help you with your other*

problem," she retorted back with her own impish smirk.

"I figured you'd make it hard on me," responded Tanell, smiling as he handed her a twenty-dollar bill, grabbing the two albums off the counter to leave.

Ashley was used to guys hitting on her all the time but she had made up her mind years ago that she had no time for men. She was too busy in her senior year at high school trying to get a scholarship. Where afterwards she planned to attend Alabama A&M and take up journalism as her major. So, when men hit on her as they always did, she would do the best she could to turn them down respectfully and Tanell would be no different.

There was a difference however. Tanell appealed to her better interest unlike any other man as he stood there smiling at her. She couldn't help but notice his mesmerizing smile with perfect white teeth on his handsome chocolate face. He stood approximately 6'2" and weighed maybe one hundred and ninety pounds she calculated as she admired his basketball player physic. He was wearing his black *Kangol* backwards on his head with a smoke gray M.C.M. jean suit covering his frame and black B.K. shoe boots on his feet. He also donned a gold rope necklace with a gold pendant shaped as the African continent around his neck. Instantly she could tell he was a street dude whom she usually never gave an inkling of a chance. She was well aware of what came with dating one. Yet and still there was an instant undeniable attraction to Tanell.

Later that day when Ashley returned home from work her mother informed her that a vase filled with 2 dozen roses was delivered for her a couple hours prior. Along with a small package and card. Wondering where it could have come from, Ashley grabbed the vase off the kitchen counter top, lifting the beautiful roses to her nose. She then opened the small package, revealing a book titled *Black Gangster* by Donald Goines. Confused, she then opened the "Thinking of You" card and read:

Dear Ms. Ashley Storm,

I hope you like the book. I noticed you was reading Black Girl Lost by Donald Goines earlier at work when you couldn't help me with your name and number (smile). Whereas now we both know we already have one thing in common because I'm a big fan of Mr. Goines myself. Actually, I've read all his books.

Hopefully you haven't already read this one but regardless it's my favorite

*because I can relate to it somewhat so
therefore I sent it to you. By now hopefully
you see there's nothing subtle about me,
that's why I'm hoping you'll take me up on
my offer for a dinner date. You can reach
me at 555-0432.*

*Sincerely,
Tanell*

"*Black Gangster,*" Ashley thought to herself
as she finished reading the card.

"*How did he get my address and name?*"
she questioned, noticing how quick he did his
homework on her. She couldn't deny she liked his
brashness and persistence so she waited three days
and called to take him up on his dinner offer. He
soon won her heart with his self-assurance and
attentive respect for her and her wishes. As she also
simultaneously captured his heart with her non-
judgmental loyalty to him and her passion for a
better future.

Now here they lay a year and a half later
with a child on the way. Ashley opened her eyes
and noticed Tanell staring at the ceiling with his
hands behind his head.

"*What you thinking about baby?*" she asked
him.

"Nothing boo, just baby names, " he answered, looking over at her with a smile on his face.

The next night at approximately 10:30 p.m., Tanell was shutting the door to the apartment building where he and Ashley shared an apartment two buildings down from Ashley's mother's building.

"Wa' sup dawg, " hollered Marcus through the window from inside his car.

"Man ain't nuthin, wa'sup, " responded Tanell as he commenced to entering Marcus' car and giving him a pound.

"Man what's up wit you, I've been trying reach you since yesterday morning. "

Tanell then without saying anything sat back in his seat with a forlorn expression on his face and sighed as Marcus began cruising.

"Yo! Wa'sup wit you dawg, you alright? "

Marcus was Tanell's best and only friend in the world. They grew up together on the west side of Baltimore in the Park Heights neighborhood. The two had been hanging together since they were 11 years old, becoming almost inseparable over the years. Mostly because they had become all the family either one of them truly had left. Marcus grew up in foster homes and group homes all throughout Maryland until he moved to Park Heights with Mrs. Etna down the block from Tanell. Tanell lived with his older and younger sisters along with their mother who was on heroine and hardly ever home. Eventually Tanell started *hustling* the same drug his mother was addicted to when he was only 12 years old with Marcus as his partner in crime.

They were soon deeply involved in the streets and by the age of 15 were doing *anything* by *any means* to get a dollar. By that age they were already desensitized to violence from seeing it as a regular occurrence throughout their formative years. Therefore, they both grew to be extremely violent, doing whatever it took to procure an abundance of the almighty dollar.

Tanell and Marcus shared the same aspirations to make it out of their poverty-stricken ghetto. Using the game as a conduit to live *want free* for the rest of their lives after being deprived of basic living necessities since birth. They soon trusted no one but each other and had experienced everything together from their first sexual conquest to their first act of violence - a corner store robbery on the East Side of Baltimore.

Within the next three years by the time they were 18, Tanell and Marcus had a major part of the heroine trade in west Baltimore *on lock*. Murphy Homes Projects was their biggest Cash Cow. Everything was going good until Tanell got caught in a police chase with twelve bricks of heroine on his way to make a drop off to one of his young workers. He ended up getting two years in the Maximum-Security Prison of *Jessup* in Jessup, Maryland. Marcus kept in touch the entire time, sending Tanell plenty money orders, pictures and novels by his favorite author Donald Goines.

When Tanell was released he fell right back in with Marcus like he never missed a second in the streets. Until they got word from a crooked cop that the local police force was looking to indict them, getting the FED's involved.

Marcus quickly and arrogantly blew the crooked cop off but Tanell never wanting to go back to prison. He immediately decided that it was time for them to leave home and change their locale. With Marcus reluctantly obliging they soon packed up and took I-83 north until they reached a city called Harrisburg, Pennsylvania. Pennsylvania's quaint capital city appeared to be a good place to make money.

Their plan was to stay there no longer than a year and move on to the next town until they made enough money to live want free on South Beach in Miami, Florida. That was until Tanell fell in love with Ashley and Marcus fell in love in with the town's cash flow, getting complacent as he always did.

Leaning back in the passenger seat of Marcus' '84 Volvo, Tanell rubbed his face and sighed before exclaiming, *"Man, Ash is pregnant."*

"Yo word!?"

"Yeah man."

"So why you stressing it yo? That's a good thing, right? Ash is a good girl and you love her right?"

"It's not that man."

"Then what is it yo? Cause you starting to annoy me wit this somber shit," said Marcus while lighting the joint he had in the ashtray.

"Man fuck you and pass the "J" before I get annoyed."

"Fo'real though what's wrong with you? Cause that's supposed to be good news for you dawg," said Marcus, passing Tanell the joint.

"Man it's just that I ain't trying bring no kid in this world and not be there for it."

"And what's that supposed to mean?"

"That means I ain't trying have a kid living the way we live and end up leaving Ash to raise the kid alone."

"Who said she gone have to raise the kid alone?"

"Man you know what comes with living the way we live and I ain't trying leave my woman with raising our child alone while I'm sitting in prison or worse, dead," replied Tanell with hint of indignation.

"So I've been thinking."

"You've been thinking what?" Marcus quickly shot back.

"I've been thinking it's time for me to be done with this life and you too."

"Man do you hear yaself?" What we gone do? Cause we ain't got enough money to just walk away and I don't know nothing else and neither do you."

"I understand, that's why I'm figuring we cash out. I figure if we hit a couple good stings with the money we already got, we should be able to just walk away and move to South Beach and open a club like we planned."

"OK now you making sense. Sounds like a plan," said Marcus in between his final two puffs of the joint.

"Damn though dawg, this new era crack money was just start to feel good."

"Yeah but now instead of waiting for it to come to us to get rich, we go take it and get rich quicker."

"Now you sound more like my main man T. You had me worried for a second dawg," responded Marcus, mischievously grinning at Tanell as he pulled into the parking lot of *Shadow* nightclub on Market Street in the Allison Hill section.

"Yeah whatever, you ain't never got to worry bout me chump. You just worry about setting up some stings where we can make the money we're

looking for," countered Tanell, shutting the door to Marcus' Volvo and walking towards the nightclub.

"Yeah I got it man but back to the good news, my main playa bout to have a kid. We gotta celebrate dawg," said Marcus, throwing his arm around his friend's neck as they made their way inside the club.

The club was packed with women and men from the front to the very back as Marcus and Tanell entered. The nightclub was the happening spot of the times. Where everybody from the main playa's in the street to the sexiest women in town frequented the club every weekend. Loud hip hop blasted from the speakers around the club the second Tanell and Marcus stepped in as the D.J. continuously yelled crowd movers into the mic like *"put ya hands up!"*.

The club had a big oval shaped bar positioned in the middle with a dance floor in the back where the D.J. was located in the far-left corner up in a booth. There was a small numbers table in the far-right corner with purple, red, and white strobe lights flashing in the darkness throughout the entire club.

Tanell and Marcus made their way to the middle of the club slapping hands and giving pounds along the way. In route to the bar, they also got evil eyes and hate filled stares from guys who didn't particularly care for them because they were from out of town and because of the money they were seeing in town. Most of the people there knew who Tanell and Marcus were because they had become major players in the game in the last year. Especially since crack had hit the town and them being two of the first to introduce the highly addictive drug to the town.

Sitting in one of the booths located in the far-right corner of the club was Smooth. Smooth's loathe for the duo was evident as he disdainfully stared at the two making their way through the club. His hate for Tanell and Marcus started a year ago when they first started moving valves of crack in the McClay St. apartments area where Smooth controlled the cocaine flow from Peffer to Woodbine Streets. His hate for them escalated when they joined in on a dice game he was participating in and winning. They joined in on the game of trips and broke the pot, leaving with $4,600 of Smooth's money and $11,000 of the other five players money. In his anger, Smooth accused the two of cheating with loaded dice, though none of the losers could prove it.

Now as Smooth sat there contemptuously staring at the two, he came to the conclusion that something had to be done about those two thorns in his side. Meanwhile as Marcus was scanning the club, he noticed Smooth's hate filled stare directed right at him and Tanell. Marcus's omnipresent mischievous smile appeared, stretching the surface of this face, as he raised his bottle of Moet' towards Smooth while simultaneously telling the bartender to send a couple of bottles back to Smooth courtesy of he and Tanell. Marcus then turned towards Tanell who met his eyes after noticing everything that had just taken place. They both then ambiguously smiled, knowing their larcenous question had been answered. Since they knew from their reconnaissance on Smooth that he'd been hustling for years and is supposedly sitting on an abundance of old money.

$¢

"Can you feel her kicking baby?" Ashley asked Tanell as he lay beside her on the couch rubbing her stomach that held their eight-and-a-half-month old fetus.

"Yeah I can feel him kicking; I told you we having a boy," he happily answered.

"No boo I'm telling you we have a beautiful little girl. I mean I would know, I am the one carrying her."

"Nah boo I'm letting you know we having a boy, that's why we should have just let them tell us what we having. So, you would know for sure like I been telling you, we having a boy."

"Whatever, it's gone be a surprise but I'm telling you we are having a girl."

"Nah it's a boy."

"Alright if it's a boy, did you come up with a name yet? Because I still want to name it Tanell Jr. if it's a boy."

"And I already told you Ashley, I don't want my son to be Tanell Jr. because I never really liked my name."

"Why don't you like your name? Cause I think it's cute."

"That's exactly why I never liked my name cause girls always thought it was cute but growing up the boys always said it was girly so I got into a lot of fights over it. I don't want my lil man going through that."

"Aww did they hurt da little boy's feelings?" quipped Ashley in a childish voice while playfully rubbing his face.

"Yeah whatever girl," replied a smiling Tanell as he pulled her into his warm embrace and kissed her neck.

"All I know is you better come up with a name then if it's a boy and you still want to name him because you ain't just naming our baby anything. But then again we don't really have to worry about that, do we? Because we're having a beautiful little girl and I'm naming her Arielle," Ashley said as she nestled into his embrace and started drifting off to sleep.

One hour and forty-five minutes later, the piercing ring of the phone awoke Tanell and Ashley from their comfortable slumber. Ashley, reading the time off the clock, noticed it was 11: 36 p.m. and wondered who would be calling at that time of night. Whereas Tanell casually retrieved the phone and answered it.

"*Hello?*'

"*Wa'sup playa, tonight's the night,*" spoke Marcus from the other end of the line.

"*Alright give me a minute to get ready then meet me in the back alley by Emerald Park.*"

"*Alright I'll meet you there it twenty minutes,*" said Marcus just before he hung up the phone as Tanell headed for the bedroom with Ashley in tow.

"*Who was that?*" she asked while leaning against the door frame to their bedroom.

"*Marcus; look boo we got something we need to take care of. I'll be back in about an hour but I promise this is it Ash', after this I'm done!*" Tanell answered, meeting her stare after putting on his black cargo pants and lacing up his black on black 6-inch leather Timberlands.

Ashley took notice of his attire and sensed danger. Wanting to voice her apprehension, she decided against it reasoning it would be futile. So, she decided to let him go and hold him to his word. Tanell had been telling her for month's that he would be done with the game soon and tonight he had gone as far as to make a promise that this was it. Her heart wanted to trust him, her intuition spawned fear.

"Alright boo, you better be back in an hour. Tell Marcus I'm mad at him for this and don't you forget you just promised me this is it…" she said while walking towards him.

"This is it baby, trust me, I love you girl." he replied after draping his black Champion hoody over his head. He then grabbed her into his arms and engaged her in a passionate kiss.

"I love you too boo. Be careful." she responded in between breaths from their passion filled tongue lapping.

"No worries boo, I'll be back in an hour." he assured her as he kissed her on the lips for the last time before leaving their apartment.

Chapter 1

The eye of the Storm

"The eye which sees smoke will look for fire."
-African Proverb

1993

It was 6:25 a.m. and as usual nine-year-old Ryat was up before everybody else in the house. He was sitting in front of the television watching cartoons as he did every Saturday morning. This was no typical Saturday morning however. The typically jovial spirit sparked by anthropomorphic cartoon characters and floating marshmallow treasures was violently disrupted by a loud banging on the door and clamorous noise just outside the front window. Ryat immediately got up to go see what it was although his grandmother told him to never answer the door. Pulling the curtain back from the window, he was immediately paralyzed in fear as he stared down the barrel of a .9 mm semi-automatic handgun.

"How the fuck do you get in here?" barked the big black detective who carelessly pointed his gun at the innocent child.

With an assortment of police and detectives behind him, the detective and his backup were angry because their attempt at busting down the big metal apartment door didn't work. Therefore, their element of surprise was botched. Meanwhile little Ryat looked on with trepidation as they unbeknownst to them were robbing him of his quintessence. All the while, the child's mind kept telling him to run, duck, or hide as he stared at the big black man pointing a gun at him. Yet his state of shock rendered him physically helpless as his body wouldn't respond to his brain from being paralyzed by fear.

Hearing the commotion, Ryat's grandmother was appalled by what she saw when she entered her living room.

"WHAT THE HELL IS GOING ON HERE?" she yelled at the detective pointing the gun as she stood there holding her beige robe together while shielding her petrified grandson behind her back.

"How the fuck do you get in here?" barked the detective, reiterating what he had just barked at the innocent child.

"Well give me a minute goddammit!" replied Ryat's grandmother as she opened her first-floor apartment door and preceded in opening the front door to the apartment building where her

26

entire immediate family occupied the three-floor apartment building. Located on the twenty-one hundred block of North 5th street. Mrs. Eve Storm lived on the first floor with her 23-year-old son Ray and her 9-year-old grandson Ryat. Her daughter Anita lived in the second floor apartment while her astray husband Carl lived in third floor apartment. Although she and her husband were separated due to his addiction, they still maintained a platonic relationship.

Immediately after unlocking the dead-bolt lock on the apartment door, Mrs. Eve was thrown against the wall as a squadron of police officers and detectives in tactical gear stampeded past her. They were headed straight for the second-floor apartment, as a petrified young Ryat stood motionless looking at the commotion in the hallway from the living room of his grandmother's first floor apartment.

"CAN SOMEBODY PLEASE TELL ME WHAT THE HELL IS GOING ON HERE?" hollered Mrs. Eve into the backs of the squadron of police and detectives that just stormed past her.

"We have a warrant for arrest for a Mr. Tyron Crosby. He is wanted in conspiracy to the murder of a police officer and he is believed to have been hiding out in the second-floor apartment of this building." said one of the officers in tactical gear as he turned around to show Mrs. Eve the warrant.

"Oh my lord!" exclaimed Mrs. Eve with her right hand over her mouth as she looked at the

warrant in the officer's hand. She now realized they were there to arrest her daughter's boyfriend for the heinous crime she'd been reading about in the papers and watching on the news for the last four days.

"*I didn't do it... I didn't do it... I swear it wasn't me!*" cried out Tyron as the squadron of police and detectives lead him out the door of the second-floor apartment.

"*Oh my Lord!*" exclaimed Mrs. Eve again as she stared at what was taking place right before her eyes. Simultaneously, little Ryat regained control of his physical extremities, quickly taking refuge behind his grandmothers back.

Looking from behind his grandmother's back, Ryat also took notice of what made his grandmother yelp as he was again put in a state of shock and paralyzed by fear. The squadron of police and detectives in tactical gear were destroying Tyron right before their eyes.

"*I didn't do it!...Please, I didn't do it!...Somebody help me!*" cried out Tyron.

"*Shut up motherfucker; you like killing cops huh?... Well how you like this, you piece of shit...huh? How you like this motherfucker?*" barked one of the white police officers in tactical gear as he repeatedly slammed Tyron's head and face into a big pipe in the middle of the hallway causing immediate swelling on Tyron's face and head.

Throughout the entire physical castigation of Tyron, there was no more sight more malicious and frightening upon young Ryat's eyes than the sight of Tyron standing there butt-naked, battered, and bruised begging for his life. All while a squadron of police and detectives took turns beating away at his body as they lead him out of the apartment building.

"Stop that...stop that you racist muthafuckers; he didn't do shit! Let him go, yall got the wrong one!" yelled Anita as young Ryat watched his aunt chase behind the squadron, pleading for them to stop their abuse of her presumed innocent boyfriend.

"Girl cut that shit out and calm your ass down before they arrest your ass too. There's nothing you can do to help that boy right now." said Mrs. Eve to her daughter as she grabbed her arm, preventing her from continuing to chase behind the squadron yelling obscenities.

Outside the apartment building the episode continued as Ryat watched the police continue their trouncing of Tyron as they threw him butt-naked and handcuffed down the concrete steps. All the while a nosy crowd formed around the building also witnessing the malicious treatment the police were exacting upon Tyron.

"NO that ain't right... that ain't right! Yall can't do that to that man like that!" yelled a heavyset woman from the crowd.

"Yall gone kill that man. This ain't justice, he innocent till proven guilty but yall won't be

satisfied til ya kill us all!" yelled an elderly black man from the crowd.

Meanwhile young Ryat stood by watching as people from the crowd made various outburst directed at the police for their malfeasance and the unjust beating they were delivering to Tyron. The officers however were careless or oblivious to the outburst and epithets directed at them as they undauntedly continued in their physical castigation of Tyron. With little Ryat looking on they threw a debilitated and unclothed Tyron in the back of one of their squad car's as if he was a heap of dirty clothes.

Right then 9-year-old Ryat was no longer petrified as he was overcome with a feeling he did not understand. Staring at the big black detective who had carelessly pointed a gun at him, his quintessence was subverted with a kindling rage.

Later that night as little Ryat got ready to go to sleep, his grandmother sat beside him on his bed right after he got under his blanket.

"What's wrong baby?" she asked him.

"Nothing." he curtly replied.

"Come on Rye baby, you know you can tell your Nana what's wrong and don't lie because I know when something's wrong with you. You've been extremely quiet and withdrawn since what happened this morning. So come on baby and tell your Nana what's wrong."

"I hate cops!"

"Don't you say that; you hear me? Don't you ever let me hear you say you hate anyone. You can't go around hating a whole group of people because one or a few of them are bad or not the right kind of people, you hear me? So don't you ever let me hear you say you hate people, OK?"

"Yes ma'am, but what if they hate me? Cause Mr. Jackson from across the street said they won't be happy until they kill us all."

"Aww they don't hate you baby and they all don't hate us. Now it is true that some of them hate people that are not like them but that don't give you an excuse to hate all of them because when you hate people or a person it only makes you a worst person because that hate you feel only affects you in a negative way and not the person or people you hate because most likely that person or people don't even know you hate them or they just don't care. As for Mr. Jackson, he has dealt with a lot of hate towards him in his lifetime to where it has made him see things differently. Which you will understand a lot more when you get older."

"But why did they try to kill auntie Nita's boyfriend?"

"I don't believe they were actually trying to kill your aunt's boyfriend but I do believe what they did was extremely wrong. But baby they believe your aunt's boyfriend did something extremely wrong. Which is no excuse for what they did to him but you just learn from that and don't do nothing

*wrong so you don't have to deal with evil cops or
go to jail, OK baby?"*

"OK Nana."

*"Now you go ahead and get your sleep for
school tomorrow. I love you baby, good night."* said
Mrs. Eve as she hugged him through his covers and
kissed him on his cheek.

"I love you too nana, good night," replied
little Ryat, smiling at his grandmother as she left his
room. Unbeknownst to her, the affect that day's
events had on his young mind as he turned over to
go to sleep was a loss of innocence that could never
be recaptured.

CHAPTER 2

*"Out of suffering have emerged the strongest souls;
the most massive characters are seared with
scars."*
-Kahlil Gibran

...1984

Twenty minutes past midnight Tanell and Marcus were sitting in a 1976 navy blue Ford Thunderbird. They were parked behind the Italian Lake Apartments in a parking lot adjacent to one of the many places Smooth resided. Tanell and Marcus had really done their homework on Smooth over the months prior and from the information they dug up on him, they learned that out of all the places he rested his head, this was where he supposedly stashed the bulk of his illegal currency. After furtively studying his goings and comings, they became familiar with his schedule.

Having had prior opportunities to move on him in the past six months, they didn't because of

Tanell's soft spot for children. Therefore, he refused
to rob Smooth while his small son and the mother of
the child whom lived in the apartment with him,
were home. So, they waited until that night since
they knew the child and its mother were in Virginia
visiting her mother. Smooth on the other hand had
been holed up in the apartment for the last two days
conducting business. Whereas to be expected from
his usual schedule, they knew he should exit the
apartment at exactly half past midnight to replenish
his workers narcotics supply and pick up from them
that day's monetary intake. Knowing this, Tanell
and Marcus pulled their black ski masks' over their
faces. Put on their black leather gloves and with
weapons in hand, they crept against the hedges
along the pathway that lead to Smooth's residence.

 Within seconds, Smooth emerged through
the doorway - brown paper bag in hand. He was met
by Marcus' .45 caliber handgun, which greeted his
left temple and Tanell's two .357 revolvers, which
sent salutations to his right temple. Smooth was
instantaneously frozen in place. He stood there in
shock, afraid to move a muscle.

 In an attempt at chicanery to disguise their
voices as native Harrisburg denizens from another
part of town, Marcus hissed,

 "Slowly back ya ass up in that door bruh, or
we murkin' you."

 Smooth quickly obliged but wasn't fooled
one bit, he recognized who it was right away.
Regardless, he was scared *shitless* and wouldn't

give them the benefit of knowing that he knew who they were for fear of his life. Internally however, Smooth quickly became enraged, cursing himself for not already executing his plan to have Tanell and Marcus out of his way.

Unbeknownst to them, Smooth had been working with the local police force for years. Reason why for years he had been able to escape the clutches of the criminal un-justice system that eventually entraps 95% of African American men that delve into peddling narcotics. For close to a decade Smooth had been secretly helping the local police force convict drug dealers while simultaneously eliminating his competition and solidifying his relationship with detective Burke. The last six months, Smooth had been secretly providing detective Burke with incriminating information regarding Tanell and Marcus' criminal activities. The irony was that three days prior, Smooth was elated to hear from detective Burke that the local police force would be serving an indictment upon Tanell and Marcus within the next week.

"Now sit yo ass on dat couch and don't try no slick shit bruh," barked Tanell as Marcus shut the door behind him. Smooth made sure he sat in the left corner of the couch.

"Now where da fuck is the weight and the paper bruh?" asked Tanell while focusing both of his guns on Smooth.

"And don't play one game or I'ma pop yo top bruh!" barked Marcus as he came from behind Tanell, putting his gun in Smooth's face.

"Listen man the money ain't here but I got four bricks of coke out back in the alley. It's in one of the abandoned looking garages in a row, the one with the red doors..." answered Smooth frantically.

"Bitch didn't I tell you not to play one game? You gone sit here and lie, where the fuck is da paper bruh? We know it's here!" barked Marcus while simultaneously cracking Smooth twice in the head with the butt of his gun.

"My word the money aint here." Smooth cried out in a high-pitched tone.

"Bitch ya word ain't shit!" hissed Tanell as he joined Marcus in the pistol whipping.

"I swear the money ain't here, I'll take yall to it. I swear I'll take ya to it!" squealed Smooth while covering his head to fend off their crushing blows.

"Alright go get the coke." said Marcus, gesturing to Tanell while training his gun on the middle of Smooth's head.

Meanwhile back at their apartment, Ashley lay on the sofa watching a rerun of the popular *Cosby* television show. When she noticed the VCR clock showed it was 12:45 a.m., almost ten minutes past the time Tanell said he'd be home. As if on cue she started feeling excruciating pains in her stomach. the baby kicking and moving rapidly and uncontrollably as if signaling an ominous sign of some foreboding event.

Tanell, reaching the alleyway behind Smooth's residence, instantly spotted the abandoned looking garage with the red doors. He quickly made his way over to it and using the keys Smooth gave him, opened the doors. After sifting through various pieces of junk, garbage, and miscellaneous items, he located the *Weis Market* grocery bag that contained the four bricks of coke. He then decided to quickly put the bag in the Ford Thunderbird since it was parked just a little distance off in the adjacent parking lot. Reaching the Thunderbird, he opened the back-passenger door and placed the bag partially under the passenger seat. While closing the door was when he heard it… the first gunshot.

Marcus, under the guise that they had caught Smooth completely off guard, made a fatal mistake by taking the focus of his gun off of Smooth.

Unbeknownst to him, the reason Smooth made sure to sit in the left corner of his couch was because he had secretly concealed a .9mm in between the cushion and the armrest, with the butt of the gun slightly poking out, off safety. Therefore, the minute Marcus turned his back and walked towards the window to peak out, Smooth capitalized, immediately reaching for his gun. Marcus, noticing the shifty movement from his peripheral, quickly spun around with his gun raised but was a fraction of a second too slow as Smooth fired his first shot Hitting Marcus square in the chest. The force from the shot knocked Marcus against the wall next to the door.

Thankful as always for his omnipresent bulletproof vest, Marcus fired recklessly in the direction of Smooth. Smooth simultaneously fired another shot at Marcus as he took cover behind the couch. With the second shot hitting Marcus in his shooting arm, he helplessly dropped his gun. He then opened the front door running with Smooth on his heels.

Meanwhile after hearing the first shot, Tanell instantaneously took off running towards the back door of Smooth's residence. Upon reaching the back door and hearing the succession of gunshots, he hurriedly ran through the house towards the mayhem with both guns raised. Making his way to the front room, he immediately noticed Smooth running towards the open front door firing recklessly. Tanell then quickly closed the distance between him and Smooth, firing three shots directly into the back of his head, instantly killing him. He then hurriedly moved passed Smooth's tumbling carcass, crossing the threshold of the front door where he witnessed his best friend sprawled on the pavement just past the hedges.

Unaware to them, after the first shot sounded in the usually quiet neighborhood, one of Smooth's neighbors immediately called the police. Whereas if a sign of twisted fate, a police officer just happened to be within a two-block radius on patrol. Responding to the call, the police officer quickly made route to the address of disturbance given by the caller. Upon reaching the residence of disturbance, the police officer quickly became aware of the macabre that lay before. He took notice of a man sprawled face down in front of the residence with another man approaching the fallen victim with two guns in hand.

Oblivious to everything around him after reaching the spot were Marcus lay face down, Tanell knelt down, dropping his guns at his side. He then turned his *brother from another mother* onto his back. Recognizing the bullet wound where a bullet tore through Marcus' esophagus, he let out a cacophony of uncontrollable wails as he held the lifeless body of his life-long friend in his arms.

The initial officer on the scene was now accompanied by backup with their guns drawn on

Tanell while continuously shouting for him to surrender and put his hands up. Yet still oblivious to everything around him, Tanell continued to kneel there with Marcus in his arms, cursing God for their abject upbringings and his unfairness in their lives. The unsympathetic police officers then subdued Tanell by pulling him away from Marcus, slamming him onto his face and stomach while restraining him in handcuffs.

Defying the laws of nature for so long, Tanell, Marcus, and Smooth wrote their destinies day in and day out. Now as always the Law of Cause and Effect had come to procure its due compensation for their life-long deeds whether good or bad. As in the reaper had come to harvest the malevolent seeds Tanell, Marcus, and Smooth had perpetually sown their entire lives.

After taking two Aspirin pills to ease her pain, Ashley fell asleep comfortably in the bed. Reminiscing of her and Tanell asleep on her couch, she was awakened by the piercing ring of the house phone. Except when she looked up, Tanell was nowhere to be found. Noticing the alarm clock read 6:12 a.m., Ashley, now confused and worried, immediately answered the phone.

"Hello, who's speaking?"

"Oh my God, lil sis you alright?" Ashley's older sister Anita frantically questioned into the phone.

"Yeah I'm alright. Why would something be wrong with me?" questioned Ashley. She was now more worried than before.

"Oh my God you haven't heard yet; turn to ABC 27 news right now! I'm on my way over there!" exclaimed Anita as she started putting her clothes on to make route to her little sister's apartment. Knowing Ashley would need consoling after digesting the abject news pertaining to the love of her life.

Meanwhile, as Ashley hung up the phone she simultaneously turned on the television, quickly flicking the channel until she got to the ABC news. The second the news appeared on the screen she was met with the shock of her life as she listened to the news anchor say:

"Breaking news; Two men dead and one man held in connection to what appears to be a robbery gone awry. In the early morning hours, the local police department responded to a call of gunshots fired in the Uptown neighborhood near Green & Division Streets. Arriving at the scene the police were confronted with suspect Tanell White holding a gun in each hand while standing over deceased victim Marcus Candon. After subduing and arresting suspect Tanell White, police then entered the residence of disturbance, leased to

known local drug dealer Larelle "Smooth" Mullins. Where upon entering the residence, police found the second victim Larelle 'Smooth' Mullins deceased. We will keep you updated on this breaking news as it unfolds; This is ABC 27 news..."

Initially in a state of shock and pure denial, Ashley grabbed the house phone and continuously tried contacting Tanell to no avail. Emotionally addled she then called *City Hall*, where her denial was overcome with facts as she was told Tanell was currently in custody and being charged with double homicide and after being processed he would be given a call. Hanging up the phone, she fell out emotionally distraught as she succumbed to the realization that the love of her life was really in police custody charged with two murders. She still sensed something wasn't right because she knew Tanell would never kill Marcus.

Hearing the relentless banging on the door, Ashley ignored it for close to twenty minutes. Then after barely pulling herself together enough to stop crying and become mobile, she answered the door where her brother and sister stood on the other side.

"Why?!... Why?!... Oh my God, Why?!" Ashley cried out as she fell into her brother's embrace. His security left her crying and sobbing uncontrollably.

"Everything gone be alright sis. Everything gone be alright, just calm down so you don't harm

the baby by stressing yaself," he replied while tenderly patting her back.

"Calm down sis, we here for you. Everything gone be alright." said Anita as she joined the embrace.

"What happened Ray?!... Ray what happened?!"

"I really don't know sis. Anita just told me everything she know."

"We only know what you know. I was just hearing it myself on the news when I called you."

"Why? Oh my God, why is this happening?... I need to talk to Tanell."

"Don't worry sis, he gone call when he gets the chance. You just calm down. Mommy's on her way over here too." said Ray as he guided Ashley to a seat on the couch.

Due to the fact that mistreatment to criminals was almost a norm at City Hall, during the booking process Tanell was denied his first phone call, which he was entitled to by law. Then after being transported to County lockup, he did three days on a quarantine block where he was locked in a vile cell for the entire 72 hours, with no shower while being fed through a slot in the door. He refused to eat the putrid looking unrecognizable meals mainly because his state of melancholy rendered him no appetite. After being poked and prodded for diseases by the medical department, he was transferred to his housing block. Upon arrival, he was met with immediate enmity from a few of

Smooth's coterie. Ignoring their hate-filled stares but remaining vigilant, he made his way straight to the phones in the day room where he immediately called Ashley collect at their apartment.

"*Hello? Who's speaking?*" answered Ashley in a low pitched depressed tone. She was then directed by an automated machine.

"*You have a collect call from…*"

"*Tanell*"

"*This is a collect call from Dauphin County Prison; This call will be monitored and recorded. To accept this call press 1, to refuse this call press five or hang up…*"

"*Tanell! Tanell! Oh my God is that you?*" exclaimed Ashley into the phone immediately after pressing 1.

"*Yeah it's me boo. You alright?*"

"*Why it took you three days to call me Tanell? Are you alright?*"

"*Yeah I'm alright boo, don't you be worrying about me. I'm gone be alright, you just worry about you and our baby. How's my lil man doing in there anyway?*" replied Tanell, doing his best to sound upbeat and self-assured for Ashley's sake.

"*She's fine and I'm trying but me and the baby need you here Tanell.*"

"*I know you and the baby need me there and you know I want to be there but right now we gotta wait and see what happens at my trial. I should be alright though boo.*"

"*I really hope you do be alright cause I miss you so much already and I can't help worrying because I'm scared to lose you Tanell...*" responded Ashley, sounding more depressed by the second.

"*I told you don't worry about me, I'm gone be alright boo, trust me,*" countered Tanell while still trying to remain upbeat for Ashley though internally his spirits were diminishing by the second.

"*Listen boo, Ray helped me find a lawyer for you, he's supposed to be one of the best. I talked to him yesterday and he said he believes he has a good chance at beating your case because he said from what he knows right now the D.A. can't really prove you killed anyone. So, he's supposed to come see you sometime this week. The only problem is he said since your charged with double murder, his fee is gone be sixty-thousand dollars and we only have twenty-thousand saved.*"

"*What's his name boo?*"

"*William Carpolus.*"

"*Yeah he's real good. I been heard of him, plus he just beat those two young boys murder case that's been in the news. I'ma wait to talk to him and I probably can come up with ten-thousand from what people owe me in the street. But I don't see no other way to come up with the rest of the money unless you can get Ray to help me get rid of something..."* said Tanell with renewed spirits after feeling like there was no way out of his current circumstances.

Being unlettered in the law, he and Ashley both fell victim to that lawyer's chicanery in giving them hope that Tanell could regain his freedom. When the lawyer already knew Tanell's chance at regaining his freedom was slim to none.

"Boo you know Ray will help you in any way he can," responded Ashley.

"Alright then you talk to him for me. I'ma write you a letter telling you everything I'ma need him to do, because I can't tell you over these phones. If Ray gone help me, when you get the letter just tell him everything he need to do and after that we should have enough for the lawyer." said Tanell just before the automated machine informed him that he only had thirty seconds left on his call.

"Alright boo I'ma make sure I call you tomorrow. Just know I love you and our child so much, you know you my heart."

"I know boo, and you know I love you so much and I miss you so much already. You better call me tomorrow, love you, bye," said Ashley with a tear drop running down her left cheek as she hung up the phone.

Three days later Ashley received a letter from Tanell detailing for her to inform Ray that there were 4 bricks of coke in a navy-blue Ford

Thunderbird parked behind the Italian Lake Apartments. The bricks were in a Weis Market bag under the passenger seat. After acquiring them, Ray was to call the number given in the letter. It was for a man that Tanell had set up a deal with, the man was supposed to buy the 4 bricks at a very cheap price of forty-thousand for all.

Two hours later after finishing the letter, Ashley sat in a state of ambivalence as she accepted Tanell's call.

"Hello, Ash, wa'sup boo?" said Tanell immediately after being connected through the line.

"Nothing, I'm just glad you called." She responded.

"Yo I just got word Ray out here, they say he came through last night. What's that about? Is everything alright?" asked Tanell, fearing the worst may have happened after they received his letter.

"That's why I'm glad you called cause Ray's P.O. violated him yesterday for not reporting his change of address and for a dirty urine."

"Damn! I'm sorry to hear that. At least it ain't too serious and he ain't run into no trouble with that other situation?"

"He don't even know about that situation because I just got your letter. That's why I was just starting to stress after reading your letter because now that Ray's been arrested I can't think of how we gone take care of that situation to get the money for your lawyer."

"I keep telling you Ash, don't worry about me and my situation cause everything gone be alright. Just stop stressing yaself for the baby's sake at least. Plus, we can just wait til Ray get out to take care of that."

"That's the problem Tanell because Ray still owe those people eighteen months and ain't no telling when he gone see the judge or when they gone release him. He could be in there until after your trial."

"Damn!... alright, let me try make something happen and I'ma let you know from there."

"Listen boo, I've been thinking I can just take care of that situation. Since all I would have to do is get the stuff, make a call, take it to whoever and get the money."

"HELL NO! Listen Ash, ain't no way I'm gone have my pregnant woman taking care of some business like that, no matter what the situation, you hear me?!" barked Tanell, realizing his predicament was dismal and at that point Ashley was the only person he could trust. Yet he refused to put her in harm's way.

"Alright boo calm down, like I said it was just a thought because there ain't nobody else we can trust and I want you to know there's nothing I wouldn't do for you. But I understand and just know I love you." she replied as the automated machine informed them of their final thirty seconds in the call.

"Ash I already know you would do anything for me but you just let me take care of this. Everything's gone be alright, you just know I love you and that baby, you know you my heart. I'll talk to you later alright, I love you...bye."

One week later as Ashley was riding back from her doctor's appointment inundated with emotions, all she could think about was how she would need Tanell there for her and the imminent birth of their child. Succumbed by these thoughts, she decided that by any means necessary she was going help the love of her life regain his freedom.

Blinded by her love for Tanell and the deceptive spiel of attorney William Carpolus, she pulled her car to a stop next to the navy-blue Ford Thunderbird parked behind the Italian Lake Apartments. Getting out of her car, she grabbed the crowbar she had on her back-seat. Making her way to the back-passenger window of the Ford Thunderbird, she swiftly shattered it with two crushing blows. She then reached through the window, unlocked the door and quickly grabbed the Weis Market grocery bag jumped back into the driver's seat of her 82 Chrysler Labaron and hastily sped off.

As soon as Ashley made it back to she and Tanell's apartment she dialed the number in the letter Tanell sent.

"Hello?" answered a man in a gravelly tone.

"Hello, sorry if I woke you but I'm calling for Tanell. He said you would be expecting my call regarding a business deal..." said Ashley.

"Oh...yea, ight but I was told to be expecting a call from a man. Who are you?" asked the man on the other end of the line after realizing that this was the call he was expecting a week ago.

"I'm Tanell's fiance and due to certain circumstances, I'll be handling the business deal."

"Ight, so you got the package?"

"Yeah, it's all here."

"Ight...meet me on Agate street. It's a little street up by Jefferson Park. Do you know where that's at?"

"I'll find it."

"Ight, what kind of car you driving?"

"A maroon eighty-two Chrysler Labaron."

"Ight meet me on Agate street in about forty-five minutes."

"OK."

Immediately after hanging up the phone, Ashley started experiencing excruciating pains in her stomach as the baby again started kicking rapidly and uncontrollably. Doing her best to ignore the pains she swallowed two Aspirin pills before leaving the apartment. She then jumped into her car and made her way to Agate Street. No matter how hard she tried to suppress the pains, they continued relentlessly. Still, Ashley did her best to ignore them. She was determined to get the money to help free the love of her life. In minutes, she sat parked on the small block of Agate Street, which was only one way in and out. She sat suppressing her pains for over 15 minutes until she noticed a man in a dark gray hooded sweat-shirt approaching her car. Though she didn't know what the guy she talked to on the phone looked like, she figured that had to be him. As the man approached, the baby in her stomach began kicking more rapidly and relentlessly. Opening the car door, the man spoke first.

"Tanell's fiancé right?"

"Yeah and you're the guy I talked to on the phone right?" Ashley responded.

"Yeah, so let's make this quick... Where's the product?" asked the man as he sat in her passenger seat staring at her rub her protruding belly.

"It's right here; you got the money right?" countered Ashley as she reached down between her legs to retrieve the Weis Market grocery bag that contained the 4 bricks of coke.

"Yeah I got the money but I need to check the product first."

With Ashley never before doing anything like this she knew nothing of the precautions she should take. Therefore, she didn't become apprehensive until he slightly snatched the bag from her after she retrieved it from between her legs. Now skeptical of him, Ashley watched him closely as he examined the contents in the grocery bag. Her fears were confirmed when he opened the passenger door and began getting out the car without even looking at her or saying anything. Thereby blinded by her unrelenting love for Tanell and her wish to help him regain his freedom, she quickly reached out and grabbed hold of the grocery bag just before the man fully exited her vehicle.

"Please…No, don't do this." she exclaimed as a teardrop ran down her right cheek. All the while she held firmly onto the grocery bag. This bag now represented Tanell's freedom and Ashley held onto Tanell's freedom for dear life.

The man now with his back slightly towards her, standing just outside the passenger door, pulled on the bag as he turned to face her with a chrome pistol grip .357 revolver in hand.

"Bitch let go of the bag!" he barked callously as she looked into his now cold-blooded eyes with a pleading stare.

Just as unrelenting as her love was for Tanell, she refused to release her grip on the bag as tears poured down her face. With a stoic expression on his face, he then recklessly and cold-heartedly fired two shots directly into her chest. Snatching the bag away from her now debilitated grip, he then quickly disappeared into an adjacent darkened alley as her atrophying body lay slumped head first against the steering-wheel. With tears of love and pain simultaneously streaming down her angelic face.

$¢

Later that night, just before lock-in time at approximately 8:35 p.m., Tanell picked up the jail-phone to call Ashley at their apartment.

"MY DAUGHTER IS DEAD BECAUSE OF YOU! YOU BLACK SON-OF-BITCH, MY DAUGHTER WAS KILLED BECAUSE OF YOU!" yelled Ashley's mother in a piercing scream, expressing her bereavement immediately after excepting Tanell's phone-call.

"What are you talking about? Where's Ashley?" countered Tanell, praying he heard her mother wrong.

"SHE DEAD YOU BLACK SON-OF-A-BITCH. SHE'S DEAD AND YOU KILLED HER!" shouted Mrs. Eve Storm in a hostile tone, expressive of her tumultuous emotions as Anita stood by trying to console her.

Meanwhile Tanell stood on the other end of the line at a complete loss for words as a man from the neighborhood whom he knew tapped him on the shoulder. He responded by raising his index finger as if to tell the man to wait a minute.

"No, no, no, ... What happened? What about the..." said Tanell in almost a whisper before being cut short.

"Muthafucka my daughter is dead because of you. I hope you burn in hell you black piece-a-

shit," barked Mrs. Eve Storm just before hanging up the phone.

Tanell now completely incredulous and at a loss for words, turned to the man who tapped him on the shoulder while he was on the phone.

"What da fuck did you want?" he hissed in a sinister tone while simultaneously clinching his jaws and fist.

"Damn man, I'm pretty sure you know by now but I meant to tell you earlier when I got off the phone that I'm sorry to hear what happened to Ashley." the man replied.

"What did you hear happened?"

"My girl Lisha gave me the news earlier on the phone that Ashley was found shot to death up by Jefferson Park around one-fifteen this afternoon. I been meant to give you my condolences... I'm sorry for what happened man..." answered the man with a look of pure sympathy as Tanell stared at him with eyes full of contempt.

Tanell then just walked off in the direction of his cell without saying another word. He then retrieved his makeshift knife that he had fashioned from a broken piece of fence with a ripped sock tied at the bottom of it for a handle. With the makeshift knife in hand, he then marched straight to the dayroom where three dudes who were a part of Smooth's coterie were playing cards. Tanell under the belief that Ashley was killed in retribution for Smooth's murder, marched right up to the table and stabbed the first of Smooth's friends in the neck.

With the other two trying to fight Tanell off of them, he was like a vulture on its prey as he stabbed them repeatedly all over their bodies. Two correctional officers who responded to the violent altercation were also stabbed repeatedly before a swarm of C.O.'s violently restrained Tanell.

In the aftermath of the mayhem, one of Smooth's friends was put on life support while the other two were put in intensive care. The two initial C.O.'s that responded were treated for multiple lacerations awhile Tanell was left for dead in an isolation cell for 11 days. Needing medical attention after almost every correctional officer in that jail commenced to trouncing him after they had him in cuffs. Breaking his ribs and right leg with him also needing stitches over his left eye and above his top lip.

Two months later while sitting in solitary confinement, Tanell was notified through the intercom to get ready because he had a visitor. Incredulous, he told them that it couldn't be possible because he no longer had any family or friends in Harrisburg or alive for that matter. Yet they assured Tanell that the visit was for him, so he readied himself.

After being transported to the visiting room alone, Tanell sat handcuffed and shackled in a small cubicle separated from the other side by a plexiglass window. Wondering who in the world could be visiting him, his skepticism was soon answered when a conspicuously pregnant woman sat before him on the other side of the plexiglass window.

"What the fuck are you doing here? And what the fuck do you want with me?" he barked vehemently as he stared intensely into the pregnant woman's eyes.

"Listen Tanell I know your situation and I'm sorry for your pain but I can't take back what happened between us that night. So, I just came here to let you know that this baby I'm about to have any day is yours." replied the pregnant woman as she stared pensively back into his eyes. Tanell's paramour was holding the phone they were talking through in her left hand against her ear while rubbing her stomach with her other hand.

Tanell then momentarily sat there reliving the one time he got inebriated and cheated on Ashley. He had regretted it as soon as it happened and was at least thankful Ashley didn't have to find out that way. Yet, still he sat there addled and unbelieving as blood tears internally streamed from the orifices of his now hardened heart.

"How do you know for sure that's my baby? You had a boyfriend and if you supposedly been thought it was my baby then why it took you until now to tell me? What is this some type of fucking joke? You know what? Get the fuck outta here right now!" Tanell growled through clenched teeth as he furiously and deplorably stared at the pregnant woman that sat before him.

With him now causing her to feel a sense of compunction, she sat there silently for a moment staring at him. Then simply hung the phone up and calmly stood to leave, staring at him compassionately before making her way out of the visiting room.

Subsequently, seven months after Ashley's death, Tanell was convicted of first degree murder in the death of Larelle 'Smooth' Mullins. He was also convicted of solicitation to murder in the death of Marcus Candon. Where he received two consecutive life sentences without the possibility of parole.

He was also later sentenced to a consecutive 50 years for the stabbing of Smooth's friends and the aggravated assault on two correctional officers.

Chapter 3

*"People living in wretched conditions often react
with violence and anger when they can no longer
tolerate the injustice of their lives."*
-Carl Upchurch

*"I'm telling you Mil, it looked like he
wanted to shoot me man, I was scared."* said 9-
year-old Ryat.

"I would have been scared too." replied
Ryat's best friend Camill Evans as they walked
home from Steele Elementary School. The
unrenovated school, due to low enrollment and a
district wide budget shortfall, was five blocks away
from the area they lived.

Ryat and Camill had basically been raised
together since they were about 4 years old. Ever
since Camill's mother suggested to Ryat's
grandmother on their second day of preschool, that
she would watch little Ryat every day after school.
Mrs. Eve immediately accepted, delighted that this
nice young woman would relieve her of having to

find and pay for a baby-sitter to watch Ryat while she worked during the day.

"He even pointed the gun at my Nanna like he was gone shoot her. Man I'm telling you Mil, I hate him but my Nanna say I shouldn't hate nobody but I still hate him," said Ryat as he looked over at his young friend with fire in his eyes. *"And it looked like they was trying kill my aunt Nita boyfriend."*

"I heard my mom talking about it, she said they brought him out the house butt-naked and everything." said Camill.

"But my Nanna also always say's what goes around comes around because you reap what you sow. So, I know something bad gone happen one day to that cop that pointed his gun at me." said Ryat, precociously pondering karmic concepts far beyond his tender age. "

"Watch he gone get his one day," he added, clinching his jaws and balling his right hand into a fist.

"Matter of fact, I'm gone get him myself one day Mil, watch."

"Man Ryat you can't get the cops, you sound crazy. Anyway, look at what I got," said Camill as he stopped walking, removing his school backpack from around his shoulders. He placed it in front of himself, unzipped it, bent over and dug around inside of it until he retrieved a coin-sized, stuffed

plastic baggy. After breaching the bag Camill dangled it in front of Ryat's face.

"What is it?" Ryat inquired.

"Drugs. The one that everybody be smoking."

"Oh it must be that weed stuff my Nana always be saying my auntie Nita be smoking cause it don't look like crack."

"Yeah that's what it's called - weed."

"How did you get it?" Ryat asked as he took and examined the stuffed plastic baggy.

"I sold some already." answered Camill calmly as he took back the stuffed plastic baggy from his friend and put it back in his school backpack.

"What?! How did you sell some already Mil?!" inquired a shocked and excited Ryat as they continued their walk home.

"Well you know how my moms be sleeping until 1 or 2 o'clock in the afternoon and how I hate waking her when she sleep cause she be waking up all grouchy and angry. Well the other day in the morning - like eleven, me and my sister kept hearing somebody knocking on the door. So, I answered it and my uncle Trev was at the door even though he ain't really my uncle, he just friends with my moms and everybody.

Well he asks me where my mom was, so I tell him she sleep thinking he was gone leave. But then he tells me she knew he was coming and for me to wake her up. So, I go wake her up even though I *was scared. I went into her room and shook her awake. She was all mad like 'boy what the hell do you want?' in her grouchy voice. I told 'her uncle Trev told me to wake you up because you knew he was coming.' She say 'oh' and then turned on her side, reached into the top drawer of the small dresser beside her bed.*

Then I see her take out a small purple bag that had gold stitching around it and Crown Royal stitched in gold on it. Then she took out two of those baggies I just showed you, gave them to me and told me to take them straight to uncle Trev and bring straight back what he gave me. So I take them to him knowing it had to be those drugs my grandma always talking about.

When I gave them to him, I told him my mom said to give it to him, that's when he start smiling saying how he was gone have to talk to my mom, then he gave me two ten dollar bills.

I'm telling you Ryat I made twenty dollars that easy. I wanted to take one of the ten dollar bills but I knew my mom would kill me, so I took the money to her then waited until she left later that day. Then I went into her room and took that baggy I showed you out of the purple bag in her drawer."

"What you gone do with it?"

"I don't know."

"Hey Mil did you get the twenty dollars for the field trip? You know you gotta give it to Ms. Borger by tomorrow."

"Yeah I know but my mom and grandma both say they don't got it because they gotta pay the bills by tomorrow and you know Kevin my sister dad told me no like he always do." responded Camill while walking with his head down.

"What about you?"

"My uncle Ray already gave me the money but I got two extra dollars you can have. Matter of fact, Mil you want to go to Weis Market on 3rd street and carry bags so we can get the twenty dollars for you? We can go down there after we get done with our homework."

"I guess..." Camill replied as he lifted his head to look at his friend.

"Hey Ryat, how did you know it wasn't crack when I showed you that baggy? You seen crack before?"

"Yeah, a few months back I seen my uncle Ray cutting this tan looking rock into little smaller rocks with a razor. He didn't know I was there at first but then he caught me peeking through the crack in the door. I thought he was gone beat me after that but he just asked what I was doing so I said 'watching you, what's that?' and he said I shouldn't have seen that but since I already did, he told me it was called crack and that it was how he made his money but that I should never want to be like him and that I better not ever deal with crack or anything wrong or illegal.

I didn't even know what illegal meant so I just sat there on his bed for a while watching him

*cut that tan rock into little smaller ones and put
them into little bottles. Then I asked him why he put
the little rocks into the little bottles and he said that
was how he made his money because each bottle
was worth ten dollars. So then I asked him how
much money he made off all those bottles. That's
when he smiled at me and said I ask a lot of
questions. Then he told me that the bottles was
worth two thousand eight-hundred altogether but
that he would probably make two thousand four-
hundred off –* "

"*Two thousand four-hundred dollars Ryat!*"
blurted Camill excitedly.

"*Yeah I know, all I could think about after
he said that was all the stuff I could buy like cars
and my Nana a new house and a whole bunch of
new Sega games. I was about to say that to him
when he stopped me from day dreaming and told me
I better not tell my Nana what I had just seen and
for me to get out of his room.*"

"*Man Ryat your uncle Ray is rich!*"

They soon arrived in front of Camill's
apartment building on Woodbine street where it just
so happened that Ryat's uncle Ray was sitting on
the steps in front of the building with a few of his
cronies.

"*Wha'sup uncle Ray, wha'sup E, wha'sup
Dollas,*" said Ryat in his coolest tone as he slapped
each man's hand with Camill echoing and doing the
same.

"Wha'sup youngens, yall just getting off school?" said Ray's friend E as he embraced both Ryat and Camill.

"Yeah..." replied Camill.

"Aye lil Ray I hear you gone be the next Michael Jordan, they say you killing em in da little league. I heard you dropped eighteen points the other day. Thas major for you to only be in the pee wee league. Back then I could only score about four points a game." said Ray's friend Dollas.

"Stop lying Dollas, you can't even score four points in a game now." quipped E as everybody started laughing.

"Man I'ma be better than Michael Jordan one day, watch!" said Ryat.

"Thas wha'sup lil Ray, Thas how you suppose to think. I'ma come to ya next game then." said Dollas as he took a small wad of cash from his sweat-pants pocket and gave both Ryat and Camill two dollars apiece.

"Here youngens, don't spend all that on candy."

"We won't, good looking out Dollas." said Camill.

"Thanks Dollas, hey one day my nickname gone be R Billions cause I'ma have all the money and his name gone be Millions..." said Ryat as he pointed at Camill.

"Man why I got to be Millions? Why can't you be Millions Ryat?" countered Camill.

"Because you already Mil," retorted Ryat as E, Ray, and Dollas choked with laughter.

"Aye Ryat you don't need no nickname because your name already means something. That's why most dudes get nicknames because it represents something about them. You don't need no nickname because your name already means something that represents you." said Ray.

"How? What does my name mean uncle Ray?" inquired Ryat as he sat on his uncle's knee.

"Your name Ryat comes from an old African folklore about a small boy who was the only survivor after his whole family and village was conquered in ancient Kemit. The small boy was found alive by a man who lived in the wilderness. The man took the child to the wilderness with him and for years raised him to be a strong warrior. Until the day came when the small boy grew to be a strong warrior and avenged the conquering of his family and village through retribution by conquering single handily those who conquered his family and village. He became king of the entire Ancient Kemit."

"Who named me then Uncle Ray?" Ryat asked, fascinated by the story of the young warrior and how their stories were analogous.

"I did. I got the name from a book of stories my dad, Pop Pop, used to read to me all the time when I was small. The book was called World Myths and Legends, African. Once I told mommy

the story when you were born she let me name
you."

"*What does retribution mean uncle Ray?*"

"*To pay someone or some people back in*
punishment for the wrongs they did you or your
people."

"*Oh...OK.*"

"*Ight, you and Camill go ahead and take*
care of y'all homework so y'all can go play later."
Ray said as Ryat and Camill made their way inside
the apartment building.

It was 6:15 p.m. in the afternoon, Ryat and
Camill had been standing in front of the Weis
Market grocery store on 3rd street for over an hour
waiting for patrons to come out of the store that
looked like they would need help carrying their
bags. Ryat and Camill would then kindly offer to
help carry their bags for a dollar.

"*How much you made already Mil?*" asked
Ryat as Camill came walking back, putting a dollar
in his pocket from the last person he helped.

"*I made five dollars so far,*" replied Camill.
"*How much you made?*"

"*Three dollars. That means we got fourteen*
dollars with all the money together plus what we
already got. That means we still need six dollars for
all your field trip money."

"I know and the street lights bout to come on, so we gone have to go home soon."

"Yeah, and I don't think we gone make the six dollars by the time the street lights come on Mil. Maybe we should just try asking my uncle Ray for the six dollars."

"Or Maybe we can sell this." Camill said as he pulled from his pocket the stuffed baggy he showed Ryat earlier that day after school.

"What!" exclaimed Ryat.

"You trying get me a beatin' from my Nana? How we gone sell that Mil? You know we gone get in trouble."

"It's easy Ryat, I told you I already sold some. I was thinking we could sell it to ol'head Roe from Hamilton street that drive that red Beemer."

"He gone tell my uncle Ray," countered Ryat.

"No he not gone tell because you know he go with my older cousin Nessa and you remember the time I beat up my cousin Tevin. That was because Roe paid me to do it. He said my cousin Tevin told his sister, my older cousin Nessa, that he seen Roe with another girl and Roe say he hate snitches. Plus, I know he smoke weed because he always is and the one time he gave me money a couple bags like this fell out his pocket."

"Oh yeah I remember when you beat Tevin up... 'ight lets hurry up and do it before the street

lights come on. " Ryat said as they started their seven-block trek in search of Roe.

Arriving at 4th and Hamilton streets eight minutes later, Camill and Ryat approached a small group of older men standing on the corner.

"Yo ol'head, you seen Roe?" asked Camill to one of the men standing there nestled in a blue and gray First Down bubble coat.

"Who you youngin?" the man countered.

"His lil cousin."

"Oh'ight, he over there sitting in his whip," said the man as he pointed towards Roe's red BMW 325i."

"What you two badass muthafuckas doing down here?" Roe asked in his usual calm demeanor after rolling down his driver's side window, another man sat in the passenger seat puffing on a blunt.

"We came to see you because I got something for you..." replied Camill.

"What you got for me lil nigga?"

"This..." answered Camill as he produced the small baggy stuffed with marijuana from his pocket.

"You can buy it."

"What! Let me see, where'd you get this from?"

"Ten dollars," said Ryat in a stern tone as he quickly grabbed Camill's arm before he could hand the small baggy to Roe.

"Yo them lil niggas is funny as shit cuz," said the man in the passenger seat as both men

choked on their smoke unable to control their laughter.

"Yo I like that in y'all. Two lil niggas about they business early, ain't that some shit. 'Ight here...." said Roe as he handed Camill a ten-dollar bill, Camill then handed him the small bag of marijuana.

"Man good looking out Roe!" said Camill.

"Matter of fact, here," said Roe as he also handed Ryat a ten-dollar bill.

"I like y'all style but don't y'all be coming around here or anywhere else no more trying sell drugs because y'all ain't ready for this shit yet but when y'all get a lil older and still wanna grind then I'll put y'all on myself because I can see y'all gone make a lot of money one day."

"Good looking out O.G., you ain't gone tell on us is you?" said Ryat.

"Man you's a funny lil nigga. Nah you ain't got to worry about me telling on you. I never tell what I heard, saw or done. Always remember lil nigga the best kept secret is taken to the grave. Now y'all lil niggas go ahead and get home for y'all get y'all asses wupped, it's getting late."

In that instance Ryat and Camill realized the street lights were on. Without any delay or hesitation, they *hauled ass* in destination of their homes.

CHAPTER 4

*"Life is a continual pattern of growth and
refinement, challenge and obstacles."*
-Dennis Kimbro

COMING HOME from basketball practice,
11-year-old Ryat and Camill parted ways at
Camill's building as Ryat made his way towards
his. He noticed from a little distance ahead that a
light-complected male was sitting on the steps of his
building, knowing it was his grandfather put a smile
on his face.

*"Wha'sup Pop Pop, what you doing out
here?"* asked Ryat as he neared his grandfather
sitting on the steps.

*"Hey boy; I'm just out here enjoying this
good weather. You coming from basketball practice
huh?"* replied Ryat's grandfather Mr. Carl.

*"Yeah, I got a game tomorrow. You coming
right?"*

*"Don't I always come to your games. You
just better learn how to pick your dribble up and*

stop dribbling so much or you'll never be good as your granddaddy once was."

"Go head Pop Pop, only reason you say that is cause back in your day they didn't dribble. All y'all did was pass the ball up and down the court cause them tight shorts y'all used to wear wouldn't let y'all dribble." countered Ryat as he and his grandfather fell into a joyous laughter.

"Hey boy, look, your uncle Ray was running around here looking for you earlier."

"What did he want?"

"I don't know. He should be in there, he said to send you to his room when you got home."

"Alright Pop Pop, see you later." said Ryat as he made his way inside the apartment towards his uncle Ray's room.

Opening the door to his uncle's room, he didn't initially see him when he looked inside.

"Uncle Ray...Uncle Ray," he blurted as he stepped inside the room.

"Aaaaahhhhhh!" yelled Ray from behind his room door as he grabbed Ryat from behind, startling him.

"Aww man you scared me, wha'sup? Pop Pop said you was looking for me."

"Yeah I was looking for you. Earlier E's lil sister told me you let some boy named Jamar punk you in front of everybody and you was scared to say anything back."

"I wasn't scared of him."

"You must have been, you let him punk you in front of everybody and you ain't do or say nothing."

"I told him like Nana always say as long as he didn't put his hands on me I didn't care."

"You sound like a punk," said Ray as he punched Ryat in the body a few times.

"You still have to stand up for yourself and don't let nobody intimidate you. Plus I heard he did put his hands on you because he supposed to had pushed you in the head."

"Man he's in the sixth grade and he's all bigger than me and everybody in school scared of him," exclaimed Ryat as his eyes started to well with tears.

"It don't matter if he in a grade higher than you or if he bigger than you and everybody else in the school scared of him," hissed Ray as he hit Ryat with a few more body shots.

"You hear me? Look me in my eyes when I'm talking to you. What I tell you about that? Always look a man in his eyes when he's talking to you. Now I'm only gone tell you this one time, you hear me? Don't you ever fear a man that breaths the same air as you. You hear me? Every man on earth bleeds just like you no matter how big they are."

"Yes sir," replied Ryat as tears streamed his cheeks while his chest heaved uncontrollably.

"Why you crying? Ballin' ya face up and puffing ya chest out like you mad. What I tell you?... Never let a person control your emotions because that means your no longer in control and you can't fight any battles angry cause then you fight distracted, leaving yourself open. Remember, always stay level headed no matter what.

Listen Ryat the only time you should fear is the natural fears God has given everybody like not jumping in front of a train because you know it will kill you. Other than that you shouldn't fear nothing but God. But it's only natural for humans to fear things they maybe shouldn't that's why God also gave us courage, which is best described as having the presence of fear with the will to go on. So always have courage Ryat, do you understand me?"

"Yeah I understand."

"'Ight now throw ya hands up like I been teaching you," said Ray as Ryat then jumped to the balls of his feet with his right foot behind his left and threw his fist into a boxing guard.

Ray was a former junior golden gloves whom since Ryat was eight years old had been teaching him how to box. Ray and Ryat than began practicing various jabs, hooks, and combinations for hours.

"What the hell has gotten into you boy?" shouted Mrs. Eve at Ryat as soon as he walked through the door after getting suspended from school for fighting.

"Nothing," responded Ryat in a shaken tone after noticing the belt strap she held over her right shoulder.

"Something must have gotten into your ass, you going to school starting fights and carrying on. I ain't raising no damn heathen! I got something for your ass though, now pull your pants down and lay your ass across that couch!"

"But I aint..."

"Boy shut up and lay your ass across that couch before I really tear into your ass!"

Mrs. Eve then gave Ryat a beaten that lasted for close to a minute though it felt like an eternity to Ryat as it was the worst beating he had ever received from his Nana. He knew he had to had really done something wrong because she rarely ever beat him without talking to him first. He just couldn't figure out why because that wasn't the first fight he'd gotten into. Afterwards, crying his eye out from the pain, he was sent to his room to do his homework. Three hours later as he lay on his bed on his back tossing his basketball in the air, Mrs. Eve came calmly walking into his room, shutting the door behind her.

"Sit up baby, come sit beside your Nana so I can talk to you," she said.

74

"Yes ma'am," he responded as he quickly obliged and sat beside her on his bed.

"Now you tell me the truth when I ask you this. Is it something that you need to tell me because your far from a bad kid and I don't want you running around here fighting and carrying on like some damn heathen."

"No ma'am, nothing's wrong with me. That boy just been picking with me for a long time now and I just got tired of it."

"Now I'm not mad at you for standing up for yourself because that's what you're supposed to do, but what really ticked me off was when I heard you were also fighting a girl too, you should never fight a female. Do you hear me?"

"Yes ma'am but that was his sister, she just started swinging on me so I just started hitting her too,"

"Listen to me when I tell you this; you are to never hit a female!" said Mrs. Eve in a stern tone.

"A male should never hit a female, ever, no matter what. Do you understand me?"

"Yes ma'am."

"Let me tell you something baby. Physically men are stronger than women naturally but that isn't the reason a true man should never hit a woman. A true man should never hit a woman because first and foremost woman gives birth to man, all man. Secondly because women are who keep man strong and balanced. Women are who men leaned on for strength since the beginning of

*time, especially black women. We are who strong
black men leaned on during slavery, Jim Crow,
segregation, the civil rights era, right up to this very
day of modern systematic oppression. Women are to
be treated like queens by their kings. Now if a
woman doesn't respect herself or her self-worth
enough to be treated like a queen, then you treat her
at her own self-worth but again a man should never
hit a female, no matter what the circumstances. If
you find yourself in a situation where you feel as
though you need to hit a female, you just simply
remove yourself from that situation. Now do you
understand everything I just said to you?"*

*"Yes ma'am and I promise I will never hit a
female again."*

*"Ok and I want you to apologize to that girl
when you get a chance, OK."*

"Yes ma'am."

*"Now that sounds more like my baby, get
over here and give your Nana a hug,"* said Mrs.
Eve as she then embraced him in a loving hug.

*"Now go get ready for dinner and do me a
favor, go upstairs and tell that aunt of yours dinner
is done since she been getting on my nerves all day
about it."*

"What did you cook Nanna?"

*"Aww just baked chicken covered in creamy
mushroom gravy, rice, green peas, and cornbread,"*
she replied with a knowing smile as he smiled back
after hearing she cooked his favorite meal,
especially the cornbread. Thanks to her, he swore

there was nothing more delectable on earth than her cornbread.

Jumping two steps at a time, Ryat was in a rush to get his aunt Anita so he could hurry back to his favorite meal. Opening her door, he walked straight in on her smoking a Newport 100 on her couch while talking on the phone.

"Ryat what are you doing?" she quickly asked him after he startled her.

"Yo auntie, Nanna said to tell you she done making dinner."

"Alright," she quickly replied.

"Hey Ryat hold up a minute."

Anita then hung up her phone as he stopped dead in his tracks, turned around and made his way on her couch.

"Mommy told me you got suspended for starting fights," she said.

"Yeah but she already beat me and talked to me about it," countered Ryat, hoping she wasn't about to give him another scolding for his culpable behavior at school.

"Yeah I bet she really beat you good too for hitting a female, didn't she?"

"Yeah."

"I know she did because she do not play that. She did the same thing to Ray when he was young. I think one of her old boyfriend used to hit her before or something because she really don't play that."

"Who Pop Pop?"

"Naw I don't think he ever hit her but I just know she do not play when a male hits a female."

"Yeah she talked to me about it, how woman gives birth to all man, how men lean on women for strength and how men should treat women like queens. I understand now and I already promised her I'll never hit another female."

"Ok that's what's up because you shouldn't hit a female. I also heard you beat that boy up real bad too, you go little Ryat," said Anita while smiling at him.

"Yeah he started so I finished it," responded Ryat, grinning from ear to ear.

"Alright Ryat but just because you can fight, don't start thinking you all tuff, starting fights and trying be a bully and stuff because no matter what it's always somebody that can beat you."

"I know, I don't be trying be tuff and I don't be starting fights. I just ain't gone let nobody punk me though."

"Alright I just wanted you to know that and not get big headed because you won a little fight," said Anita with emphasis while grinning.

"Forreal though Ryat I know you growing up fast and before we know it you'll be a man. I'm saying this because you a good boy and I don't want you getting caught up in the same bullshit most dudes around here get caught up in. So always remember this little bit wisdom I'm 'bout to tell you because it probably be the only wisdom I ever be able to give you anyway. Remember this though you

can't let people control your actions by controlling your emotions."

"So what you telling me? Not to stand up for myself when somebody trying to punk me?"

"No what I'm telling you is to never let that somebody out-think you. What I mean is don't let anybody control your actions by antagonizing you, you don't always have to react. Always think before you act whether you going to regret it or not."

"Oh alright, I understand."

"Alright, come and let's hurry and get down there to dinner before mommy kill both of us for taking so long."

After dinner that night, Anita helped Ryat clean up and do the dishes. She then left for one of her friend's house as Mrs. Eve retired to the living room to watch an episode of *Murder She Wrote*. Ryat truly loved Anita because she was always more than an aunt to him. She never treated him as if he was a subordinate. It was almost as if she was his big sister, whom cared about his wellbeing so much she never wasted a chance to show it since he was a baby. Knowing this, he could never understand why she never gave birth to any kids. Curious about the fact, he decided to ask his grandmother about it.

"Nana can I ask you something?" he questioned as he sat on the sofa beside Mrs. Eve.

"Yeah baby, what's wrong?"

"No nothing wrong, I just was wondering why auntie Nita aint got no kids because I think she

would be a good mom. She's always been good to me and other kids," said Ryat as Mrs. Eve sat surprised by his question then suddenly a sense of melancholy washed over her. She then began to stare off into space with a forlorn expression.

Noticing his grandmothers quick change of demeanor, Ryat asked,

"What is something wrong Nana? Did I ask something wrong?"

"No baby you didn't ask anything wrong, it's just that... it's just that... it's just that your aunt Anita already had kids before."

"What?! When?! Where they at?!" blurted Ryat as he stared at his grandmother with a surprised expression.

"Listen baby calm down," said Mrs. Eve as she regained her composure, fully understanding his shock,

"I figured you'd be older before you heard about this but yes your aunt Anita already had kids once before, actually the oldest was only six months older than you."

"What happened to them?" asked Ryat in a shocked and incredulous tone.

"Well baby, she had two of them, the oldest was four and the youngest was two when it happened. And trust me your aunt was a good mother but one day as always your aunt's then boyfriend, the youngest child's father, stayed in some mess. Well on that particular day someone came banging on your aunt's door, telling her that

her boyfriend had just been shot on the corner. So, she then quickly shut her house door leaving her kids in the house alone for the first time.

She ran to the corner to check on her boyfriend and as she stood on the corner checking on him, out of nowhere her house burst into flames. By the time she got back to her house, she tried to go in and help her children but it was already too late as the whole house was in flames... them two babies died," said Mrs. Eve as she wiped tears from her eyes and tried to remain strong for Ryat's sake.

Sitting there aghast, Ryat couldn't help it after hearing such a shocking and sad story. He sat in utter disbelief with tears streaming down his face.

"What happened? How'd the house catch on fire?" He finally worked up the strength to ask.

"To this day nobody knows, they never actually found out what started the fire. But listen baby, your aunt still to this day isn't really able to accept it or deal with it so I ask that you don't bring this up to her."

"I won't," replied a somber Ryat as he continued to sit there in a state of bewilderment while Mrs. Eve joined in on the moment of silence with him as she resigned to staring into space with a forlorn expression.

Ryat just couldn't believe what he had just heard about his loving aunt. Such a tragic revelation yet in a sense he finally understood why his aunt always seemed sad even when she looked happy.

Always giving off the vibe of never being truly happy.

Punishment was really starting to get to Ryat, especially after being stuck in the house for the past two weeks with his grandfather Mr. Carl. Even though Ryat loved his grandfather deeply, he hated spending long periods of time with him because for some reason Mr. Carl was always acting weird like something was wrong with him. For instance, Mr. Carl would come out of his room at certain times all excited while acting paranoid, like looking out the window repeatedly as if someone was always coming after him. Then he was always picking up little pieces of white lint and crumbs checking it to see if it was something he always seemed to be looking for. Ryat once heard his aunt arguing with her father about him having a crack addiction. So he figured that's what must make him act so eccentric. Never-the-less Ryat had been stuck with his grandfather during most weekdays since being put on punishment for getting suspended from school. So when his uncle Ray came rushing through the door, Ryat eagerly followed him to his room.

"Wha'sup unc? Pop Pop keep acting all crazy and its boring man."

"Yeah Pops be on some other stuff when he on that shit. When you get off punishment anyway?"

"In two days, I can't wait either."

"So wha'sup man, you never told me what happened when you went back to school."

"Nothing really happened except everybody was acting like they my friends now but I know better."

"OK you learning and I know you staying humble, right?"

"Yeah," responded Ryat as he then turned, noticing the shiny object protruding from his uncle's jacket pocket. The jacket hung on his closet door as Ray was getting his outfit together for what he was gone wear out that night.

"What's that?" asked Ryat as he moved closer to get a better look of the prominent shiny object in his uncle's jacket pocket.

Realizing what his nephew was talking about, Ray stared at him intensely for a moment, contemplating what to say or do.

"What's this?" asked Ray as he grabbed the object from his jacket pocket and held it for Ryat to see.

"Yeah... that's a gun right?" answered Ryat as he looked on curiously.

"Yeah and I'm showing you this cause it ain't no use lying to you when you basically already seen it. But I'ma tell you like my daddy told me, a man should never possess a gun unless he need it and he should never put it in his hands unless he

know he gone use it with no regrets. But you don't
have to worry bout that cause you going to school
and make something of ya'self as long as I got
something to do with it," said Ray as he then took
the gun, wrapped it in a towel and put it in his
hiding place in his closet while Ryat intently looked
on.

CHAPTER 5

*"The future changes quickly into the past at a
control point called the present moment."*
-Danny Cox

Sitting on the porch in front of 11-year-old
Ryat's building was Ryat and four of his friends
since kindergarten. Camill sat at the top of the steps
with Potta, Melvin, and Hochee occupying the rest
of the porch. They were debating sports as always
when a pale blue, kitted-out, '94 VW Jetta with 16
inch BBS rims came riding by.

*"I bet you we beat y'all Melvin. Y'all ain't
got nobody but you and the boy Brian,"* stated Ryat.

*"You crazy Ryat, we gone beat y'all bad in
the championship next week cause for real the
Bombers ain't got nobody but you and Mil for
real,"* countered Melvin.

*"Yeah right! We got a whole team and we
already beat y'all once. Y'all just couldn't stop me
and..."*

"Oh shit yo! That's my whip right there!" shouted Hochee as he stood up pointing at the pale blue Jetta riding by them.

"Dang Hochee, that joint is cold," said Camill as he stood with the rest of them admiring the car riding by them.

"Hey let's go down Emerald, I got something."

"What you got Mil?" asked Ryat as they all began stepping away from the building in destination of Emerald Park.

"Just wait and see," countered Camill.

After reaching their destination, the crew found a seat on one of the benches in the middle of the park. While sitting under the tent like structure, Camill pulled a small stuffed plastic baggy from his pocket. Along with a White Owl cigar and lighter from his other pocket.

"What you got that for Mil?" Inquired Ryat.

"I stole it from my mom's drawer. You know how she always got a lot of this, so I took it so we can smoke it," replied Camill while looking around the table at their faces to see their expressions. He knew none of them never really smoked weed before even though they all fronted as if they had.

"Here let me roll it," said Potta.

"Man where you know how to roll from, you ain't never smoked weed," retorted Camill.

"Man you crazy, I been smoking wit my big cousin since I was in the 3rd grade."

"For real?" exclaimed Ryat as he looked at his friend knowing he was most likely telling the truth because Potta did anything he wanted with his mother being a crackhead and never showing much care for her son.

Camill then reluctantly handed the small baggy and *White Owl* cigar to Potta. With all eyes on him, Potta cracked the cigar down the middle, dumped the tobacco contents out, licked around the cracked cigar shell, put the weed inside and rolled the blunt like a pro to their collective amazement.

"Here let me light it," said Hochee while reaching for the blunt from Potta's hands.

"Nah I got it, you don't even know what you doing. You ain't never smoked before," retorted Potta as Camill handed him the lighter.

Potta then put the blunt to his mouth and as he inhaled, he lit the blunt and exhaled a small cloud of smoke. He then took the blunt from his mouth and passed it. Hochee took it and instantly took a strong pull. Which lead to a quick attack of coughs and hacking as he doubled over from the attack.

"Man you can't be pulling all hard like that, you ain't ready for that. You got to take small pulls at first," quipped Potta in between his laughter as they all laughed at Hochee's expense.

Camill then took the blunt from Hochee's hand and began to take two shorts pulls from it. Afterwards smoothly inhaling and exhaling his last pull, he passed the blunt to Ryat who then took his first pull from the blunt which ended in a small fit of coughing. He then went to hand the blunt to Melvin who'd been quiet the entire time.

"Man go 'head Melvin, your dad can't see you. So you ain't gone get no beatin," said Potta after noticing Melvin's hesitancy.

"Yeah go head Melvin, you aint scared, are you?" chimed in Hochee.

"Man I ain't scared," countered Melvin as he reluctantly took the blunt from Ryat's hand and inhaled the smoke from the blunt.

After smoothly exhaling to every one's surprise, Melvin took two more smooth pulls from the blunt before passing it to Potta again. They then all passed the blunt around two more similar rounds of them inhaling and exhaling the smoke until the blunt diminished. Afterwards they just sat around the table staring awkwardly at each other in silence for close to ten minutes until Ryat broke the silence.

"Man yo Potta you ugly as fuck!" he quipped before falling out in a fit of laughter as Camill, Melvin and Hochee looked at Potta for a second before they also burst out laughing uncontrollably. Even Potta couldn't help but laugh before replying.

"Man Ryat go ahead wit your baseball head," he retorted in between laughter.

"Yo you do look like a baby monkey though Potta," quipped Camill in a giddy tone before they all burst out laughing again.

"Go head Mil wit those dusted Nikes," Hochee chimed in.

"Man I know you ain't talking Horton. What type of Spanish name is that anyway? What happened to Hector or Jose and what the hell is a Hochee?" countered Camill as the rest of the boys were bent over in laughter, they were almost ready to urinate on themselves.

"And you big head, look at his head, I bet you your picture's even heavy cause of that big ass head," quipped Potta in a giddy tone while pointing at Melvin's head as they all continued in their perpetual laughter.

Fully taking in the experience, Ryat loved the way the marijuana made him feel. The euphoric feeling coupled with the feeling of indifference it gave him made him fall in love with the potent earth extraction. Each boy refused to leave the park until they came down off their highs. So they all mischievously goofed around with each other and others in the park until their highs dissipated over an hour later. While walking home from the park they were all slap boxing each other back and forth when a gold *kitted-out* '94 BMW came riding by them.

"Damn yo you see that joint, that's my car right there," stated Ryat as he pointed at the car.

"Dang yo, I was gone call that joint, that car is dope yo," said Melvin.

"Man watch, one day I'ma have a car like that 'cause I'm have a whole bunch of money when I get older," said Ryat.

"Yeah I'ma have a bunch of money too," said Camill with a bunch of *"me too's"* echoing the same.

"I know I'm gone have a bunch of money cause I'm going to the NBA," said Melvin.

"Man I don't care how but I know I'ma have a whole bunch of money cause like my granddaddy always said if it don't make Dollers then it don't make sense," said Potta.

"Yeah my Pop Pop always say that too but he ain't never got no money," said Ryat as they all found laughter in his comment before entering the corner store.

Inside the store each boy grabbed more sweets than they ever ate in one month. To the point where even after they spent the few dollars they had, Potta and Hochee both stole extra candies from the store.

Returning back to Ryat's porch a half an hour before the street lights came on, they all sat on the porch tearing into the candies and chips like they'd never tasted such a delicacy before in their entire lives. In the midst of their sugar inundated feast, Mr. Carl came bursting through the apartment building door and walked down the steps in a hurried agitated state. It was as if he was yearning after something that was to never be experienced or seen again. Ryat truly hated to see his grandfather in this state because he'd come to understand that his grandfather was chasing a high never to be recaptured again. Though there was no other man in his life whom he respected more, he couldn't understand what could make such a strong and smart man fall victim to such a powerful addiction. That destroyed so much and broke even the strongest man down to the lowest form of existence.

Ironically Ryat's current state of marijuana induced high that was slowly dissipating helped him in a way understand his grandfather's current plight. As his marijuana induced high lifted his spirits and put him in a careless euphoric state. That for a short time period, let him live worry and care free, though his worries were minor. He could only imagine what types of struggles and pain his grandfather's powerful high helped him escape in brevity. Yet and still Ryat vowed to himself that night that he would never become such an addict where life and reality became mired in a mind altering cloud of smoke.

"Come on Ryat, you gone be late for your game. The championship at that," said Ray as he stood in the doorway to the apartment building, waiting to take Ryat to his basketball championship game.

"Here I come," shouted Ryat while running from inside the apartment to catch up with his uncle.

They then commenced to walking up Woodbine street in route to the Y.M.C.A. where Ryat's little league basketball championship was being held. Accompanying them was Ray's best friend Dollas whom kept joking with Ryat about his selfishness with the ball in games.

"I'm saying, I know you nice youngen but you gotta pass the ball when five people on you and the rest of ya team is open," said Dollas.

"Man go head Dollas, I do pass the ball."

"Aye Ryat you do be gunning, that's why I already told you to make sure you pass the ball out the double team to the open man cause that's how y'all lost those two games to the Rebels and Hoopers," Ray chimed in.

"Yeah I know," replied Ryat as he stopped in front of Camill's building, just as Camill came rushing out of his building door to join the group on their way to the game. Arriving in front of the Y.M.C.A. building, Ryat's team was outside the building with their coach talking strategy. So he and Camill immediately fell into the fold and began listening to their coach's strategy as Ray and Dollas made their way inside the building to find a seat for the game. Meanwhile, as Ryat was standing outside listening to his coach, he took notice of an angry man pulling up in front of the building in a purple

Cadillac. Thinking nothing of it, he just looked on as the angry man stormed inside the building.

A short time later Ryat and Camill's coach decided it was time for them to enter the building and prepare for the game. Yet as they were entering the building the people inside abruptly started screaming and running for the exits as the loud echo of a gunshot rang throughout the building. Within the abrupt mayhem and stampede for the door, Ryat noticed the angry man who just pulled up in the purple Cadillac, calmly walking within the crowd towards the door. Just as the man calmly walked by, Ryat met his eyes as he walked in the opposite direction of where everybody was running from.

Moving off of pure impulse and no explainable reason Ryat walked towards the mayhem. Entering the gym, he made it just in time to see his uncle Ray laying on the ground while Dollas knelt over him doing something that Ryat couldn't make out. Standing there stunned, suddenly everything around young Ryat began moving in slow motion as he struggled to comprehend what lay before him.

"Yo get out of here Ryat! somebody get him out of here!" shouted Dollas after noticing Ryat standing behind him witnessing his uncle struggle for his entitled portion of the atmosphere's air.

Ryat barely heard any of Dollas words as he continued to stand there in a trance until his coach began pulling him away towards the exit. Obliging,

Ryat still in a semi-trance let his now excited coach hurriedly usher him back out of the front doors.

"Come here boy; you OK? Where's your uncle?" asked Ryat's grandfather Mr. Carl, who had just arrived to see Ryat's game but after noticing the melee immediately became excited trying to locate his loved ones.

"Uncle Rays on the ground," answered Ryat as his grandfather loosened his embrace, looking him in the eyes.

"What!?" exclaimed Mr. Carl.

"He's in there on the ground coughing."

"Aww shit! Listen you stay right here, I'll be right back," said Mr. Carl right before he took off towards the inside of the building. Just before he could get inside the building he was stopped short by the police who had just arrived with E.M.S.

"I'm sorry sir but you cannot go inside here," said one of the officers who was doing his job trying to get the scene under control.

"Listen my son is in there and I think he may be the person who got shot, I NEED to get inside there," countered Mr. Carl as he feared the worst and frantically wanted to get to his son's aid.

"I'm sorry sir but at this point there is really nothing you can do. If your son is the victim you will be notified but at this point I cannot let you enter this building."

"Goddamit that is some bullshit and I'm telling you I NEED to get to my son!"

"Sir I am sorry but I cannot let you into this building. Now what I need you to do is move across the street with the rest of that crowd or I will be forced to arrest you."

"God damn this is some bullshit!" yelled Mr. Carl as he walked over to Ryat and guided him across the street to stand behind the demarcation set up by the police.

Taking in the entire scene, Ryat looked on as the EMS and police were frantically at work with a noisy crowd harking for information. It was then as he was surveying the scene that he again laid eyes on the angry man with the purple Cadillac. Except this time the man appeared to be calm as he stood beside his vehicle talking to a few police officers. Intently watching, Ryat looked on as it appeared that the man was explaining himself to the officers whom one of which was taking notes with a pen and a pad. Then as Ryat attentively watched, the police confiscated from the man what appeared to be a gun. They then arrested the man with no struggle and put him in the back of one of their squad cars. Looking out the window of the squad car, young Ryat met the man's eyes briefly again before the man bowed his head towards his lap.

Seconds later, EMS workers came rushing out of the building with a man on a stretcher, Dollas following closely behind with blood now on his blue and white Tommy Hilfiger shirt. He immediately began running towards Mr. Carl and Ryat the second he laid eyes on them. Explaining to

Mr. Carl in horror what had just happened. Mr. Carl then instantly told Dollas to take Ryat home and inform Mrs. Eve of what had just taken place. Mr. Carl then rushed to be with his son in the ambulance as Dollas lead Ryat home with a heavy burden on his chest in having to explain to Mrs. Eve that her only son had just been shot.

"Did that man shoot uncle Ray?" asked Ryat in an eerily calm tone with his head bowed as they walked home.

"What?!" exclaimed Dollas as he was awakened from his melancholic trance…

"Was the madman in the red shirt with the purple car the one that shot my uncle Ray?"

"Ye…yeah," answered Dollas reluctantly as he still couldn't believe what just happened.

"Why?"

"Huh?…uh…because…" stammered Dollas unsure of what to say as he was still struggling to understand what happened.

"They were uh…arguing."

Eight minutes later, Dollas and Ryat arrived inside Mrs. Eve's apartment. To where Dollas commenced to the unbearable task of explaining to Mrs. Eve that her son had been shot. After hearing the horrific news, Mrs. Eve immediately put her right hand over her heart, chanting,

"Oh, my Lord!" Mrs. Eve hollered repeatedly.

She then hurriedly grabbed her purse and car keys, rushing for the door in route to the

Polyclinic Hospital. Meanwhile, Ryat sat on the couch in silence with Dollas sitting at the other end of the couch, both of them in their own personal melancholic trance.

"What's up y'all?" said Anita as she came bouncing through the door with a *HECTS* shopping bag in her hands minutes later.

"Why y'all sitting there looking like somebody died?"

"Uncle Ray just got shot." said Ryat as he looked up at his aunt.

"What?!...When?!...Who did... Dollas what the hell happened to my brother? And oh my God, where is he at?" exclaimed Anita as she looked at Dollas intensely.

"Man this is crazy man... that dude Victor George shot him a lil while ago up the Y," responded Dollas in a depressed tone as Ryat paid special attention to the name Dollas mentioned.

"What! Oh my God! I know he didn't shoot my brother over that bitch Bree? Oh my God I told my brother to stop messing wit that stinking bitch," wailed Anita as she began crying uncontrollably.

Just then, Ryat, Dollas, and Anita all became silent as they listened to the local news anchor give an update on Ray's shooting:

"Just in ladies and gentlemen; it has been confirmed that Raymond Storm of the twenty-one hundred block of North 5th Street was pronounced dead in route to the hospital. As just reported

minutes ago Mr. Storm was shot in the chest inside the Y.M.C.A. on 6th street by a Mr. Victor George. Unfortunately, the details surrounding this tragic event have not been released as of yet but will be forthcoming and we will keep you updated; this is..."

"OH MY GOD! NO... NO... NO... NOOOOO..." wailed Anita.

Ryat and Dollas both sat aghast on the couch as they all fell into their own personal state of mourning while silently in denial. Until a broken Mr. Carl came through the door a half an hour later in a state of complete bereavement. For Ryat, the anomalous sight of his grandfather so broken confirmed for him that his uncle was actually deceased. At that point he then fell into a fit of crying and sobbing uncontrollably as Mrs. Eve came through the door moments later. Anita immediately ran to her mother wailing as everyone else just kind of looked in her direction, expecting Mrs. Eve to be most visibly torn. Although internally she was tormented and torn by her only son's death externally she seemed eerily calm because as fate would have it over the years she'd dealt with so much trauma that she'd become numb to the anguish it caused.

Ray's funeral was held six days later at the United Methodist Church at 2200 Nth 6th street. There was a big turnout between family and friends but the biggest turnout was from a bunch of mourning female acquaintance of Ray's. Where ironically as fate would have it, Ray lost his life over a female acquaintance of his. As was told to his family, Ray lost his life after being confronted about sleeping with Victor George's woman. Detectives told Mrs. Eve that a heated argument ensued to where Ray was subsequently shot. The Courts later concluded that Victor George acted in self-defense because of Ray's prior firearms convictions. Coupled with the fact that two witnesses testified at Victor's trial saying that it looked like Ray was reaching for a gun although there was none found at the scene. Dollas knew the truth though as he told Ray's family that Ray was only reaching to take his beeper off his hip in order to fight Victor. Subsequently Victor was only found guilty of involuntary manslaughter and sentenced to a short prison term of two and half to nine years.

Tanell had just spent the last five years of his life in isolation, unable to differentiate between an hour and a day. His numerous violent assaults on inmates and staff over the years was what landed him in such a position. For which his most recent assault before being isolated resulted in a correctional officer having to take an early retirement due to nerve damage caused by Tanell.

Tanell's reasoning for his malefic impetuosity was that he no longer had anything to live for. After being torn from a natural existence for the past eleven and a half years, he gave up all hope while his appeals each dried up like an autumn leaf. His only contact with the outside world was an occasional letter from his older sister in Baltimore who wrote him maybe once a year. Guilt was Tanell's greatest tormentor though after the death of everybody he truly loved. He felt that life could get no worse.

The day of Ray's funeral was such a traumatic experience for 11-year-old Ryat as it was the first funeral he had ever attended. The most grievous part was that it was the funeral of someone he admired and loved so deeply. Later that night he was sitting in his late uncle's room in a melancholic trance when he was suddenly compelled to look inside Ray's closet. Going straight to his uncle's hiding spot, he found what he was looking for. Retrieving the bundled-up towel, Ryat took it from its hiding place and placed it on his uncle's bed where he then began to unravel the towel revealing a chrome pistol grip Glock 40. Ryat then just stared at the gun for a while remembering everything his late Uncle told him regarding guns.

Ryat then became extremely timid as he looked at the gun remembering the crux of his uncle's warning against him and guns. Yet the more he thought about his late uncle the more he became enraged. All of his uncle's reasoning's against him and guns went awry as Ryat then began to remember one thing his uncle told him about and that was *retribution*. In that heated moment, Ryat secretly vowed that he would repay Victor George one day, he then took his uncle's gun to his room and placed it inside the stereo speaker that he took from Ray's room just days before.

Chapter 6

*"No man is the same after an agony; he is either
better or worse, and the agony of a man's
experience is nearly always the first thing that
opens his mind..."*
-Oswald Chambers

    In the couple of years since Ray's death each
of the Storm's found their own way of dealing with
the trauma that seemed to be repeatedly inflicted on
their lives. As Mrs. Eve's motto was *you never learn
to get over or except it, you just learn to deal with it
the best way you can.* She therefore dealt with the
continuous pain weighing heavy on her heart by
keeping herself busy so she didn't have idle time to
harbor on such pain.

    She began working more hours on her job,
then straight to bingo most nights and when she
wasn't doing either of the two, she was at church.
She also seemed to always be cleaning around the

house ceaselessly. More shocking of all, unbeknownst to her, was when Ryat found out that his grandmother had also began smoking weed as a coping mechanism. He started noticing her peculiar behavior after coming from the basement most nights so he quietly snuck down behind her one night. Receiving one of the few shocks of his young life as he furtively watched her puff on the small joint between her fingers. Though shocked, he never mentioned it because he fully understood and was just happy to see that it relieved her, if just for a short time, from her sense of disquietude as she seemed serene after coming up from the basement most nights.

Mr. Carl dealt with his pain strictly through his crack addiction. In the couple years since Ray's death, he went from a moderate functioning addict to a full-blown crack addict. Fiendishly seeking to walk the clouds through crack smoke with every breath he took. He no longer could hold a job because of his ceaseless crave to escape reality. Therefore, he did petty hustles all day in the streets just to at least make a meager $10. So, he could for a short time live in the subjective realm, tap dancing on rain clouds as if mocking the analogous nature of his family's last name to their grievous plight.

His appearance became a sad sight as he looked like an alley bum no longer concerned about his upkeep. Where he was once a strong, lean, well-built man, he now barely held any resemblance of his old self as he became so skinny he was beginning to resemble an actual apparition. He became completely eccentric as Ryat along with the rest of his family barely saw much of him anymore. They all hated the full crack addict he had evolved into and how he went about living his daily life. Yet, they all understood Mr. Carl experienced more pain than the average man could bear therefore crack became his coping mechanism.

Meanwhile, Anita became engrossed in bettering herself and her circumstances since Ray's death. Unlike the rest of her immediate family she refused to dwell in self-pity or become entrapped in an insidious depression. Achieving a better future became her nepenthe as she refused to continue to look at life through myopic eyes. Therefore, she enrolled at Harrisburg Area Community College (H.A.C.C.), taking up Business and Financial Services as her major. Looking to become a marketing manager in the near future, she gave her all to her school work. When she wasn't occupied by her rigorous school schedule, she worked as a telemarketer for an advertising sales company. She no longer smoked weed or drank because she believed she no longer needed them to cope and they only hindered her effectiveness regarding her school work and future planning. She even found herself a good man named Keith who treated her like a queen and was looking towards a future with her. He even had a good job as an industrial truck and tractor operator.

Thirteen-year-old Ryat on the other hand took Ray's death the hardest as fighting became a conduit for him to release his new-found omnipresent anger. He just always seemed to be angry or pensive since his late uncle's passing. Therefore, he became antisocial, only speaking when spoken too, mainly only to family and friends. He initiated fights with other peers restlessly, earning himself the title of trouble maker whom only the bad kids in the neighborhood were allowed to hang around. Seeing the path he was headed down, Dollas would catch him in the neighborhood every so often and talk to him about staying on the straight path regarding school and his future. But it was to no avail because every time Dollas would talk to him it went in one ear and out the other as Ryat only thought about smoking his next blunt or causing some type of mischief.

Mrs. Eve knew of his fighting and trouble-making but didn't get on his case that much about it because he still made the honor role in school every report card. Also, she along with the rest of the family figured it was only a phase he was going through since his uncle's passing. Yet, little did they know the fire that was kindled in him four years prior was now at a simmer.

Walking out the back door of their apartment building, Ryat was surprised to see his grandmother on the back porch, sitting on the step smoking one of her beloved Virginia Slims.

"Hey baby, where you headed?" asked Mrs. Eve the second she looked back and saw Ryat coming through the backdoor threshold.

"I wasn't really headed nowhere Nana, I was just bout to run to the store on Fourth and Woodbine," answered Ryat as he sat beside his grandmother on the step.

"You seen ya granddaddy lately boy?"

"Not since three days ago when you was at work. He came in that morning and made like ten big ole burnt pancakes like he ain't ate in years."

"Go figure, I should have known, that's why I only go half box of Bisquick left," said Mrs. Eve followed by a short chuckle.

She then commenced to smoking her cigarette as they sat in silence for a while until she noticed the pensive look on his face.

"What's wrong baby? You look like something is troubling you."

"It's just that I been thinking bout my mom a lot lately Nana, things like what was she like and stuff."

"She was a beautiful person inside and out and she would have been so happy to see the beautiful boy you've turned out to be."

"I was just looking at her picture on my dresser, the one she was pregnant with me in, and I

just started thinking about her. I just wish I would have gotten the chance to know her. She looked like such a happy person. Do you think she was happy to be having me?"

"Boy your mother was so happy when she found out she was having you, couldn't nobody tell that chile nothing, she talked about her unborn baby all day long. Boy she was extremely happy to be having you, she couldn't have been more excited."

"Yeah?" responded Ryat in a somber tone, then after taking a deep breath, he hung his head low and said,

"I just wish I could have known her man. I just wish I could feel happy like she used to be."

"What do you mean baby? I know you miss her and your uncle and this makes you sad and even mad at times but you're young. You won't be sad or mad all the time, you have plenty of time to be more happy then you've ever been."

"I don't know Nana; I just feel like I have anger all the time. It's like when people be happy I just be mad."

"At what baby? Well let me tell you this baby, anger leads to hate and hate leads to suffering and destruction and I'm here to tell you this baby, the last thing you need any more of in your short life is suffering. So, like I've told you in the past, you need not hate anyone or anything but first and foremost you have to get all that anger out of you boy, everything is gone be alright in due

time. You gone grow up and everything that you've been through is only gone make you a better man and give you a better appreciation for life."

"I know Nana and hopefully I will make you, my mom, and uncle Ray proud one day."

"Oh you will baby, you will," responded Mrs. Eve with a smile just before Ryat gave her a hug, got up and made his way to the store.

Ryat and Hochee were standing in back of the buildings on Woodbine street, leaned against a car in the parking lot. Watching as the rest of their friends and other neighborhood boys were about to start a game of basketball on a makeshift court fabricated out of milk crates and wood boards posted from light-pole to light-pole.

"Yo come on Ryat, you gone be on my team," blurted Melvin.

"Man I don't know how many times I'm gone have to tell you I DON'T play fuckin basketball no more. That bullshit ass game don't mean nothing to me no more," replied Ryat.

"'Ight man damn, it's cool. I'm just gone grab fat boy right here," Countered Melvin as he gestured towards a fat dark-skinned boy standing by the side.

"Yeah you, you on my team."

"Yeah Melvin, we good, ain't nobody trying play wit yall niggas," said Hochee as he commenced to lighting the blunt he and Ryat were about to smoke.

*"Man go head Hochee, you just mad cause
you trash and ain't nobody trying pick you,"*
chimed in Camill as he was shooting the ball before
the game got started.

"Yeah whatever Mil, you trash nigga,"
retorted Hochee as he passed the blunt to Ryat.

Ryat and Hochee then stood there taking
turns on the blunt while watching their friends play
basketball for over an hour when suddenly Potta
and his older cousin Lati came walking up. With
Ryat and Hochee instantly taking note of Potta's
new look as he came walking up in a new leather
Avirex coat with a fresh pair of *Jordans* to match.
Which was a big transformation since everybody
was used to seeing Potta in faded hand-me-downs
as he was always known as one of the little dirty
kids from the neighborhood.

"Yo what up Ryat? What's good Hochee?"
said Potta as he gave both Ryat and Hochee five
with a half hug embrace.

"Ain't shit, what good wit you though cuz?"
replied Ryat after breaking their embrace.

*"Yo Potta I'm 'ight but man you the one
that's good, looking like a balla and everything,"*
said Hochee as Potta stood there gloating, knowing
his friends were admiring his new attire and look.

*"Yo what up Ryat and Hochee? Y'all niggas
look higher than a muthafucka. Where can I get
some of that fire y'all was blowing?"* said Lati after
hanging up his cellphone.

"Ain't shit, yo what up Lati? We grabbed that fire from the dude Bone on Maclay," answered Hochee after he and Ryat broke their embrace with Lati.

"It's all good though wit me my niggas. I'm just trying get this paper wit my big cuz," said Potta as he showed off a small wad of twenties from his pocket.

Ryat just kind of stared at the small wad of cash, realizing his hunch was correct as he initially figured Potta must had started hustling. Which explained his new fly attire and him hanging around Lati all day and night.

"Damn word!" exclaimed Hochee as he seemed to be enamored with the thought and sight of Potta in his new fly threads holding a small wad of cash.

"Yeah word. I'm saying Hoch, what you know 'bout them cooks?" asked Lati as he pulled a sandwich bag filled with smaller blue bags containing small beige rocks from his pocket. He then tossed the baggy to Hochee who stared at its contents as if admiring its potential profit.

"Damn yo, how much is this?" asked Hochee as he handed the baggy back to Lati.

"A lil under seven hundred dollars' worth. I had just grabbed a quarter ounce and just made a quick sell for eighty," replied Lati.

"Damn man yall dudes getting money!" said Hochee excitedly as Ryat looked on nonchalantly, not too enamored by his friends' choice of income.

Ryat knew hustling wasn't for him because he knew Ray wouldn't have had it if he were alive and the mere desire to hustle drugs he knew Mrs. Eve would kill him for. So, he simply looked on as his friends gloated about their new-found hustling endeavors. Though Lati had been hustling for a little over a year as he was two years older at age fifteen. He began hustling drugs at the tender age of fourteen. For mainly the same reasons his thirteen-year-old little cousin Potta was now hustling at such a tender age. Both of their parents weren't really a part of their lives. Whereas both of Lati's parents had been incarcerated since he was nine. While Potta's mom who was Lati's mom's sister, was a full-blown crack addict who barely existed in his young life. He also basically had no memory of a father because his was murdered when he was just a few months old.

"So what's up, y'all dudes trying get some paper? I'll put y'all on y'all feet with enough to get y'all a ball if y'all hustle it right and then I'll hook y'all up wit my ol'head Bo who y'all can start picking up off," said Lati while staring at Ryat and Hochee.

"Nah I'm good, I ain't really trying get into that shit cuz," replied Ryat.

"Yo I'm good too man, I ain't really ready for all that right now but good looking out though cuz," echoed Hochee reluctantly, just as Camill and Melvin came running up all sweaty.

"Yo what up Potta and Lati? What's good wit y'all dudes man? I see y'all fresh ta death," said Camill as he and Melvin embraced both Potta and Lati.

"Yo what up y'all? Why ain't you come ball wit us Potta so I could bus ya ass," said Melvin.

"Yo man go ahead Melvin. You think you the best in everything. I'ma get wit all y'all later though, I gotta be out real quick," said Lati.

"Me too," echoed Potta as they both gave daps to everybody and made their way around the corner in misguidance to peddle the devil's pebbles in order to acquire the root of all evil.

"Yo I'ma be out too cause my dad supposed to be taking me to the Cougars game tonight," said Melvin after Potta and Lati had just stepped off.

"'Ight then cuz, we get wit you later," responded Camill as they all gave Melvin five with half hug embraces before he went on his way.

Ryat, Camill, and Hochee then began walking to Hochee's house on 5th & Camp street to play video games. Camill then began inquiring about Potta's new threads and the fact that they hadn't been seeing much of him lately. That's when both Ryat and Hochee filled Camill in on their friend's new-found hustle.

"Word cuz! Potta grinding? That dude is crazy but I ain't surprised, especially since Lati been hustling for a minute now," said Camill.

"Yeah Potta and Lati offered to put me and Hochee on our feet," said Ryat.

"Word! What y'all say?"

"Man I told him I'm good cause that really ain't for me plus my Nana would kill me if she found out I even thought about it," replied Ryat.

"Yeah I told him I'm good too but I ain't gone lie man, I wanted to get put on my feet for real after seeing them wit that money. But I know my moms would kill me and have me going to her church everyday instead of just on Sundays. But I do need to make that type money to help her wit them bills she always praying about, that God ain't help her with yet," said Hochee.

"Yeah I feel you Hochee cause I wish I could make some real money to help my moms and grandma out because it's like they struggling every month to keep a roof over me and my sister head. And my sister dad Kevin living with us, making all types money in the streets but the only person he look out for is my sister. Man, I swear I hate dude. I get tired of hearing my moms begging this dude for a couple dollars to help wit the bills. Oh yeah, and I ain't gone front though, I would stay fresh ta death everyday if I could make some real money," said Camill.

Ryat, Potta, and Camill were in Ryat's living room playing Golden Eye on Nintendo 64. Admiring the weaponry in the game, they all talked endlessly about the various assault rifles and handguns as they played the game.

"*Yo I'm telling y'all, I'm getting me one of those M-16's and one of those revolvers one day,*" blurted Camill.

"*Man you always talking bout what types guns you gone get. What you need a gun for Mil?*" asked Ryat as his mind drifted to the gun in his possession, which belonged to his late uncle. He couldn't help but think of the words of his late uncle regarding guns.

"*...a man should never possess a gun unless he need it and should never put it in his hands unless he know he's gone use it with no regrets...*"

"*Man I just like guns. What's wrong wit that? And I am gone get some guns one day just in case because you never know Ryat. That's why everybody carry a gun these days. Shit, my mom even carry a gun when she bartends at night, I seen it. I think it's like a baby three-eighty cause it's small and she keep it in her bra,*" responded Camill.

"*Damn yo Mil, Ya mom is a G,*" quipped Potta.

"*Shit look at Mr. Tony from down the street, he carry a gun everyday and he work,*" said Camill.

"*How you know?*" countered Ryat.

"*Cause he told me all about it one day after I seen it on his hip in its holster when he paid me to help him wash his car. He said he got a gun permit. He said he carry it because people these days don't*

*care about nothing or nobody and will harm you
while you're walking with your mom and will harm
her too without a care in the world."*

*"Yo word cuz, I feel that because those
niggas down on da ave. jumped my cousin Brian
and his moms and all she was trying do was break
up the fight. That's why I copped this lil thirty-two
right here,"* said Potta as he showed off the small
silver revolver he concealed in his waistband.

"Oh shit yo! Let me see that joint!"
exclaimed Camill excitedly as Potta handed him the
gun.

*"Yo man put that shit up for my Nana come
in here and kill all of us,"* hissed Ryat as he
remembered the fact that his grandmother was right
outside the door in the hallway sweeping the stairs.

Mrs. Eve had been sweeping the stairs to the
apartment building for the past twenty-five minutes.
She started with the back-hallway stairwell first,
working her way to the front stairwell where she
was currently sweeping. She was on the second
flight when she began feeling acute heart
palpitations. She immediately dropped the broom
she was holding, grabbed her chest with her right
hand and the banister for support with her left. Then
before she could understand what was happening to
her, she suddenly lost consciousness. Collapsing,

her limp body fell down he entire second flight of steps.

"Oh shit yo, you hear that?" blurted Camill, referring to the loud noise coming from just outside the door.

"Oh shit! Yeah!" exclaimed Ryat, instantly thinking of his grandmother as he immediately ran out the door with his friends in tow.

"OH SHIT!... NANA!" shouted Ryat as he looked up from the bottom of the stairwell and saw his grandmother laying limp at the bottom of the second staircase flight.

"OH SHIT YO!" echoed Camill and Potta.

"NANA!" cried out Ryat as he flew up the stairwell to aid his fallen grandmother just as Mr. Carl came rushing out of his third-floor apartment. Seeing what was causing all the raucous, Mr. Carl cleared the two stairwell flights in record breaking time to aid his fallen wife.

"Ryat GODDAMMIT call an ambulance. Hurry up!" shouted Mr. Carl frantically as he immediately picked Mrs. Eve up off of the ground and carried her to the couch downstairs.

Six minutes later, an ambulance pulled in front of their building with emergency personnel rushing from the ambulance towards the inside of the building. Awhile Mr. Carl and Ryat stood by frantic as E.M.S then rushed Mrs. Eve from the building on a stretcher.

Moments later while in route to Polyclinic Hospital, Mrs. Eve was diagnosed as experiencing cardiac arrest. Where upon arrival at the hospital, a group of doctors and nurses immediately took over and began performing cardiopulmonary resuscitation. They restored Mrs. Eve's breathing, though she remained unconscious as they strapped her with I.V.'s and hooked her to an oxygen machine. Meanwhile Mr. Carl, Ryat, Anita, and Keith sat impatiently in the waiting room, frantically awaiting to hear about Mrs. Eve's status.

They were relieved a half an hour later when they were informed that Mrs. Eve pulled through. But would remain in intensive care for further medical care unit until she was well enough to be moved.

CHAPTER 7

"A man's strength is to know his weakness."
-Russell Simmons

Ryat had just entered the hospital and was in the gift shop buying his grandmother a bag of her favorite *Werther's* candy. He had been doing the same thing around the same time for the past five weeks his grandmother had been in the hospital. Except this time, while in the gift shop he noticed a girl around his age inside the gift shop also. What initially intrigued him was that it was during school hours, where he was usually the only kid in the hospital at that time. Though he immediately noticed the girl had a beautiful pure cinnamon skin tone with wavy hair that was held together by a colorful bobby pin down to the small of her back. He also took notice of how beautiful her facial features were the moment she turned around and smiled sheepishly at him. Blushing, he smiled his infectious smile, noticing the girl had sort of a quiet innocence about her that intrigued him even more.

"How you doing? My name is um-uh...Tiffany," she nervously spoke in a soft quaint melodic tone.

"Yeah wha'sup, my name is Ryat," he calmly replied still smiling.

"I was checking you out at first because you the first person I've seen my age around here in the last five weeks I've been coming here. But then I noticed how pretty you are, so that's why you caught me checking you out so hard."

Smiling shyly, she said,

"Well my older sister just had her baby an hour ago so my mom let me take off from school and be here."

"That's wha'sup; you must have a tight family. My grandmom is on the fifth floor, so I been hanging out around here since she had her heart attack five weeks ago."

"So your mom let you be here every day like this, even when you supposed to be at school?" Tiffany asked.

"Well my grandmom is pretty much my mom."

"Oh Ok . so how old are you? Uh...Riot, right? Like in Riot, R-I-O-T."

"Yeah it's Riot but it's spelled R-Y-A-T and I'm thirteen."

"Oh ok, I like your name, it's cute. And that's funny because we're the same age."

"Oh yeah, that's wha'sup, so let me get your number then," countered Ryat boldly with his signature infectious smile highlighting his pubescent facial features.

"Oh my God, I'm not really allowed to talk to boys on the phone," she responded in a regretful tone.

"Well are you allowed to talk to your girlfriends on the phone?"

"Yeah."

"Well all that means is that I can't call you but you can call me and act like you talking to one of your girlfriends. So can I give you my number and you call me?"

"Yeah," answered Tiffany, intrigued by his manly confidence as he then quickly scribbled down his home number and handed it to her.

"I usually be home any time after ten," said Ryat right after handing her his number.

"Oh my God, you must just do what you want since your grandmom has been in the hospital," she responded with a sheepish smile.

"Well I have to be off the phone by nine."

"Oh 'ight," said Ryat returning her smile.

"So just call me at eight tomorrow cause I'ma go in early just for you."

"OK."

"Yo Tiffany, come on. We about to leave, I been running around this hospital looking for you for the past ten minutes," shouted a fat dark-skinned man as he walked towards them.

"Ok, here I come."

"Who's that?" inquired Ryat.

"My big brother Avery."

"Yo come on Tiffany and who is this lil boy?" said Avery as he approached them.

"Nobody Avery, he just helped me find the Happy New Born cards in the gift shop because he basically work here."

"Oh 'ight, come on then," retorted Avery as he quickly turned his back in route to leave with Tiffany in tow.

Just then Ryat was getting ready to turn and head towards his grandmother's floor, Tiffany quickly turned around and made a phone signal with her right hand against her ear and cheek, mouthing words,

"I'm gonna call you."

"Wha'sup Nana," said Ryat in an excited voice accompanied by a broad smile after walking through the door of his grandmother's hospital room.

"Oh my God boy! What did I tell you about coming here during school hours? I done told you over and over and I'ma have to curse your aunt out because I done told that darn Anita to make sure you're going to school and not coming here during school hours," said Mrs. Eve while raising her decibel level a bit as she lay in her hospital bed.

"Calm down Nanna, aunt Nita thinks I'm at school because I leave the house like I'm going to school right now because I can't focus and learn any work as long as you in here. But I promise as soon as you get out of here I'ma study even harder at school," responded Ryat as he handed his grandmother the candy he had bought for her.

"Boy are you crazy? Telling me some got darn mess like that. Talking bout you can't learn because I'm in here..."

"For real Nana, I can't, that's why I come here every day until you get out because all I can think about when I'm at school is you being in here and until you get out of here I ain't gone be able to focus on my school work. It's like, when I'm at school no matter how hard I try to focus, my mind is here with you."

"Boy you are too much but I want you to understand that I understand that you worry about me but I am going to be alright because the good Lord is going to make sure of it. Now you on the other hand will not be alright and there will be nothing the Lord can do to stop me from whupping your narrow ass if you don't take your behind to school and learn all you can because learning is like healing, it happens over time. Your never done learning boy and your education is important for your future, so I don't want to hear all that you can't focus mess. You better take your behind to school or else, do you understand me boy?"

"Yes ma'am."

"Now I know you've been getting into a lot of trouble around the neighborhood. I didn't say much cause you were doing good in school and your uncle had just passed. But now you're not even going to school and your using me as an excuse. I refuse to let you turn into one of these heathens, running around here ignorant with no respect and no future. Now I'ma tell you this, you will either drive yourself or be driven. Don't let the winds of circumstance blow you in any direction."

"Yes ma'am but it just so happens you'll most likely be out of here by the time I go back to school because tomorrow is the beginning of spring break," countered Ryat followed by his infectious smile he knew his grandmother couldn't resist no matter how mad she got at him since he was a toddler.

"Oh my Lord boy you are entirely too much, now come here and give your Nana a hug before I pull my strap out right now and wup you for growing up so fast," said Mrs. Eve with a lovingly wide smile as he immediately walked over and embraced her in a loving hug.

"Yo Mil, Wha'sup?" said Ryat after entering Camill's apartment building and seeing him sitting at the top of the stairwell with another boy around their age, smoking a blunt.

"Yo Ryat wha'sup cuz? You just come from visiting your grandmom cause I ain't seen you all day?" responded Camill.

"Yeah," responded Ryat after making his way up the stairwell and embracing Camill in a half hug handshake.

"Yo wha'sup sun," said the brown-skinned boy sitting with Camill while extending his hand towards Ryat.

"Yo what up cuz," responded Ryat as he took the boy's hand into a handshake.

"Yo Ryat, this is my man Bryce, he just moved here about three months ago. We been chilling out here in the hallway off and on for about a month now," said Camill, pausing for a second to inhale the weed smoke, then after exhaling he continued.

"He good people though and he real dude."

"No doubt what up Bryce? Where you from cuz?" said Ryat as Camill handed him the blunt.

"Yo word ta mutha sun; what is up wit all this crab talk? Yo Mil, don't let me find out all of a sudden that you niggas is crabs," said Bryce while intensely staring at both Ryat and Camill as Camill then began laughing hysterically.

"Yo Mil what the fuck is so funny and why is ya man over here bugging bout some shit I don't even understand? Like cuz, what the fuck you so mad about CRABS for?" hissed Ryat at Camill then Bryce, awhile Camill continued laughing even

harder as he bent over in hysterics while trying to catch his breath.

"Aye Ryat...Aye yo Ryat hold up for a second..." said Camill as he struggled to control his laughter.

"Yo Ryat, Bryce is Blood. So he thinking we Crips cause we always saying cuz." Finished Camill before erupting in laughter all over again.

"All nah Bryce, we ain't Crips. It ain't even no Crips and Bloods in the Burg that I know of. That's just how we talk uptown cuz," said Ryat.

"Oh 'ight sun I'm understanding. But Yo Mil the shit wasn't that funny sun," countered Bryce.

"Sheiiit," retorted Camill as he wiped his eyes after gaining control of his laughter.

"Yo y'all niggas can't front, that shit was hilarious cause Bryce you really thought we was Crips but this nigga Ryat thought you was really talking about crabs...real CRABS."

They all then just looked at one another before falling out into a violent laughter.

"Y'all dudes is high as fuck now," said Ryat just before inhaling the blunt he had just realized was burning in his hand the entire time they were going back and forth.

"Yo Bryce I can tell I'ma fucks wit you like that, especially since you and Mil already cool. So you blood huh? I can tell you must be from somewhere in New York cause how you talk."

"Yeah I'm Damu, straight seven-thirty. From Harlem sun, Polo Grounds, my moms move me out here trying get me away from my other seven-thirty niggas up top. But that shit won't change me sun, I'm Damu for life and always gone be down for whatever, N.T.G.!"

"Yo Ryat I told you he a real dude, he wild too. I can't wait for Hochee and Potta to meet him cause I know they gone fucks wit him heavy wit their crazy assess," said Camill.

"Yeah they gone love him. Yo what up wit Melvin? I ain't seen him since his pops found out he be smoking weed wit us."

"Yeah man, you know his Pops went hard on him. I seen him three days ago, after school. I tried to get him to come ball wit me and Bryce down Emerald but he said his Pops got him on punishment and said he couldn't hang around us no more."

"Yeah sun looked all shook up, word," chimed in Bryce.

"Damn yo, Mr. Varner do be going hard. I just hope my boy still be able to chill wit us though," said Ryat.

"But anyway, yo Ryat what up wit girly Tiffany you told me you met about a week ago while visiting your grandmoms at the hospital?" asked Camill.

"Oh...she cool cuz. She live down on Calder street so I been going down there kicking it wit her a lot lately."

"Oh shit, sun blushing. She must be tuff sun," quipped Bryce.

"Damn cuz, let me find out she got my main man whipped already," quipped Camill as he and Bryce broke into a slight laughter.

"Yeah 'ight," countered Ryat curtly while twisting up his face and sucking his teeth.

"Yeah whatever, you still my mans even if you is a sucka for love," retorted Camill just before he and Bryce broke into an all-out fit of laughter at Ryat's reaction.

"I'm saying though I know she got friends, hook ya homies up."

"Yo Mil I know you ain't calling nobody a sucka for love when Essie done had you whipped since like the third grade and you already know she got you too scared to even look at another girl. So I don't know why you fronting, talking bout hook you up wit something."

"I'm saying though," countered Camill as a wide smile began to stretch the surface of his face, *"I love her cuz."*

"Yo I told you he's the one who's really whipped Bryce, look at him," said Ryat as he and Bryce laughed at Camill's expression of young love.

Later that day, Ryat, Camill, Hochee, Melvin, Potta, Lati, and Bryce were all sitting on a bench in the middle of Emerald Park, holding a conversation while passing blunts in succession.

"Nah I'm good," said Melvin while bouncing a basketball close by the bench as Potta tried to pass him the blunt.

"Yeah Potta chill out, you know Melvin just got off punishment after getting his ass wupped for getting caught blowing wit us," quipped Hochee, drawing chuckles from a few of the fellows.

"Man I ain't get my ass wupped. My Pops just gave me the talk on how I got to stay focused and how that shit just alters your mind state, making you careless, lazy, forgetful, and shit like that," countered Melvin.

"If you got ya ass wupped, you got ya ass wupped, I'm saying I used to get my ass wupped when I was a toddler." quipped Potta while laughing at his own remark.

"Man y'all niggas need to fall back. Shit I wish I had a Pops like Melvin that stay on my case and kept me focused," said Lati as he sat up on the back of the bench, puffing on a blunt.

"Shit man, my Pops been locked up my whole life," said Camill.

"Yeah man I feel you Mil, my Pops is dead. My Nana say my Pops died when I was a baby but she don't tell me no more than that cause she say she protecting me that way," said Ryat, expressing the same forlorn expression as Camill while sitting up on the back of the bench.

"I feel y'all man cause my pops is a cold-blooded deadbeat, he don't give a fuck about me or my little brother and sister. If you ask me it be

better if he was dead," said Hochee with a nefarious look on his face.

"Sun I watched my father die two years ago, right in my projects up Harlem. That's why my moms packed us up and moved down here," said Bryce with fire in his eyes as he puffed on the blunt.

"Yeah man... my daddy dead too." Said Potta in a hushed tone while looking off in space pensively.

They all then sat around in a state of melancholy, not saying much to one another until Melvin said he had to be home before 8 p.m., where they all then went their separate ways.

"Hello?"

"Can I speak to Ryat please?" asked Tiffany from the other end of the line.

"Yo this is me; how you don't know my voice yet?" responded Ryat.

"Because your voice sounds deeper on the phone and the one time I called I thought your aunt's boyfriend was you when he answered the phone."

"Oh 'ight but for the record I don't sound nothing like my aunt's lame ass boyfriend. Anyway, so wha'sup wit you girl? Me and my mans seen

your friend Kelly at my man Melvin's game earlier."

"Oh my God Ryat, why your aunt's boyfriend got to be a lame? Why because he isn't a street person?"

"Because he just is. Why you so worried about it? It ain't like he's your boyfriend cause I thought that was me."

"It's just that you don't like nobody."

"I like you."

"Ok Ryat, I guess that's just the way you are."

"No doubt."

"So what happened at your friend's game? You better not had been smart to my friend Kelly."

"Nah she cool, she was there wit her cousin I guess. She spoke so I spoke back but then my man Bryce started feeling her so I hooked them up."

"Bryce? Is that the New York boy you hang wit?"

"Yeah."

"He better not try play my friend Ryat," said Tiffany.

"For real Ryat, stop laughing, it ain't funny."

"Nah she cool, my man Bryce real dude."

"Alright Ryat, anyway is you still coming over my house tomorrow after I get off school. My mom and brother ain't gone be here."

"Yeah I'm coming over after I leave from visiting my grandmom. You know I can't wait to get

over there and get some of that sweet potato pie while ya moms and brother gone," said Ryat while smiling into the phone.

"Boy you are stupid," said Tiffany while smiling coyly into the phone.

"I'll see you tomorrow, bye."

Walking from the elevator on the fifth floor of the hospital where his grandmother was being kept, Ryat found doctor Pascal coming out the room of one of his other patients.

"Excuse me, Dr. Pascal," said Ryat, walking towards the doctor.

"Yes young man, Mrs. Storm's grandson correct?" responded Dr. Pascal.

"Yeah, um when you think she'll be able to go home because it's been two and half months since she's been here and it seems like there's nothing wrong with her so she should have been able to go home."

"Well young man, your grandmother is a very strong woman so you probably wouldn't know when something is wrong with her because she doesn't even know most the time but for the most part her condition has been up and down since she's been here. So, we've been running continued test to make sure she's in the best possible condition before we send her home. As of late though it seems

we may have to keep her longer and give her some alternative treatments. Because it seems as of right now her overall health is in a regressive state. As a matter of fact, I have some basic questions I have to ask her before we take her for some more testing. So why don't you come with me as we go through this process."

"Alright," replied Ryat, incredulous as to what the doctor had just told him regarding his grandmother's health.

Dr. Pascal and Ryat then proceeded inside Mrs. Eve's room where she lay propped up in her hospital bed. With a meal tray positioned across her midsection, sitting on the tray stand that was connected to the bed. Turning abruptly towards the noise of the people entering the room, a broad smile spread across Mrs. Eve's face at the sight of Ryat. He immediately became apprehensive because though she always smiled, this smile seemed unfamiliar. Coupled with the fact that she usually never greeted him with a smile at that time because he was supposed to be in school. Walking towards her he became even more apprehensive as he noticed the glassy look in her eyes just before he embraced her in a hug.

"Hey baby, I'm glad you've finally made it. They've been wanting to take me home for a while now but I told them we have to wait for my baby to get here before we go anywhere," said Mrs. Eve as they broke from their embrace.

"What? Who? What you…" Ryat barely got out, befuddled, before being cut short by Dr. Pascal. Who stood close by Mrs. Eve's bed holding a clipboard with pen in hand.

"Sorry Mrs. Storm but I have to ask you these questions before we take you for testing in a minute, Ok," said Dr. Pascal.

"Goddamit, I told you I don't need no more damn test! My kids have come to take me home and I'm going Goddammit," replied Mrs. Eve, taking on a combative tone.

"Kids?" mouthed Ryat in a low audible.

"Mrs. Storm I'm sorry but I have to ask you what is your full name?" asked Dr. Pascal.

"Goddammit y'all been asking me this question over and over like I'm crazy or something."

"Please answer the question Mrs. Storm."

"Goddammit my name is Eve Mae Storm. Now y'all can stop asking me that Goddamn question because I'm not crazy and it isn't like y'all haven't been known my name."

"All right Mrs. Storm and your home address is what?"

"Goddammit I'm done answering these stupid questions. Ask my daughter, Ashley tell them where we live, 2119 north 5th street."

"What! Nana! What you talking bout?! Ashley? My m-… she's de-… she's not here!" exclaimed Ryat in a state of bewilderment.

Ryat then looked towards Dr. Pascal for answers but was met with an impassive look from the doctor as his gaze fell back to his clipboard. Ryat immediately got the impression this was the reason for the basic questions and the test to come.

"What you mean baby? Ashley is right here, so is my Ray."

"Aww man Nana, what do you mean! Nobody's here but me, you, and Dr. P..." said Ryat before cutting himself short as he stared at his grandmother with her glazed eyes and eccentric demeanor, she looked like an aberration of her normal self.

Tears began to well in his eyes as he began to feel an immense intangible pain while staring at his disoriented grandmother.

"Baby why are you crying? What have I always told you? Times make the man, not the other way around. Nothing is wrong baby; your Nana is alright. I'll be home soon, OK baby?" said Mrs. Eve with a familiar smile that gave Ryat a semblance of his usual grandmother.

"All right Mrs. Storm, it's time for your testing. So, we'll be taking you downstairs to the third floor at this time," said Dr. Pascal as a nurse came in the room with a wheelchair to help Mrs. Eve into.

"Sorry young man but testing will be in excess of an hour and we are not permitted to let visitors to our testing area. So, you can wait in our

waiting area young man or maybe you can go and come back later."

"Alright... I guess I'll just come back tomorrow because visiting hours is over in a few hours...Alright then Nana, I'll see you tomorrow, OK?" said Ryat as he then moved to embrace his grandmother in a loving hug.

"Alright baby, now you be sure to tell your aunt Anita that I don't need her to come and get me because Ashley and Ray have already come," said Mrs. Eve as Ryat was pulling away from their embrace.

"Uh... O... K... Nana, bye, I love you," stammered Ryat just before turning to leave in a melancholic state.

"Bye baby, your Nana loves you more."

Later that day Ryat had just finished telling his aunt Anita about the events that transpired earlier that day at the hospital. All while Anita sat back into the couch simply taking in everything her nephew had told her. Incredulous to everything she had just heard, Anita could not understand why her mother could have been so aberrant.

"I just don't get it Ryat, what do you mean she was talking like my sister and brother were right there in the room?" asked Anita as she took a deep breath and looked Ryat in the eyes.

"Man I'm telling you aunt Nita; she was talking crazy like she wasn't herself but she seemed so happy when she mentioned them. I'm telling you man it scared me like Nana was losing her mind or something. I just think she been in that stupid hospital too long. I wish they'd just let her come home with us," responded Ryat as he held back tears from the vision of his strong-willed grandmother seeming so vulnerable.

"Oh my God, I can't believe this but I know one thing; I will be at that hospital first thing tomorrow morning. I don't care if I got to take off work for the day because I have to find out what's really going on with my mom," said Anita as if almost thinking out loud.

At 9:35 p.m. that night, while Ryat sat on the couch watching a program on television, the phone rang. Anita, walking by the phone at that present time, answered it.

"Hello, may I ask who's speaking?"

"Hell, hi um am I speaking with Ms. Anita Storm?" asked the person on the other end of the line.

"Yes, this is her."

"Ms. Storm this is Dr. Pascal and I'm afraid I have some terrible news to deli..."

"NO! NO! PLEASE NO!" Anita abruptly cried out.

"Ms. Storm I am so sorry to inform you that your mother has passed away at approximately nine-twelve p.m. this evening."
"OH MY GOD, NO! NO! NO! this can't be. NOOOOOOOOOO! PLEASE GOD NO!" wailed Anita barely dangling the phone at her ear as Ryat's acuity immediately lead him to realize what had happened. The only reason his aunt would be breaking down at that point on the phone.
"NO! NO! NO! PLEASE GOD NO!" Anita continuously wailed into the phone while confirming the inevitable for Ryat.

His loving grandmother had passed away. With tears streaming down his eyes, Ryat just simply looked on in a familiar trance as his aunt bewailed ceaselessly.

Six days later at Mrs. Eve's funeral proceedings, Ryat sat in his familiar pensive trance between his grandfather and aunt, in the front row of the proceedings. Hundreds of people showed that Ryat had never seen before, mostly well-meaning older people that knew Mrs. Eve for years. His pensive state at that moment was him harboring on the irony of his grandmother's death. The irony being that she died of a heart attack, where he believed she literally died of a broken heart. After so many years of intangible pain inflicted on her heart, Ryat believed the pain began to weigh so heavy on her heart that she literally died of a broken heart. These depressing thoughts and his trance was interrupted when he realized the proceedings had come to an end as people began filing out of the funeral home. Some in destination with him and his immediate family to watch as his grandmother was laid in her final resting place.

While heading towards the parking lot, Ryat was approached by a meek older black woman.

"Ryat, I'm so sorry about what happened to your grandmother but do know that she is in a much better place, I can assure you of that. By the way how are you holding up baby? I know it must be hard," said the woman as Ryat looked into the eyes of the woman he knew as Mrs. Mary from his grandmother's church where Mrs. Eve was Daughter Ruler and a Trustee.

"Mrs. Mary, how do you really know?" asked Ryat while staring intensely into her eyes.

"Really know what baby?"

"How can you really tell me that my grandma is in a much better place? Why because of God?! Man, my grandma always talking bout God gone see us through everything but he ain't never did nothing to help my family," exclaimed Ryat while still holding Mrs. Mary in eye contact as his began to well with tears.

"Aww baby listen I understand why you could feel like that but you must believe that God is with you and he had been whether you notice or not. But one day you will come to know this just like your grandmother knew because sooner or later God will bring self-sufficient people to the place

where they have no resource but him – no strength, no answers, nothing but him, without God's help they're nonexistent."

"*I know this Mrs. Mary... it's just that...It's just... man I miss her so much, I need her man,*" bewailed Ryat as he became completely vulnerable for the first time since his grandmother's death. Tears streamed his face and fell from his cheeks as Mrs. Mary embraced him.

"*Everything's gone be alright in the long run son, you just have to believe it will and know that you can come to me if you ever need anything. You want to know how I'm so sure she's in a much better place? Because your aunt told me what happened in the last hours of her life when you were at the hospital. I want you to know your mother and uncle WERE there that day."*

"*WHAT?!*"

"*Yeah baby, see they were there because like she said they were there to take her home. That's what happens when people like her pass, God sends their angels to take them home peacefully."*

Standing over the plot as his grandmother was being laid in her final resting place at William Howard day Cemetery in Steelton, Ryat stood with a forlorn look on his face. Awhile his ambivalence

lead him towards anger as he began to feel
abandoned. Right then fire flashed in his eyes as the
fire that was kindled in him when he was just nine,
then a couple years later came to a simmer, was
now ablaze.

Chapter 8

"The Gods see what is to come, wise men see what is coming, and ordinary men see what has come."
-Apolonius

Tanell had just finished reading Nathan McCall's book *"Makes me Wanna Holla: A Black Man in America"*. He placed the book inside his footlocker and then laid back on his bunk. As he did most days lately, he then began to ruminate. Reflecting on his life and how he had arrived at this point. After almost a decade and a half in the penitentiary, with most of it spent in long term segregation units throughout the Pennsylvania D.O.C.

He knew his life and thought process needed a drastic change if for nothing more than the serenity of his soul. After so many years removed from society, mostly spent in solitary confinement, he had been doing a lot of introspection and what he arrived at today was probably when his pessimistic outlook on life began.

He remembered it as vivid as yesterday's crescent moon aligned with five stars positioned around it as he gazed from his cell window. It was the day his very own father was murdered right before his young eyes. Ironically by his older sister's father over their mother.

His father was a good, honest, hardworking man who loved his mother dearly and would do anything for her. His mother was actually an honest church going woman at the time. Whom at a very young age fell in love with a young street-slick man named Sam whose past time was spent robbing banks.

By age seventeen, Tanell's loving mother Celia gave birth to his older sister Sonya, whom Sam was the father. A year after Sonya's birth, Sam was arrested for a few bank robberies and sentenced to nine years upstate Maryland. Within a year of Sam's incarceration, Celia met and fell deeply in love with Tanell's father Wallace. Where she genuinely loved him in an honest, good-loving way, not the type of puppy love she shared with Sam. Eighteen months later Tanell was born and Celia married Wallace a couple months later.

Tanell's formative years were bread in a loving household where he loved his pure-hearted, nurturing mother tremendously. Yet, his love and bond with is good-natured father went out of his way to edify and teach him early the benefits of being a real man. Tanell would never forget the times his father would take him to the garage with him for *'Take your child to work day'* and they would work together on an old engine block for hours.

Tanell's life took a drastic change during the summer in his seventh year of life. When his older sister Sonya's father Sam came home from the penitentiary a very angry and bitter man. While inside Sam's hurt over Celia's new found love and marriage caused him to sever all emotional ties to the outside world. Therefore, he gave up contact with his daughter and her mother, becoming a very rancorous man. Learning nothing while incarcerated, he went home with the same immature mind state he went in with. Therefore, he came home promising revenge on Celia for betraying his love. The very day he was released back on the streets of Baltimore, Sam immediately went and bought himself a .38 special revolver. The next few days he spent tracking Celia down to her address in the Park Heights section of west Baltimore.

That day would be like none other for young Tanell as he sat on the front porch playing with his toy truck set when a tall burly, dark-skinned man came walking up the steps and rudely nudged past him. The man noticing Celia's sudden appearance in the doorway began to yell boisterously at her.

"Celia, where the hell is my daughter? Tell her to pack her stuff, she's coming with me!" he barked as he stepped closer and swung the screen door open.

"Oh my lord Sam!" exclaimed Celia in a gasping whisper with her right hand covering her mouth.

"Sam I'm glad to see you are home and have come to see your daughter but this is not how you do it, I mean she hardly knows who you are."

"And who's fucking fault is that?" barked Sam.

"Sam you are the one who decided to cut all connection to your daughter while you were in there. I tried to see to you and her bond," responded Celia while backing into her house away from the monstrous man she once knew to have a much smaller frame.

"Yeah it's my fault huh? Ain't nobody tell you to go off and get married!"

"Listen Sam I decided to move on with my life and live, we were young, you have to understand. Now this is not the way you go about getting back into your daughter's life, you have to let her get to know you first."

"Yeah right whatever! Where the hell is my daughter! She's coming with me right now and you never have to worry about seeing her ever again," barked Sam as he pushed past Celia into the foyer of her home and began yelling for his daughter.

"No Sam! You are not just gone take my daughter," exclaimed Celia. Trying to muffle her imminent cries as she ran up the stairs to her daughter.

"Celia I am leaving here with my daughter! There's nothing you can do about that and you will never see her again," barked Sam adamantly, knowing taking their daughter from her would hurt her deep, just the way he had planned.

Just then Wallace was pulling in front of his home in his midnight blue '69 Buick 225. Where as soon as he emerged from his car in his oil stained Winston's Garage jumpsuit, he immediately noticed his son running towards him.

"What's wrong son?" he immediately inquired, sensing something was wrong from the panicked look on his son's face as neared him.

"Daddy, come on, hurry! Some man is trying to hurt mommy, you have to get him dad!" exclaimed young Tanell as Wallace instantly rushed past him, making a mad dash for the wide-open door his home. Where as soon as he crossed the threshold inside his home he heard a man shouting boisterously.

"Celia let go of my daughter right now or else," shouted Sam as he pulled on one arm of his 9-year-old daughter with Celia holding onto her daughter's other arm for dear life.

"Please Sam, why are you doing this? Please! Why are you doing this to our daughter?!" sobbed Celia as she held onto her wailing daughter.

"What the hell is going on here? You let go of my Goddamn daughter?" shouted Wallace, the minute he walked into the dining room where the tug of war over the child was taking place.

"YOUR DAUGHTER?! Do you know who the hell you are talking too? This here is MY DAUGHTER chump and you better beat it while I get MY DAUGHTER and take her with me for good," barked Sam as he in the fraction of a second let go of his daughter, spun around on his heels and was in Wallace's face.

"Daddy!" screamed Sonya while reaching for Wallace as her mother held onto her.

"Woman you got MY DAUGHTER calling this negro DADDY!" hissed Sam as he was now staring Celia down contemptuously. He then pulled his gun from his waist beneath his shirt and barked,

"Celia let go of my daughter right now or else!"

"Hold on brother, you don't have to go about this like this," said Wallace, trying to placate the situation as Sonya wailed ceaselessly in her mother's grasp awhile young Tanell stood on the opposite side of the dining room observing the entire ordeal.

"Fuck this, let go of my daughter right now Celia," hissed Sam as he began to pull at his daughter's arm again.

"NOoooooo! PLEEease!" bewailed Celia as she steadfastly held onto her daughter.

Though Sam never really intended to physically harm anyone, his jealous rage controlled him, thereby inducing him to act impetuously. He clenched his teeth and before he truly assessed his actions beforehand, he swung his gun swift and hard. Hitting Celia square on her temple, knocking her out cold, snatching his wailing daughter from her debilitated grasp.

"What the…" gasped Wallace just before he instinctively attacked Sam in a grapple, trying to wrestle the gun away from him.

With the quick attack, Sonya was able to break free from Sam's grip where she then immediately ran to her frightened brother and held onto him for dear life.

"Save us daddy!" exclaimed Sonya in between cries.

Just then Sam overpowered Wallace, breaking his right arm free which was gripping the gun. Awhile Wallace continued to tussle for the gun, Sam in his rage, impetuously pushed the barrel of his gun into Wallace's chest and squeezed the trigger four times. Wallace in wide-eyed horror held onto Sam until he could no more as he fell to the ground holding his chest.

"DADDY!" screamed Sonya as Tanell stood shaking from the horror that laid before his young eyes.

Wallace who was seconds ago fighting for his family's safety, was now losing the fight for his life. Awhile Tanell watched his father's chest heave as if it was being lifted by invisible strings and then fell back to normalcy like all the air had just left his body. Wallace died right before his children's eyes.

"Come on Sonya, time to go," said Sam as he quickly grabbed a wailing Sonya from her hold on her brother.

Meanwhile Tanell just stood there in complete shock and utter horror as he watched the now panicked looking Sam forcefully take his distraught older sister. Tanell then ran to his perpetual hero's side and cried out loudly while trying to help him up as he thought that was all his father needed.

"Come on daddy!" Pleeease daddy come on, get up!" wailed young Tanell as he tried ceaselessly to pull his father up from his sprawled position on the ground.

Tanell continued this relentlessly until police and subsequent medical personnel arrived twenty-one minutes later.

Tanell remembered vividly when the detective pulled him away from his deceased father. Where they then tried uselessly to get information from the distraught child as they took his mother from the home on a stretcher. Tanell would also never forget how long they just let his father lay there as it seemed they did nothing but look around him.

Days later, Sam was arrested for the murder/kidnapping and Sonya was found safely but the ensuing years only became a nightmare for young Tanell. As his loving mother Celia was never the same after the tragic death of her only true love. Heroin had begun to take on a new wave in west

148

Baltimore with Celia quickly becoming a disencumbered addict. Using her heroin addiction as a coping mechanism over her love Wallace's death. She soon turned to tricking for cash in order to replenish the source of her addiction. Becoming pregnant to an unknown trick, she subsequently gave birth to Tanell's younger sister Evalyn. To where Tanell soon felt the burden of having to step up and help his family. So, he took to the streets a very angry and desensitized pre-adolescent. Evolving into the very confused volatile man that lead to him being in his current predicament.

Tanell's rumination and deep introspection was interrupted by the intercom in his cell.

"Hey White; you taking your yard?" Asked the C.O.

"Yeah," replied Tanell as he got up from his bunk and made his way in front of his cell door. Where two correctional officers suddenly appeared, ordering Tanell to turn around and place his hands through the slot in the door, to which Tanell obliged and was cuffed. Then lead by the two latently bigot C.O.'s to an upright coffin-sized cage outside for his one hour of yard recreation. Where once inside the small cage, Tanell breathed in the only natural air he would be able to inhale for the next 23 hours.

"T, what up dog" said a light-skinned man in the cage adjacent to Tanell's.

"Yo T, what's good homie?" echoed another man in a cage whom was in the middle of a callisthenic workout when Tanell entered his cage.

149

"Another day black man, another day," said an older black man in one of the cages further down.

"Yes sir, another day brother Rahja X. Aye what's going on fellas?" responded Tanell to all who greeted him.

Tanell then took three steps to the other side of the cage where he grabbed onto the gate and took in another deep breath. Gazing at the morning sky, he began to regress to his previous thoughts of his late father. As he did often, he wondered how life may have been had his father not been murdered that dreadful day. Whereas always he surmised that he would have become a good man had his father had the chance to be the protagonist in his life.

Chapter 9

*"We stand in Heaven's own light and cast
the evil shadow of self, and say it is the devil."*
-Gerald Massey

Following the death of his grandmother, like a moth to a flame, Ryat took to the streets unconsciously at the tender age of fourteen. Becoming a truant, he hardly ever went to school anymore. Only occasionally to show off his latest sneakers and outfits which he acquired from his new street hustling endeavors. He was now living with his aunt Anita who tried her best to preach to him about his missing school and his new-found hustling but his quick transformation into a gamin induced him to ignore everything she said and spend most of his time in the streets.

While standing on the corner of Moore & Forest streets with Camill, Potta, Hochee, and Lati, Ryat stood waiting with his friends for buyer after buyer of the insidious crack rock. After securing and executing a sale to a nomad looking man in a dilapidated, rust stained beige truck, Ryat noticed a brand new snow-white '96 Acura Legend rolling towards him down Forest street. The Acura then pulled to a complete stop right in front of him and as if on cue the driver's side window rolled down.

"Ayo lil Ryat, get in," said Dollas from behind the wheel of the new Acura.

"Oh yo, what up Dollas?" said Ryat as he proceeded to get in the car on the passenger side.

"So what's good wit you lil cuz?" said Dollas as he began to pull off.

"Man I been chilling. But yo Dollas this Ac' is the shit cuz," said Ryat while admiring the inside of the brand-new car.

"Yo, you must be moving major weight like da streets talking."

"Listen, always only believe hardly none of what you hear and only half of what you see. Anyway, yo what's really been good wit you lil cuz? I ain't seen you since Mrs. Eve's funeral but I seen Nita and she told me you out here hustling and as I can see for the most part it must be true."

"Yeah man, it is what it is. I gots to get it how I'm living," retorted Ryat as he slouched in the passenger seat and began to crack a Vanilla Dutch Master cigar down the middle.

"Oh yeah, is that right? Look at you; you done took to blowing heavy and all. I just hope you ready to accept everything that come wit this shit since you a man now 'cause you know Ray wouldn't be letting you wild out like this."

"Yeah well, Ray ain't here no more so I gots to play the game how it go and I don't plan on losing," quipped Ryat as he commenced to dumping out of the window the tobacco from inside the now split cigar.

"That's some bullshit cause the game is rigged, if you don't play is the only way you can't lose."

"Yeah I hear you Dollas but like I said I gots to play the game how it go, it is what it is," countered Ryat, unwittingly shrugging his shoulders while lacing the hollowed cigar with marijuana.

"You right, I guess you know everything then. Just know this; he who cannot listen, cannot learn. Anyway, I heard you out here grinding for the dude Roe from Hamilton street."

"Yeah I ain't really grinding for him, I'm just basically picking up off him."

"It's all the same lil cuz, You good out here though? Cause I know how these dudes around here get," said Dollas while peering over at Ryat.

"Man I'm good, I'm saying I had a lil run in wit a couple ol'heads cause they don't be trying let the young dudes get money for real. But they don't really bother a couple of us young dudes cause of who our folks be like Ray being my uncle and Kev

being Mil step daddy. The only person be trying tell me I can't grind on da block is ol'head Bo because I'm the only youngen out here not really picking up off him," said Ryat while puffing on the blunt he had just rolled where he then made a gesture in passing it towards Dollas.

"Nah, I'm good, I really don't fuck wit that shit, but you don't worry bout Bo. I'ma holla at dude."

"Man I ain't worried bout that nigga, I got something for him," retorted Ryat while continuously puffing on his blunt.

"See you got to know when to move and when not to move, it's the sign of a good general and right now is not the time for you to be moving cause you not in his league. So, like I said I'll holla at dude," countered Dollas while turning the staring-wheel to bend the corner.

Ryat and Dollas then continued to Ride around conversing until time elapsed them and before they knew it, it was almost midnight.

"Yo where you want me to drop you off at lil cuz?" asked Dollas.

"Yo drop me off on da block fam," responded Ryat while looking as if he could barely see because his eyes were now chink from his marijuana induced high.

"Man I'm dropping you off at your crib. You don't need to be on the block every second. Let it breathe, that's what's wrong wit yall young dudes,

that's how you catch a case or get caught up in some left-handed shit."

"Man yo Dollas it really don't matter cause if you drop me off at my crib, I'm still just gone go straight to da block anyway."

" 'Ight cause as always you right. I guess you just gone have to find out the hard way. Anyway, earlier you said something like, you got something for Bo. So what you packing now too?"

"I'm saying I really don't be packing crazy but yeah I be holding cause shit be getting crazy out here. Shit the fiends just as crazy as the stick-up boys, they'll murder a nigga for nothing. Shit word is, it was a fiend who beat that youngen from da Ave into a coma bout a few bags," responded Ryat just as Dollas was pulling back up to the spot on Forest street where he had picked him up.

" 'Ight lil cuz, I'ma holla at you later. Just remember what I said, he who cannot listen cannot learn. The game is rigged lil cuz, if you don't play is the only way you can't lose," said Dollas as Ryat was letting himself out the passenger door.

" 'Ight Dollas, I'ma holla at you later fam," said Ryat right before shutting the door to Dollas' car.

"Yo Ryat what up cuz? Yo who was that? That AC' is crazy!" shouted Lati as soon as Ryat emerged from the car.

"Yeah what up cuz? I ain't seen you since earlier, that AC' is crazy," said Camill.

155

"Yo what up Lati and Mil," responded Ryat as he embraced them both in a half hug handshake. *"Yeah that Ac is hot huh? That was Dollas' new whip."*

"Damn, that was Dollas? I ain't seen him in a minute. What's good wit him?" asked Camill.

"Ain't shit really, he was just hollering at me bout some shit."

"What was that he was banging right before y'all pulled up cause that shit was hot?" asked Lati.

"He said it was some new dude from New York name Jay-Z. He said dudes ain't really up on him down here like that. The song was called 'You can't knock the hustle' wit Mary J. on it but that whole tape is fire, I just had him playing that whole joint back. I think the tape was called Reasonable Doubt, I'ma have to cop that joint."

"Oh yeah I heard that song, that joint is fire. Big Bo was putting me D wit it. Dude talks that real street, get money shit. Matter of fact, yeah that's dude wit the dead president's joint. Plus I seen Bigg on Rap City telling Big Lez how that was his dude," said Lati.

"Word, damn I'ma have to peep dude out cause Bigg is my mans," said Camill.

"Aye yo auntie, auntie right here, I got you," yelled Lati at a scraggly looking woman wearing what looked to be at least three pairs of sweat pants, the outer pair a dingy gray color. With a dirty bright colored First Down coat on, walking in a pair of terribly run down white Reebok

Classics. She was also sporting what looked to be a dingy black t-shirt tied turban style around her head.

Lati immediately made his way over to her and served her the escape she was looking for from her self-made hell. After receiving the two dimes of crack rock for the only $15 to her name, she walked away so hurriedly that it almost looked as if she had broken into a run, except her knees never bent. As quickly as she came, she was gone, like a second in time you can never get back.

"Yo Mil, where Potta and Hochee go?" asked Ryat.

"Potta road out wit Bryce when he came through in a fiend float and Hochee went in a couple hours ago, you know since he started grinding his moms been hounding him. So, you know he trying keep her cool by not staying out crazy late," responded Camill.

Ryat, Lati, and Camill stood out all night on the corner, peddling the devil's pebbles in the form of pea-sized insidious crack rocks. Obstinately, the three adolescents continued to sell the detrimental drug well into the early morning hours. Until Camill's newly acquired *Omnipoint* flip phone began to ring. Where after answering it and talking briefly with the person on the other end of the line, he looked to his friends and informed them what the call comprised.

"Aye yo I'm out cuz. That was Essie, she about to open her back door for me while her folks sleep," said Camill.

"Hold up Mil, me and Lati going walk you over there," said Ryat as he had just turned from serving two black occupants in a royal blue 1990 Saturn.

"Yea, hold up real quick fam," said Lati as he jogged to an abandoned white Dodge Dynasty parked two cars from them. Where he retrieved from on top of the driver's side rear tire, a .380 semi-automatic handgun.

"Aye yo. Let me hold the burna cuz," said Ryat as Lati jogged back towards them and simply handed him the pistol. Ryat then tucked it perfectly into the right pocket of his black *Carhart* coat.

The three then commenced to making their way to Camill's girlfriend house near 4th & Peffer streets. After arriving at their destination on Peffer street, Camill quickly gave his friends dap then snuck into his girlfriend's house through the back door.

"Man I should have did like Mil and set up some cheeks for da night," quipped Lati.

"I feel you cuz, he got me ready to try and wake Tiff up," said Ryat while smiling at his own remark as his friend commenced to laughing.

A little past 2:30 a.m. was when Camill crept into his girlfriend's house. Meanwhile Ryat and Lati decided to hang on the corner of Logan and Peffer streets where a speakeasy located just a block away began to provide them with some customers.

Ryat was serving a petite unkempt woman in an alley on Logan street when a tall dark-skinned man approached Lati in a pair of blue jeans that were extremely too tight and stopped at least an inch above his ankles. The man had long feet in a pair of unrecognizable run-down sneakers, his right foot hung halfway out of one. He donned a faded Cowboys hoody under an unbuttoned dingy blue jean jacket. With a teal green water-damaged Ray's Café baseball cap pulled snugly over his head, the brim just above his eyebrows.

"Aye youngen, what you got for eighty?" asked the man in a deep raspy voice.

"I'm saying I got twelve dimes for you ol'head," responded Lati as he pulled a sandwich bag filled with bagged dimes from his pocket.

"Come on youngen, all you can do for me is twelve? Come on youngen, you can do better than that, I got eighty here," said the man in his deep gravelly tone while eyeing intensely the sandwich bag in Lati's hand.

"'Ight, dig it ol'head, I can do you fourteen; that's it. And I'm looking out," said Lati as he reached in his sandwich bag to retrieve the 14 dime rocks from the bundle.

"'Ight youngen, I can do that. Give it here."

"Hold up ol'head, where the fuck is the eighty dollars? Show me the money before I give you anything!" said Lati with a slight scowl on his face as he noticed the man's ambiguous behavior and shifty eyes.

"Muthafucka give all that shit up before I kill yo little ass!" roared the man in his deep raspy voice as he held his hand in his jean jacket pocket as if he was holding a gun. He then quickly reached his other hand out and tried to snatch the sandwich bag from Lati's grip.

"Man fuck that! You ain't got no gun you fucking crackhead, I'll fucking murda you. Let go of my shit!" barked Lati defiantly as he struggled to free his drugs from the man's grip.

"Muthafu..." hissed the man through clenched jaws just before the shot rang out, ending their tussle. Just as Ryat was emerging from the shadows of the alley after serving the unkempt woman who had just seconds before departed from the other end of the alley.

Within a fraction of a second of realization as his friend was falling face first into the pavement, Ryat instinctively pulled the .380 semi-automatic handgun from his coat pocket. The man, oblivious to Ryat, began running while clutching Lati's drug filled sandwich bag in his left hand, with his right hand still clutching the gun in his jacket pocket. His Jacket pocket now had a hole through it from the penetration of the .32 revolver bullet. Ryat then within that millisecond began to fire recklessly towards the man's back as he was rounding the corner into an alleyway. Once the man was out of his sights Ryat quickly stepped over to his friend's side. Where upon kneeling, he realized the inevitable, that his friend was dead.

Panicking, Ryat immediately stood, unconsciously dropping the gun by his friend's side. He then took off running into the night faster than he had ever run, trying to escape the macabre in which he was just involved. Three and a half blocks away from the incident, he stopped off in an alley to catch his breath. A million thoughts began to run through his mind as he suddenly became conscious of the gun he had dropped unwittingly. He then contemplated running back to retrieve the gun but knew it would be futile because police were likely already on the scene by now.

Fearing the worst as to how the gun could connect him to the crime, he began experiencing tremors. Confused as to what to do next, in this panicky state, he became unable to move. Until he noticed the black form fitting cotton gloves on his hands, which he had been wearing all day. He then took off again like a wild rabbit when a human gets too close. Running nonstop until he reached the back door of the apartment building where he called home and felt the most secure.

He quickly made his way inside to the first-floor apartment where he now lived with Anita. Once inside his room, he removed his clothes from his body as if they were on fire, placing them in a backpack he never used. Scared and confused, he fell into a state of delirium where again a million thoughts began to run through his head. He tried to take a shower to calm his nerves but it was to no

avail as he stood under the water naked and
trembling.

*"What if they think I killed Lati?...Aww
man I can't go to jail...I can't do life...What if
somebody seen me?...What if they find out I had
the gun even though I had on my gloves?...Damn
man, I should have never told Lati to give me the
gun, then maybe this wouldn't have
happened...They gone know somebody else was
there...Somehow they gone find out I was
there...Aww man what about that lil lady I
served?...Shit, she gone tell them I was there and
they gone think I killed Lati...Aww shit I need to
get away from here... where am I gone go?...I
don't even have any money to go on the run...Shit
I got to do something cause they gone think I
killed Lati...Nobody will believe me..."*

Ryat's thoughts ran wild as his young mind
lead him into becoming more rattled from his
insidious talk.

Now out of the shower sitting on the edge of
his bed with just his boxers and socks on. He rolled
and smoked a blunt to calm his nerves but it only
exacerbated his delirium and paranoia. It became so
hard for him to think straight that he couldn't even
lay down for a minute. He began pacing while
frequently looking out of the window.

It was 7:13 in the morning when Anita walked into the living room and noticed Ryat sitting on the couch in his underclothes.

"Boy what you doing sitting here staring at the walls? Turn the T.V. on or something. You probably high, I told you that shit gone do damage to your mind," she said still half sleep.

"I'm just chilling aunt Nita."

"You need to be taking yourself to church today with me and Keith."

"Nah I'm good, I'm just gone fall back and probably chill in da crib all day," responded Ryat while doing his best to remain calm and not make his aunt Anita apprehensive.

"Well maybe that's a good thing that you finally staying home for once and not running around in those streets all day and night like you ain't got no sense. I'm telling you, you ain't gone be satisfied til them streets reach up and give your lil ass a hard slap or worse," said Anita as Ryat stared off into space, thinking of the irony in the words she had just spoken,

"And another thing, boy you gone take your ass to school tomorrow too."

"Man I do be going to school."

"Boy, don't you sit there and lie to me. I know you don't be going to school because first off, they still sending fines here in mommy's name from you missing school. And secondly, do you really think I don't know that you leave here like you going to school but instead go hang in one of those

building hallways selling drugs until school lets out."

"*Alright, I'm going go to school tomorrow. I promise.*"

"*Yeah OK, you just better,*" said Anita as she was walking out of the living room.

At 9:25 a.m., Ryat was still sitting in silence in the living room while sporadically pacing and checking the window. When the phone began to ring endlessly, paranoid he sat afraid to answer it until he calmed himself enough to speak in an even monotone.

"*Hello?*"

"*Hello? Yo is that you Ryat?*" said Camill excitedly from the other end of the line.

"*Yeah yo, wha'sup?*" responded Ryat as his heart raced a mile a minute afraid of what may come next.

"*Aye yo what happened wit you and Lati last night?*" asked Camill as Ryat immediately began to panic while trying to think fast and remain calm.

"*Ain't nothing happened. I came to the crib after we left you, and Lati said he was going to the crib too. Why? Wha'sup?*" responded Ryat while beginning to tremor slightly.

"*Aww man you ain't heard yet? Lati was killed last night,*" said Camill with evidence of melancholy in his tone.

"What?" exclaimed Ryat in a high-pitched tone, trying his best to sound shocked and incredulous.

"Yeah man...shit crazy, they say somebody else got murdered too but I really don't know to much more than that cause that's all Potta said his folks was told so far."

"Damn man, that's crazy...not Lati. They saying somebody else got murdered too?"

"Yeah man, I thought it was you when I first heard but they said it was some other dude, nobody really knows who yet though."

"Damn man, not my boy Lati, this shit's crazy fam," uttered Ryat in a low audible as once again his mind began racing to the extreme.

Ryat immediately surmised that the other dead man had to be the man he was shooting at. Which quickly put him back in a state of delirium where insidious thoughts permeated his mind. He began to dither, wondering if he should make a mad dash for the door. Knowing the first place the police would look for him was at his home.

"Aye yo, me and Bryce on our way over there, then we can walk over to Lati and Potta's grandmom's house," said Camill.

"Nah Mil, I'm fucked up after hearing this. So I'ma just fall back. This shit is crazy, Lati was my mans. I ain't really ready for all that right now," responded Ryat while cursing himself internally for not running and hiding out away from home when it was still dark out.

"I feel you man; this shit is crazy...by the way I didn't tell nobody y'all had walked me down there to my girl's house or nothing because I figured I don't want to get questioned by the D's bout something I really don't know about."

"I feel you fam,"

"Yeah... 'ight then homie, I'ma holla at you later."

" 'Ight then, " responded Ryat as he hung up the phone partially in denial over the mere fact that he may have killed a man.

He sat musing over all the possible outcomes of the situation when before he knew it, time had elapsed him and the clock showed it was two minutes until noon. Still extremely paranoid he decided to turn on the T.V. to the local news to see if they were covering his friend's death. To his enlightenment coupled with trepidation, as soon as the local news came on, the macabre in which he was involved the night before was the main topic.

Ryat listened as the news anchor told of a man and an adolescent being dead in what detectives deemed as drug related. The anchor reported that detectives believe 42-year-old Lenard Bagley and 15-year-old Lati Elliot killed each other in what is believed to be a drug deal gone awry. Detectives on the scene found Lati dead on arrival with a single bullet wound to the chest. Clutching 14 bags of crack rock in his left hand with a .380 semi-automatic handgun lying beside him, close by his right hand. Lenard Bagley was found just a few yards away in an alley dead on arrival from four bullet wounds to his back, which it appeared that he was shot from the gun lying near 15-year-old Lati Elliot. Lenard Bagley was also found clutching a sandwich bag containing 42 bags of the same crack rocks Lati Elliot held. Also, clutching in his other hand was what appeared to be the same gun that killed 15-year-old Lati Elliot.

Ryat could not believe what he was hearing. Initially he felt despair for his friend along with trepidation over the fact that it was true that he had killed a man. He became paralyzed in dread for a second until he realized that he may be absolved from all involvement in the incident. For which he figured the best thing to do was like Roe had once told him, that the best kept secret is taken to the grave. Therefore, he would not tell a soul anything about his involvement knowing it might lead back to him. He also decided it best to lay low and act normal to everything around him.

Mr. Carl came rushing in from the cold, hastily taking off his old blue London Fog coat only to reveal a waist length yellow and red jacket underneath.

"Hey boy, What ya doing there?" he said as he was removing a wool hat from his head.

"Ain't nothing Pops, I'm just falling back. What's good wit you though? You look like you freezing."

"Yeah boy that hawk is out today. So how you making out? I heard what happened to your

friend," said Mr. Carl while cutting his eyes at Ryat just before walking towards the kitchen.

"Yeah man, that was my boy Pops. That shit is fucked up," responded Ryat as he got up from the couch and followed his grandfather into the kitchen.

"Yeah I told Lenard not be messing wit those kids," said Mr. Carl, calmly breaking an egg into a bowl.

"Yo Pops you knew that dude Lenard?"

"Yeah I knew him and I told him a time ago to leave those kids alone but he just wouldn't. That's why when Sylvia came back and told me what happened... shit I wasn't surprised. I feel for that lil boy though and his family...Lenard had it coming."

"Sylvia?!"

"Yeah she was there when it happened. She told me how her and Lenard planned the robbery and her job was to distract the other kid while he robbed the other one," replied Mr. Carl, impassively while whipping the eggs in a frying pan.

"She said something 'bout another boy? Who? Did she say what he looked like?!"

"Nope, not really," answered Mr. Carl then pausing for a second as he studied his grandson's face before turning to finish scraping eggs into his plate from the pan.

"And believe you me when I tell you she won't be telling anyone else about what happened. Because the minute I told her how she could get

charged as an accessory to the murders since she helped in the robbery. No sooner than that she put herself in a crack coma where no sooner than after that she died from an overdose...just that quick. Shit and if you ask me the way I see it like I told her is them boys done killed each other, ain't no sense nobody else going down behind it."

"*Yeah...yeah I feel you Pops,*" said Ryat while breathing a half-sigh of relief internally.

"*Listen here boy I got something to tell you and you listen good if you know what's best for you. You must find your own unique pathway in the world; the masses, or majority, never do. Until you set the tone for your own existence, you will follow others, who are in turn following you,*" said Mr. Carl while staring intensely into his grandson's brown eyes. Ryat simply stared back, taking in the wise words of the man he knew without a doubt held his best interest at heart.

Chapter 10

*"When a man does something that is
complimentary to his character, it is virtually
impossible for him to hide this thing, keep it to
himself, keep from telling it to those he wishes to
impress; this is natural egotism, the need for
attention and flattery asserting itself."*

-George Jackson

It had been three months since Lati's funeral
and Ryat along with the rest of his friends were
taking it hard. Ryat had been staying home from
school and away from the streets more often lately.
His aunt Anita held such sympathy for him due to
his traumatic experiences thus far that she figured
his staying home so much was a result of his
grieving. Therefore, she decided not to chide him
about missing school.

Ryat, Potta, Hochee, Camill, and Bryce were
sitting in the living room during school hours,
smoking weed and playing *Playstation*, all while
Anita was at work.

"Yo man, I swear I wish that nigga Leonard didn't die so I could get that nigga myself but you know my cuz was a G, he took that mothafucka wit him!" said Potta while taking the blunt from Hochee's hand.

"Yeah…I feel you," said Ryat who was playing Camill in the new *NBA Live '99.*

"Yeah man, I miss my nigga and I swear that fat nigga Bo been acting extra funny towards niggas ever since my nigga died. That fat nigga been shorting us grams and shit, plus I feel like since Lati died the nigga think we just a bunch of nut-ass in-the-way ass youngens runnin' wit our heads cut off." Said Hochee.

"Word sun, that fat nigga been acting mad funny sun, like he don't even want us on da block no more. And sun, I can't stand the way the nigga Rip and his lil squad treat the nigga like God and sun them niggas think cause we young that they run shit on the block and they 'let' us get sales." said Bryce in between puffs of the blunt.

"Well you know they say Lati might have been Bo's son, so I don't think the fat nigga would have fucked wit us if it wasn't for my cuz." Said Potta.

"Word?" questioned both Ryat and Bryce.

"Yeah man, word is my aunt was creeping with the fat nigga back in the day and Lati's Pop might not be his real pops. My uncle had told Lati a while ago. The fat nigga never said shit about it but you can tell he knew by the way he treated Lati

cause Bo known to be a type-grimy dude but he been looking out for Lati from day one. Now that my cuz his dead, I guess the fat nigga see us like Hochee said, as some in-the-way-ass young niggas wit our head cut off," responded Potta.

"Damn that's crazy man... But fuck that nigga Bo, you can just grab from my O.G. Roe. Fuck that nigga, he ain't going to stop us from grinding," said Ryat.

"See Ryat, you've been all cooped up in the crib for the last few months, having Tiffany over here every day, that you ain't up on what's poppin in da streets. Roe got booked last week. They say the Feds ran up in all his spots and got major work. He was supposed to have been coming across the bypass in his new Benz when the feds boxed and bagged him. Word is he had a bird and a half in a book bag in the backseat, he supposedly was on his way to take that shit to some dude from out Bellevue Park. Dude is the one who supposedly set him up, supposedly dude is some young nigga from out there that get money," said Camill.

"Damn word! That's fucking crazy, Roe is my ol 'head, he keep it real twenty-four seven. I can't believe some bitch ass nigga would set my O.G. up like that," responded Ryat while clenching his jaws and punching his right fist into his left palm.

"Yeah well believe it my nigga cuz Roe be lucky if he get a hunnit years," quipped Hochee.

"Damn man," said Ryat in a low audible while hanging his head.

Later that night, Ryat was in his bedroom laid across his bed on his back in just his tank top and boxers. Tiffany sat in a T-shirt with her back against the headboard as they held a conversation.

"For real Ryat everything ain't always funny. That is messed up how your friend Bryce did Kelly, she really liked him and he just go and get her pregnant and then tell her she got to get an abortion. He shouldn't have got her pregnant because her family and their religion don't believe in abortions," said Tiffany while hugging a pillow and scowling at Ryat.

"Nah Tiff, I was just laughing cuz Bryce tried telling us he stopped messing wit her cuz her underarms be stinking... I ain't know she was pregnant," countered Ryat while still giggling.

"Alright well stop laughing Ryat because it is NOT funny."

"'Ight... 'ight, you right that shit ain't right and I'ma holla at him because real talk, I don't believe in abortions either."

"You don't believe in abortions Ryat?"

"Nah, not at all," replied Ryat as he turned on his side, propped his elbow, and raised up on it a little to look her directly in her eyes.

"Nah Tiff I don't believe in abortions but it's not because of religion or anything. A few years ago, my grandmother told me the story of how my mom held onto her last breath so I could be born, she died as the doctors were removing me from her. So, I feel like if my mom wouldn't have fought for me to be here, I wouldn't. So, I believe all babies should have the chance to live like I have. I feel like

*my grandma always said, that a baby is a blessing
from God and if God don't want you to have the
baby then that's why there's miscarriages."*

"Oh my God Ryat... *That was so deep, I
can't believe you just told me that about your mom.
I know it must really hurt to talk about her,"* said
Tiffany with tears welling in her eyes as she held
his stare, then released the pillow she was hugging,
leaned over, and hugged him around the neck.

A day later around 9:35 a.m., Ryat had just
woken up to use the bathroom when he heard a loud
knock at the door. Walking out of the bathroom on
his way to get the door, he almost bumped into his
aunt who was headed in the same direction.

*"I want to know who the hell that is
banging on my door like that this time of morning?
I'm telling you right now right, it better not be one
of your little ignorant ass friends because if it is
I'ma lay into his ass and then yours,"* said Anita,
half groggy while tying her robe at the waist.

*"I don't know who that could be, it can't be
one of my friends cause they would never bang on
the door like that. I ain't even know you was home
though. Why you ain't at work?"* responded Ryat as
he made his way to the front window, looking out to
see who was banging on the front door.

*"Why you want to know? Today is my day
off. Who is it?"* countered Anita noticing the
petrified look on his face after looking out the
window to see who was at the door.

After pulling the curtain back from the
window, Ryat laid his eyes upon what looked to be

two detectives and a cop. Banging on the door was a tall, white, bald- headed, plainclothes looking detective. He was burly, wearing a gray blazer, white dress shirt, blue and gray striped tie, black slacks, with a clipboard in hand. Standing beside him was a petite white woman with spiked blonde hair. Wearing a black business suit with what looked to be a detective's badge around her neck. Standing to her left with his hands on his hips looking back at Ryat peeking through the window was a white male cop in full uniform.

"Boy what the hell you done did? What the hell you standing there looking all scared for?" inquired Anita as she made her way to open the door

"Nuth...Nuthin, I don't.. know... Why they here," stammered Ryat as his mind raced back and forth over whether to run or stand and act normal.

"Hello, how are you doing? May I ask what you all are here for?" asked Anita, immediately after opening the door to greet them.

"Ms. Anita Storm, right?" Asked the petite detective looking woman who is now holding open a file folder and looking back and forth from it towards them.

"Yes," answered Anita.

"And that would be your nephew, fifteen-year-old Ryat Storm, standing to your right, am I correct?" asked the woman, still looking back and forth from them to the dossier she held in her hands.

"Yes and Excuse me but may I ask what this is about?" countered Anita while Ryat stood behind her feeling a sense of déjà vu as he experienced

trepidation to the point of almost becoming paralyzed by fear.

"Well ma'am, me and my partner here, John Copeland are with Child Protective Services. Our offices were notified approximately one month ago by the Harrisburg School District regarding Ryat here and his many absences from school," said the woman, revealing the C.P.S. credentials hanging around her neck.

"Ok AND... I know he has missed a lot of school this year but that's only because we have experienced a lot of tragedy in our family lately but I can assure you he'll be back in school soon without missing any more days," said Anita, slightly agitated just as her boyfriend Keith came up from behind her and stood by her side.

"Well ma'am, you see it's normal that we are notified about children missing many days from school and we usually recommend that the parents are fined. But upon investigation into Ryat's background and family structure, I am sorry to inform you..."

"Excuse me but what my partner is trying to say is that after our investigation, we learned that Ryan's parent-guardian, a Mrs. Eve Storm, passed away eight months ago. With that, we learned that you, Ms. Anita Storm, is the person listed as looking after Ryan unofficially. But with regards to what took place with your chil..."

"WHAT THE HELL ARE YOU TRYING TO SAY? AND DON'T YOU DARE BRING UP MY CHILDREN MUTHAFUCKER!" screamed Anita at

the big bald-headed man who had just rudely interrupted his partner to speak

"Nita, calm down, just let the man speak," said Keith as Ryat stood half shocked yet relieved that they weren't actual detectives.

"I'm sorry ma'am but as partner was trying to say, we're sorry to inform you that given your history with your children and your failure to accept rehabilitative counseling thereafter, the state of Pennsylvania has deemed you unfit to be Ryat's guardian. Therefore, we have to take Ryat in our custody. I am so sorry about this ma'am," said the female C.P.S. agent while crossing her arms, dossier in hand, then tilting her head slightly and pursing her lips.

"What?!" mouthed Ryat indirectly, now completely in shock.

"AWW HELL NO! Yall are not about to take my nephew anywhere! I'm all he has, yall ain't taking him nowhere with this bullshit! I can take care of my nephew goddammit!. So y'all can go on and get the fuck off my porch," screamed Anita while attempting to shut the door in their face.

"Excuse me ma'am but you're going to have to calm down or I'm going to be forced to arrest you," said the police officer in full uniform right after blocking the door with his foot so Anita couldn't shut it.

"Now at this point there is nothing you can do to prevent us from taking this young man into our custody. You will have your chance to prove your case and stability in court but right now this young man has to come with us."

"OH HELL NO! HELL NO! You can arrest me because I am not about to just sit here and let you take my nephew."

"Come on Nita, calm down, calm down before you get yourself locked-up. Come on baby now calm down," said Keith while doing his best to restrain Anita.

"What the heck is going on here?" inquired Mr. Carl, sternly as he walked up on what was happening in front of his home that involved his family and what looked to be the police.

"They trying to take Ryat daddy!" yelled Anita towards her father, then looking towards the C.P.S agents, she shouted,

"Yeah there's my dad, he can take care of Ryat since I'm so fucking unfit."

"What?... Why y'all trying to take my grandson? What is this about?" asked Mr. Carl, stepping up on the porch with the C.P.S agents and the officer, as they stared repulsively at the extremely unkempt man's appearance.

"I'm sorry to inform you also sir but we are here to take Ryat Storm into our custody per a court order and as my file here indicates, you also have been deemed, as of right now, unfit to be Ryat's guardian," said the female agent after looking Mr. Carl from head to toe and reverting back to her dossier.

"This can't be right, this can't be happening," said Mr. Carl in a hushed tone indirectly as if thinking out loud while standing there shaking his head with his hands on his hips.

Meanwhile Anita continued to scream irately at the agents as Keith did his best to mollify her.

"Nah man, fuck that! I ain't going nowhere wit yall!" barked Ryat.

"Please young man do not make this hard on yourself," said the burly male agent as he moved to grab hold of Ryat.

"Man get ya fucking hands off me cracker!"

"Get your fucking hands off my nephew, you fat cracker bitch!" yelled Anita as Keith restrained her.

"Please young man, I do not want to have to put my cuffs on you," said the police officer who had joined in on the tussle with Ryat to take him into their custody.

Ryat then realizing the best thing for him was to oblige, he did so without much further resistance. The two C.P.S agents and the police officer then walked him to the agent's silver Crysler Town & Country van. Anita stood in the doorway crying profusely as she felt completely defeated. Mr. Carl stood with his head hung low wondering how his family could have been dealt such a terrible hand by God. He then began thinking of how bad he needed an escape. It seemed like the entire neighborhood was watching the scene as the C.P.S agents took Ryat into their custody. As the van was pulling away down the street, Ryat was looking out the window pensively. He noticed, standing on the edge of the curb as they road by, Tiffany staring at him with an addled expression on her face. He stared back at her ineffably as tears began to stream her face. She then took off running in the direction of his family who were still standing on the porch agonizing as Ryat road out of their sight.

Thirty-five minutes later, the silver Chrysler Town & Country van pulled to a stop in front of a three-floor home on Orange street in Lancaster, PA. The house had white vinyl siding and looked to be a well-kept place with its immaculate front lawn.

"Ryat I want you to understand we are so sorry we had to do this and take you away from your family. I pray it is only temporary and you can go back with your family soon. But for now, you will be placed in this foster home here," said the female agent after turning around in her passenger seat to look at Ryat sitting in the back of the van.

"Yeah, from what I hear young man, you will be in very good hands as I've heard the people that run this home are two of the best people you could ever meet," said the male agent from the driver's seat while looking at Ryat through the rear-view mirror.

"Yes their names are a Mr. Mathew and Marjorie Hodge," said the female agent after referring to her dossier.

"Man look, fuck y'all and Mr. and Mrs. 'Hog' or whatever the fuck. Y'all don't know me or really give two fucks about me and don't worry your-selves to much because I'll be back with my family soon enough. So let's just get this shit over with for now," countered Ryat, then displaying a mischievous smirk across his face while intensely staring back and forth into both of their eyes.

The female agent impassively looked away from Ryat as she exited the van. Whereas the male agent narrowed his eyes with a scowl on his face as he exited the van from the driver's side. Ryat then exited the van from the back-driver's side sliding door. He was then escorted by the two agents into the foster home of Mr. and Mrs. Hodge.

Chapter 11

"Each thought that we become aware of is complete in itself. The problem is understanding the direction that the thought is moving. Every degree of true knowledge brings us closer to the reality of our own existence, and each thought is in possession of some form of sound knowledge that enhances our intellect and gives rise a new order of thinking. To think is to be in possession of progressive knowledge that leads to a new order of intelligence. The mind is alive when it thinks and asleep when it doesn't."
-Rahman Shadi

Once inside the Hodge residence, Ryat was immediately greeted by the repugnant smell of what seemed to be a foul mixture of underarm sweat, medicine, and wet dog. He was then greeted by Mrs. Marjorie Hodge who was an obese woman with a gregarious smile spread across her marshmallow face. Walking up beside her, Mr. Hodge looked like one of those scary old pastel men from the horror movies as he greeted Ryat. He also looked to be at least twenty years older than Mrs. Hodge with his slick-back silver hair and stolid marble face on a frail frame.

"How are you doing Ryat? We are so happy to meet you, don't worry hun I know it must be hard for you right now. But I'm sure it will get better for you as we promise to take good care of you," said Mrs. Hodge with her hands crossed pleasantly across her forearms, smiling that smile that was already beginning to annoy Ryat.

Apathetically, he just stood there staring intensely back and forth between the couple.

"So Ryat, where's your clothes hun," asked Mrs. Hodge.

"Well since agents double 0 dick and cunt abducted me from my family I don't have nothing but the shit on my back."

"Given the extreme circumstances in which we had to extract Ryat from his family we were unable to retrieve any of his clothes but our office will be giving you a two-hundred-dollar voucher to take him shopping for clothes," said the female agent as the male agent stood by clenching his jaws while furtively glancing at his watch.

"Did you hear that Ryat? It's alright, we get to take you shopping," said Mrs. Hodge with a jovial emphasis at the end.

"I ain't no fucking charity case, I don't need shit from y'all. I got my own clothes already. What da hell y'all expect me to do wit two hundred dollars anyway. Plus, don't even worry yourselves cause I won't even be here that long anyway," countered Ryat.

"Young man now I can see your upset right now behind what took place and you may have plans to run away from here but I can't allow that. Now it may be hard for you the first few weeks but you just know it will get easier. Now follow me so I can show you where you'll be staying," said Mr. Hodge motioning for Ryat to follow him as Mrs. Hodge lead the agents out the door

Ryat was led by Mr. Hodge to a room on the second floor near the bathroom. Inside the room laid across the bottom bunk of the two sets of bunk-beds was a brown-skinned stocky kid that looked to be at least 17 years old. Mr. Hodge introduced the kid as Earl Summers and told Ryat that Earl would help him get acclimated. Mr. Hodge then left but not before warning Ryat that he would be keeping a close eye on him.

"Wha'sup man, I guess you gone be staying right here over top me," said Earl as he got up and patted the empty mattress on the bunk above him awhile Ryat simply stared at him Apathetically.

"Look man I'm cool but I know how you must feel right now so you can just holla at me when you ready," said Earl as he sat back down on his bunk and commenced back to reading his new Sports Illustrated magazine.

The rest of that day Ryat was introduced to the rest of the 8 kids under the Hodges care. Refusing to speak to any of them, he simply stared them in the eyes when they tried to speak to him.

That night was the hardest for Ryat as it was the first one he had ever spent away from family. He laid on his back with his arms crossed behind his head atop the sheet-less mattress that he refused to make. He stared at the ceiling in the dark with thought of his family occupying his mind. Wondering as he did often growing up, the *what if's*, had his mother been alive. He wondered if he would have been different in the way he handled situations from how he could have grown. He then thought about his uncle Ray and all the lessons on manhood he tried to teach him in such a short span. A tinge of pain crossed his heart as he thought of his late uncle as images of the man that murdered him play across his mind's eye. Ryat then again as he did once before swore vengeance upon the man that murdered the man who was more like his father than his uncle.

He then began to muse over his late loving Grandma, never forgetting the many life lessons she and calculated him with. Missing her nurturing and undying love, he became overwhelmed with emotions. Tears begin to fall from his eyes prolifically as he mourned his deceased loved ones silently while staring at the ceiling emotionally distraught. He began to curse God for the omnipresent black cloud he felt God placed over his family's lives as if enjoying the analogous nature of such to their last name. Extreme emotional pain washed over him as he laid there lonely, crying like a two-month-old baby. His thoughts rested upon the fact that he believed if his mother, uncle, or grandmother were still alive he wouldn't be in his current predicament and feeling so lonely.

Over the next couple of days Ryat remained silent and withdrawn from the rest of the inhabitants in the foster home. He paid close attention, though silently, to each of their attitudes and characters, to their mannerisms. Remembering the lessons his grandmother taught him about body language being eighty-five percent of communication, that the smallest of actions can give you an inkling into a person's true character.

Earl seemed to be the best natured of the kids in the house with his amicable personality. There were also four other boys; Pete, Dave, Eddie, and little Jeffery. Pete and Davey were brothers who couldn't have been more of such polar opposites. Pete carried himself with a smug, pompous jock attitude while Davey was more reserved and soft spoke. Physically, their white skin was the only trait they had in common, Pete stood 6 '1" with a running back's physic, red hair and spoke in a brogue accent. Davey a year younger than Pete at 15, stood 5'3" in a small frame with bushy black hair and glasses on his face. They both slept in the room with Ryat and Earl on the other set of bunkbeds.

Little Jeffery was the youngest in the house by far, he looked about ten years of age. He had a definitive birth mark on his right cheek shaped like the state of Georgia. Seemingly quiet and pensive, he appeared as a very sad boy yet the simmer in his eyes told Ryat another story.

Eddie was like Tiger Woods to Ryat, a black boy who hated being black. Like Tiger, they resembled in temperament and character in the way Eddie carried himself, spoke, and had such strong affinity for white women. Ryat quickly noticed in him how he went out of his way not to identify with the black man while in turn doing everything to acculturate himself with everything white. Ryat had also heard him two days prior talking to Earl about his preferences in woman. The way he talked as if black women were not attractive and white women were of superior beauty irritated Ryat and slightly angered him. Ryat could never understand how a man that came from a black woman found an entire other race more beautiful. He even noticed that Eddie and Samantha may have been fooling around in clandestine from the way they would furtively flirt with one another.

Samantha was one of the three girls who were under the Hodge's care in the foster home. She also just happened to be the Hodges only biological child though she bore no resemblance to her mother and little of her father. She had her father's deep set eyes and slender frame yet she was more like her mother in personality. It was very conspicuous to Ryat that she was their child before it was alluded too, given the polarity in treatment she was given aside from the other kids.

The other two girls under the Hodges care were Leslie and Asaria. Leslie reminded Ryat of the many Goth kids he'd seen depicted on television. She wore the black heavy makeup around her eyes, black nail, long jet black hair that covered half her face and ratty clothes. Though she was more of a recluse and reserved than any other kid in the house, she stuck out to him the most. Asaria was what Ryat liked to call a Spanish fly because she was an extremely attractive Latina. She stood about 5'2" in a voluptuous frame with long dark wavy hair that hung down to the mid of her back.

Ryat swore her face bore the dimensions of an angel though she was no angel by a long shot. Which made her less attractive to Ryat with her virulent attitude, it seemed to him that she was always bitter and angry. Which to him was understandable on the surface yet he would never be able to understand how such a beautiful female could always be so bitter. Regardless though he knew Camill would trip over himself after seeing her, especially since he adulates Latina's.

The thought of his best friend instantly made him feel homesick. He wondered what his friends were up to and what they were doing with themselves at that specific time which caused him to miss their friendly boyhood coterie immensely. He then smiled at the thought that no doubt they were up to some kind of mischief and debauchery. The thought of Lati then crossed his mind and once again a tinge of pain crossed his heart. He pictured his late-friend's joyful spirit and assertive personality. The entire incident surrounding Lati's death gave him a sense of ambivalence as it humbled him more and more each day yet it desensitized him wholly in regards to human life. Thoughts of his girlfriend Tiffany then crossed his mind and he couldn't help but envision the last image he saw of her standing there looking emotionally distraught as they took him away. He knew she truly loved him and unlike some people like his aunt would categorize it as "puppy love", he truly loved her too. She was the only person those days he felt totally comfortable being vulnerable around. Though societies standards told them they wouldn't last because they were too young and unexperienced, he envisioned a long amorous future with her. He even pictured having a family with her one day. A vision of her dimpled smile flashed across his mind's eye and put a smile on his face.

Later that day, Ryat was told he could make a few phone calls but was forbid to call his aunt or grandfather. This enraged and tempted him to run away from that place right then and there. Yet he thought wise of it and knew that wouldn't be the right time because he had never been outside of Harrisburg and didn't even really know where he was at. Over the days he had been there he had already grown to hate the many strictures Mr. Hodge had in place. The way he was so prying and controlling angered Ryat. Therefore, he decided against a phone call, looked Mr. Hodge in the eyes with contempt then simply went to his room stewing with rage.

Noticing Ryat's extreme anger as he came through the bedroom door. Earl immediately surmised what must had happened as he had gone through the same routine before. Therefore, Earl decided to let Ryat cool down before he offered him some advice and help. Ryat was on his two hundred and fifth push up of twenty reps a clip when Earl began speaking in an even tone.

"Hey Ryat, dig it man I know what you're going through and what just happened and I know you most likely don't want to talk about it right now. So, I won't get into all that right now but I just wanted you to know if you really want to talk to your family tonight I can help you with that," he said, turning his head away from the T.V. he was playing Playstation on and looking towards Ryat

Ryat immediately stopped mid pushup, looked up at Earl with a dubious look then replied,

"Straight up! Cause for real man this got me ready to..." cutting himself short Ryat then grunted, clenching his jaws as he stood to his feet, eyeing Earl.

"Yeah man straight up, even though we ain't supposed to have one and the Hodges think I couldn't possibly come up with the money to get one, my uncle got me a cell phone the last time I visited him. I've had it for three months now. I keep it hidden from the Hodges 'cause you can already see how they are and how they be searching," said

Earl as he got up, retrieved the phone from its hiding place inside a hole in his pillow, then handed it to Ryat.

"Look ma man just go in the bathroom, turn on the exhaust fan on and talk low so they don't here you and try not to be too long in there 'cause my unc' say he don't want to be getting no crazy high bills."

"'Ight, good looking man," said Ryat with gratitude written in his eyes as he stared at Earl then made haste to the bathroom with the cell phone in hand.

Ryat immediately dialed his aunt's number and was elated the moment he heard her voice on the other end of the line. She was just as elated to hear his voice when he blurted her name from excitement as soon as she answered the phone. He immediately commenced to telling her how much he missed her and about everything that had transpired with him up until that point. He then began to tell of his plans to run away and how he would be home soon. For which she then countered by emphatically telling him to not run away because it would only make things worse. She then told him how she had hired a lawyer and had begun to take the counseling sessions she was supposed to take years ago. Telling him that her lawyer said that it would take no more than two months before she regained custody of him. He then promised her that he would never miss another day of school once he got home. She then told him that Tiffany had been calling every day since he was taken away. Wanting to know where he was and how he was doing and for Anita to tell him that she loved him when she got a chance to talk to him. He responded by telling his aunt to tell Tiffany that he loved her too and would write her about everything. He then began blushing from the other end of the phone line as his aunt playfully chided him about their puppy love. They then commenced to saying their good-byes and *I love yous* but right before they hung up she made him promise that he wouldn't run away.

After giving the phone back to Earl and thanking him emphatically, Ryat then did as he did every night since he had been there. He had made a point to stay away from everybody there, so he would just lay atop his bunk with his hands behind his head ruminating, while staring at the ceiling. He thought about what his aunt had told him and decided to go along with the program until she got him out of there and back in her custody. Therefore, he decided he would be less of a maverick and try his best to adhere to the rules and regulations.

The next day he started by finally telling the Hodges what sizes he wore so they could get him the few clothes, he held back from laughing in their faces at the mismatch off brand clothes he was so used to seeing *corny* white people wearing. They told him that since there was only three weeks of school left that they weren't going to sign him up right then. Yet he was gone have to take some sort of extra curriculum activities, so he chose to join the local football team and go to their tryouts and half-a-day summer camps. As he figured that would keep him away from the house the longest during the day. The Hodges were startled when they initially mentioned basketball and he sternly yet solemnly said no while intensely looking them both in the eyes. Unbeknownst to them they had hit a deep nerve with him.

Over the next month Ryat tried his best to be congruous with the Hodges but the maverick in him refused to comply totally. He refused return back at the house every day and do most of the chores around the house they would tell him to do. He would only keep his personal area clean and adamantly told them over and over that he would only clean his home and that wasn't his home. He also refused to participate in most meals and activities with them and the other kids in the house, as he would justify this by explicitly telling them that they were not his family. That he did not care to and would most likely never see any of them again once he left there. Though he had begun to build a solid bond with Earl.

The moment Earl helped him in time of anguish and need opened Ryat's well-guarded heart to friendship. That coupled with the fact that Ryat ended up being around Earl most of his days there, being as though they were bunk mates and Earl was star of the football team he was trying out for. In turn, Ryat had learned a lot about Earl since they had become friends. He had learned that Earl told him how he hadn't seen his mother since she had put him up for adoption. That she had ran to California to become some dream of a star she held. Yet the last Earl had heard about her, was that she was a dope junky and a prostitute in Hollywood. He told Ryat how his uncle was the only family that cared about him but since his uncle was handicapped, the State wouldn't award him custody of Earl. When Ryat asked why he had never Run away or if he had ever thought of it, Earl responded by telling him how his current situation provided him with a chance to take advantage of school and his God given gift in football. He told of his plans to get a full scholarship through football and hopefully make the pros. Though if he didn't he would still take advantage of the scholarship and end up with a solid career and life no matter what.

Ryat admired Earl's integrity and confided in him the details of what lead up to him being there. He told him of how his grandmother had raised him after his mother had passed, then how his grandmother passed a year ago. Telling Earl about how like his uncle the State recently decided his aunt and grandfather were unfit to have custody of him. Yet his aunt had hired an attorney and she would have custody of him soon. Ryat only gave Earl the bone of his family's plight and left out the flesh for fear of revisiting deep anguish and becoming too emotional. He did however tell Earl of how he was there when his uncle was murdered and seen the man that murdered him. He then told him how he promised himself that he would get retribution for the murder of his uncle one day. The good nature and morality of Earl made him want to try and convince Ryat otherwise. Yet the fire in Ryat's eyes when he spoke of reprisal dissuaded Earl.

Earl then told Ryat as much as he knew of all the kids back stories under the Hodges care. He told him how like himself most of the kids there had been under the Hodges care for years since they were very young kids. For some strange reason after hearing their grievous back stories, Ryat began to feel more comfortable in the house. As he felt for the first time there were kids his age who could identify with his plight and his emotional anguish.

Chapter 12

"With every adversity comes with it the seed
of equal or greater benefit in return."
-Napoleon Hill

Three months had gone by since Ryat was put under the Hodges care and he was still refusing to acclimate himself. There had been two continuances for his custody hearing and he was becoming more impatient and rancorous by the day. Aside from the other children in the house whom he considered products of their parents' misfortune like himself, he simply grew to hate everything about that house and the Hodges. He sensed the Hodges were only into taking in foster children for the money therefore he hated their fake attitudes, and their fake care and concern. He felt that anyone with half a brain could see that they only really cared about Samantha. He held enmity towards Mr. Hodge for a plethora of reasons but mainly because there was something in his eyes that Ryat couldn't quite make out. Yet it deeply bothered him, especially when he looked at little Jeffrey.

Little Jeffrey was one of the only other people Ryat had begun to take a liking to in the house besides Earl. Jeffrey had become sort of like the quasi little brother that Ryat never had but had longed for. Ryat soon began to embrace him as such shortly after their intimate encounter. It had been a month since he and Jeffrey first began to build a bond with each other after Jeffrey had gotten into a fight on the last day of school. Ryat had been walking back towards the Hodges' from the park three blocks away when he saw little Jeffrey beating up a kid his age and size. Then just as Ryat was approaching simply to watch the fight, a kid around his size and age jumped in the fight from the small crowd and began punching on little Jeffrey to help the other kid. Ryat then quickly intervened, making quick work of the older kid. Immediately after the fight was broken up, Ryat and little Jeffrey began to form their bond.

Ryat soon learned how much they were alike in their Collective outlooks on life and their similar sense of abandonment and loneliness. He even began to notice how they could even almost pass for real brothers as they share the same toffee complexion and like personality. He also learned how Jeffrey had been put up for adoption when he was a baby and had been bounced around throughout the state of Pennsylvania from foster home to foster home.

At that present moment, Ryat and Jeffery were in the room Jeffry shared with Eddie on the third floor playing *Playstation*.

"Aye lil Jeffery, let me ask you something. How can you put up wit that weird ass dude Eddie?" asked Ryat with a sly sneer on his face.

"I hate that weird ass dude man. He thinks he's White; always talking about Black people like he aint one. See those pictures right there?" responded Jeffery as he pointed towards the top of a small dresser.

"He keep those pictures up like those white people is his real family. He always talking about how great they are. He always talking like those two white people are his real parents when they the ones that supposedly kicked him out of their homes after raising him til he was twelve."

"How come he talk so highly of them if they got rid of him? That's definitely some weirdo shit."

"Well when Onix was here he told me that they got rid of Eddie cause he was infatuated more with the mom than just as a mother because he would always pop up when she was getting naked."

"Yo...Yo...I can see some shit like that with this weird dude." stammered Ryat as they did their best to recover from the laughter that erupted between them.

"Yo that so fits dude character, but yo who's Onix, "

"Oh he used to be here when I first got here. He was cool and he was the only dude I spoke to since I been here besides you."

"What happened to him?"

"Him and Mr. Hodge had a fight and Mr. Hodge had him sent to Juvie. You know how Mr. Hodge be on some private eye shit around here. Onix always said he was a freak but they fought because Mr. Hodge had caught Onix trying to run away a couple times so he started threatening Onix and Onix just snapped, punching him in the face and calling him a freak. But Mr. Hodge ended up taking him down with some type of military move and kept him there until the cops came and locked Onix up."

"Damn man, Mr. Hodge be on some ex-private eye shit. That muthafucka seem like he be watching my every move and I be feeling like he be watching me when I aint even in the house."

"He probably is that's why I hate him man. I woke up one day in the middle of the night and he was just standing over top of me, staring at me with this crazy look in his eyes."

"What?! He was just staring at you? What did you do?"

"The shit scared me at first because I had only been here like six months and I was only nine at the time. I tried to run away a week later. I was two blocks away when he just popped out of nowhere throwing me in that dirty ass van and brought me back here, threatening me about if I

tried to run away again I won't get out of Juvie 'til I'm twenty-one like Onix."

"Damn...Word?"

"Yeah man and Mrs. Hodge aint no better cause she sneaky and shit too. One day I caught her following me from the baseball park and I think she be reading my mail...plus, she be stinking anyway."

"Damn lil' Jeff, I feel you though. She do be stinking, smelling like underarms and ass." quipped Ryat after a short chuckle.

"Yo Ryat man, I done told you to stop calling me Jeffery, my name is Boody Boo."

"I'm saying, that's what everybody around here be calling you, so I guess I'm just used to hearing it."

"I told you I don't like none of those people man, that's why I let them call me by my government, whatever, I don't answer or speak to them anyway. But I'm cool with you so call me by my name Boody Boo."

"Yo I fucks wit you too lil Boody boo." Said Ryat with a sarcastic emphasis at the end.

"Is it alright if I just call you lil Boody? Yo what type of name is that anyway? I mean like, where did you get that name from?"

"My mom." said Jeffery in a hushed tone as he stared straight ahead at the TV with a now solemn look on his face.

"Damn, word? I'm saying, I aint tryna get all deep in your personal but how you know that's the nickname your mom gave you if you told me you

never really got to meet her cause she gave you up for adoption when you were a baby?"

Jeffery then turned towards Ryat, staring at him pensively.

"Because of this..."

Jeffery retrieved a children's book from his top drawer and handed it to Ryat. The book was small and thin with a cartoon picture of a mother duck and her ducklings. The title read: ***The Search for Mother Goose's Lost Duckling***.

"I've had that since I was a baby, they've made sure to send it with me everywhere I went since I was born." said Jeffery while staring pensively at Ryat.

"Go ahead and read the inside cover."

Ryat did as he was told.

To my beautiful son; my heart. Know that I love you more than my own life. That's the reason I pray you can one day understand why I had to make the decision I made. I pray the best for you and pray with all my heart that the decision I made affords you a better opportunity at life than I could have given you. Please just know that your mother loves you and just as the sun and moon are always in the sky, my heart and mind will always be with you. I love you so much my beautiful son, you will always be my Boody Boo.

Sincerely with Love,
Your Mother "Karen"

After reading the inscription on the inside of the book there was an awkward silence between the two as Ryat began to think of the day his uncle told him of the significance in his name. He then instantly felt a sense of melancholy wash over him.

"Do you ever think of her?" asked Ryat in a barely audible tone as he passed the book back to Boody.

"All the time." replied Boody in a hushed tone while staring towards Ryat with glazed eyes.

"And I'ma find her one day."

"How?" inquired Ryat, almost absent-mindedly as his mind became inundated with thoughts of his own late mother.

"Well my mom gotta be from Philly because that's where my birth certificate say I was born at. So I'ma go there one day and find her." Answered Boody, now staring at the inscription in the book himself; his young eyes glistening. Again, he looked at Ryat pensively.

"Hey Ryat, do you ever think of your mom?"

"All the time..." replied Ryat while staring off into space ruminatively as he was now thinking about the *what ifs* had his mother been alive.

Ryat then thought of the picture of his mother he usually woke up to every morning when he was home. He became angry as he thought of another reason why he hated his current predicament.

Since his first few weeks there Ryat had been writing Tiffany at least twice a week. With her writing almost every day. He also called her occasionally on the cell phone. Although, he really didn't like talking to her on the phone because she would always end up crying before they hung up. He would then always have to reassure her that he would be home soon. He had also spoken to Camille twice on the phone. Which put a smile on his face each time as Camille would tell him the humorous stories about the mischief he and their friends were up to.

Ryat had just gotten off the phone with his aunt and was elated to hear that a custody hearing date had been scheduled for the week of the following month. He told Earl quickly thereafter and promised him that he would send him enough money to compensate him for his generosity and letting him use his phone. Earl expressed how glad he was for him but told him emphatically that he never looked to be paid for helping. Ryat then ran to the third floor in hopes to find Boody in his room to relay the good news but when he looked in there Boody was nowhere to be found.

Just as he was making his way back downstairs, he happened to walk past Leslie and Asaria's room and was instantly frozen in place from what he saw as he glanced in. Standing with her back to him in a bow-legged stance was Asaria. She stood at the foot of her bed fixing her long wavy hair into a ponytail. She was wearing tight purple booty shorts which accentuated her perfectly shaped round mound, a tight pink belly shirt and *Life Saver* candy colored striped ankle socks on her small feet.

"Yo, why you so fucking evil?" asked Ryat with a sly smirk on his face as he was now leaning against the door frame staring at her lustfully.

Asaria then spun around on her heels quickly and after seeing Ryat leaning against the door frame she stared at him with a startled expression for a moment, then after fixing her face nefariously, she retorted,

"Why are 'you' so fucking evil?"

"I ain't evil, I just don't fuck with a lot of people," he calmly retorted followed by a wide smile while staring at the beauty of her smooth warm brass complexion and sinuous shape as she stood there indignantly.

"Well I guess I don't fuck with a lot of people either. Why you so bothered with me anyway? And why are you spying on me fucker?" She snapped indignantly as a slight Spanish accent became more resonant.

"Calm down Lady of Rage, I just happened to be walking by when I seen you and decided I wanted to know how a chick so angel faced and sexy can be so evil like, 'all the time'." Answered

Ryat as he walked over and sat on her bed as if it belonged to him.

The indignant expression that was written on her face was replaced with slight confusion then surprise as she watched this boy two years younger than her seem so confident and self-assured. She then looked at him from head to toe and said,

"Muthafucka, I don't know what makes you think you can just barge in here like you own the world. And put my remote down!"

"That really doesn't look good on you."

"And now you got the nerve to disrespect me?! You don't know me bitch! You better get out of here before I end up cutting your ass!" Asaria snapped, narrowing her eyes and twisting up her face after looking at herself from head to toe self-consciously.

"That definitely don't look good on you. Dig it, I'm just saying that mean grill you keep on your face all the time don't look right on you. I told you your face is too angel like for all that evil on it." he countered placidly while staring at her. Then, with a shrug of the shoulders he turned towards the TV and changed the channel.

"I just think you'd look ten times better if you smiled more."

"Angel-faced huh?" Asaria retorted sarcastically as she plopped down on her bed staring at Ryat. Suddenly, realizing that he had appealed to her like no other boys her age or of any age had. Noticing the infectious smile on his face as he

looked back at her, she couldn't help but smile too. She tried to repress it by bringing her left hand to her mouth.

"See, that definitely looks good on you.... almost goddess like. Nice teeth by the way."

"Oh my God, I hope this isn't what you call your game."

"Not at all, I don't have 'game'. I'm just a realist, plus I already got a girl."

"Realist huh? So what, you're a gangster?"

Turning his face up into a sly grin as he continued to stare at her he responded,

"Nah, I just speak how I feel."

Then, after a short pause and shrug he continued,

"I guess that's just the way my grandma raised me."

An awkward silence then ensued between them as they both suddenly became uneasy and unsure of what to say next. Although the both of them were surprisingly comfortable in each other's presence. She simply sat there staring at him amiably while he turned the channels on her TV as if it were his.

"Yo Asaria, where you from?"

"Harrisburg," she answered as he quickly turned around looking at her wide-eyed and incredulous

"What? Why you looking at me like that?"

"Nah, its just that you the only kid here that I've met that's from where I'm from."

She then brightened up, slightly surprised as well.
"Oh yeah? So you're from Harrisburg too? What part?"
"Uptown."
"Oh, I'm from the Hill. We used to live on Thompson Street." Asaria said more solemnly now as she looked down at her dangling feet and asked Ryat in a hushed tone,
"Hey Ryat, how did you end up here?"
"That's crazy cause I was just about to ask you the same thing."

Ryat then commenced to telling her in brevity how he ended up under the Hodges care. They then talked introspectively for the better part of two hours sharing their back stories and some of their most intimate thoughts with one another.

He learned that she had been in the Hodges care since she was thirteen years old, after her father was sent to prison when she was twelve. She told him how her mother then moved her to Reading, Pennsylvania where her mother ended up getting strung out on dope and began leaving her home alone for days at a time; until her mother didn't come home for two weeks.

Asaria had become so accustomed to her mother leaving her home alone that she didn't realize how long her mother had been absent. Until there wasn't one morsel of food left in their apartment and she began to starve 3 days before she noticed two uniformed police officers and a plain clothes officer knocking on their apartment door. At the sight of them she became so scared as she remembered when her father was taken away. Therefore she climbed out onto the fire escape, jumping down the black metal steps two at a time and then ran off into the street in search of her mother. Asaria would then end up living in the streets for three and a half weeks while looking for her mother. Eventually a philanthropic elder woman that she met at the church took her in. Asaria had showed up to the church in hopes to receive some free food. The lady seeing the young unkempt child, begin to ask questions that Asaria being scared and emotionally distraught hesitantly answered, telling the woman everything. The woman genuinely concerned for the child's well-being, took Asaria in and promised she would do her best to help her find her mother.

Two Days Later Asaria and the *Angel Lady* were sitting in the woman's living room watching television when the woman stepped into the room accompanied by, to Asaria's surprise, those same two cops and plainclothes officer that showed up to her mother's apartment. The plainclothes officer turned out to be a Child Protective Services agent who explained to Asaria that her mother had died from an overdose therefore she would be taken into their care. Asaria, then crying profusely, was taken from that house kicking and screaming for her mother.

Ryat almost lost control of his emotions and cried the tears Asaria was suppressing as she told her melancholic story. This made him feel closer to her more than anyone he could think of since his late grandmother. Suddenly just as she had finished speaking and tears began to stream from her cheeks, he wrapped his arms around her from the back and pulled her close. Both of them in their own respective trances, stared off pensively in silence towards the walls, eyes glistening.

Over the next few weeks they became almost inseparable as their friendship blossomed into one that Ryat never knew could exist between a male and a female. It was clearly platonic though more intimate than any of his other friendships. Their conversations were straight-forward yet so deep and honest that they would often joke with each other that they were the same person of opposite Sexes.

When he asked her if she ever planned to run away she told him no because she had lived on the streets before and would rather be under the Hodges care where she could take advantage of school. Also, explaining to him that she planned to enter the Independent Living Program the next year for foster kids, where they could enter right after their 18th birthday. The program would then put her in her own apartment and assist her every step of the way while teaching her life skills.

Two days before his custody hearing Asaria became reticent and distant towards him. When he asked her what was wrong, she was straightforward with her response. Telling him that he was the first genuine friend she had since she was a small child and it was going to hurt her to see him go although she knew it was best for him. He promised her that he would always keep in touch with her and she responded it still wouldn't be the same.

The day of the custody hearing Ryat was so excited to be going home that he decided to be nice to the Hodges as they rode together to the courthouse in downtown Harrisburg. Once inside he was even more elated to see his aunt after so many months away from home. He sat eagerly throughout the three-hour hearing in anticipation of being reunited with his loved ones. Only to be let down when the judge awarded temporary custody to the Hodges and rescheduled the subsequent hearing a year from that date.

Chapter 13

"Nobody can give you freedom. Nobody can give you equality or justice or anything. If you're a man, you take it."
-Malcolm X

    Ryat sat aghast and in shock at the judges' decision to the point he became unconsciously unaware of everything that transpired thereafter. He vaguely remembered his aunt's reaction except for when she directed here final outburst towards him.
    "You know Ry', you just do what you gotta do and you'll be home wit your family soon. To hell with that dese people talking about."
    Anita shouted.

Arriving back at the Hodges' residence, Ryat dealt with a plethora of mixed emotions. As he mainly fluctuated between extreme depression and anger. Especially since he could have sworn he saw Mr. Hodge smirk when the court awarded them temporary custody. Especially when they were going over the details of the payment plan for them for the time Ryat would be under their care.

As soon as Ryat came through the door, Asaria came from the kitchen immediately trying to console him as best she could. It was to no avail though as he told her he needed to be alone while removing her arms from around his neck. Soon thereafter, he ended up in the basement where he had been going often when he needed some solitude. He stayed down there for hours simply sitting on top of the dryer in the back while musing over his current predicament. He stayed in this reclusive state for over six hours when suddenly he thought about his Aunt's last words to him. The peculiarity of them moved him to capriciously jump off the dryer and run up the steps.

Reaching his destination in the room in which he resided, he noticed Davey sitting at the small desk by the far wall.

"Ayo Davey, where Earl at?" asked Ryat impatiently.

"Whoa!" bellowed a startled Davey as he spun around in his seat, hearing the urgency in Ryat's tone.

"Hey man look, I don't know but hey check it out. Little Jeffery was looking for you earlier. He looked a little messed up dude, because he supposedly found out Mrs. Hodge had been withholding mail from him that you know he believes it was probably his mom trying to find him like he wishes so he went crazy on her and Mr. Hodge. That's when he came looking for you after hearing what happened with you. But then after not finding you he thinks you ran away when you had the chance. So dude it's only a guess but I think he decided to run away before Mr. Hodge locks this place down like Fort Knox."

"Aww shit," exclaimed Ryat just as Earl was coming through the door and confirming what Davey had just said after hearing a portion of their conversation that Boody had indeed run away.

Ryat's depression was than exacerbated as he quickly came to the conclusion that there was nothing he could really do. Quickly remembering why he had run up to the room in the first place, he asked Earl to use his phone and made his way to the bathroom. After leaving the bathroom he seemed surprisingly serene as he entered the bedroom handing Earl his phone back and quietly finding a seat atop his bunk.

It was around 11:15 p.m. when Ryat laid back in his usual way with his arms behind his head on his back, looking up at the ceiling. He lay there for hours in the same position as it seemed to be another normal night for him at the Hodges'. Until around midnight when he became restless as he jumped out of his bunk and began standing and sitting in different places throughout the room. He would even sporadically look out the window like he had seen his grandfather do so many times before when he was in the throes of a crack induced high. Ryat continued his routine for the next three hours while the other boys in the room slept soundly.

At approximately 3:30 a.m. a light flashed repeatedly outside the window. Ryat immediately grabbed the flashlight he had on the table, took it to the window and clicked it on and off three times. The repeated flashing lights outside the window then stopped as Ryat began to open the window.

"Ayo Ryat, what's up man?" inquired Earl in a groggy voice as he sat up on his bunk looking towards Ryat.

Initially startled, Ryat spun around from the window looking at Earl. He quickly realized he had awakened him. Then in a half elated and slightly sorrowful tone, he answered,

"I'm out man."

As Earl got up he looked at Ryat oddly for a second then smirked and said,

"I knew it wouldn't be too long."

Ryat then smirked himself and replied,

"Yea..."

"Alright man," said Earl as he moved to embrace Ryat, pulling away from one another Earl said,

"You just be cool out there man. I know you've told me how you're tired of living in poverty and your family suffering the effects of it. So you plan to get money by any means. I'm just saying don't let your desire for a better life cost you your life because Ryat, there's more to life than the value placed on it monetarily."

"Yeah man I hear you and I heard that before but I can't accept that because all my folks that died, died broke and never really got to experience that happiness and freedom that money affords in this capitalistic society. So like I told you before, all I know is if it don't make dollars then it don't make sense." countered Ryat as he then climbed out the window and hung from the second floor windowsill.

Letting go of the windowsill, he landed on his feet and quickly ran in the direction the repeated flashing lights had come from. He knew this was the only way he could make a second getaway from the Hodges' residence. As he knew after 9 p.m. Mr. Hodge locked that house down like a Detention Center. Mr. Hodge double bolt-locked every door in the house and set the alarm system to prevent anybody from coming in or going out. Right now, even if he got one of the doors open that alone would undoubtedly sound off in no time and Mr. Hodge would just as quickly have the police there to impede any plans he had to make a sound getaway.

Ryat ran at breakneck speed through the narrow alleyway on the side of the house until he reached the vehicle from which the repeated flashing headlights have come from. He ran straight for the passenger seat door but was surprised to see someone was already occupying that seat. Upon quick examination, he noticed it was Camill who was supposed to had been the driver.

"Ayo Ryat come on man hurry up and get in the back." said Camill, noticing Ryat's confusion and hesitancy.

Ryat then quickly obliged. Once inside he realized to his surprise that Dollas was actually the driver.

"Yo what up Dollas? What up Mil?" said Ryat, elated to see both friends.

"Yo wha'sup my nigga?" responded Mil, just as elated while reaching back and clasping Ryat's outstretched hand in an embrace.

"Yo what up champ? Ain't seen you in a minute," said Dollas placidly as he also briefly clasped Ryat's outstretched hand in an embrace.

"Yeah man it's been like six months. I can't wait to get back home, I hated this shit fam."

"A Ryat, you sure you want to do this?" asked Dollas while staring at Ryat through the rearview mirror.

"Ain't no doubt in my mind, didn't you just hear me? I hated this shit man!" replied Ryat with more of a seriously explicit expression on his face.

"Alright then I can respect that. Understood. Just know that tough times don't build character, they Define it. Adversity introduces a man to himself." said Dollas philosophically.

"No doubt."

"Ayo Ryat, when you called me, Dollas just so happened to be riding through the hood, so I told him what was up and he said he'd bring me down here to get you. I'm glad too man because I probably wouldn't have made it. We ended up getting pulled over on the way here but you know Dallas got his L's so we was cool, but you...Oh shi...." Camill shrieked as an abrupt clatter against his door startled him. He had his gun out in a fraction of a second and positioned himself to fire through his door.

Ryat quickly realizing what was about to happen, immediately grabbed Camill's arm and shouted;

"Yo Mil chill! Chill yo!"

"What da fuck yo!" blurted Camill, excited and slightly addled.

"Nah yo, just chill." said Ryat as he rolled down his window.

"Yo Boody, What's up? Why you creepin' up on us like that outta nowhere?"

"Aye Ryat man, you gotta take me with you." Responded a desperate sounding and panicky

looking Boody as he stood outside the SUV in front of Ryat's window.

"Hold up Ryat, you sure you ready for this? I'm just saying, because you can barely take care of yourself right now." said Dollas while staring intensely at Ryat through the rearview mirror. Ryat stared back as he digested his words and briefly pondered them.

"Yeah man you could probably go to jail or some shit." Mil chimed in.

"C'mon Ryat I ain't got nowhere else to go and you know I can't go back in there. I'll take care of myself man, you just gotta take me with you." plead Boody.

"Nuff said man, hurry up and get in." said Ryat.

"Good lookin' out man." said Boody as he jumped in the SUV just as Dollas was pulling off. Camill then cut his eyes at Ryat as he slouched in his seat.

"So yo, where he going to stay Ryat? Cause I know you ain't bringing him just to live on the streets." said Dollas placidly as he kept his eyes on the road.

"Wit me."

"And where would that be since I know Child Protective Services will be looking for you."

"We gone stay at my pops."

"Hold up, I thought that's where you already live with the rest of your family."

"Nah, my pops live in the apartment on the third floor and the only address they got for me is the apartment on the first floor, my Grandma's apartment where I grew up. That's where my auntie live now."

"Oh alright, you should be alright then but damn, all this time I thought y'all all lived in that first-floor apartment."

The rest of the ride back to Harrisburg they all rode in silence as they each concentrated on their own thoughts. The moment they arrived back in the city, the iridescent street lights of downtown captured Ryat and put him in a trance. In reverie, he realized how much he missed his hometown, with its unique identity and big city similitude. He had always wondered how other more eclectic cities got all the adulation as well as the abasement as if the same things happening there weren't happening in other places. Given its contrast, he knew the same beauty they emanated and poverty they experienced could be found in his city.

They arrived in back of the building Ryat grew up in at approximately 4:15 a.m. and although it was still dark outside, Ryat thought there could be no better vision.

"Alright, y'all hurry up and get out before Anita see me dropping y'all off and be coming for my head!" said Dollas as he pulled to a stop in the back alley next to a children's playground.

"Alright Dollas, good lookin' man, I'ma get at you." said Ryat as he embraced Dollas with a handshake then emerged from the SUV with Boody in tow.

"Yeah, I'm a holla at you too Dollas. Good lookin' out." said Camill as he also quickly embraced dollars with a handshake then exited the vehicle.

"Ayo Ryat..." said Dollas with his window rolled down as Ryat, Mil, and Boody began to walk towards the back of the building.

"Wha'sup?" responded Ryat as he turned around to face Dollas.

"Aye look man, though I don't condone it, you done made your choice so now you either go hard as you can out here and get out just as quick or take your ass back to those people's house and follow that route for your life. Just don't be out here risking your life and freedom for next to nothing."

"No doubt, I feel ya." Replied Ryat while nodding his head, fully understanding the validity in the words as Dollas pulled away.

Ryat and Camill then parted ways as they both promise to meet up later in the day. Right then made his way inside the building with Boody in tow. Now standing in front of the first-floor apartment door, he became slightly afraid and apprehensive as he wasn't sure of how his aunt will react to seeing him on the other side of the door, especially so early in the morning.

Fighting against his apprehension and fear, he knocked on the door with his head hung low. After two more short knocks on the door it opened as he lifted his head cautiously to face his Aunt on the other side of the door.

Anita looked at Ryat sternly for a moment then fixed her face into a relieved smile and said, *"What took you so long?"*

Chapter 14

"It is the first duty of every man not to be poor."

-George Bernard Shaw

Ryat had been home for little over a week and had been relishing in every minute of it. The moment he introduced Boody to his aunt and grandfather they immediately took him in after hearing his story. Ryat and Boody had been staying with Mr. Carl in his two bedroom third-floor apartment. Though it was as if they were living there alone because Mr. Carl was hardly ever home and when he was he would sleep for a short period of time and be right back out the door.

Child Protective Services had been by to visit Anita twice and both times she told them she knew nothing about Ryat running away or his whereabouts. She even pretended to be angry and cursed them for taking her nephew away from his family only for him to end up missing. To their knowledge they had no idea that Boody was also living only two floors above with Ryat as they were under the guise that Boody had ran away by himself prior to Ryat's disappearance from the Hodge residence.

Ryat decided the last thing he wanted was for Child Protective Services to take him back into their custody. So, he had been laying low the entire time he had been back home. After initially meeting up with his friends the day after returning home, he hadn't seen them since. Though they also instantly took to Boody the minute he introduced him to them as Boody immediately commenced to ingratiating himself with them also. He had even been seeing more of them than Ryat. Since Ryat for the most part had been spending most of his days and nights at Tiffany's house.

After being home for about a week and a half, he decided to go outside and hangout with his friends. Especially after witnessing the landlord talk condescendingly to both his grandfather and aunt about their past due rent. When Ryat asked his aunt about her struggles with the rent she explained to him that all her bills coupled with her school expenses had her basically living paycheck to paycheck. Sometimes without enough to cover the entire rent bill. Yet she told him that the bills would be paid regardless, especially when her boyfriend Keith got his check in the next couple of days since he had taken to helping her with her bills. Ryat then talked briefly with his grandfather about his struggles paying rent. Mr. Carl told him bluntly that they would be getting kicked out soon, because he was $1600 behind in past due rent and had no way of paying it. Hearing this deeply troubled Ryat and slightly angered him as he pondered what seemed to be his family's perpetual struggles. Suddenly right then and there is when he made up his mind that he was tired of his family living a marginal existence financially. Therefore, he planned to improve their circumstances the only way he knew how garnered from his social engineering in acquiring a dollar by any means necessary.

He was walking up Woodbine street from his home when he saw most of his friends sitting on the steps in front of Mil and Bryce's building. Whereupon approaching and greeting them with half hug handshake embraces, he immediately sensed something was wrong from the miserly expressions on most their faces.

"Ayo what up wit y'all niggas?" he asked enthusiastically as he had just finished shaking Potta's hand.

"Ain't shit. Yo what up Ryat? Niggas is happy to see you, you been gone for a lil minute," responded Hochee while lifting a blunt towards his mouth.

"Y'all niggas don't look happy to see me. Why y'all sitting around here looking all pissed and shit?" countered Ryat as he looked from face to face for an answer.

"Man cause shit's crazy sun, ain't no bread coming through" replied Bryce, then looking past Ryat down the street as if hoping for a fiend to come up the block looking to buy some crack.

"So why y'all ain't on da block? Y'all know don't no bread really come through here cause niggas usually catch it on the block before it come around here," inquired Ryat with an addled expression on his face as he looked at Mil for an answer.

"Cause man Ryat shit done got crazy since you been gone. First off man we got into some shit wit dese niggas from the Southside at one of those Clubhouse parties. Shit got crazy wit them niggas so we had a few shootouts, that's when Hochee got shot in da calf about two mon..."

"Hold up, yo Hochee you got hit in da leg?" interrupted Ryat, excitedly while looking intensely at Hochee.

"Yeah man but that shit ain't bout nothin cuz, I'm smooth, plus we got the nigga that hit me," replied Hochee while pulling up his pant leg and showing off his bullet wound to Ryat.

"Anyway man after all that the shit made the block hot, especially after Bryce over here pistol whipped a fiend almost to death for trying to give him fake money. Then after all that Bo wouldn't sell us no more work, then had his lil toy soldiers Rip and em come tell us we couldn't hustle on da block no more. I'm saying we was ready to take them niggas to war but you know we ain't really ready for all that cause the nigga Bo got major paper and a gazillion toy soldiers ready to do whatever he say. So, we been around here trying get at a dollar but like you said don't know bread really come through here cause them niggas on da block usually catch it before it do," said Mil, taking the blunt from Potta and inhaling it deeply.

"Damn yo Mil, why you ain't tell me all this shit was going on when I was calling you?"

"Cause man I figured you was already dealing with your fucked up situation so it wasn't no use telling you bout the fucked up shit wit us."

"Word sun, you had your own shit to deal wit," Bryce chimed in.

"So who y'all been coping off since that fat nigga won't sell y'all no work?" asked Ryat.

"We been coping work off Mil step daddy," quipped Potta with a sly smirk on his face.

"Man I'm not gone keep telling you that nigga ain't my step daddy," barked Mil while staring at Potta intensely as they all began laughing.

"Straight up cuz, fuck that nigga! I hate that pussy. I'm telling y'all he lucky he my sister daddy cause I would been bodied him."

"I feel you though, that nigga is a snake. He been charging us crazy like we some young nuts cause he know won't nobody else sell us work cause Bo done gave the word," said Hochee.

"Damn, what he been charging?" asked Ryat.

"Fifty-five for four and a half," responded Hochee while shaking his head slowly.

"Damn cuz that's crazy! He's straight disrespecting. But that's crazy y'all all only coping four and a half together after all this time."

"Shit ain't been right man. Like you said don't no money really come through here and it ain't like we can cop off somebody else."

As Ryat was listening to Hochee something caught his attention out the corner of his eyes. Directly looking at it, he noticed Potta and Boody had jumped up off the porch running full speed towards a blue Ford pickup.

After realizing what was taking place, he said, *"Yo what the fuck is this? Y'all got lil Boody out here hustling too? And that's crazy the way they look fighting over a sell like savages for food."*

"Look sun, that's how shit is out here now. They got us like savages out here trying ta eat sun,

word," responded Bryce with an indifferent shrug of the shoulders

"Man that's crazy but fuck all that, why y'all got lil Boody out here grinding? He's only eleven. Man I knew I shouldn't had left him wit y'all niggas," said Ryat just as Boody and Potta came walking back towards them with Potta busy counting the money from the sell.

"Man Ryat ain't nobody got him doing shit yo, he out here just like us. He made his own choice and who are we to stop him," said Mil as he passed the blunt to Ryat.

"Yeah sun you can't be da nigga daddy," quipped Bryce.

"Yeah Ryat I'm cool man," said Boody in a hushed tone with his head down

"You cool?" hissed Ryat while puffing the blunt and staring at them intensely.

"'Ight fuck it then."

"Oh shit hold up, there go that fat nigga right there," said Hochee while pointing towards a brand new black Eldorado that was cruising up the block towards them. They all stared as the sleek black Cadillac came riding by them, Rip in the driver's seat smirking at them. While Bo sat in the passenger seat looking on apathetically.

"I swear ta God sun I'm ready ta murda dat fat nigga," snarled Bryce while gripping at his gun and stepping towards the end of the curb, staring at the car with loathe.

"Nah yo chill Bryce, we gone have our day," interjected Ryat.

"Man fuck dat sun, I ain't bout to keep letting dat nigga treat us like we a bunch of bitches. Word, I'll murda dat nigga first sun. Fuck dat sun, dat fat nigga ain't no threat, he got a fucking ponytail!" Bryce continued to growl as his friends abruptly fell out laughing.

"Yo Bryce now I remember why I missed you... yous a funny nigga cuz," said Ryat in between laughter

"Yo word Bryce yous a fucking nut," quipped Potta while barely containing his laughter and choking off the blunt smoke.

"Straight up though sun, dat nigga look like Bruce Bruce," retorted Bryce, ending with a smirk.

"Yo Bryce you shot out. But yo listen y'all know we can't really fuck wit that nigga til we get our weight up. So I been plotting on this nigga my girl brother be hustling for. He's a next nigga and supposedly touching major paper on da low down midtown. He got like two dudes with him and they hustle out of a house down by Penn and Calder. I've been laying on this dude for the last week and I know we can get him, plus I already stole his number out my girl brother phone. So y'all niggas be ready and strapped tonight and I'ma put y'all D wit everything else," said Ryat.

"Yeah sun we can just meet back here at my crib since y'all know my moms won't be here cause she work da third shift. But yo Ryat now I remember

why I missed you sun, cause you always making sense about us making some dollars, you feel me sun. Unlike this dumbass nigga Potta over here who couldn't make cents out of a million dollars," said Bryce, smirking as the rest of the gang snickered.

"Yo Bryce fuck you cuz, I get money," retorted Potta.

"Nah yo for real though I ain't gone be able to make it cause my moms been on me like crazy ever since I got shot. So to keep her from having a heart attack, from stressing over me, I told her I would make sure I be in the house by ten-thirty," said Hochee.

"Aww shit sun, did y'all here that shit? Hoch over here talking bout he got to be in by his curfew or his mommy gone wip his ass," quipped Bryce as all the guys except Hochee commenced to laughing again.

"Yo that ain't what I said chump, don't be twisting my words. I go in out of respect for my moms which you wouldn't know nothing about," countered Hochee as he stood up off the porch.

"Yo don't get mad at me sun cause you the only gangsta I know that still gets his ass wupped by his momma," retorted Bryce with a sly smirk on his face as Hochee stepped towards him with his hands up and they began slap boxing.

Hours later back at the apartment in Ryat's room that he now shared with Boody, he and Boody both were preoccupied with their own thoughts and actions. Ryat lay back on his bed staring blankly at the ceiling, while concentrating his mind on the hit he and his friends had plans to execute in just a couple of hours. Boody on the other hand sat upright on his blowup mattress counting the money he had made from that day, hustling.

"Ayo Boody you ever think of yo daddy, like who he was or what type of man he was?" asked Ryat suddenly while staring at the ceiling.

"All the time man, actually when I find my mom, besides me getting to know her, that's one of the first questions I'ma ask her," replied Boody as he folded $230 into his pocket.

"Why Ryat? Do you think a lot about what type of man your daddy was?"

"Yeah man, all the time."

Chapter 15

"The violently oppressed react violently to their oppression. When their reactionary violence, their retaliatory or defensive violence cannot be effectively directed at their oppressors or effectively applied to their self-liberation, it will be directed at and applied destructively to themselves. This is the essence of Black-on-Black."

-Dr. Amos N. Wilson

Around midnight, Ryat, Mil, Potta, and Bryce were sitting in gray '91 Chevrolet Corsica parked three houses down from their intended target. Potta had bartered the car for a few hours from a crackhead for $40 worth of crack. They were dressed down in black, each possessing a different type of pistol. They also wore different styles of black ski mask with black form fitting cotton gloves on their hands.

Ryat pulled out a cellphone he had stolen from an elderly white crack fiend's car earlier that day. He then pulled out a little piece of paper he had written a number on that he then dialed into the cellphone.

"Who dis?" answered a man from the other end of the line.

Ryat then answered in a voice he had been practicing for days,

"Yo Juan, this is me dog; big Avery."

"Oh what's up dog? I didn't recognize your number. You sound like you sick or something."

"Naw I'm just tired. This is my new phone, I lost my last one but look I need some food. I ain't got no more and I got people waiting."

"What you trying to eat?"

"I got an appetite for the same thing as last time."

"Oh 'ight, just come around da crib. You know like usual, come through the back, I'll get the door cause Vance and Ben just went on a run."

"Cool, I should be there in like five minutes. I'm coming around da corner from da crib now."

Ryat then hung up the cellphone telling his partners it was a go as planned. He, Mil, and Bryce then exited the vehicle leaving Potta at the wheel as the getaway driver. He was known amongst them as the most skilled driver from his previous car stealing days where the police never caught him in a car chase.

"Yo you out there?" answered Juan.

"Yeah I'm standing out back right now," replied Ryat in the makeshift voice.

"'Ight here I come," said Juan, then after a few seconds he swung the back door open recklessly.

"Yo big Ave."

"Shut the fuck up nigga," barked Mil in a muffled tone due to his ski mask as he stuffed his 9mm. handgun in Juan's face while backing him into the middle of the kitchen.

"What the fuck is the..."

"Didn't he say shut da fuck up," hissed Bryce in a muffled tone as he banged Juan across his head with his 50. Caliber Desert Eagle.

"Nigga we asked da questions and you answer them straight or we murda you."

"You know why you here so don't play games. Where da fuck is da money and work?" asked Ryat calmly as he pointed his pistol-grip 44. Magnum revolver in Juan's face while staring at him apathetically.

"Man fuck this, yall don't know wh- ...AHHhhhhh......AHhhh...AHHhhh shit, come on... Al'ight AHhh AHHh.." screamed Juan as he fell to his knees from Bryce abruptly pistol whipping him almost unconscious.

"'Ight man listen I swear I don't keep no money here but I got a bird outback in my car, I swear."

"'Ight take us to the coke then you can take us to the money. How that sound?" asked Ryat while staring down at the bloodied face of Juan.

"'Ight, 'ight cool, just let me live man," pleaded a battered Juan who was on his knees shielding his head with his forearms as if to ward off anymore possible blows.

"Yo I got the crib," said Mil with Ryat nodding to him in agreement, he then commenced to ransacking the house. While Bryce pulled Juan to his feet as he and Ryat lead him out the back door.

A short distance from the back of the house in the alley was where Juan's forest green S500 Mercedes Benz was parked. Bryce forced him into the driver's seat as he got in the passenger seat and Ryat got in behind Juan.

"So where that shit at nigga?" hissed Bryce with the barrel of his gun pressed against Juan's cheek.

"It's right there in the detergent box," answered Juan as he pointed towards a small dirty clothes hamper with a box of Tide on top in the backseat next to Ryat.

Ryat then grabbed the box of Tide detergent and bust it open. A brick and a half of crack fell out in the mist of the soap powder spilling out all over the back-seat. Ryat then snatched the dirty clothes out the hamper revealing a Tec. 9. And two handguns under all the clothes. Ryat then pulled the backpack from off his back and put the crack and guns inside.

"So what you wasn't gone tell us about the guns huh? What you thought you was just gone somehow get one and body us, huh?" asked Bryce through clenched teeth, then looking towards Ryat as Ryat nodded towards him after catching his eyes. Indicating for Bryce to knock Juan out with his pistol as planned so they could make a clean getaway.

"AHHhhh shit...AHhhh shit..." yelled Juan as Bryce commenced to hitting him atop the head with his gun. Juan then growled, *"AHhh shit.. I swear to God."*

"You swear to God what nigga?" hissed Bryce as he stopped briefly from hitting him to stare at him intensely in anticipation of his answer.

"Man I swear to God dog yall lil niggas don't know who yall fucking wit cause I'ma murda you and all ya lil homies," replied Juan in a low growl of a whisper as he stared back at Bryce odiously.

Ryat heard Juan's statement just as he had grabbed the door handle to exit the car. He then instantly flashed back to that last night with Lati. In an impetuous haste he placed the barrel of his 44. Magnum to the back of Juan's head and unflinchingly pulled the trigger. Blowing a fifty-cent piece size hole through the back of his head. Bryce in an instant shock quickly pushed Juan's slumped body against the driver's door off the steering wheel to stop the horn from continuously beeping. He then immediately looked back at Ryat meeting his stare, noticing the stolid look in his eyes. Bryce now beyond his brief startled state, with his eyes smiled at Ryat nefariously as they both commenced to exit the vehicle. Then as Ryat was shutting the car door behind him he looked back and noticed that just before Bryce shut the passenger door he pointed his gun back inside the car and fired three more shots into Juan's body.

They both then took off running back towards the house in destination for the getaway car. Mil came running out the back door of the house as they were crossing through the back yard.

"Yo wha'sup? I heard shots," inquired an excited Mil as he jumped down the small flight of stairs and fell in line behind them running towards the getaway car.

"Ain't shit yo, come on," replied Ryat curtly as he was running full speed through the alley on the side of the house.

"Yo he wasn't lying, wasn't shit in that crib but three-hundred dollars," said Mil almost out of breath just as they reached the Corsica where Potta sat impatiently. The moment each of them sat inside the car before they could even shut the door, Potta sped off.

Ryat sat unfazed by what had just taken place as he stared out the car window with an impassive look on his face while they all road in silence.

They had just pulled to a stoplight at 6th & Riley streets only a half of block away form where they were to ditch the car in the Jackson Lick building's parking lot. When each of their eyes were instantly attracted like mosquitoes to light to a brown-skinned man's jewelry. Potta then immediately pulled into the gas station where the man had just gotten out a white Lincoln Navigator with 24' Dasani rims. Whereupon closer inspection the gang noticed the man's gaudy jewelry was a thick gold Cuban link necklace with a diamond encrusted pendant the size of a small saucer plate. The charm looked to be a representation of Mary holding baby Jesus in the manger. The man also wore a diamond encrusted watch and bracelet. While the other two passengers in his truck looked to be donning the same type jewelry except their chains had smaller different styled pendants.

"Yo we gots ta get those niggas sun," blurted an excited Bryce from the back-seat.

"We definitely gots to get them niggas, they stuntin crazy and I need that ice," said Potta while staring down the brown-skinned man with the gaudy jewelry as he got back in the driver's side of the Navigator.

"Man yall niggas wilding. We just came up. Ain't no need to draw anymore heat to us plus look at all these people out. They most likely going to the same place as those niggas. Yall know it's club

night, they probably all bout to hit the Bucks real quick," said Mil.

"Man fuck all dat cuz, we already hot. Ain't no better time than now to get these niggas for they ice. Fuck all those people going out, that's why we masked up. Plus that's how we gone catch em slippen, in the parking lot of da Bucks. So what's good Ryat, you down?" countered Potta as he turned back to look at Ryat for his reply, Ryat then simply looked at him and gave an indifferent shrug.

"'Ight then Mil you just grab da wheel when we jump out on dese niggas," said Potta as Mil then cut his eyes at him.

Potta then surreptitiously followed behind the white Navigator a short distance to the parking lot adjacent to *Roebuck's* bar. Being as though there were a plethora of patrons in the parking lot either going in or coming out, the gang went totally unnoticed to the occupants in the Navigator. As the Corsica doubled parked behind the Navigator immediately after the Navigator found a parking spot. Just then in the fraction of a millisecond, every door to the Corsica swung open as Ryat, Potta, and Bryce emerged with their guns drawn. They quickly accosted the occupants of the white Lincoln Navigator as the other people in the parking lot began running and screaming in fear of the masked gunmen.

"Yeah go head, I triple dare you nigga," hissed Potta with his gun raised at the occupant in the back-seat. Whom a millisecond to slow, was

reaching at this waist for his gun. Which his sitting position impeded him even further as it made it more difficult for him to possess his gun before the gang accosted them.

"Yo what's this bruh?" inquired the startled driver of the Navigator as Bryce stood in front of him with his .50 cal. Desert Eagle pointed in the center of the man's face.

"You know what it is sun, give up everything or lose ya fucking life," barked Bryce as the man in the passenger seat whom Ryat had his gun trained in on began to plead with the driver to just give everything up. Whom quickly relieved himself of his jewels and money, handing it to Ryat. Who had the passenger put it in the backpack off his back which was now in his left hand with gun still in his right. Ryat then ordered the man out of the truck and to lay on the ground as he relieved him of the pistol in his waist-belt. Potta quickly followed suit by relieving the man in the back-seat of everything then making him lie face down on the pavement. Bryce on the other hand was having a little more difficulty as the driver began to become slightly obstinate.

"Man fuck this bruh, do ya lil ass know who I am nigga?" blurted the driver while starring at Bryce belligerently whom had the driver's door open now ordering him out of the truck.

"You see that' da problem right there sun, everybody swear they somebody. All you had ta do

was give up da ice, now you just bout to be a dead nobody on ic..."

"*Fuck it cuz, kill dat nigga, we gots ta go,*" snarled Potta from the other side of the truck with his gun still trained on his victim as Bryce impulsively was just about to pull the trigger when Ryat stepped towards him shaking his head.

"*Nigga give that shit up,*" hissed Ryat through his mask as he stared the driver dead in the eyes.

The driver then quickly relinquished himself of all his money and jewels as the look in Ryat's eyes compelled him more than anything else. It was the pernicious tint over them that told him his life meant more than money and jewels. After successfully relieving the men of their possessions and making them lay face down on the pavement, the gang quickly jumped back into the Corsica as Mil immediately sped off.

They then took the juxtaposed alley straight down to 7th street, making a right, they only road two blocks before making a right back up Boas street. Riding at a moderate speed until they were back on 6th street where they road a block back towards the crime scene before pulling into the parking lot of the Jackson Lick Towers. Only two blocks from where they had just committed their last robbery. They then pulled into a parking space and watched for a few seconds as cop cars sped past them en route to the location where the robbery had taken place. They all then got out of the Corsica and walked towards two different rental cars. Mil and Potta got inside a silver '99 Chrysler Sebring with the backpack containing the fruit of their robberies as Ryat and Bryce got inside a dark blue '99 Chevrolet Impala. Ryat then told Mil and Potta to take the backpack back to Bryce's house and that he and Bryce would be there soon after they dumped their guns.

The two cars then took off in separate directions as Ryat and Bryce headed across the river towards the 21st plaza. Ryat figured they could grab some food from his favorite fast food spot Wendy's over in the plaza as they would have to go across the river anyway to dump their guns. The moment they reached the middle of the Harvey Taylor bridge, Ryat rolled down his driver's side window and tossed his 44. Magnum over the bridge into the water of the Susquehanna river. He then looked towards Bryce wondering what was taking him so long to dump his gun. Bryce then informed him that he couldn't part with his baby therefore he wasn't dumping his gun. Ryat was ready to chide him about his stupid decision but then decided against it with a simple indifferent shrug of the shoulders.

Chapter 16

> *"If oppression be so hard to bear, that a
> wise man is made mad by it… then a series of those
> things, altering the behavior and manners of a
> people, is what may reasonably be expected."*
> **-John Woolman**

One week had passed since the robberies
and things were slowly beginning to change for the
crew. They continued to keep a low profile while
only hanging inside the buildings on Woodbine
street. Yet they were beginning to see more money
than they had before from their previous petty
hustling. Due to the fact that the day after the
robberies they all sat in Ryat and his grandfather's
apartment cooking, breaking down, and cutting the

kilo and half of kilo into $20 rocks. This took them 6 hours until they had broken all the crack down into peanut sized pebbles and stuffed them into diminutive baggies.

They then began giving out samples the very next day at Ryat's suggestion, against Potta's dissent to give nothing away for free. The tactic worked out great for the crew as the crack ended up being some of the best on their side of town. Which lead to crackheads running up and down Woodbine street looking for the young boys with *'dat good shit'*. The crew even further proliferated their sales when Mil suggested they sell the $20 crack rocks for $10 since it was all profit thereby doubling their clientele that way and making the money faster. Before they knew it, they had acquired more traffic up and down Woodbine street than they ever expected or had ever been seen on the block. Within that first week they had sold half of their crack supply, quickly making $31,000. More than any of them had ever seen in their life up until then.

Enamored by their quick earnings and the impressions of the ultimate Hustler inculcated on them through rap videos and older Hustlers, they couldn't wait to show off their immediate mediocre success. Therefore, each of them except Hochee in Boody, decided to buy used cars with their portion of the money. Boody, barely able to see over the steering wheel couldn't drive well enough yet and Hochee decided to give most of his illegal earnings to his struggling mother who needed it due to her extreme debt. She accepted the money against her wishes for him to stay out of the streets and even began to unleash her grasp on him as she felt he was already out of her control.

To further flaunt their new-found hustling success' the young gang knew that in order to make a real impression on the streets they needed jewels. Gaudy necklaces like those worn in the videos and by the other Hustlers. Therefore, each of them jumped in their new used cars and headed towards the East Mall. Hochee's older cousin had told them that an Italian man named Joey, who owned a jewelry stand in the middle of the mall, would trade in any jewelry for a small percentage. This is what the game plan was to do with the jewelry they acquired during their robberies. Ryat and Boody road in Ryat's black Oldsmobile Cutlass, while Mil road alone and his blue Acura Integra. Potta also rode alone in his blue Buick LeSabre while Bryce and Hochee road in Bryce's fire red Volkswagen Jetta. Each car was equipped with new tent, rims, and sound systems.

Upon arrival at the back of the East Mall, they all quickly parked, filing out of their cars with Mil holding the backpack containing the jewelry. They then entered the mall and in no time found a suspicious-looking jewelry stand in the middle of the first floor. Standing in the middle of the circular stand surrounded by a plethora of omnifarious jewelry were two manila-complected men. One of the men, apparently older, with slicked-back hair that was greying, wearing a silk gray button-up, the top two buttons were purposely left unfastened to show off his gray chest hair. He also wore a pair of silk black slacks.

The other guy who appeared to be the youngest sported a spiked-up hairdo that was faded on the sides. Wearing a sky-blue dress shirt with the sleeves rolled up showing off one of the most diamond-encrusted watches any of the boys had ever seen.

"Ayo, which one of y'all dudes is Joey?" asked Ryat after a few moments.

"That would be me." Answered the younger of the two men as the older man stood off to the side staring at the young band of misfits. Whom to him didn't even look old enough to have a job to buy jewelry. Therefore, he stood leerily close by the emergency button.

"Yo, we was told we could come see you about trading our old jewels for some new shit," spoke Ryat for the crew as they all stood there in anticipation of the man's response.

"Well let's see what you got," said Joey in an incredulous tone as he too now stared at the boys leerily.

His dubious stare continued for a few seconds until Mil walked up to the counter and began pulling the jewelry from the backpack. Joey's avarice eyes then quickly brightened as he stared at the diamond encrusted chains, bracelets, rings, and watches being pulled from the backpack.

"Well yeah, I believe I can help you guys with this..." said Joey with a broad smile now stretching the surface of his face.

Simultaneously the older man's apprehension also quickly dissipated but for another reason, as the youngest of the band of Misfits pulled out a large sum of money and began telling him how he was looking to buy a *'big Iced-Out chain'.* The older man's greedy mind quickly began plotting on how he could sell young Boody as much jewelry as possible to relieve him of the large amount of money. Boody, being the one with the most money left, planned to buy his own jewelry as the other boys bartered the stolen jewelry.

"Aww yeah, I really like what y'all got here..." said Joey in a high-pitched kind of whisper as he held one of the diamond bracelets in his hand, examining it with what looked to be a small magnifying glass type device.

"So what can you do for us?" inquired Mil.

"Aww man, I can do you guys good, since this is good quality stuff. I'm only going to charge you 15% interest away from the usual 20%. Which means I could treat each piece here, piece for piece, and require a substantial dollar amount. But let's say I trade you piece for piece on just the three chains and two rings, I then would keep the two bracelets and 3 watches as my interest without you having to pay any dollar amount." Joey replied with an impish tint over his eyes as he stared out at the young boys for a response. He figured their

response would be in his favor. He surmised they wouldn't be able to comprehend the business side.

"Nah yo, we ain't feeling that deal sun. How about you let us pick up five chains with charms and then you get to keep the rings, bracelets, and watches?" Bryce quickly spoke up.

"I...ahh...I don't know about that..." responded Joey while slowly shaking his head and pursing his lips.

"Man, yes you can 'cause I know we should be able to get two or three of those chains just for this chain alone," countered Mil as he pointed towards a row of chains inside the glass in casing then picked up the big diamond encrusted Cuban Link necklace with the large diamond encrusted pendant. Joey's eyes suddenly glistened even more as he stared at the large chain and pendant which to him looked like an action figure size representation of Mary holding a baby Jesus in the manger. He began to salivate at the thought of getting that piece of jewelry for next to nothing. Yet just then as Mil was holding the large chain up for Joey's inspection, the older man turned towards them briefly in the midst of his sales pitch to Boody. Then, just as he was getting ready to turn his head away from them, a look of shock and trepidation washed over his face as he stared at the large chain.

"No, no, no...No I'm sorry but we can't take this stuff. We can't do business with you." The older man quickly said with a panicked expression on his

face as he moved in front of the boys and motioned for them to pack up the jewelry and leave. Confused, both Joey and the boys all stood there looking at him addled until he pointed towards the large chain and said, *"I'm sorry but we can't take this stuff. I know who's that is, he just finished making payments on it."*

The gang stood there with their mouths agape for a split second just before Potta mouthed the word *payments* and the gang broke out laughing. Each of the boys laughed, except for Ryat, as he stood there silently staring back at the older man. Joey also didn't laugh as he began to rub his head in slight frustration and confusion. He simply watched in angst as his father was turning down one of the best deals they'd secured all year.

"Listen man, you may have sold someone a chain like this one but this is my chain and all of this is OUR stuff. So you can take it or we can just take our business somewhere else," said Ryat in a matter-of-fact tone.

"No, that's the piece I sold the man and I'm sorry but we don't want anything to do with that," countered the old man in a resolute tone as he then pursed his lips and furrowed his forehead. Then looking towards Boody, who he was just about to secure a nice sell with, he said, *"I can still do business with you young man and sell you that piece at the price we discussed."*

"'Ight fuck it, you believe what you want. We'll just take our business somewhere else. Yo

Boody, we out, dese muthafuckas won't be getting none of our paper. " said Ryat while intensely staring into the older man's eyes as he began to place all of the jewelry back inside the backpack.

The older man quickly cut his eyes towards Boody, who simply shrugged his shoulders as the man then realized that he had just lost out on a significant sale. Still he stood resolute while watching as the boys begin to leave.

"Hold on one second guys, let me speak to my father quickly before you leave. " Joey said before the boys were away from the jewelry stand.

The boys then turned around as Joey was pulling his father to the side. Joey then begin to emphatically explain to his father why they couldn't let such a good business deal slip away from them. He explained to his father how much potential profit they can make off that one chain alone and how it could never lead back to them. As long as they didn't show or sell it at that display stand as it turned out their family owned two other jewelry stands at two different malls in the city. After taking the second to ponder his son's words and the possible monetary gains, the older man reluctantly agreed to let his son handle that as he set off to the side.

Joey then informed the boys, to his delight, as it showed in his eyes, that his father had agreed to let him handle the business with them. He also informed them that he would accept the deal of them picking 5 chains of their choosing for all the jewelry in the backpack. Each of the boys then picked out their own individual chain with pendant as Boody paid for his.

Then as they were all leaving the jewelry stand sated with their jewelry, Joey looked towards Ryat and said, *"Hey, let's just say this transaction never happened."*

"Understood." replied Ryat with an impish smile on his face.

The boys then, after an hour of shopping for clothes, left the mall. Each of them were adorned in their own chain and pendant. To them, through the ghetto osmosis, a chain represented the image of a real man or real niggas as they affectedly called themselves.

Later that day, the boys were sitting in Bryce and his mother's apartment playing the new NBA Live '01 on *Playstation*. They were gambling for $20 a game. After losing five different games throughout the night, Bryce abruptly threw his joystick across the room and cut off the game.

"Yo, that's some sucka shit Bryce, turn the game back on man. You can't get mad cuz you a bum." quipped Hochee, who had just beaten Bryce in the game. The rest of the boys broke out in laughter at Bryce's expense, triggered mainly by their marijuana induced high.

"*Man fuck that sun, yall niggas ain't just gone keep bussing my ass on my shit, in my house,*" blurted Bryce. "*And ain't shit funny su...*"

"*Oh shit yo! Hold up! Hold up! Look!*" yelled Mil excitedly while pointing towards the T.V. which was showing the local news. All the boys then immediately quieted themselves and looked towards the T.V. screen which showed an image of a Breaking News banner across the bottom. With a picture of police tech's surrounding a green Mercedes Benz.

"Yo turn it up! Turn it up!" blurted Hochee as Bryce quickly obliged.

The gang then listened intently as the newscaster began to speak:

"*Again, I'm Amy Hannigan for Fox news, reporting live from where as I reported earlier. I'm on the scene of where just hours ago detectives found the decomposed body of a man inside this Mercedez Benz, seen behind me. The man appeared to have been murdered as detectives report, they believe he was left dead inside this vehicle for approximately the last week and a half. We've just learned that police have identified the man as a Juan Malone of south fifteen street. Robbery has not been ruled out as the motivate but detectives deem it highly unlikely because he was still wearing some of his jewelry and when detectives searched the vehicle they found an enormous amount of money and drugs. To be exact, from what I was told detectives found one hundred fifty thousand dollars*" *and five kilograms of crack cocaine, which has an approximate street value of close to two hundred thousand dollars. Again as I reported earlier police have not made any arrest nor do they have any suspects or leads on who could have committed such a horrendous crime. So we ask if you have any information or leads please do not hesitate to contact detectives at the number listed at the bottom of your screen. I'm Amy Hannigan reporting live for Fox forty-three news."*

The gang sat apathetic throughout the entire broadcast until towards the end of the woman's report when she mentioned what detectives found. Each of them then sat mouths agape, staring at the T.V. with an incredulous shocked expression on their faces.

"Yo that's crazy Mil and Essie bout to have a youngen," said Hochee as he and Ryat were riding around smoking blunts in Ryat's car.

"Yeah that's crazy; Bryce already got one. My niggas just having kids," responded Ryat just before taking another puff of the blunt.

"So Bryce claiming Kelly's buck finally?"

"That nigga ain't got no choice now, the blood test done came back and the buck's his."

"Word, that lil boy look just like him anyway. You next nigga."

"Next for what?"

"You already know what I'm talking bout, you and Tiff, I already know yall gone be having a buck soon."

"Aww nah, she on dat pill. I ain't trying have no kids right now, I'm too young, I'm only sixteen. I'm all about a dollar right now, you feel me,"

"Word, I feel you cause if it don't make dollars, it don't make sense," said Hochee as they were riding down Emerald street behind a school bus as school was just letting out.

With the music blasting, they sat behind the bus as it pulled to the bus stop and began letting out school kids. They both sat bobbing their heads to Fabolous' *Keepin It Gangsta*, as other adolescents walked by in droves looking towards the tinted vehicle trying to surmise who the young boys were that occupied the tricked-out car.

"Oh shit yo, there go my nigga Melvin," blurted Hochee as he turned the music down.

"Where?"

"Right there, look at that nigga standing there looking like a straight square wit his bookbag on," said Hochee while pointing towards Melvin through the window.

"Yo roll ya window down so I can holla at my nigga," said Ryat as Hochee obliged by rolling down the passenger side window.

"Yo Melvin, what up my nigga? Get in," yelled Ryat through the passenger window from the

driver's seat as the other adolescent onlooker's whispered about who was driving the vehicle.

Melvin then walked towards the vehicle slowly with his head ducked and eyes squinting, all in an effort to figure out who was calling him from the vehicle.

"Yo it's us nigga, what you don't know ya own homies now school boy?" blurted Hochee as Melvin got closer to the car.

"Oh shoot yo, Hochee! Ryat! that's yall?" blurted Melvin as he was now standing outside the car looking in.

"Yeah nigga it's us, get in," responded Ryat as Melvin acquiesced.

"Al'ight yo I see yall dudes is balling now, yall all iced out. Plus yo this whip is in, I'm feeling the rims. Yo Ryat this you?" inquired Melvin as they were pulling away from the bus stop.

"No doubt," replied Ryat while bobbing his head lightly to the music.

"Damn yo, yall dudes is getting money now huh? Those chains are chunky, I know yall paid something nice for 'em," said Melvin, infatuated with his friend's new found ghetto affluence.

"No doubt we getting money nigga and you squad so you suppose to be getting money wit us," said Ryat just before pulling his cellphone from his pocket and conversing with one of his clientele.

Melvin then looked at his friends with their new jewels, nice clothes, latest sneakers and fly cars and vacillated for a split second between if he should start hustling or not. He became momentarily enamored with their new auspicious lifestyles, mainly attracted to the fast money, cars and females who were sure to come with the superficial aspects of the lifestyle.

"So real talk, what's good Melvin? You getting down wit us and getting this money?" inquired Hochee just as Ryat was ending his phone conversation.

"Nah yall, I'm good. I'm just trying finish high school and do my thing on that football field and on that basketball court," replied Melvin after snapping from his ephemeral daydream.

"Yo come on Melvin, that sound like Mr. Varner talking. You a lil too big for him to still be wupping ya ass," quipped Ryat as he thought to himself, that his friend had to be stupid to turn down such a chance at easy money, knowing he could use it and the freedoms it could afford him.

"Yeah Melvin man, it's to much money out here to be getting. You wasting time wit all that bullshit school and sports shit, that ain't gone help you right now. Your folks are struggling just like ours, I know you tired of that shit. I'm telling you Mel we on our way wit dis shit," said Hochee.

"Nah yall, that just ain't me and nah Ryat my dad don't wup my ass like you need yours wupped. I just ain't trying disappoint my father because he done sacrificed so much for my family and he's the one that keep me focused," said Melvin as he momentarily thought of his father and all his

lessons about the morals, principles, values, and integrity that a real man possess.

"*I feel ya homie, you still my nigga even if you want to be broke ya whole life,*" quipped Ryat with a broad smile on his face as he pulled to a stop in front of Melvin's house.

"*Yo Ryat whatever man, I'ma holla at yall later ight,*" said Melvin as he shook both of his friends hands and commenced to exiting the car.

"*Yo Melvin, don't you got a game coming up soon?*" asked Hochee right before Melvin's body was fully out of the vehicle as Melvin nodded his head.

"*Al'ight my nigga we'll be there to watch our boy run all over them niggas,*" said Hochee as Ryat began pulling off with Melvin walking towards the front door of his house.

In no time the gang had sold all the crack in their possession. They now desperately needed a connect to which was becoming harder and harder for them to find. Mainly because the tension between them and Bo had exacerbated as he began to take notice of their quick success. Which was starting to cut into his profit as some of his clientele were going to the young boys for their cheaper prices. Therefore, Bo put out word to all the major distributors in city, that with an imminent war brewing with the young insidious gang, anyone who supplied them would also be an enemy of his. For which most of the local distributors took heed to this advice and refused to sell to the young gang knowing how pernicious Bo's small army could get. The guys who didn't heed Bo's words and were still willing to supply the young gang, were ironically incapable of covering their order.

The gang therefore refused to buy from anyone who couldn't cover their entire order for many reasons. Mainly because it would substantially cut into their profits and most likely cause them to no longer be able to undercut the street market. Therefore they would lose all of their clientele to Bo and as a result be no longer able to compete with him. Instead in the interim, Potta, Bryce, and Hochee robbed a few of the guys who had refused to sell to them. Meanwhile Ryat and Mil was left with the task of finding a connect because they knew they wouldn't be able to continue robbing and run their drugs at the same time successfully. Especially since they had made a lot of new enemies with the robberies.

Meanwhile Ryat had made some time to sit down and write Earl back at the Hodges and send him a $500 money order. Ryat thanked him for his respect, help, and comraderies while he was under the Hodges care. He also informed him that he was doing good and that the plans he had divulged to him while there was coming to fruition. Ryat then ended the letter by informing Earl that he would forever have love for him. He then sent the letter off under a fictitious name, he was sure Earl would be able to decode.

Ryat then also took some time to write Asaria to whom before he knew it, he found himself opening up to her about his current circumstances and the things going on in his life. He ended the letter by telling her that she would always be one of his best friends and how he hoped to hear from her soon.

Chapter 17

"When you deal with the past, you're actually dealing with the origin of a thing. When you know the origin, you know the cost. If you don't know the origin, you don't know the cause. And if you don't know the cause, you don't know what the reason, you're just cut off, your left standing in mid-air. So the past deals with history or the origin of anything; the origin of a person, the origin of a Nation, the origin of an incident."
-Malcolm X

In possession of almost $70,000, Ryat and his crew still couldn't find a connect with Ryat becoming more desperate by the day to find one. Especially since his friends were becoming more ruthless by the day with the pernicious robberies they were committing just to keep drugs flowing through their block.

They were like a savage pack of hyenas with an insatiable hunger for more. Which Ryat was sure would draw the attention of the police soon, aside from the retaliations being exacted on them daily. By enemies they couldn't even single out as they now had so many. Most of these enemies were becoming more and more afraid of the young virulent gang. Even little Boody was proving to be just as or even more vicious than the rest of the crew.

Ryat and Mil we're sitting in the living room of the house on Jefferson street that Mil had just helped his mom put a down payment on. They were laid back smoking blunts, watching Half Baked on DVD, while continuously trying to contact Dollas on his cell phone in hopes that he would help them in their quest to find a connect.

"Man this nigga Dollas is like a ghost, only being seen or heard when he wants you to see or hear him. I've been hitting this nigga sell for like 2 days straight and still no answer no nothing." said Ryat.

"Word yo, that nigga is like a ghost, but yo dig it, I ain't tell you how hard this nigga has been hating on me since I helped my mom get this spot. He keeps putting hatin ass shit in her head like I'm going to have cops running up in here soon or some kidnappers trying to grab her or my sister because of the shit I'm doing in the streets. And you know

she listened to everything this nigga say so she stay tripping on me now and got my Grandmom's trippin too.

That's why I don't even really come around here that much and this nigga got the nerve to say to me one day all sarcastic like, 'son what you don't want to get money with your daddy no more.' Then he smirked like he had just said some of the flyest shit. I told that nigga like, nigga you ain't my daddy, never was, you just my sister Daddy and I never was getting money with you. Yo tight-ass was too busy robbing me and my boys. Yo, you know after I said that the nigga acted like he wanted to rumble?

I was about to blow dat nigga head off when my mom jumps in and you know she took his side talking about he is my daddy because he supposedly took care of me when my real daddy ain't nowhere to be found. Man I just left after that," said Mil in between puffs of the blunt he was holding.

"Man that nigga just hatin cause you doing shit for ya folks that his tight ass never thought about doing."

In fact, all of the boys were helping out their loved ones in one form or fashion with the profits from their illegal endeavors. Ryat had helped his aunt out of her strenuous financial situation and took over the bills at his grandfather's apartment. Hoochee continued to give his mother most of his earnings to help her out of debt while Potta took over the bills at his grandmother's house. Bryce also helped his mom out, buying her a car so she no longer had to take the bus or walk to her two jobs. Which she refused to quit at least one at his request.

As Ryat and Mil continued their conversation, Mil's mother came walking down the steps carrying the hamper full of dirty clothes.

"Camill, what did I tell you about smoking all out in the open like this, in my living room. My mom could be coming through that door at any time and what if the cops were to show up on the doorstep for some reason and smell that shit?" She immediately chided Mil the moment her foot hit the bottom step.

"Alright mom, I hear you," replied Mil as he exhaled smoke while cutting his eyes at her then reclined further back into the couch.

"Obviously, you don't hear me good enough cause you continue to do things your way but you'll learn. Anyway boy, here pass me that," she responded after sitting the hamper down and walking towards Mil who nonchalantly complied in passing her the blunt. She then took a small puff and exhaled smoothly.

"Yo how you doing Ms. Evans?" greeted Ryat with his signature smile spread across his face. Which he couldn't suppress whenever he saw her whom he secretly had a crush on since he was five, though he would never tell his best friend.

"Boy how many times I'ma have to tell you to stop calling me Ms. Evans like I'm all old or something. I told you to call me Nia like everybody

else. But anyway, how you doing boy? Looking more grown every time I see you," she replied.

Lania Evans was definitely not an old woman in any sense and was very much a beautiful woman. Whom still had her youthful figure and face. As she was only 32 years old after having Mil when she was only 16. Ryat had always found her beauty mesmerizing and even though he knew she was forever off limits he still couldn't help his lust whenever he saw her.

"I am grown... Nia," quipped Ryat, a smile still plastered across his face.

"Boy listen to you trying sound all grown, you ain't grown yet and when you are you probably gone wish you weren't. So boy enjoy your youth while you have it," Nia replied, then as she stared back at him for a second, she blurted, *"Oh my God you have his smile!"*

"What?" Ryat responded, still smiling yet simultaneously twisting up his face, befuddled.

"Boy I know you've heard it before, you have Tanell, your dad's smile. So when was the last time you went and seen him?" responded Lania as both Ryat and Mil now sat addled. Ryat's eyes getting bigger with confusion written all over his face.

"My dad?..Tanell?..Seen him?," he mouthed in a low audile while staring bewilderedly towards the ground.

"OH MY GOD!...You don't know?...They never?...Oh my God!...Oh my God!.." exclaimed

Lania, her left hand covering her mouth as she instantly realized what she had just done. *"Yo what you know bout my dad? He's supposed to be dead! What do you know?"* asked Ryat becoming more incensed by the second as Lania stood there unresponsive with an empathetic look on her face. Then as Ryat stood staring at her, he barked, *"Yo what the fuck do you know bout my father?!"*

"Yo Ryat, watch who you talking to like that nigga, that's my mom," barked Mil as he stood facing Ryat.

"What nigga?!!" countered Ryat as he indignantly glared back at Mil.

Then as Ryat stood glaring at Lania who was now sitting with her head bowed in between her hands, he exclaimed, *"Man fuck this, I'm out."*

Ryat then stormed out of their house, got in his car and sped off, tires screeching. He drove recklessly until he reached the apartment building where he was raised. Marching straight inside the first floor apartment, slamming the door behind himself. Ryat instantly noticed Anita and Keith sitting on the couch eating while watching something on the television. Meanwhile, Mr. Carl, was also sitting on the other end of the couch munching down on a plate of fried pork chops, corn on the cob, and mashed potatoes with gravy. Startled by the door slamming, they all looked towards Ryat the moment he walked in.

"Boy what the hell is your problem? Don't be slamming the door like that. Good you made it on time though cause the food still hot but you gone have to make ya own plate," said Anita.

Ryat then just stood there glaring at them for a moment before saying in a low growl, *"I thought my father is supposed to be dead. Yall fucking told me both my mother and father died in a car crash when she was pregnant with me and that I was the only survivor because she held on til they successfully delivered me. So why the fuck am I hearing that my father is alive? ...Hunh? ...Hunh? ...Why?"*

Completely stunned, they all just stared at him for a second as Keith looked to be the most confused of them all. Anita ready to chide Ryat for raising his voice and cursing, couldn't as she now could no longer chew the food in her mouth.

"My Lord, I knew it would be coming to this soon," responded Mr. Carl as he pensively stared towards Ryat while slowly shaking his head.

"What are you saying pops? So are you basically telling me that my father is alive and y'all been lying to me my whole fuckin' life?!"

"Listen boy, I understand your anger but you goin' have to calm down so I can talk to ya now."

"Nah man, fuck th..."

"Listen Ryat, like Daddy said, we understand your anger but you're not just going to sit here and be all disrespectful, you were taught

better than that. We always knew one day it would come to this and we would have to tell you the truth about your father. You were told what you were told because Mommy wanted to protect you from the truth for as long as she could." Anita sternly interjected.

"Protect me from what truth?"

"She wanted to protect you from the truth that everybody believes that your mother was murdered because of your father. That's why mommy always told you your father was also dead even though he's somewhere in prison serving double life."

"What?!" exclaimed Ryat. *"And now I'm finding out my mother didn't die in a car crash, that she was murdered? And that she was supposedly murdered because of my father and he's alive somewhere serving double life? Aww man, what the... Aww man."*

Ryat then sat confused and heartbroken on the couch in a complete state of shock.

"Listen son, I understand, it's hard for us to even have to relive this right now but you must know so I'll tell you as much as we know. See son, your father was to had supposedly killed two men during a robbery, he was caught on the scene. Meanwhile your mother was pregnant with you and one day, months later, she was found shot in the chest inside her car. Now son, there was some truth to what you've been told most of your life because by the time they found her she had lost a lot of

blood and doctors said she should have died within the first two minutes after being shot. But that girl... " Mr. Carl's voice became almost a whisper as he choked up for a second while Ryat sat there with tears now streaming his face.

Anita also sat covering her face with her hands as she cried silently. All the while, Keith sat completely shocked listening to one of the most tragic events he'd ever heard, events that would crumble any family.

Regaining his composure somewhat, Mr. Carl continued.

"But boy that girl, she was a fighter and she held on for dear life for over two hours until you were successfully delivered. Then my baby... My baby... She... She... Passed away."

Silence then permeated the room as for the first time Ryat watched his grandfather, whom he'd never seen in such a vulnerable state, break down crying.

Ryat then wiped the tears from his face with his shirt and with fire in his eyes he looked towards his aunt and calmly asked, *"Who killed her?"*

"The cops they never found out who did it but they believe like everybody else, that she was murdered in retaliation for one of the men your father killed because that man was a major guy out here in the drug game and supposedly had a lot of money and people who would kill for him at the drop of a dime. That's why mommy never told you about your father being alive somewhere in prison

because she blames him for everything that happened to your mother" responded Anita as she did her best to wipe the tears and melancholic expression from her face with the bottom of her shirt.

Ryat then calmly stood from the couch and commenced to leisurely walking towards the door without saying another word.

"Hey Ryat man, you gon be alright?" asked Keith, solemnly after clearing his throat as Ryat had just opened the door to leave.

With flames flickering in his pupils and a malefic smirk on his face, Ryat slowly turned towards Keith, meeting his empathetic gaze and responded.

"Yeah I'll be alright man. Ain't no sense in crying when it's raining."

Meanwhile, Tanell had just been released from solitary confinement. Spending the last sixteen years of his life in long-term segregation units throughout the Pennsylvania Department of Corrections. In order for him to be released from isolation he had to sign a contract with the warden of that particular penitentiary. In the contract Tanell signed off that he would refrain from any harmful behavior towards staff and or inmates. If he were to violate this contract in any way he could be resubmitted to solitary confinement where he would spend the rest of his natural life. This, Tanell believed would be a non-issue as he was now a humble, selfless, and submissive man of spiritual consciousness.

Tanell had years ago, accepted God into his life and though he still suffered in agony from the losses of his true love, best friend, and unborn child, he resolved to completely submit himself to the will of God.

$¢

After hearing such life-altering, shocking news, Ryat solemnly rode around the city in his car chain smoking blunts while musing over the news he had just ingested. He rode for hours in a quasi-trance as the marijuana permeated his system, soothing in brevity a modicum of his mental anguish.

It was almost 2 o'clock in the morning as he was riding down Swatara Street in the South Park neighborhood when he suddenly saw a face out of his driver's side window that had him thinking the drugs were starting to make him hallucinate. He therefore slowed down his car while rubbing his eyes and looked out of the window towards the face of the unkempt man. The man looked to be a crack addict on a mission to procure the mechanism of his vice. Right then and there as Ryat strained his eyes, he couldn't believe what, or better yet, who he was seeing.

He then quickly yet surreptitiously pulled his car further down the dark lit block and parked. Jumping out of his car with his gun in his hand, Ryat salivated at the thought of killing this man. He figured it would permanently cure a large aspect of his mental anguish.

Ryat, with the blood in his veins boiling, then swiftly walked in the direction of the man with his gun firmly gripped by his side. He was about five feet away from the man when he began to raise his gun at the man. The now startled man stopped abruptly, staring at Ryat in wide-eyed horror. Just then, coincidentally as if a sign of fate, a police car pulled out of the alleyway that separated Ryat and the man by the five-foot distance.

Ryat then quickly pulled down his gun and tried his best to hide it against the back of his right thigh as the cop was looking towards the other man skeptically. The cop then dubiously looked towards Ryat as the other man commenced to turning back the other way and swiftly walking off. Ryat then, with anger burning inside of him, had in his mind for a second that he could quickly kill the cop then catch and kill the man before he got away. As he surmised that nobody would find out, it was extremely dark and they were the only people in the area. Yet, Ryat being of a rational mind and not letting his emotions control his actions, quickly decided against his pernicious first thought. He simply looked at the cop dead in the eyes resolutely and kept walking in the direction he was already in route to. Simultaneously the cop pulled off slowly out of the alleyway. Watching Ryat in his rearview mirror as he calmly walked past the rear of the squad car.

Ryat continued to walk down the street as if he were on his way somewhere until the cop's squad car bent the corner and was out of sight. Ryat then ran to his car at full speed, got inside, and ducked down in the seat just before the apprehensive cop had pulled back around the block. Through his tinted windows, Ryat watched as the cop slowly road back down the street, intensely looking back and forth between his driver and passenger windows.

Once the cop had finally turned off the block, Ryat then pulled off and instead of going home he rode around the South Park neighborhood, then, the entire Hill section in search of the man whom he had just moments ago, salivated at the thought of killing. He subsequently came up empty in his search and cursed himself for not acting more hastily in his kill.

It was approximately 9:30 a.m. that same morning as Ryat was asleep in his car parked behind an apartment building on Maclay Street. The ringing of his phone suddenly awoke him. After answering it, he was met with Dollas on the other end of the line telling him to meet him at Jimmy the

Hot Dog King in the Uptown Plaza. Ryat obliged and immediately made route to meet the man whom he figured was exactly the person he needed to speak with after all he had learned. Once he reached the Plaza's parking lot and parked his car, Ryat made his way inside the dining room where he found Dollas paying for the order he had just received to go.

"Yo Dollas, what's good cuz?" asked Ryat as they embraced in a half-hug-handshake.

"What's good youngen? I know you most likely hungry the way you been running these streets wit yo tank on empty so I grabbed you something to eat too. Just grab you something to drink."

"Yo, good looking fam."

"No Doubt!" replied Dollas as he commenced to making his way out the diner to his brand-new silver Range Rover.

Ryat then quickly ordered himself an orange juice and joined Dollas in his SUV.

"So what's been good wit you youngen? I noticed you been trying to get at me a lot lately. You alright?" inquired Dollas as he handed Ryat the food he had bought for him.

""Yeah man I've been trying to get at you for the longest. At first it was just about me trying to get you to help us catch a connect but man shit's been so crazy I don't know where to start..." replied Ryat as he cracked the lid on his sausage, egg, and pancake meal. Then, suddenly after his first bite, a

malefic tent washed over his eyes as he thought of all he had learned the day before.

With his eyes blazing, Ryat narrowed them at Dollas and asked,

"Yo, why you ain't tell me that nigga Victor that killed my Uncle Ray was out here running around?"

Dollas, still chewing his food, then look towards Ryat for a moment without saying anything. Then, as he casually set back in his seat, he coolly replied,

"Yeah so you seen him? I'm surprised it took you this long. He's been out here for the past three and a half years. Especially since he's now one of the biggest crackheads in the city. I'm surprised he ain't came through your block looking for some of that good low priced shit y'all been selling up there."

"Yo Dollas, what type of fucking shit is that to say?! Yo, you sitting here all cool while nigga that murdered ya best friend has been walking the streets for years?! What type of shit is that? That nigga supposed to been dead! But you know what? It's cool! I want to do the honors anyway and I almost had the nigga last night but he got lucky cause a cop showed up. Then I couldn't find him but it's cool now that I know I wasn't tripping when I seen him because now I know he out here and I'ma catch his ass sooner than later and I'ma body that nigga like you should have been done!" shouted Ryat as he then pulled the gun from his waist,

holding it in his hand for Dollas to see. He continued.

"And I'ma make it special too. Yeah, do this look familiar?"

Dollas just sat there for a moment analyzing Ryat and the gun he had just pulled. He then responded in a cooler resonant tone.

"Ryat calm your ass down and put that fuckin gun away. What I keep telling you about guns? See, you all heart and half a brain. That's the problem with stupid muthafukas who worship a gun, they tend to be more reckless, reason why they almost always end up dead or in jail. Sun Tzu said it best in The Art of War 'weapons are instruments of ill-omen, only to be used when unavoidable.' Ryat I keep telling you, you have to think and be more calculating."

"Man yo Dollas I don't give a fuck about all that. What you telling me now? That I ain't supposed to kill the nigga that murdered my uncle right before my eyes and basically got away with it? Man fuck that! And fuck all that Sun whoever peace talk cause if Ray wouldn't have left this at home then maybe he'd still be alive!" countered Ryat as he gestured towards Ray's .40 caliber in his right hand.

"That's why I keep mine on me. A nigga aint just goin catch me slippin. Fuck that! I feel like as long as I got my piece, I'll experience peace eventually."

"See that's your problem, you think you know everything."

"See nah, that's ya fuckin' problem. That nigga should have been dead. What type of fuckin' best friend are you?"

Dollas then losing his cool responded by shouting,

"That's how much you fuckin know Mr. Smart Guy gangsta! The nigga is dead!"

"What da fuck do you mean he's dead? I just told you I seen the nigga yesterday and he sure wasn't no fucking ghost."

"See first off calm yo ass down and listen to what I got to say. I tell you this shit cause I love you as if you are my nephew but this shit don't go beyond here.

"Now I keep telling you how you have to be more calculating in your thought process. Now just think if I would have been bodied that dude like you keep saying? Everybody and their mom know Ray was my best friend and that I was there when that dude killed him. Man don't you know the cops would have been put that body on me if for no reason than the ones I just gave you. So now that one dude would have took both Ray and me from our families and Ryat I got kids I'm trying to be around for.

"It's about my kids and their future. Don't get it fucked up I loved Ray and promised to avenge his death like you. That's why I keep telling you to be more calculating in your thoughts and moves. So when I say dude is dead already, I say it figuratively because he is dead, his soul just ain't depart from

his body yet. As in, he's what you call The Walking Dead."

Ryat simply sat there listening intently with a dubious expression on his face while trying to make sense of what Dollas was saying as he continued,

"See, I used to have this girlfriend when I was in Middle School. I don't remember why we broke up or anything but we lost touch. I had run into her some years ago and we hit it off immediately on a friendly note and I was quickly reminded of how thoro she was. She was my first love.

"So when she told me how she had contracted AIDS and couldn't afford her medicine I was shocked initially because she was still beautiful and had a body. Then I felt sorry for her. So I kept it real with her and help buy her medication as well as I stayed friends with her. She would always profess her love and loyalty to me even though our relationship wasn't on that level.

"So once I got word that dude had come home and was down the halfway house on 4th Street I asked her if she would seduce the dude and make sure she gave him AIDS and without any questions she started playing the job where they had him working. And to let her tell it, it was easy to seduce him after the first time she flirted.

"Just as I expected of him after just coming home from prison, that he would be thinking with his little head instead of his big one. So she fucked

*him raw and to make sure she gave it to him she
fucked him over ten times. Soon enough he called
her on a tirade about how he got AIDS and she was
the only person he was sleeping with.*

*"I then just simply relocated her. It was easy
cause she gave him the wrong name and everything.
It's fucked up though cause she died from that shit a
year ago. But the good news is that's how I know he
ain't got long because she already had full-blown
AIDS when she fucked him and AIDS mutates and
gets worse as it's transmitted from person to person.*

*"That's why I say he's dead or better yet,
dying the worst type of death, a slow painful death.
That's why he's running around here smoking all
that crack to escape his pain. But it don't matter cuz
he die everyday he wake up,"* said Dollas with his
eyes focused on the road as he crossed the Maclay
Street Bridge.

*"Damn, that's some deep shit and it's even
more deep cause the nigga killed my uncle over a
bitch. Now he die everyday cause of a bitch. Yo,
you's a diabolical dude. I feel you though."* said
Ryat, even though he didn't mean it because he still
felt that the man that murdered his uncle wasn't
dying fast enough.

Then, within that second his mind shifted
gears, anger coupled with confusion washed over
his face as he looked towards Dollas and said in a
low tone,

*"Ayo Dollas, you know my mom was
murdered and that my pops is still alive upstate?"*

276

Caught off guard, Dallas slightly swerved his SUV as he looked towards Ryat with a stunned expression on his face. Then, as he regained control of his vehicle and relieved himself of the initial shock, he simply focused his eyes back on the road and calmly replied in a solemn tone.

"Yeah man."

"So why you never told me?"

"Same reason nobody else ever told you and you just finding out now, because Mrs. Eve felt as if she needed to protect you from the hurt as a boy and tell you all about it when you became a man. And I had no choice but to respect that... Your moms, she was good people though.,"

"Yeah, I've been hearing that my whole life... I just wish I could have gotten to meet her," said Ryat in a solemn tone as he looked outside the passenger window. Then with silent rage in his tone, he looked towards Dollas and asked, *"You ever heard who might have killed her?"*

"Nah, cause trust me, the muthafucka would have been dead. The hood loved Ashley. Man, so many people showed up to her funeral, that's why I think they never found who did it because nobody could imagine who would do some shit like that to her. All anybody could come up with was that it was a retaliation for your pops killing Smooth."

"Yeah, my aunt and grandpops already told me that. So Smooth was the dude's name? They say my pops killed two people though."

"Nah man, ya pops just caught a bad rap. Everybody know he ain't kill his right-hand man Marcus. That whole situation was crazy but he basically got stuck with that body cuz he only had a PD, cuz any lawyer would have beat that one. Matter of fact, now that I remember, the one thing I did hear besides it was retaliation was that your moms got robbed for some birds that supposedly belonged to ya pops. Word is, she was trying to sell them to help him get a lawyer. But then after word got out that your pops stabbed a few of Smooth's men up out the county and made one of them a paraplegic, everybody I guess just chalked it up as if your mom really was killed in retaliation even tho detectives couldn't prove it."

"Damn Dollas, so you saying my moms could have been murdered during a robbery?" Inquired Ryat with an incredulous look on his face as he thought of the irony in his mother possibly being murdered in a robbery. As well as his father killing during a robbery and how all that related to him. How he could remain so apathetic when exacting the same trauma amongst others like Juan.

"Yeah man, and to be honest with you, me and Ray never really believed it was retaliation because the only reason dudes fronted like they was loyal to that dude Smooth was because he had money and kept those dude's pockets lined right. But we could never really see anybody retaliating like that for him because he was a snake and those dudes love for him wasn't real." responded Dollas

278

as he kept his eyes focused on the road while continuously trying to suppress his true emotions about the things he was revealing to Ryat.

Ryat then just simply sat in silence, entranced as he thought of all he had learned thus far regarding his mother's traumatic death and his father's incarceration. Suddenly his thoughts centered on all the death and pain his family had suffered thus far as his mind momentarily drifted back to the day his uncle told him the meaning behind his name. Ironically, the analogous nature in which the tale behind his name corresponded with his life seemed almost prophetic, because just as the man in the tale of his name avenged those he loved, so would he.

Flames flickered in his pupils and violence course through his veins. The fire that was kindled in him when he was just nine years young, which had come to a simmer after his uncle's murder, then a roaring blaze after the passing of his grandmother, was now an inferno that raged and his young heart.

Chapter 18

"Tis better to have loved and lost than never
to have loved at all."
-Alfred Tennyson

Later that night after Ryat had spent the remainder of the day alone musing over his lost loved ones, he went and picked up Tiffany from her home. Wasn't long before they found themselves at the Comfort Inn Hotel just off Route 22. Ryat then within the intimacy of them being alone in the hotel room confided in his first true love. Revealing all of the shocking traumatic news he had recently learned regarding his mother and father.

All the while though Tiffany knew without a doubt that these new shocking revelations had to be tearing him apart, he didn't show one sign of it. As his face remained calm and his eyes betrayed the rage that lie within them, she knew his heart was heavy with pain.

Therefore, she hurt for him and wanted nothing more than to fix him and his hurt in every way. Even though she knew him good enough to know at this point it would be next to impossible. Reason why when he became distant after they made love, she understood and let him go be by himself. Ryat ended up on the balcony, only wearing his maroon silk boxers, sitting in a comfortable reclining veranda chair, smoking a blunt.

He sat staring into the midnight sky with the smoke form his blunt slithering into the air, it began to drizzle. Then within minutes the rain started to pour with him having no cover as the balcony had no roof. Yet instead of Ryat going inside to shield his half -naked body, he seemed to get more comfortable as each rain drop cascaded down his exposed toffee complected flesh.

Laying in the bed completely bare, Tiffany looked away from the television and through the glass sliding doors to see Ryat sitting comfortably on the balcony in the rain. Partially confused and partially concerned, she jumped up from the bed and walked briskly towards the balcony. Careful to shield herself from the downpour, Tiffany slid the glass door open slightly.

"Ryat, what are you doing sitting out here in the rain like this? Come inside," she said continuing

to shield herself behind the glass door as he swiveled his neck to see her standing there in the nude with the moonlight highlighting her beautiful cinnamon tone and hour glass figure.

"Come here..." he calmly countered, now staring lustfully at her.

"Oh my God Ryat, are you crazy? It's raining and I'm naked, I ain't coming out there."

"Man, stop trippin girl, it's warm and can't nobody see you. Come here. Trust me. It feels good."

She then without any further hesitation opened the glass doors and stepped onto the balcony with him. He watched as she moved to sit on his lap while raindrops cascaded down every part of her nude body.

They both stared into each other's eyes for a moment then broke into a light chuckle. Tiffany then asked him, *"forreal though Ryat, what is up with you and this rain?"*

Ryat then became serious as a solemn look came into his eyes while continuing to hold her gaze. *"On some real shit though Tiff. You might think I'm tripping. But I feel like being as though when it rains, the rain comes from above. So this is the only time I can feel at peace and feel close to my deceased loved ones again."*

Tiffany then, while continuing to stare deep into his eyes, vicariously felt his inner pain and understood his heartfelt logic probably better than anybody could. She knew it just wasn't the marijuana induced high that compelled him to utter such words, that those words were genuinely the fruit of his heart. She then turned her body to straddle him and leaned into him as their mouths met and their tongues were in no time intertwine in a passionate kiss.

This fervent kiss continued for seconds which felt like an eternity of experiencing love for them. She then began to follow raindrop trails down his chest with her tongue. He then tenderly pushed her back and began to sensually suck on her neck. Then with his tongue, he followed the trails of cascading rain drops down to her nipples. Where he tenderly nibbled and sucked all over them.

Tiffany then stood over him panting as she removed his now soaked boxers then reclined the Veranda chair all the way back as she did a sexy squat above him in a catcher's position. Putting her hands on his chest for support, she then slid down onto his shaft as the tip of his rock-hard manhood parted the silky warm lips of her vagina. She then began to move herself up and down on his shaft while controlling the depth and pace of the penetration. Simultaneously, she leaned back to stimulate her clitoris as he reached forward to caress her breast all the while the euphoric sensations made their fervency even more intense as the rain poured and the warm breeze enveloped them in their lovemaking.

$¢

"Real talk though Mil, you know I ain't mean to disrespect your mom's like that," said Ryat as he and Mil were riding around town three hours after Mil's girlfriend Essie had just given birth to their daughter.

"I told you already you don't even have to mention it cause I already know you ain't mean it. You was just fucked up after what you heard. Man, that shit would have fucked me up to."

"No doubt."

"Ayo but Ryat let me ask you something. After finding out all that and Dollas done told you that your mom's might not have gotten killed because of your pops, is you gone and see him? Like, see what type of dude he is?"

"Nah, not at all cause I still feel like she did get murdered because of him even if she did get killed during a robbery. Because what type of dude sends his pregnant woman to get rid of some work for him so he can get a lawyer. I mean, I might go check that nigga out one day and trust me it won't be nice but right now I gots to make shit right because somebody goin' pay."

"No doubt, I feel you fam and we definitely gone track down the nigga that killed her and body that nigga but first we goin' find this nigga Victor and buss his head."

"No doubt!" replied Ryat with a slight smirk on his face as he salivated at the thought of exacting his revenge. Smiling at the fact that his best friend had his back like his spinal cord.

"Ayo but fuck all that right now cause I just can't believe how beautiful ya daughter is."

"Man nigga what you thought she was goin' look like? Look at me." responded Mil with a sarcastic smile on his face.

"Man nigga, go head wit yo black ass. You know she got her looks from Essie." countered Ryat as they both commenced to laughing.

"Man fuck you nigga." retorted Mil in between laughter. *"But nah on some real shit, did you hear about Hochee and his Pops?"*

"Nah not really. I mean, Boody was trying to tell me some shit about it at the crib but I had too much shit on my mind to really pay attention to what he was rapping 'bout."

"Well man... Yo dig it! Guess who his pops is first off? Yo you know ol'head or Oilcan who always be coming to the block to cop a few bags?"

"Yeah yo, I know the dirty ass Ol'head. He always got some shit in a book bag that he done stole from Rite-Aid that he be trying to sell. Oh shit yo, you telling me that's Hochee's dad?"

"Yeah cuz, that's crazy right? Especially how Hochee usually be right on the block most those days dude came through and he would act like he ain't even know dude but it makes sense now

*because Hochee would never serve him. Well
anyway, a couple of days ago Oilcan came through
the block but he ain't have no money so wouldn't
nobody fuck with him. Hochee didn't even see him
because he was sitting on the steps with his head
down counting money.*

*That's when Oilcan walked up to him and
snatched the baggie with Hochee work in it off his
lap. Yo, Hochee jumped up looking like he was
going to kill Oilcan. You know the rest of us was
bugging off that shit. That's when they started
wrestling and Hochee slammed him then stood over
him and pulled his gun out.*

*That 's when we found out Oilcan was his
dad cause Oilcan started yelling on the ground like,
Horton Diaz Junior, this is how you goin' do ya
father? You goin' kill me???*

*Yo my word Ryat, me and the rest of the
niggas couldn't believe what we was hearing and
Hochee was still standing there looking like he was
going to kill his pops. And yo Ryat, I believe he
would have if I ain't step in and grab him. Shit, you
should have seen Bryce and Potta, you know them
niggas don't give a fuck about nothing and they
even got Lil Boody like that now.*

*Shit, Bryce even said some shit like, 'fuck it
Hochee body the Nigga'. So you know I'm on some
shit like, yo chill Hoch dats ya pops!' The whole
time though Oilcan was still on the ground yelling
at Hochee like, 'muthafucka I brought you in this
world and I'll take you out!' That's when Hochee*

was like, 'not if I take you out first!' And that's when he really looked like he was goin' pull the trigger, right before I grabbed his arm and snapped him out of the little trip he was on."

"Then all of a sudden Hochee snatched away from me and literally knocked his Pops teeth out his mouth with his gun and told him 'nigga you ain't never been a father to me! Fuck you, my moms made me a man and if you ever come around us again I will kill you!"

"Damn yo, that's deep but it don't surprise me though cause Hochee always talked about how he hated his junky ass Pops for beating on his moms and never helping her raise them," responded Ryat while continuously looking in his rear and side-view mirrors.

"Word cuz that shit was crazy," said Mil as he was now also looking in his side-view mirror. Then suddenly he shifted in his seat, grabbed his gun from his waist, cocked it and said, *"ayo Ryat you see that purple Lex behind that truck that's behind us, it look like it's following us."*

"Yeah I see it, I noticed it coupled of blocks ago," replied Ryat as he too grabbed his gun from his lap and gripped it in his palm as he attentively watched the Lexus through his rear-view mirror. All the while, thoughts of his gang's numerous enemies and who it could be ran through his head.

He then maneuvered his car to see if the Lexus was really following them or if they were just being paranoid for being conscious of their many enemies. Yet sure enough their suspicions were right as the Lexus followed them into the gas station on 17th & Derry streets.

"Yo hold up Ryat, that's a bitch driving that jawn... she just got out her car and look like she walking towards us. Damn, she bad as shit too," said Mil as Ryat had just parked his car by a gas pump and poised himself to shoot first and ask questions later.

Yet when the woman got out of her car and began walking in their direction, something told Ryat it wasn't what he thought. Still he kept a firm grip on his gun as a precaution because he knew of too many men that died after letting their guard down for beautiful women. He had learned this lesson as early as when his grandmother used to force him to go to Bible study as a kid and he learned the story of Samson and Delilah.

The woman was definitely stunning though as she sensually sauntered towards them in a pair of Manolo Blaniks the same color as her car. Also wearing black pin striped form fitting Prada pants, showing off her thick thighs and juicy hips. As the Prada blouse she wore showed off one of her beautiful smooth almond complected shoulders and the Chanel shades only added to her mesmerizing appearance.

When she got closer to his car, Ryat stepped out, not concealing the pistol grip chrome .40 caliber he held firmly by his side.

"It ain't that type of party baby, I come in peace. So you can put that away," said the woman as she stood like a stallion before him with one arm across her midsection and the other gesticulating towards his gun.

"Yeah so how am I supposed to know that? You the one coming after me," responded Ryat sternly as he noticed through all her beauty that she was definitely a woman at least two times his age. Though you couldn't tell by looking at her, he figured she was in her mid-thirties.

"I mean come on baby, look at me. Do I look like I come for a gun battle?" she countered with an impish smile on her face. Then playing on his male ego, asked, *"What you've never been approached by a beautiful woman?"*

With a sly smirk now on his face, he replied, *"yea whatever, so what you want with me so badly that got you following me for blocks like you da police or a nigga trying murk me?"*

"Well your name is, Ryat right?"

"See now you REALLY starting to sound like da police."

"Alright so since I take it that you are Ryat. My name is Grace and it just so happens I have been trying to contact and find you for a couple weeks now but you seem to be one of the hardest young men to track down and I take it you want it like that, therefore that would explain the gun and your watchful eye."

"Alright so get to your fucking point already cause you are really starting to sound like some type of fucking police psyche."

"Well to the point, my brother really wants to see you but like I said before; you were hard to find until I got a description of your car, so..."

"Alright, so who is your brother that wants to get wit me so bad?" inquired Ryat as his mind already wandered to the fact that he needed to immediately get a new car.

"Roe."

"Oh shit, damn, Roe's ya brother? That's my OG. What's good wit him?"

"Well it just so happens that I found you right on time because I go to see him tomorrow morning and he really wants to see you."

"'Ight, cool, I 'm down. Here, take my number and call me when you ready to come pick me up,"

"Alright, so you just be ready when I call you at 5:30 in the morning and I guess I'll actually be seeing you in about seven hours," said Grace as she accepted his number then just as quickly turned on her heels and sauntered back to her car with. Her hips swaying to each of her rhythmic steps. As the sensual movements accentuated her voluptuous backside, Ryat looked on with eyes full of lust.

At 5:25 that, next morning; Ryat received Grace's call half asleep and in ten minutes she was parked in front of the hotel he was staying in.

In no time, he was in the passenger seat of her Lexus in route to see Roe. He then began asking her questions about the visit as he'd never been to visit any one in jail in his life, therefore he had many apprehensions.

Grace joked about his age and told him that since he was only 17 that she was already listed on her brothers visiting list as his guardian, so he would be OK. Chuckling at her quip, he asked what he could and couldn't wear inside the prison. Grace informed him that as long as he didn't have any drugs or weapons on him that he would be fine.

He then pulled out his gun to her surprise and informed her that he almost forgot he had it on him until she mentioned weapons. With a scowl on her face while giving him the evil eye, she asked him what would possess him to bring a gun with them. He simply replied that he didn't leave home without it. She countered with indignation and reluctantly told him that he could place his gun in her glove compartment until they were done visiting her brother.

Ryat complied, he opened her glove compartment to store his pistol. Yet the minute he opened the glove compartment, he immediately noticed another pistol already in there and beside it was what proved to be a silver badge with the letters *H.P.D.* embossed at the top of. it and the numbers *8426* embossed at the bottom.

"Oh shit! So what the fuck! You ARE the police?! So, what the fuck is this, a set up bitch?!"

blurted Ryat as he tightened his grip on his gun and narrowed his eyes at her.

Slightly rattled by the nefarious tone his voice had taken on, Grace nervously looked from him to the tightened grip he held on his gun. While simultaneously his head swiveled in many directions as if looking for other police in the area.

"Yes, I am a police officer and soon to be detective for the Harrisburg Police Department but that doesn't change the fact that Roe is my brother and the fact that he really wants to see you. And he entrusted me to make sure that it happens because he knows he can always trust me because cop or not I'm always going to be there for my brother because he was for my family when we were being raised and basically living under barbaric conditions. Yes, he is who he is and he's done what he's done but he has always been for family and his sacrifice is the reason I'm in the position that I am in. So no! This isn't a set up," responded Grace resolutely as she stared him in his eyes with the same resolve.

Ryat then believing her love felt spiel about her brother, released the grip he held on his gun and acquiesced by placing it in her glove compartment.

"Alright yo whatever, this shit is just crazy though," he said with an addled look on his face.

Approximately two and a half hours later, Ryat was sitting next to Grace inside the visiting room of Lewisburg Federal Penitentiary in

Lewisburg Pennsylvania. They were patiently waiting for Roe to be escorted to his visit with them. After a dreadful 45 minutes of watching other inmates put on a superficial show of content and happiness for their families, Roe finally walked leisurely through the doors of the visiting room. Wearing a tan colored khaki suit, equipped with a wide smile, he hugged his sister first, with them affectionately sharing their sibling pleasantries upon greeting one another. He then greeted Ryat with a brotherly embrace as Ryat caught a hint of his *Cool Breeze* fragrance oils.

For the next 45 minutes, Ryat sat silently across from Roe as he conversed with his sister concerning their family and other personal matters. Roe then shifting his attention to Ryat, smiled mischievously before speaking.

"Damn youngen, look at you man, you look like you done became a man overnight since the last time I seen you. Plus, I'm hearing a lot about you out there," he said as he stared at the young man sitting across from him.

Ryat sat wearing a pair of blue denim *Girbaud* jeans, navy blue and yellow number 13 *Jordans* on his feet, with the same color *Girbaud* designer shirt to match. Yet what intrigued and caught Roe's attention, was the solid gold diamond encrusted chain and pendant that Ryat donned around his neck. The pendant was the size of a grown man's fist and displayed a representation of a baby angel with wings sprawling, on his knees in prayer.

"I don't know what you been hearing bout me, I'm just trying get at a dollar," responded Ryat, returning Roe's mischievous smile.

"Look at you man, I knew you was gone be a problem one day," said Roe while still smiling as he crossed his arms and shook his head.

"So what's up wit you youngen'? I can see from that ice around ya neck that you doing al'ight for yaself."

"Yeah and I can see that you still the man no matter the circumstances cause you the only one I see in here rocking a pair of six inches on a visit while everybody else got on those black army looking shoes."

Roe then just simply responded with another impish smile, his arms still crossed staring at Ryat.

"Aye so what's up wit lil Camill, I hear yall got a vicious lil crew taking shit over. I know Bo ain't feeling that."

"Mil chilling and what can I say, Bo had his time," replied Ryat, while becoming leery of where the conversation was headed.

"But anyway, what is up wit you? Word is some nigga ratted on you and set you up."

"Oh so it's Mil now huh?" replied Roe accompanied with a light chuckle.

"Boy y'all young niggas done grew up, I seen it when y'all was pups, like I said, I knew y'all was gone be a problem one day. But yeah anyway

man, I was ratted on and set up by one of my young niggas I put on and helped get his folks out the hood."

"Word, damn that's fucked up. I heard the nigga is from the Parks and that he still out here living life to da fullest after ratting on you," said Ryat while holding eye contact with Roe. He then bent over towards him and whispered.

"Yo just give me the nigga's name and it's handled for nothing cause you my OG. I'll never forget when I used to come pick up lil quarters off you and you would ride around and give me the game."

Roe then leaned back in his seat with his seemingly omnipresent impish smirk and responded,

"See that is kinda ironic that you say that cause you couldn't imagine how bad I wanted the nigga dead and I even put money on his head but word always got back to me that the nigga could never get caught slippin. But then just a few weeks ago I got word that he was found murdered and none of my men were the ones who done it."

'Word? Who was da nigga?" inquired Ryat.

"Juan Malone," answered Roe while staring intensely into Ryat's eyes.

Ryat sat aghast for a split second in shock, then just as quick showed nothing but apathy as he stared back at Roe without saying another word.

As he began to wonder how much Roe knew, he suddenly also became conscious of Grace sitting beside Roe and the fact that sister or not, she was still the police.

Roe then noticing Ryat's eyes shifting incredulously back and forth between him and his sister said, *"Anyway youngen, not only did the nigga rat on me and set me up but he was one of the only people who knew where my main stash house was. So, he got to my shit before I could and got me for all my work. As karma would have it though when they found him dead, the cops found a lot of it in the trunk of the car he was found dead in.*

The irony is that the detectives think it was a professional hit cause the best kept secret is taken to the grave. The killer ain't take nothing. But I know that he was simply caught slippin and robbed because I know my shit and word got back to me soon after he was bodied that some of my shit was on the streets."

"Oh yeah, word? So is that why you wanted me here? To look into that for you?" inquired Ryat as he intensely studied Roe's eyes and body language.

Roe responded with a smirk while holding Ryat's eye contact. Then after a short pause he said, *"Nah youngen, that ain't why I had you brought here. Actually I want to help you because like I told you before I been hearing alot about you lately, especially how you got your block doing numbers. So when I got word that you were looking for a connect, I felt it my duty to extend my help."*

"So how can you help Roe?"

"Well youngen it just so happens I still got peoples out in D.C. from South America that trust my word and judgment. So they've already gave me their word that they'll supply you some of the best shit and even throw in consignment if need be. All you have to do is contact them and work out the business end. So, the minute you leave here, Grace gone give you a number and you handle it from there. *Don't worry about taking care of me, I'm good, and what can I say; I almost feel like I owe you,"* said Roe as he then mischievously smiled with a glint in his eyes that Ryat couldn't help but catch as he sat there silently, taking it all in.

"Oh yeah and for the record youngen, you can trust Grace, trust me, she's gone help you in any way she can on the strength of the love she see I got for you."

"No doubt," responded Ryat as the visiting room correction officers were calling Roe's last name to signify that his visiting time was up. Roe immediately stood and gave his sister a loving hug and goodbye as well as embracing Ryat in a brotherly hug.

"Always remember youngen, the best kept secret is taken to the grave." whispered Roe in Ryat's ear.

"Understood," replied Ryat while slightly nodding his head and staring Roe in the eyes as they broke their embrace.

"Yo what's up wit you girl?" answered Ryat after noticing that it was Tiffany who was calling him on his cellphone.

"Nothing, what you doing? Where you at?" she quickly countered from the other end of the line.

"I'm at the crib. I just got back from seeing my Ol 'head. But I'm saying though, what's up wit all the questions? Something wrong?"

"Well Ryat it's just that I need to see you cause I got something I need to tell you."

"Man come on Tiff you know I hate when people do that, If it's that important you mines well tell me now instead of having me worry about nothing."

"It's not nothing Ryat! And since you can't wait til you come see me. I'm pregnant!"

"Oh shit! Damn word?!" exclaimed Ryat almost breathlessly as he immediately became afraid for the first time in a long time.

"Yeah WORD Ryat! I'm pregnant" countered Tiffany almost indignantly.

"Um uh...I thought...uh never mind...well uh um I-I I'ma come see you later. I-I got something to do real quick," stammered Ryat as he rushed to hang up the phone immediately after his last word.

He then sat back on the couch afraid and confused, too many thoughts occupying his mind space.

Not only did Ryat not go see Tiffany later that day but for the next three weeks he completely avoided her all together. All of her many calls for the first two weeks he would ignore. Convincing himself that he just needed some time to get his mind together.

Meanwhile his street endeavors rose to a new level as he immersed himself in the streets as if he was a part of the mixing combination for the asphalt. Where after visiting Roe, and Grace giving him the number to the contacts out in D.C., he immediately called them the next day and set up a deal where he was to take a trip to Washington in order to secure 5 bricks. He would pay for three at a much cheaper number than local prices and get two on consignment.

The trip back and forth with the product seemed to be the only obstacle. It quickly became a non-issue after Ryat convinced Grace to be his driver for a small fee to which she obliged without the slightest objection.

Reason being besides on the strength of the love she seen her brother had for him, she herself secretly found herself attracted to the young man and his air of purpose.

After the first day of receiving the product, Ryat, Mil, Bryce, Potta, and Hochee quickly laid the foundation to their empire. With all opposition being met with iron showers, the young gang quickly made a name for themselves and took over majority of the crack trade uptown. Just as quick a power struggle war broke out with the old guard of Bo and his minions.

Just as fast the war ended with very few casualties, mainly to block runners on both sides. Bo's incarceration being the cause of the war ending so abruptly after he took a plea bargain with the Fed's for thirty months from a prior drug trafficking with firearm indictment. Which resulted in Ryat and his crew taking over the entire reigns of control in the crack trade uptown. Their business quickly expanding throughout the city.

After weeks of avoiding Tiffany, Ryat was riding in the passenger seat of Bryce's new fire red '02 Lincoln Navigator, when he decided to call her. As the phone rang he suddenly became excited at the thought of being a father which he couldn't wait to tell her and apologize for abandoning her for the past three weeks.

"Hello?" Tiffany finally answered after 6 rings.

"Yo um...uh Tiffany what's up, this me," he said, suddenly becoming nervous as he thought about how she must feel after he avoided her for so long.

"So what do you want?" she calmly countered, emotionlessly.

"I uh um...just wanted to...uh" he stammered then paused shortly, not knowing what to say. *"So I mean um.... How's the baby?"*

"What baby?" she quickly and calmly countered apathetically.

"Wha-what do you mean? I... I thought you were..."

"Yeah well there ain't no baby no more because I refuse to have a child to somebody who's not gone be there for my child. So my sister took me last week to get an abortion," spat Tiffany vehemently as she finally broke down in her first show of emotion.

"Huh? Wha-what?" replied Ryat confused and caught completely off guard.

Then with a raw show of emotion, his anger got the best of his rational as he suddenly experienced a certain feeling of perpetual hurt all over again.

"So you just gone kill my baby?! You already know how I feel about abortions," he barked before pausing for a second while simultaneously closing his eyes briefly and rubbing his right hand over his face.

"Bitch you know what, I don't ever want to see you again in my life, I suggest you lose my number," he hissed, then hung his phone up angrily as Bryce looked on apprehensively.

Chapter19

> *"Just as a lump of coal can be transformed*
> *into one of the world's most valuable gems, a*
> *human being can vastly increase his or her own*
> *value to the world."*
> **-Dennis Kimbro**

Over the next two and a half years, Ryat and his crew power and ascendency in the game was unmatched. They controlled half of the weight distribution throughout the city and had 23 blocks that garnered the most of their profit. A few of these blocks were located in each section of the city, which they ran meticulously like a debauch Fortune 500 company. Each block having its own latent hierarchy from general to soldier where all problems were handled internally as well as the reward and punishment system. Unless a problem impeded progress to the point where Ryat, Mil, Potta, Hochee, or Bryce had to step in and give a universal order to all. Like when the police kept knocking off the block runners with guns and finding their dime bag packages in used chip bags amongst debris as if they were tipped to the method being used. Which always ended with those block runners getting lengthy prison sentences. Until Mil came up with the solution to pay each local mailman from those respective blocks a nice sum for a copy of their mailbox keys. Which he then gave to each block lieutenant and ordered them to have their block runners only keep no more than 20 dimes at a time in their possession. Whereas the lieutenant would then keep the main stash inside the mailbox, replenishing his workers supply when they ran out. Meanwhile the lookouts were the only ones to possess a gun in order to protect the block.

Therefore, if and when the police crept up on the block before the lookouts could alert, the lieutenant would simply walk away without getting caught with anything and the workers if caught could get charged with nothing more than a misdemeanor simple possession. To which the block lieutenant would simply return to the mailbox later that day, open it up with his copy of the mailbox key and retrieve the stash.

Things couldn't have been going any better for the crew as they had acquired all the material possessions they had ever wanted and had moved their loved ones into nice places outside the city.

Yet with all his new-found affluence from the game, Ryat unlike his crew was far from being satisfied as thoughts of retribution continued to occupy the better part of his mind space. He had spent the last few years trying his hardest to come up with any information as to who killed his mother, which he always ended up back at square one. Awhile he hunted Victor like a lion after a gazelle, it began to seem as if Victor had become a real live apparition, always heard of but never seen. Still Ryat remained patient with his lust for the blood of those who killed his loved ones as it was what fueled his rage and ambition day after day.

The relationship with the connect out in D.C. couldn't be going any better for Ryat and his crew either. He had built a solid trustworthy relationship with them. The more money he generated for them, the more liberal they became with the product. Which made the needed *re-up* trips less frequent as the money and product became more prolific. Initially Ryat had no problem taking the monthly trips to the Potomac Gardens housing project in Washington D.C. Where on G street between thirteenth and Penn, he and Grace would simply park their used car that hid the re-up money in a stash spot under the backseat. They would then exit the vehicle, and walk down the block a little until they found the used van they were looking for. The keys would always already be in the ignition. Which they would them simply get inside the van and commence their trip back to Harrisburg with multiple kilos of crack hidden inside stash spots throughout the interior of the van. Ryat had only ever actually met the connect in person twice which each time strengthened his revere for them in how they ran their operation so fastidious and business like. With a clear set of values, principles, rules, rewards, and punishments. Which Ryat had conveyed to his crew in helping them incorporate it into their operation which was the key to taking them to the next level.

The only real pressure in the whole ordeal for Ryat was the trips back with the product because he knew if he was ever caught with such an amount that he would never see daylight again. Which he and Grace had almost come close to one trip when a state police truck, with a K-9 in the back, pulled them over. As the officer made his way to the driver's window, Ryat sat in the passenger seat paranoid knowing that regardless of the stash spots, if that k-9 got to sniffing the van, they were over. So, he sat poised with his .40 cal. firmly gripped on the side of his seat, already making his mind up that the moment the cop got too suspicious he would 86 him and take his chances on the run. Awhile Grace knew his thoughts, she feared the worst yet she handled the situation so effortlessly when the officer approached the window that Ryat quickly realized how much of a great asset she was.

The minute she rolled down her window, the fat pale-faced state troopers' racism was written all over his face. Which he made no show of hiding as he spoke condescendingly to Grace in explaining how she had a busted taillight and how she knew she shouldn't be driving under such conditions.

Grace let him go on with his bigot diatribe for a few minutes while she remained calm in her seat until he made the first threat to have the van searched. That's when she showed him along with her license and registration, her badge. Informing him that she was a detective from Harrisburg, Pennsylvania and that She and her son was on their way back from visiting Georgetown University where he had just gotten a scholarship to attend. Which she ended by informing him in a sardonic way that she fully understood her rights and would like her ticket so she could be on her way before she missed her 'Officers Ethics' meeting which she was hosting. In seconds the bigot state trooper's entire façade instantly changed as he suddenly became servile in defense. He praised Grace for her great work and how nothing more than a simple warning would be warranted as he handed her back her license, registration, and badge. Immediately making his way back to his k-9 truck while wiping the sweat from his brow awhile Grace and Ryat broke into a laughter as they pulled away.

That's the day their platonic relationship became sexual. It happened after they left the officer by the side of the road, immediately in route to find a car repair shop. Where after finding one a few miles ahead, they ended up waiting almost two hours to have a simple taillight fixed. Which by the time it was done they had already decided to spend the night at the nearby hotel and finish the trip in the morning. This would be the first time they had ever spent a night in a hotel on the road together. Before they had furtively flirted with each other, she would always negate his advances and her sexual desire for him with quips like, "boy I'm old enough to be your mother." Which he would always take in stride until that day in the hotel where the sexual tension got the best of both of them.

Once inside the hotel, they stayed in two different rooms that were joined by a locked door separating them. On one side of the door, Ryat lay on his back sprawled across the bed in just his tank-top and boxers. He laid there smoking a blunt with lascivious thoughts of Grace running through his mind. On the other side of the door, Grace sat Indian style on her bed, wearing only her soft pink lace panties and bra to match. She was watching a re-run of 'Law and Order' while sucking on a jumbo watermelon Lolli pop for which she had an innocuous addiction too since she was a child. All the while she also sat secretly hoping that Ryat would make one of his sporadic sexual advances. Which she planned to accept without the slightest sign of reluctance. Suddenly in the middle of her lustful thoughts, her desires were to be answered with a silent knock on the door as if Ryat was a mind reader.

Opening the door, she stood there half naked like a stallion while sensuously sucking on her Lolli pop with eyes full of hungry lust as she stared at him. Ryat stood on the other end of the door in his tank-top and boxers, eyes slanted with a reddish tint. An impish smirk spread across his face just before he spoke.

"Since you always talking bout you old enough to be my momma and seeing how you called me your son to that officer. I figured I could sleep in your bed cause I'm scared in here by myself."

Meeting his impish smirk with her own, Grace stepped to the side as he stepped past her taking off his tank-top in the process. Throwing it on the floor as she immediately ogled his body in admiration of the art depicted on his toffee completed flesh. Tattoo's that gave her a better inkling into who he really was and his pain. His entire back was covered with the angel of death standing hauntingly behind two prominent gravestones which one read R.I.P Raymond "Ray" Storm, followed by a short epitaph and the dates commemorating the years of his short life. The other gravestone read R.I.P. Lati Davidson, followed by a short epitaph and the dates commemorating his young life also. Each of his shoulders also had different depictions of black female angels with different names under each of them that Grace couldn't make out from the position in which he was standing.

Now on top of the bed laying on his back with his hands behind his head, Ryat smirked mischievously as Grace stared him down with eyes full of hungry lust as she removed her bra. Revealing the most beautiful mahogany brown D-cup breast he'd ever laid eye's on, instantly arousing an erection out of him as he now stared hungrily at her erotic hardened chocolate nipples. Then without any more words being exchanged between the two, she slowly sauntered towards him while sensually sucking on her Lolli pop. Reaching him she then straddled Ryat and began sensually kissing him. Then as she bent back a little, wetting the Lolli pop with her mouth, she began a sensuous trail with it at his neck, across his shoulders and chest, down to his belly button, removing his boxers in the process. She then began erotically tracing the candy trail with her tongue, savoring the taste of his flesh mixed with the watermelon flavor. All the while it drove him rapturously crazy as it felt as if she was stimulating every sexual nerve ending he possessed. Grace continued this trail with the wet Lolli pop down the inside of his thighs to his knees. Where she would then follow this trail with her tongue and mouth. Making him pant and tremor for the first time in his life. Sensually sucking the candy off his knees, driving him mad, Grace ended by lapping his erection up with the wet Lolli pop, taking him deep into her mouth. Getting into a good sensuous rhythm for a short while before he couldn't take it no more. Pulling himself out of her mouth, he jumped up from the bed frenetic, in shocked pleasure.

"What? You can't handle it baby boy," Grace quipped in a sexy whisper in between giggles.

"Oh so you think it's a game," Ryat countered with a sly smirk as he stepped towards the bed, pulling her to the edge and flipping her over onto her stomach.

He then removed her panties as she lie on her stomach on the bed with her legs slightly open and her knees slightly off the edge. He then standing behind her at the end of the bed, lifted her legs up towards him, until he was able to enter her tight warm silky wet love opening from behind. She then bent her legs, and wrapped them around him, locking her feet together at the ankles.

Simultaneously he held her with his hands, resting her on his thighs as they instantly fell into a synchronous rhythm with her meeting his every thrust. She moaned and gasped awhile he filled every inch of her love opening. Creating for her a euphoric sensation as he over stimulated her G-spot. Then just as they both were about to reach their peak, Ryat pulled out, maneuvering himself onto the bed.

He then laid on his back and ordered her into the reverse cowgirl position, which she immediately obliged and in no time, they got into a rhythm as she bounced up and down, gyrating her hips with him meeting her every motion. She then skillfully with him still inside her, turned her body around to where she was now facing him. This drove him crazy as they fell right back into rhythm. Grace then slowed up the pace and in one swift motion reached over into the nightstand beside the bed and placed her detective badge around her neck. Which hung erotically between her juicy butter brown breast on a thin sliver chain. Yet her attempt at creating an even more erotic ambiance for him, back-fired when it immediately caused a cessation to his ecstasy. Her act awakened in him his seemingly innate loathe for police.

Just the sight of the badge created in him a hate for her that he couldn't seem to control. He began to feel as if he was faking it just not to alert her to his deep seeded hate.

Therefore, he pulled her towards him while still in rhythm and snatched the badge from around her neck and threw it across the room. Which this only heightened her ecstasy as she believed it was just a mere way of him showing his dominance, which she loved. Whereas the second the badge was out of his sight, the rapture returned for him and even heightened as they both simultaneously reached their peak in the form of a euphoric orgasm. They then both collapsed onto the bed completely exhausted.

Yet this was the turning point in their relationship in more ways than one as Ryat could no longer suppress his indirect loathe for police. Though he knew he could never reveal this to her because she was such a great asset and because he knew she could bury him if she felt she could no longer trust his actions. Therefore, He continued his sexual tryst with her occasionally but knew that in order for her not to pick up on the subtle signs of enmity, he wouldn't be able to take those trips with her. So he convinced her that it would be best for her to take Boody on the trips with her because he was younger with a younger face and physique which would make it easier for him to pass as her son just in case certain circumstance presented themselves again. Thereby the only time he would have to take the trips with her would be when the connect wanted to see him directly. She easily took the bait and obliged to the arrangement, where he then awarded her with a pay increase which Grace readily accepted.

Sitting on the edge of the roof of his brand new tricked-out aqua blue Jaguar XF with his legs hanging off the side, Ryat was eating a pint of beef lo mien. While simultaneously talking to a female whom stood sexily in front of him. Potta then pulled up beside him with the beats banging in his money green GMC Denali, setting off nearby car alarms as Fabolous' *'Breath'* blared from his stereo system.

"Yo man, turn that shit down nigga. Can't you see I'm trying handle business," hollered Ryat into the passenger window of Potta's car while smiling from ear to ear.

"Man fuck that bitch cuz, she gone fuck you regardless. What's up wit you though? You seen Bryce? I was supposed to meet da nigga up here an

hour ago but I had got caught up and now he ain't answering his phone," responded Potta after turning his music down and leaning towards his passenger window from the driver's seat. Meanwhile the female standing in front of Ryat sucked her teeth and snapped her neck at this comments.

"Yeah he was up here but him, Mil, and Boody went somewhere like twenty minutes ago. They most likely rolling to Melvin's game together. I'm gone pick up Hoch in a minute and we gone meet them there. I know you going? Cause tonight you know our boy gone show his ass for those scouts."

"Yeah I already know my boy gone show his ass, you know I'm going. I'ma meet yall niggas there then."

"Ight den, I'ma holla at you later," said Ryat as Potta pulled off down the street. Ryat then resumed back to talking to the sexy woman that stood before him scantily clad.

Rounding the corner on 6th & Curtain streets was a detective in a navy blue Chevrolet Caprice. Whom instantly became angry the minute he saw the bejeweled young man sitting atop a high priced luxury car. Which the detective was sure belonged to the young man even though he wasn't listed in the data base as the vehicle's owner. This enraged the meager salary earning detective as he cruised by the young man staring bitterly into his face. Ryat returned his stare with an almost mocking smirk which further enraged the detective as he thought of how much he hated the young man whom carried himself as if he was Mr. Untouchable.

Staring back at the detective who glared at him, Ryat couldn't help but wonder where he knew that face from as he prided himself on never forgetting a face. Yet the more he pondered where he knew this apparently loathsome detective, he came up blank. Until it suddenly occurred to Ryat that the detective may have been one of the one's who arrested him a year prior and charged him with drug trafficking. After he was pulled over in his neighborhood during a sting operation around election time. Which Ryat had no problem stopping for them after securing his pistol in it's stash spot. Believing that he would just receive a simple ticket and be on his way.

Yet when the detectives searched his car they came up with 98 grams of crack in a zip lock bag. Surprised, Ryat swore it wasn't his but was still arrested. The D.A. on the case immediately asked for an outrageously high bail considering the charge, which from the onset Ryat smelled a fix. Knowing it wasn't his narcotics because by then he barely touched the drugs he pumped into the city's debauch arteries.

Ryat then hired two of the best attorney's in the state, whom in two months' time, beat the case for him at the preliminary hearing. Receiving clandestine help from inside the police force and mainly because Ryat's passenger at the time of the incident, a female acquaintance of his testified that she had the drugs inside the vehicle unbeknownst to him. Which Ryat's lawyer's convincingly persuaded the district judge of such, getting all charges against him thrown out at the chagrin of the Harrisburg Police Department. The most amusing aspect of the whole ordeal for Ryat was when upon his release he was held on a detainer Children and Youth Services had put on him. Agents double O dick and Cunt as he called them, whom he hadn't seen since they dropped him off at the Hodges, picked him up from the prison and escorted him to the youth detention center. Ryat spent the next two days there for running away from the Hodges but was shortly released because of his age. His lawyers wasted no time in getting him emancipated as an adult because of his age being 19.

Wherefore after surmising that the loathsome detective whom glared at him had to be one of the detectives who unsuccessfully tried to put him away with a setup, Ryat put on an arrogant smirk and glared back at the detective. For which the detective took umbrage and almost jumped out and harassed Ryat for such an insolent act but the detective suppressed his impetuous loathe for the young man. Understanding that it would be futile to harass him now, knowing that in due time he would have the last laugh or better yet the last arrogant smirk.

An hour later, Ryat and Hochee sat parked inside his car at the gas station on 6th and Division Streets. They sat engrossed in rolling blunts with their eyes focused on what they were doing, not noticing the person walking up wildly to the driver's window. Until suddenly a loud thud mixed with a clamoring against the window instantly put both of them in a state of shock and trepidation. As they figured they had got caught slipping and therefore would be paying the price with their lives via an iron shower, especially if karma had decided to rear her ugly head.

Within those few terse seconds Ryat's mind wandered a mile a minute as he cursed himself for getting caught slipping in such a vulnerable position. Meanwhile Hochee's only thought was making it out of that situation alive so he instantly grabbed for his gun on his lap and maneuvered himself to shoot back at whoever. Until just as quick within those long-standing seconds, Ryat lifted his head to face his attacker and immediately shouted for Hochee not to shoot. Whom obliged yet looked up at him reluctant and confused. Ryat explained that it was only some crazy chick while simultaneously he was opening his driver's door to confront the woman.

Whom the minute she saw Ryat emerge from his car with rage in his eyes, she immediately broke down crying while covering her face with her hands and mumbling over and over, " *Oh my God, I'm so sorry. I'm so sorry, I thought… I thought… you were my… oh my God… oh my God.* "

Befuddled, Ryat stared at her with a confused look, then within that same second he took notice of her sinuous figure as he looked her from toe to head. The second his eyes finally made it to her face and met her eyes, they both looked on shocked at one another.

"Asaria?"

"Oh my God!.. Ryat?"

"Yo Asaria...Damn Yo! What's good? I ain't seen you in forever it feel like. Where'd you come from? And why you trying break my windows?" inquired Ryat as he looked at her, almost incredulous that she was actually standing before him.

"Oh my God Ryat, that is you. I can't believe this," she responded, just as shocked while looking him from toe to head.

"I didn't mean to almost bust your windows. I didn't even know that was you in there. I actually thought it was my boyfriend who I just had found out was cheating on me. He has a car just like this one."

"Damn yo I really can't believe this is you Ria. I ain't seen you in years. It's got to be fate that we meet again like this. Plus I can't believe of all females you let some nigga have you out here all distraught like this," said Ryat as he stepped closer to her, admiring her natural beauty as he suddenly realized how much they both had grown since they last saw one another and how much he had missed her companionship.

"Yo what happened to you after I left? I wrote you so many times but you never wrote back.

I just figured that funky ass Mrs. Hodge wasn't giving you my letters."

"Ryat I got all your letters," she responded placidly with the look on her face suddenly changing as she stood there.

"So why you never wrote me back then?
Inquired Ryat with an addled look on his face.

"Because Ryat you just up and left me there by myself and you never even said goodbye before you left!" snapped Asaria as she now glared at him.

"Damn Ria I'm uh...Damn Ria I'm sorry I ain't know. I ain't mean to just leave you like that. You right I should have at least told you goodbye before I left but at the time my mind was just on getting the fuck away from that place."

"You know what Ryat, there's no need to explain. It is what it is, I told you how you were the first real friend I had ever really had. Then you just up and left me without even saying goodbye...You know what Ryat, never mind, I got somewhere to be anyway," said Asaria, then abruptly turning on her heels, she stormed off towards her car.

"Yo hold up Ria," Ryat immediately blurted as he quickly stepped behind her, grabbing her by the arm, spinning her around on her heels to face him.

"Come on Ria, damn I said I'm sorry, what else you want me to do? I really meant that shit or I wouldn't have said it and you know it."

"Look Ryat, whatever, I got to go. It was good seeing you, bye," said Asaria with a grimace

on her face as she glared at him while standing indignantly with her arms crossed.

Suddenly a smile commenced to stretching the surface of his face which further angered her as she stared at him with a grimacing confused look.

"What the fuck is so funny Ryat?" she spat vehemently.

"Yo Ria, how many times I'ma have to tell you that mean grill don't look good on your angel like face?"

With her menacing facial expression softening and a smile threatening to stretch the surface of her face, Asaria responded, *"yeah whatever Ryat."*

"See I knew the Ria I know is still in there somewhere. Go head you can smile. You know you missed me like I did you. Your right though I could have at least said goodbye but I tried explaining myself in those letters but I guess that wasn't good enough. So let me make it up and take your bad ass shopping and to dinner or something."

"Ryat I don't need your money! I never wanted anything from you except for your friendship but I guess you showed me how much that meant to you when you just up and left me without even a goodbye so you could come back here and live out your 'gangster' dreams. Well I guess your living your dreams now but don't try to throw none of your money at me, I ain't one of your ghetto smuts Ryat!"

With his eyes locked in on her piercing stare, he slightly nodded his head after her emotional diatribe. Remaining silent for a split second to take in everything that she had said.

Then as he continued to hold her stare, he said, *"no doubt, I feel you Ria. But don't let my actions in not even at least saying goodbye and my haste from me wanting to get away from the Hodges be a reflection on how much your friendship means to me. Granted my decisions may not have been clearly thought through but at least give me room for error as a boy."*

Suddenly with a smile finally stretching the surface of her face, Asaria continued to hold his contrite stare for a moment before hugging him tight around his neck and in almost a whisper, she said, *"Ryat I missed you so much."*

With his arms now wrapped tight around her waist, he replied, *"I missed you so much too Ria and didn't even realize how bad til just now."*

Chapter 20

"For what is a man profited, if he shall gain the whole world, and lose his own soul?"
-Matthew 16:26

Over the next four months the concept of Ryat and Asaria reinforcing their friendship was only the beginning of what quickly blossomed into a love affair that neither of the two thought could ever really exist. It happened almost naturally as the leaves changing colors in autumn. Especially shortly after they had reacquainted with one another and she left her boyfriend. With them being single and intimately spending endless hours together, quickly reminded them of what made their platonic friendship so strong and intense. As in how they both shared almost the exact same personality and how they shared the same intangible pain among the many other things they had in common. This understanding made them nostalgic in remembering the running joke that they shared between them that they were the same person of opposite sexes. Which made it only natural in how their platonic friendship transcended into a full-fledged love affair as they became inseparable. For the first time since he was a child, Ryat's main emotion wasn't anger triggered by his lust for revenge.

She learned from him everything that had transpired in his life during their years apart. As he learned the same from her and was intrigued as to the path she had taken in life. Graduating from college with biochemistry as her major. Which lead to her current intern position on Three Mile Island as a biochemist who assisted biological scientist in their laboratories.

Where all her studying beyond school to further enhance her career is what really intrigued him in more ways than one. As he enjoyed helping her study while learning all he could regarding different poisonous agents in the process.

In no time Ryat had moved her into a condo in the newly erected state-of-the-art LITTENHOUSE SQUARE just across the river from downtown. Which was a 31 residence/31 story building complete with exclusive full-floor residences, over 4,000 square feet per residence, fully customized floor plans, and soaring 10-foot ceilings. Featuring oversized window walls, and expansive terraces which all gave off spectacular 360° unobstructed skyline panoramic views of the city. The building also included such luxuries as a state-of-the-art fitness center with lap pool, sauna and hot tub. Private elevators that opened directly to each individual unit, and 24/7 concierge that resided on-site. With the building's most impressive feature being the European designed, fully automated, state-of-the-art parking system. Where cars are automatically guided to a retractable floor that gently lowers the vehicle to be stored below ground. When leaving, an automated retrieval process is initiated. As a person descends the elevator, their vehicle is brought to them so that they can drive straight out. The owner being the only person that ever touches their car. Which all this is protected by a state-of-the-art security system, complete with guards stationed 24/7 on the main floor of the building.

This being almost a dream come true for both Ryat and Asaria who grew up living a marginal existence financially. Which Ryat told her was his reason for hustling so hard to escape from. Now that he had tasted affluence, he swore never to be broke again because to him wealthy people are born with choices whereas poor people are born to a struggle. A struggle that had claimed most of his loved ones along the way and one that had him almost as heartless as the tin man in his quest for a dollar.

Asaria restored love in his hardened heart so he went out his way to show her that. By showering her with gifts and taking her on endless trips to places like the islands of Turks and Caicos.

When Asaria broke the news to Ryat that she was expecting, he instantly became overly exuberant. More excited than she thought he would be at the prospect of them having their first child. Savoring forever deep in the crevices of his mind that beautiful sunny April morning when she awoke him to breakfast in bed and revealed to him the good news of their expectancy. He impetuously by 2 p.m. that afternoon had her on a plane en route to a luxurious resort in Aruba. Where on the white sand beaches of that resort he swore his fidelity to her and the best possible future for their family. Which caused her to break down in his arms in a raw show of emotional bliss.

Whereupon their return from their brief vacation of celebration, Ryat couldn't wait to break the good news to his boys. Which made them all just as happy as him if for nothing more than to see a sense of joy in him that they hadn't seen since they were kids. Therefore in celebration they decided to make that night one to remember by doing it big on the town. So each of them pulled out their most luxurious vehicles, donned some of the most expensive suits money could buy and took Ryat to the most lavish club in all the city called 'NEXT LEVEL'. A place where all the major players in the city frequented, bumping shoulders and partying the night away with high end doctors, lawyers, accountants, small business owners, etc. In order to get a table an individual had to buy at least 3 bottles which the cheapest started at $150 and the

V.I.P. section was a whole other experience. It was located on the top floor, complete with exotic female dancers on one side of the floor. Giant HD screens from floor to ceiling made up the walls. Which changed the ambiance every 25 minutes by changing themes, giving the entire floor a different look and background. Making it feel as if a person had frequented at least 6 different 21st century lavish clubs throughout the night without even knowing it.

Mil, Bryce, Potta, Hochee, and even young Boody made it their business to show their comrade a night to remember. As they had reserved two tables in the V.I.P. section of the club with each table having four of the sexiest female exotic dancers popping their derrieres and doing tricks the guys thought were humanly impossible. The crew sat around the tables like a powerful conglomerate ceaselessly popping bottles of Dom Perignon, Patron, and Rose. Which in no time drew the attention of some of the most beautiful women patronizing the club at that time.

As the beautiful women descended upon them, the guys accepted them with open arms. The women only made the celebration party more live. Each of the guys had at least two beautiful women all over him except for Ryat. Who politely declined all the beautiful coquette's advances, deciding that he would indeed enjoy his night to the utmost. As it was rare he went out but he wouldn't jeopardize his fidelity to Asaria. That was until the most beautiful milk chocolate female he had ever laid gaze upon approached him with persistency in her eyes that he could not deny. Not to mention she had one of the juiciest derrieres and voluptuous bodies he had ever seen. Snuggle fit inside a white Dolce & Gabbana dress, standing statuesque in a pair of platinum colored Jimmy Choo heels. Complimented by a beautiful flawless milk chocolate face. With a beauty mark just above her juicy pink lips on the left side of her face which only added to her appearance. Her short Halle Berry hairstyle being just as intriguing and alluring.

Her attraction to Ryat was fully justified as anybody with partial vision could see that out of all the guys he was the most prominent. She couldn't help but notice him as he stood beside one of the tables sipping on a glass of Rose while eyeing the female dancers. To her it looked as if the clothes wore him to look good as he stood esteemed in the color of royalty. Wearing a purple, with cream pin stripes, double breasted suit from the Roberto Cavalli collection. A softer purple dress shirt underneath, a cream colored silk Cavalli tie, with a pair of off-black suede Louis Voutton shoes gracing his feet. A diamond encrusted platinum Presidential Rolex on his left wrist accentuated by a diamond stud signet ring sitting prominently on his pinky finger. He also sported diamond encrusted platinum cufflinks that read D.B.D. Which was all the more appealing to her through the lenses of his midnight black, vintage '83 Targa Cazal shades. His signature infectious smile only complimenting his appeal to her as she couldn't help but smile back at him.

"I see you're the man now," said the woman in a sultry voice as she came within a foot of him. *"Damn I must have missed that part. By the way where did you say you know me from again?"* countered Ryat in a sardonic voice while staring her down intensely.

"Just like I figured, you really don't remember who I am, do you?" she responded, still smiling as she switched into a more sexy stance with her left hand on her hip.

Now glaring at her dubiously as he tried to remember where he could have known her from, Ryat kept coming up blank just before saying, *"nah to be honest I don't but please enlighten me as to where I know your sexy ass from."*

"July."

"What? July when?"

"July, my name is July. Does that spark your memory?"

Standing there still confused, Ryat squinted his eyes and thought hard while staring at her until it hit him. July and Jamar, they were twins who he went school with and who just so happened to be the same twins he had beat up in the 5th grade.

"Oh shit, damn July that's you?! Damn! Get the fuck outta here!" he replied as he stood there shocked, eyeing her down where he noticed that same beauty mark on her face that was once the

reason all the boys in school deemed her ugly. It now only accentuated ber beauty.

Damn ain't this some shit, the ugly duckling has definitely grown into a beautiful swan. Thought Ryat as he now stared lustfully at her.

"Yeah it's me Ryat. And don't worry I get that a lot these days," said July with a smirk now plastered on her face as she stared back at him.

"Damn July, you know what though," he responded as he became more serious and his mind began to trail off. "I'm glad I finally seen you again after all these years because I promised my grandmoms years ago that I would apologize for putting my hands on you."

"Aww come on Ryat you can't really think I'm worried about that, we were kids."

"Yeah I feel you but I promised my grandmom. Plus I really mean it when I tell you I'm sorry for putting my hands on you back then because you are the only female I ever put my hands on. And as a man I just want to make it right."

"Aww ain't that sweet," she cooed with a smile on her face while flirtatiously and seductively staring him up and down.

"Yo you was always crazy girl," countered Ryat with a smile stretching the entire surface of his face as his mind told him to decline her advances before they got too strong to block yet his carnal appetites swayed him differently.

As the night carried on and the guys enjoyed themselves even more, Ryat and July found themselves getting closer and closer as his carnal lust had him with his guard down. They furtively flirted the night away as she gave him every inclination that she wanted him to badly cap the night off by parting the lips of her love opening. Which was becoming more appealing to him as the night wore on coupled with the alcohol beverages she seemingly made sure he had plenty of.

With the night coming to an end, Ryat and the rest of the guys met up in the parking lot, heading to each of their respective vehicles. With the parking lot being filled with patrons from the club, the crew made plans to end the night off at a local Jamaican restaurant as Ryat and Mil made their way to his midnight black S600 Mercedes Benz. Suddenly just as Ryat had opened his driver's door and Mil took a seat inside on the passenger side, a silver Lexus, GS460 pulled horizontally to a stop just five feet from the back of his car.

"So what's up Ryat, you gone meet me at the Hilton or what?" asked July in her most seductive voice while hanging her head from the driver's window of the Lexus.

"To be honest wit you July as much as I want to go to the Tel wit you and buss yo ass, I can't," answered Ryat while staring intensely into her eyes as he came within 2 feet of her Sedan. She sat staring back at him impassively from the driver's window.

"Oh Ok Ryat, so your not going to the hotel with me tonight."

Suddenly Ryat's clairvoyance kicked in which most people in the hood called 'Spidy Senses'. He suddenly became apprehensive of her demeanor coupled with how she had put such emphasis on what she had just said. All while simultaneously holding her cellphone open at her ear. As if trying to convey under the guise that she had put someone on hold while she spoke to him briefly. All the while she was secretly keeping someone abreast on what was taking place. Which this leery feeling immediately prompted Ryat to reach for his .40 cal. Tucked at his waist where within that split second is when he heard it. The roar from the engine of a Suzuki GX1000 that seeming as if by the speed of light pulled to a stop about 8 feet behind him.

Mil seeing it first but unable to react within that millisecond it took for the masked gunman on the back of the motorcycle to open fire on Ryat with the twin .45 handguns he held in each hand. The first shot hitting Ryat in his upper right thigh, completely throwing his leg from under him. With the second shot, a fraction of a millisecond later, hitting Ryat square in the mid of his back. Which the inertia from it instantly knocked him to the ground. Another bullet pierced his right shoulder on the way down with a succession of bullets following as one just missed his head. Mil within that split second the shots first erupted finally made it from the passenger seat of the Mercedes with his 9mm Sig Suager in the air firing at his best friend's assailants on the motorcycle. Whom immediately sped off the minute Mil's first shot sounded off.

Bryce, Hochee, and Boody who were all riding together, immediately realized what was taking place on the other side of the parking lot and quickly began a hot pursuit of the fleeing motorcycle. Which two blocks into the pursuit they quickly, to each of their chagrin, realized they were no match for the lighting speed of the motorbike inside Bryce's fire red Range Rover Sport. All the while Boody, in rage, hung out the back driver's side window firing recklessly with a baby mac. 11.

Meanwhile Ryat lay face down in the asphalt of the parking lot clutching his .40 cal. in his right hand. Only having enough energy, as the motorbike sped off, to lift his head in time to see the stoic expression on July's face as she looked down at him emotionlessly while pulling away from the scene. Everything in him wanted to react but though his brain gave the commands, his body was in to much of a dying and debilitated state to comply. He was suddenly lifted from the ground by Mil and Potta whom quickly carried him to Potta's awaiting Honey colored Cadillac CTS. Where once Ryat was positioned safely in the back seat of the car, Potta immediately sped off in destination of the emergency room of the Polyclinic Hospital. Meanwhile the female whom Potta had just met that night and had plans of taking to the hotel, sat in the passenger seat of his car going crazy. After seeing all the blood and macabre she frenetically and frantically screamed things like, *"oh my God he's gone die,"* and *"oh my God, oh my God he's dying! God help... Oh my God I can't believe this is happening."*

All the while Ryat's head lay in Mil's lap as he began coughing up blood awhile tears simultaneously fell from Mil's eyes. Thoughts of who could have committed such an assassination attempt on his brother from another were the only thing occupying his mind's space. One thing was for sure though, that whoever did it would pay the cost with their lives.

Contrary to cliché as it would have one believe that every man on the brink of losing his life suddenly his entire life flashes before his eyes. Ryat on the other hand wondered why this wasn't such for him as he began to suffer from pulmonary hemorrhaging and lose consciousness. The only thing his mind center on was what it would be like on the other side. Like was there really a heaven and hell and if so is heaven really a paradise where there's never any worry, pain, and suffering etc., or is hell really a lake of fire or some type of eternal torture. Ryat then suddenly became genuinely afraid for the first time since he was a child because he knew without a doubt that if there really is a heaven and hell, he was no doubt on a one-way trip to the latter.

2 weeks, 3 days, 11 hours, and 19 minutes later was when Ryat awoke from his coma. The first

face he saw upon waking was that of his aunt Anita whom instantly became excited.

"Oh yes God, he's awake! Yes! Ryat your awake, oh my God," yelled Anita excitedly while jumping in place like a little girl. Which instantly put a smile on his face despite the instantaneous pain he began to feel in his upper torso and right thigh. In that terse timeframe after hearing Anita's joyous yelling, Keith and Asaria quickly rushed into the room. Smiles immediately spreading across the surface of their faces at the sight of the virile life that showed in Ryat's eyes as he lay bandaged on the hospital bed with tubes attached to a few different parts of his body. Anita immediately began talking to him in an excited and fast manner. She professed her love for him and how happy and grateful she was that he had made it. Also informing him that his grandfather had been to visit him a few times throughout the weeks since his coma but that he really couldn't handle it so he continuously ran back to the streets in search of his nepenthe which came in the form of a crack rock. She then briefly chided him about his lifestyle and how that life-threatening incident should be a big enough sign for him to leave that so-called game alone. Anita then ended with thanks to God and laid a loving kiss on his forehead, stepping to the side so that Asaria could finally speak to her man. Whom instead stood there silently staring at him intensely with tears welling in her eyes.

*"Wha...what's up baby? It's cool now baby,
I'm good,"* said Ryat in a raspy voice while trying
his best to appear strong in such a debilitated state.

Asaria continued to stare at him as tears
began to stream down her cheeks before
responding, *"no Ryat no, you are not good. Nothing
about this is good. Your living a life that is not good
which almost cost you your life and our child's
future. So what's good about that? Huh Ryat? This
is why I've been begging you for the last I don't
know how long that it's time you gave up that life. I
mean Ryat no sooner than I told you that we were
having a baby, I get the news that you died TWICE!
And then I've had to sit by for the last 3 weeks
crying my eyes out and praying to God while your
in a coma that was told to us indefinite. So what if
you would have never waken up or died Ryat? What
was I supposed to tell our child about it's father?
HUH RYAT? WHAT? Our child needs you more
than anybody Ryat. I just want you to know that
Ryat, because a father is a girl's first love and a
boy's first hero."*

"Yo you right Ria, I'm sorry," whispered
Ryat through both his physical and intangible pain.

Suddenly three detectives and a cop march
into Ryat's hospital room. Completely disregarding
Anita's immediate pleas for them to return later and
interview Ryat. Instead they instantly confronted
him impassively with a barrage of questions. To
which after telling them that he was simply walking
into his car when shot after a night out partying, he

answered every question thereafter with a simple, *"that's all I know."* Which instantly enraged the detectives as they convinced themselves that he knew more. Therefore after realizing that they would get nothing further from him they resulted to threatening him with persecution if and when he retaliated. One of the detectives whom Ryat recognized as the one who glared at him when riding through his block was now glaring at him in a more threatening way as if he wasn't already the half-dead victim.

As soon as the detectives departed from the room, Anita's boyfriend Keith decided to speak to Ryat. Whom Ryat had become quite fond of over the past few years and respected as a man's man.

"Hey youngen I'm glad to see you here finally, I didn't doubt one minute whether you'd pull through. Don't worry I won't say much cause I know you about heard enough for one day. But what I will say is that you should listen to that girl of yours, she's a good one and everything she said was right. Especially about that child. Now like I said before I'm glad to see your alive but outside of that, your gone be alright, right?"

"No doubt. Ain't no sen-"

"Yeah, yeah, I know, like you always say ain't no sense in crying when it's raining but what if that rain is a hurricane threatening to destroy your life."

Chapter 21

"He who is not getting better is getting worse."
-St. Ignatius

IN THE ensuing months as Ryat struggled to recuperate at a secret location in the city after checking himself out of the hospital prematurely against doctors wishes, mayhem broke out in the city. With Mil, Potta, Bryce, Hochee, and Boody being the sole exactors of the havoc that the local news and newspapers deemed as some of the most violent months to ever hit the city. There were multiple shootings almost every day. The crew left no stone unturned in trying to find out who attempted to assassinate their brother. Any enemy that they could think of was either tortured for information that they most likely didn't have or was simply greeted with an iron shower anywhere at any given time of the day.

Boody even showed how vicious he could be when he got word from a local hood rat that some young boy from her neighborhood was bragging to her about how he participated in Ryat's assassination attempt. Boody didn't waste a second, he kidnapped the boy who was around his age and took him deep into the woods. Instantly the young boy became obstinate in refusing to speak anything he knew and told Boody to do what he was gone do because he was going out on his feet, not on his knees. Which Boody made sure to make a mockery of as he shot him repeatedly in both his feet and eventually buried him alive, on his knees.

Potta was brought in by detectives on one occasion after a tip involved him in one of the shootings but was eventually let go shortly thereafter because as he put it, *"they didn't have nothing solid to charge him with."*

It had been 7 months since Ryat's shooting and the complete chaos that had erupted in the city as his crew continued ceaselessly to get to the bottom of who was behind his murder attempt. All of which July Johnson was fully aware of, reason why she had relocated to a brownstone on Princess street in York Pennsylvania.

July grew up in a single parent home with only her mother to struggle raising her and her twin brother. At an early age without a father to teach her true value and self-worth., she observed her mother time and time again use her sexuality to get from men what she wanted. This in turn is what created in July the ideal that money is the measure used to determine her relationships with men. Which in turn made her very self-serving, materialistic, and willing to do almost anything under the sun in order to acquire the root of all evil.

It was around midnight when July had finally made her way home after spending the better part of her day at the hairdresser. Taking her Prada boots off at the door and dropping her Fendi bag on the sofa, she commenced to making her way through her house towards the kitchen. Turning on all the lights in the process. Once inside the kitchen she made herself a beef & broccoli hot pocket. Then with it on a plate in hand, she made her way up the stairs towards her bedroom. Suddenly the minute she stepped into her master bedroom and turned the light on, she was met with the shock of her life as her mouth sat agape and her body became frozen in place. Dropping the plate containing the hot pockets all over the floor as she laid eyes on a sinister smiling Ryat who sat across her bed holding a bottle of Rose in his left hand and his .40 cal. handgun in his right hand.

"Now now why would you do that July?" asked Ryat in a sardonic tone as he looked towards the broken plate and hot pockets laying in front of her. *"I bet you could have used some of this here to wash that down. Hey look I didn't mean to startle you, I just figured we could finish off where we started at. That's why I brought the bottle and don't worry about the gun I'm just a little paranoid these days. I mean you could understand that right?"*

"Uh uh umm Ry...Ry...I umm di... I'm uh sor-" stammered July.

Ryat then noticing how she kept cutting her eyes back towards the door as she struggled to get her words out, he said; *"look July I have no plans on shooting you. but if you force my hand I promise you I'ma put seventeen holes all through that pretty designer blouse you got on. So why don't you just come over here so we can finish where we started off."*

July then complied, making her way over towards her bed, sitting right where Ryat was patting the bed next to him for her to sit. He then grabbed the two glasses he had sat on her night stand beside the bed and poured them both a nice full cup from the bottle of Rose he held. Afraid, she quickly accepted the drink and drowned it to Ryat's surprise all in an effort to appease her fears. He then poured her another drink, put the bottle down and commenced to running his left hand in a sensual manner all over her curvaceous body.

"Now I'ma ask you a few question July and I want you to be totally honest with me and don't play one game because like I said, just don't force my hand and I won't have to use this here gun. Now the first question is who the fuck had you set me up so they could catch me slippin and try and out me?"

"Um uh... my brother had me-"

"What?! Your brother?!" exclaimed Ryat as his mind wandered off wondering what her brother wanted him dead for? He refused to believe it was

because he had beat him up in the 5th grade. *"Man what the fuck ya brother want me dead for?"*

"No, no it's not like that, see my brother got busted a few years ago and had got sentenced to twelve years in the Fed's for drug trafficking and firearm charges. Well last year him and a guy known as Bo became celly's and all I know is next thing my brother introduces me to the guy. Who instantly started looking out for me and having money brought to me. He sorta like became my man. Then next thing you know he already knows I know you from when we were kids, I guess from my brother. But then next thing you know he comes home like nine months ago and he's telling me how he needed me to set you up because you and your crew were in his way. But Ryat you have to believe that I didn't want them to kill you, I'm so sorry they shot you up like that. I really am glad your alive though."

"Oh yeah is that right?" replied Ryat in almost a hiss with a malefic smile on his face as he was now massaging her breast with his left hand.

"So who was that you were talking to on your cell phone just before I was shot."

"OOoohh ooh ahh," she moaned as he now had two of his left-hand fingers in her Prada pants and inside her very wet and warm love opening. *"OOoohh ooh...his...his name...is oooh...Rip. He was the one on the back of the motorcycle...that shot you? He had some young boy riding him...*

ooh, but I swear I'll help you get them back, just give me fifty thousand dollars. "

Ryat instantly twisted his face up in mocked amusement at the irony and audacity of her actually offering to help him get his revenge for anything, let alone that amount of money when he literally had her life in his hands.

Scandalous gold digging bitch!, he thought.

He then snatched his hand from between her legs and stood up with a nefarious scowl on his face as he glared at her. Now pointing his gun at the middle of her forehead. She now laid wide eyed with her legs open while staring back at him in shocked horror.

He stood there wanting so bad to blow her brains out as he then suddenly lifted those two wet fingers that just came out her pussy towards his nose. Which was one of his many idiosyncrasies since the very first girl he had sex with. Meanwhile July laid confused while continuing to stare at him in wide eyed horror, praying that he would not kill her.

Suddenly she began to feel funny, experiencing light headedness, nausea, and excruciating pain in her lower back. Whereas Ryat after sniffing those two fingers let out a light cough while simultaneously twisting his face up in disgust from the repugnant smell those two fingers emitted. Which were inundated with her pussy juices.

He couldn't believe the irony in that this woman whom he considered to be one of the walking dead since he was shot, literally smelled like it.

Even more was that he couldn't believe how such a beautiful woman could end up so vile in character as well as her insides having a rotten egg, fish, and vinegar smell as if her soul had been escaped her body and descended into the valley of death. She then suddenly grabbed her heart now staring at him in a petrified wide eyed horror. Confused she wondered from the look on his face if he had put something up her pussy which was making her feel as if she were dying. Her heart felt like it was getting ready to explode as he glared back at her with his face still twisted up in disgust.

Then suddenly as he stared at her he realized what was happening. The poisonous agents Tetraethyl Lead & Potassium Chloride that he had mixed into the bottle of Rose were taking their effect. Which had sort of the same effect as the lethal injection.

A malefic smirk instantly appeared on Ryat's face as he watched her die slowly as all her internal organs synchronously shut down. Her chest heaved for the last time as she took her final breath. He then wanting to spit on her immediately decided against leaving any of his DNA on the scene for forensics. He gave an added sinister smirk as he heard Dollas in the back of his head telling him how he had to think and be more calculating.

Bennett Green AKA Bo was the middle son of three boys Carol had given birth to just before she died in '87 from the AID' s virus. With no father around to teach and model what a real man was because carol never really knew who any of her children's father were. Bo and his brothers were left for his 66 year old grandmother to raise. She tried her best but by the time adolescence hit he was already too rebellious. He soon found himself deeply immersed in the streets.

His entire existence now revolved around his status on the streets. Which was all that occupied his mind daily as he made his way to the blue Lincoln Navigator that awaited him out in front of his trap-house on 19th street. The second he made it inside the truck, he greeted Rip with a pound, whom was driving.

Meanwhile simultaneously from underneath a Honda Accord parked two cars in front of the Navigator and from underneath a Dodge Caravan parked two cars behind the truck, rolled two masked gunmen in all black. With a third masked gunman in all black suddenly appearing from a dark alley beside the house. A salvo suddenly erupted as each gunman took aim at the Lincoln Navigator with a barrage of bullets in succession, just as Rip was about to pullout of the parking space. Rip and Bo both did their best to take cover inside the vehicle from the attack. Yet it was pretty much to no avail as each gunman shot with an intent to make sure those two didn't live to see the next minute of the day.

Each gunman shooting with such a voracity that each shot slammed into the truck with such force that the truck began to rock in place on it's wheels. With the gunman on the side of the truck, about 7 feet away in the middle of the street, unleashing a hail storm of iron from an AK-47. Awhile the gunman standing about 8 feet from the back of the truck shot with a deadly precision from his .50 cal. Desert Eagle handgun.

At the front of the Lincoln Navigator was the third gunman who shot with a virulence dead set on retribution. He calmly walked up on the truck while firing rapidly from a glock .45 in his left hand and a nickel-plated pistol grip .40 cal. handgun in his right hand. He then suddenly jumped atop the hood of the truck, lowering the glock in his left hand at his side. He noticed through the front windshield Rip curled up on the floor in the front driver's seat whom already looked ravished by bullets. The gunman then shot two more times into Rip's body with his .40 caliber. He then narrowed his focus on Bo who just happened to be peeking at him with a petrified look in his eyes. He peeked from between his arms which were wrapped around his face as he sat on the floor of the truck between the passenger and driver's seats. The gunman then standing on the hood of the truck expressed a sinister smirk under his mask just before he pumped 4 bullets through the windshield into Bo's head from his .40 caliber.

The three gunmen then disappeared into the darkness around the corner onto Boas street where a fourth man awaited them in a black Dodge Intrepid. They all then made a quick getaway as Bo took his last breath on the same streets he used to define his existence. The same stoic streets that just made his existence trivial. The same streets that never did nor would ever literally belong to him or any other man in the game no matter how much power he procured while on those streets.

Chapter 22

> *"Any man without principles that he is ready and willing to die for at any given moment is already dead and is of no use or consequence whatsoever. "*
> *-William Cooper*

IT HAD been weeks since the mayhem throughout the city had subsided. Leaving only the local detectives and police force with an agenda. Yet Ryat could care less as he felt comfortable enough to be seen in the streets for the first time since he was shot. Being seen is something he put extra emphasis on. He cruised the city on that beautiful sunny day in his newly purchased pearl white Audi R8 Spyder. With the top back, he rhythmically bobbed his head to the beat of 50 cent's song *'Many men'*. Simultaneously singing along with the tune, *"Many men wish death upon me, blood in my eyes dog and I can't see, I'm just trying be what I'm destined to be, and niggas trying take my life away!..."*

Ryat then made his way through his neighborhood, parking in front of the apartment building he had been raised in. Finding a seat on the porch, he sat reminiscent while smoking on a blunt of purple haze. Dollas suddenly pulled to a stop behind his car and parked as he then got out of his Cadillac Escalade and made his way over to the porch, taking a seat beside Ryat.

"What is good wit you youngen?" asked Dollas as he stuck his right fist out for a pound.

"Ain't shit Dollas, I'm good. What's good wit you though?" responded Ryat as he returned the pound.

"Yeah I can see you good, ain't no doubt about that, shit you looking better than before. And by the looks of that new spaceship you got right there even Stevie Wonder can see you good. But I've been wanting to holla at you youngen cuz I've been hearing your name nonstop in these streets. You hot youngen. I'm telling you, your hot! And I'ma tell you like grandma would say, boy you getting a little too big for your britches. Youngen listen to it when I tell you it's bout time you cash your chips in before you shoot your load. Like I keep trying tell you, don't let your desire for a dollar cost you your life."

Ryat furtively rolled his eyes into the back of his head, not really wanting to hear any of Dollas conscious spiel. His ignorance and arrogance combined induced him to counter with, *"man Dollas, man I told you I'm good. I ain't worried bout all that bullshit. I'ma get what my hand calls for no matter when I decide to cash my chips in. So until then I'm running the fucking table and I'm riding, I ain't hiding. Don't blame the clay for what the potter made."*

"I guess your right cause as always I can't tell you nothing because I guess your truth is your truth and everything that you say is true cause obviously nobody can tell you different. But before I roll out of here let me ask you do you really trust all those young boys you run wit?"

"Ain't no doubt, them is my brothers. I would die for them as I know they would do the same."

"Alright younqen and I trust your judgment but remember what I'm about to tell you, that people are like tea bags, you never know how strong they are until they're in hot water."

"No doubt Dollas, I'ma make sure I remember that but I know without a doubt that my brothers are loyal."

"OK, understood but you just be smooth out here and think more about that lil boy you and your girl are about to have. I'ma holla at you later, you be smooth and think first"

Later that day as Ryat was cruising through the Southside his cellphone suddenly began blowing up with a bunch of calls simultaneously. Addled as to why, he quickly answered after the next ring.

"Yo what up? Who dis?" he immediately inquired upon answering.

"Yo Ryat this is me Hochee. My nigga, where you at?"

"Why? What's up my nigga, why you sounding all frantic and shit?"

"Because yo the whole damn national guard it seem like just ran down on Mil in front of his crib while he was sitting on the porch playing wit his daughter., Niggas don't know why they booked him yet but the way they came full force like that it got to be big. Me and Bryce on our way down B-more right now to lay low until we find out what's good. We done already talked to Potta and Boody and they getting ghost too. We suggest you do the same fam until we find out what's good."

"Damn! Word!...Al' ight yeah yeah no doubt, I'ma holla at yall niggas later. I'm bout to go underground til we find out what's good," replied Ryat as he hung up his phone wondering and worried as to why his best friend was just arrested.

Not even two minutes after talking to Hochee, Ryat was flying down Hanover street in a hurry to get out of dodge. At the corner of 13th & Hanover streets is when he was suddenly boxed in by two U.S. Marshal vans, too police cars, a K-9 truck, and 3 Chevrolet caprices with a paddy wagon pulling up the rear. Ryat instantly began to panic but with a cooler head prevailing he realized that he pretty much had no escape. So instead, satisfied that his gun was in it's stash box inside the car, he leaned back in his seat and calmly took a pull from the blunt that was burning in his ashtray ever since he put it down to answer his cellphone.

By the time he took his third pull from the blunt he was snatched from his vehicle by what seemed the entire second shift of the police department. He was then read his rights and lead away in the paddy wagon just as quickly without knowing any reason why but could come up with at least a hundred reasons if he wanted to. Yet not knowing why he had been arrested with such force worried him to no end but he refused to let them see him sweat so he remained impassive as if all this was just another day on the job. He was then lead by detectives from the back of the paddy wagon through the police station to an interrogation room. Where he was then cuffed to a table and left with nothing but his thoughts for over an hour. Which created a panic in him similar to how he felt after Lati' s death yet and still he refused to show it, knowing they were watching. So he looked on into space with a stoic expression on his face for 97 minutes until two detectives finally walked into the room. One of the detectives he recognized while the other calm looking one he had never seen.

"So how are we doing today Mr. Storm?" asked the calm looking detective the second the door shut behind him.

With a smirk now gracing his face, Ryat answered, *"I can't speak for yall but me I'm doing good, especially once yall get my lawyer William*

Carpolous down here. And yeah that's attorney William Carpolous as in the best in the entire state, ranked number six in the country."

"Is that right Mr. Storm? I'm not sure you want to go that route just yet though. I mean don't you at least want to know why we brought you in like this?" spoke the more calm looking white detective as the burly black detective stood to the rear corner of the room glaring at him.

"Nah, truthfully I don't give a fuck, Yall can tell that shit to my lawyer. Until then I don't have shit else to say," countered Ryat with an impassive look on his face and a shrug of the shoulders as he stared the detectives in the eyes.

"I don't really think that's the route you want to go Mr. Storm because we have enough to put you away forever. As I'm sure you already know we arrested your friend Camill Evans A.K.A. Mil too, he's in the next room and I'm pretty sure he's thinking more about himself right now after hearing all of what he's looking to be charged with. Now listen Mr. Storm we're looking to charge you with a slew of crimes from robbery, drug trafficking, all the way down to murder or should I say murders. First and foremost that being the murder of a Mr. Bennett Green A.K.A. Big Bo and the attempted murder of a Mr. Eric Bryant A.K.A. Rip. And yes you heard me right Attempted Homicide because yes Mr. Bryant survived and he's told us all we need to know about your involvement in his attempted murder and the murder of Mr. Green.

*You see Mr. Storm this is the only chance
I'm going to give you to help yourself because we're
the love Ryat. We're the love Ryat, the D.A. they're
not going to show you no love, the jury they're not
going to show you no love, the judge he's not going
to show you no love. We're the love Ryat, we're the
love, help yourself now. If you weren't the shooter
tell us who was, if you aren't the leader of your drug
organization tell us who is. See what I'm telling
you Ryat is right now is the time to help yourself, I
mean what do you plan on doing with yourself in
twenty, thirty, forty, shit fifty years from now? You
really want to spend all those years in a
penitentiary somewhere? Don't you want to be there
for that little boy your girl is about to have? Yes
and you can fix your face because of course we
know about your pregnant girlfriend, there's alot we
know about you that you may think we don't. So
again I'm going to extend our love to you because
like I keep telling you Ryat we're the love so help
yourself now because no one else is going to give
you any type of love from here. So do us both a
favor and help yourself now Ryat because we're the
love Ryat, We're the love, help yourself now!"* said
the white detective in a charismatic spiel complete
with the mannerisms to captivate and arouse the
trust of any average person.

Ryat sat with many thoughts running
through his mind, the main one being the fact that
Rip had survived contrary to what he had been lead
to believe. Yet there was no possible way that Rip

could say he seen him or anyone for that matter do anything. Then there was the fact that if the detectives really had all they needed to charge him with all those crimes and put him away forever then why would they need him to talk. The marshmallow face detective did know a lot more than he should.

What the fuck did he mean by robberies, murders, and drug trafficking? Shit how much do these muthafuckas really know? Thought Ryat.

Ryat then fixed his eyes from detective to detective before putting his head down and responding.

"Al'ight I'll do yall a favor if yall do me a favor first," he said almost inaudibly as he slowly lifted his head.

"And what would your favor be Ryat?" eagerly answered the fat face white detective as a smile formed for the first time on the face of the black detective.

"Hold my dick while I piss," countered Ryat as a malefic smirk suddenly appeared on his face. He then looked from the white detective whose face was now beet red towards the black detective whose smile immediately turned into a snarl.

"Why you black piece of shit, I ought to...I promise you muthafucker that bastard child of yours will be calling someone else daddy because you'll be spending the rest of your fucking life behind bars" barked the white detective as he angrily rose from his seat awhile the entire time Ryat sat laughing.

"Calm down detective Jenson, calm down. Why don't you step out the room for a minute and get yourself together while I have a go at him," spoke the black detective for the first time while rolling up his shirt sleeves as the white detective obliged by leaving the room.

Ryat sat laughing even harder at the detective's intimidation tactic.

The black detective then slammed his hands down on the table just in front of Ryat to get his attention before speaking.

"So you think this is funny huh muthafucker'? You think your so tuff huh muthafucker'? Your just like your punkass daddy. Yeah that got your attention didn't it, yeah I know, shit I should of shot your little ass when I had the chance. Oh yeah I see that really got your attention now. And see let me tell you something, when foster care came and took you from your family, that was my doing, and when they found that crack in your car where you luckily beat that case, that was also my doing. But don't you worry you little punk muthafucker because I'ma do you just like I did your daddy after he killed my nephew, that's make sure you never see daylight again. And guess what I'ma do your little bastard son the same way after he grows up to be just like his little punkass daddy," hissed detective Burke as he glared into Ryat's eyes.

Ryat sat stunned glaring back at the detective. The same detective he recognized as the one who glared at him that day as he rode through his block. The same detective who stood in his hospital room glaring at him as if he was supposed to die. This being the same detective whom Ryat finally realized and recognized as the first man to point a gun at him on that eventful morning When he was just 9 years old. which was the first time he had ever experienced a paralyzing fear. All of which first ignited the fire that burned inside him, which shortly thereafter came to a simmer, then ablaze, with it now being an inferno that raged violently in his heart as his blazing eyes bore into the detective.

At that point Ryat wanted nothing more than to break free from those cuffs and strangle that greasy black reptile to death. What furthermore made the blood boil in his veins was the fact that the detective just admitted to causing so much pain in his life, making mention of some sort of retaliation against his father. A man Ryat didn't even know. The worse part was the fact that the detective had diabolical plans of carrying out this retribution on his own unborn son.

"Yeah I figured I'd get your attention now you little piece of shit. Now we'll really see who has the last laugh after I bury you under the jail," said the detective, laughing to himself as he left the room.

Ryat was then lead from the interrogation room by the white detective to the booking area. He was then charged with first degree homicide and attempted homicide, an indictment that only named he and Mil as co-conspirators in the death and attempted murder of Bo and Rip.

The next 21 months before their trial was pure hell on earth for both Ryat and Mil during their incarceration in county lockup. They refused to eat any of the repugnant meals, living only off of commissary junk food. The living conditions were even worse as they were spiritually debilitating. A place where mental torture was the ideal. In hopes to induce' the average man to expeditiously accept a plea deal in order for that man to escape county hell as quick as possible. Ryat and Mil suffered this with no doubt in their minds that they would be home soon after being acquitted at their trial. Which they just knew was a given with their high paid lawyers and the mere fact that Rip could not truly say he seen anyone shoot him or Bo. Though it constantly bothered both Ryat and Mil as to how Rip came up with them two as his assailants. They often wondered what type of story could he possibly tell to convict them.

Yet there was no greater intangible suffering experienced by Ryat than the birth of he and Asaria's son only one month into his incarceration. Raymond *"lil Ray"* Storm was what Asaria named their child after Ryat's late uncle whom she knew he still carried a lot of pain over. The first sight of little Ray behind the plexiglass in the visiting room conjured up in Ryat an immense powerful love for another being that he had never known.

This love in turn became the source of a great deal of suffering for him as he couldn't even touch his son and the probability of him never being an integral part of little Ray's life emerged as the brunt of his agony, The same could be said for Mil who suffered just the same after every visit through the plexiglass window with he and Esmerelda's beautiful 3 year old daughter.

Still there was no greater pain and agony experienced by both Ryat and Mil during their incarceration than when they both were called to the Chaplain's office and told of Hochee's murder. Which completely devastated them as they learned that their brother through love had been shot in a shootout outside a local club. His killer instantly went on the run but was found 5 month's later in south Jersy shot to death from a .50 caliber handgun.

Potta had come through the County on a gun charge that had derived from a domestic dispute with his girlfriend where she called the cops and they found a pistol on him. Ryat and Mil rode him to no end for getting caught up after putting his hands on his girl which Potta denied to no end. Potta then began catching them up on the intimate happenings of the crew since their incarceration over a year prior. He told them how he and Bryce were still running wilder than ever especially since Hochee 's death. Then telling them how Boody had a bunch of young boys under him that called themselves the "YoungBullz" whom Potta said were even more vicious in the streets than they were. When asked by both Ryat and Mil why Boody called his gang the *YoungBullz*, Potta replied by telling how Boody said because they be rammimg 24/7. This caused them all to erupt in laughter. Potta ended by telling them how Melvin had sat the bench his whole first year in college at Nebraska State until their star player got injured. They put Melvin in the game and he instantly lit up the scoreboard. This put a smile on Ryat and Mil's faces as they thought of their childhood friend who seemed to be on the fast track to legitimate success. Suddenly they both Ryat and Mil wished they could turn back the hands of time and do it all over again and follow a path parallel to Melvin's.

Potta was shortly thereafter transferred to another block after his bail had been lowered at his preliminary hearing. He was unable to bailout because of a probation detainer from a previous case that just so happened to involve a domestic dispute.

After 21 months of incarceration in County hell, Ryat and Mil's trial finally commenced. Which to them felt like a gift from God in ending their suffering as they were convinced they would emerge victorious, gaining their freedom back. The first few days of trial though introduced them to a whole new level of spiritual torture as they quickly realized how mentally exhausting the process was. Especially the more it hit home for them that their lives literally hung on the tip of those twelve juror's tongues. Still the overall trial seemed to be going their way as most of the D.A.'s witnesses were expert witnesses that could only at best intricately describe the egregious nature of the crime. They could not, just as Ryat and Mil knew none of the witnesses on the D.A.'s witness sheet could not directly link them to the crime. It seemed to get even better for them when the prosecution's chief witness Eric "Rip" Bryant took the stand and continuously got caught in several lies about the crime in question. Still Ryat and Mil could not believe the story he told when he testified that he had seen their faces. Lying about them being urnnasked walking down the street when they spotted him and he spotted them. Where he then reached for his pistol in self-defense, explaining the gun police found on him inside the truck. He testified that he and Bo then immediately realized they were out-gunned, therefore they instantly took cover inside the truck when Ryat and Mil opened fire.

Ryat and Mil's defense attorney's decimated Rip's fictitious story piece by piece so much that he began to stutter when questioned by them. He then resulted to crying on the stand and showing off his numerous bullet wounds to gain the sympathy of the jury. Which put a smile in both Ryat and Mil's eyes as they looked at each other sharing the same thought.

Look at this fakeass gangster snitch crying like a bitch, I thought you were hard nigga.

The second Rip left the witness stand Ryat and Mil felt good and was repeatedly assured by their attorney's that they undoubtedly had the case beat. That was until the D.A. took to the floor and called to the stand their final witness.

"The prosecution at this time would like to call to the stand a Mr. Lurelle Mullins Jr.," said Chief Deputy District Attorney Mitchell Horassico.

Ryat and Mil sat calmly waiting for him to be done with his presentation after fighting so hard in a losing battle to put them away.

Suddenly, the witness' name began to ring bells to Ryat. Yet he couldn't figure out where he knew it from though he had already seen it on the D.A. 's witness sheet. He had figured it to be just another expert witness. That was until Potta walked through the trial room doors escorted by the same two detectives from Ryat's interrogation whom made it their point to sit directly behind he and Mil. Both Ryat and Mil's mouths sat agape with pure shock written all over their faces as Potta sauntered across the courtroom, taking a seat at the witness stand.

Mil and Ryat could not believe in their wildest dreams what was taking place. Even more so because they never even realized that it was one of their childhood friend's real name on the witness sheet all the while.

In that moment, detective Burke leaned over in his seat until his mouth lay on Ryat's ear where he then whispered, *"I guess my great nephew ain't*

*like it too much when I told him everything,
especially how yo daddy was the one that murdered
his daddy."*

Ryat sat even more stunned at the diabolical
detective's words as he instantly remembered where
he knew the name Lurelle Mullins from. In an
attempt to narrow down his mother's killer, he dug
up the names of the men his father was in prison for
killing. Ryat then suddenly and vicariously felt his
father in his same similar predicament a generation
prior, a vulnerable mis-indoctrinated product of his
surroundings and early childhood experiences.

Ryat and Mil watched helplessly and in
shock as Potta raised his right hand, being duly
sworn in just before presenting his testimony
for the prosecution.

Chief Deputy District Attorney Mitchell
Horassico: *Mr. Mullins, can you state your full
name for the record?*

Potta: *Lurelle Mullins Junior.*

Mr. Horassico: *And do you go by any other
name besides that as in a street name or nickname
of any sort?*

Potta: *Yes uh I've been known as Potta my
whole life.*

Mr. Horassico: *And Mr. Mullins would you
say you know the defendants Ryat Storm and Camill
Evans pretty good?*

Potta: *Yes, uh I've been friends with them
since we were kids.*

Mr. Horassico: *Okay Mr. Mullins, in regarding the death of Mr. Green and the attempted homicide of Mr. Bryant, were you present with your childhood friends on the night in question when they committed this crime?*

Potta: *Yes.*

Mr. Horassico: *Okay and Mr. Mullins can you please explain to the court what transpired on that night in question.*

Mil sat confused in total shock and rage at what was happening, glaring at Potta the entire time, whom averted his eye contact. Ryat on the other hand sat emotionally conflicted, not even thinking of revenge or hate. Only hurt for both him and his childhood friends for being mere victims of ghetto osmosis, systematic chicanery, and a misinformed upbringing.

Meanwhile Potta told a story totally contrary to the one Rip told. He testified that he, Ryat, and Mil sought out Bo and Rip for revenge in Ryat's shooting. Dramatizing how Mil and Ryat accosted the two surreptitiously with a barrage of bullets in an understanding that they were to kill the two with Potta being the getaway driver.

Both Ryat and Mil sat defeated and totally betrayed as Ryat began to suspect if Potta was going to tell everything then why he never mentioned Bryce. Which caused him to wonder if Bryce knew of Potta's infidelity and was somehow in cahoots with him. Ryat didn't know what to believe anymore or who to trust after being raised upon so many lies, half-truths, and now disloyalty by one of his most trusted comrades.

It started looking better though for Ryat and Mil when their lawyers had their turn to cross examine Potta. They caught him in numerous contradictions regarding his testimony and caused him to also stutter on the witness stand. After Potta left the stand Ryat and Mil felt confident once again that they would be acquitted. Especially after both of their attorney's in their closing arguments painted a colorful picture for the jury of the fact that they were told two totally different stories by both of the prosecution's key witnesses. Where they asked the jury to keep in mind during their deliberations whether or not; the two totally different supposed truths could possibly cohere into one truth in convicting Ryat and Mil beyond a reasonable doubt.

Ryat and Mil were then escorted back and forth day after day from the courthouse to County lockup for a week and a half while the jury deliberated their freedom. In the interim, the first chance Ryat got, he contacted Bryce about Potta testifying against them. For which Bryce told him, over the phone, how he had already found out from Asaria and how he was beyond shocked to find out. He growled as he detailed how bad he wanted nothing more than to make Potta pay but that Potta was currently still in the County being held in protective custody.

Ryat then shocked Bryce by telling him in a melancholic tone not to pay Potta back for his disloyalty. Suggesting that Bryce just cut him off but let him live. Meanwhile Bryce sat addled as he listened to Ryat on the phone sounding depressed while for the first time not wanting to seek revenge on someone that had wronged him.

It had been a week and a half since the beginning of deliberations as Ryat and Mil finally sat in the courtroom with their attorney's awaiting their verdict. The jury foreman then stood and read off the verdict sheet to the courtroom. He first read that the jury had found both Ryat and Mil not guilty of first degree murder. For which they both instantly became elated barely hearing the rest of what the foreman said as he also read that the jury had also found them not guilty of second degree murder. But that the jury had found them to be guilty of third degree murder and attempted homicide. Ryat and Mil instantly came down from their ephemeral highs after hearing the final verdict. Confused, they wondered how they could be found not guilty of first degree in the case but guilty of third degree. Which their lawyers explained that the jury must had decided to go with the victim Rip's story where they could then only render a third degree verdict because Rip's story did not connote any type of premeditation.

Ryat suddenly felt lonely like his first night in foster care as he turned to stare into the faces of his distraught family. He then made eye contact with Dollas in the back of the courtroom as he heard in the back of his mind, Dollas always saying, *"youngen you can't let your desire for a dollar cost you your life."*

Chapter 23

*"I have never met a man who has given me
as much trouble as myself."*

-D.L. Moody

THE WAIT for sentencing felt like pure
attrition on the mental faculties of Ryat and Mil as
they felt like it was a prelude to the beginning of the
end. Though the prospect of appeal gave them a
modicum of hope, they still felt as if their ending
was just beginning. Which became even more
depressing for them as they realized this ending was
coming before they were 21. An age that most
young men in the hood celebrate to if they are able
to make it their alive and free. Wherefore Ryat
decided he would go out with a bang by
implementing one of the most calculating acts of
retribution he had ever conjured. He sent a message
to Grace hoping she would acquiesce in helping him
execute his well thought plan.

A week after sending her the message, he
was called to the front of the jail where he was

placed in a bullpen until being escorted to a small room with no windows or cameras. A small table sat in the middle of the room with an empty chair on one side of the table and Grace sitting in the other chair on the opposite side of the table. Her hair was pulled back into a ponytail with a stern expression on her face. Wearing an elegant light-blue Cristian Dior blouse with her detective badge hanging gracefully from her neck over her blouse. A black business woman's attire Cristian Dior skirt laid ever so heavenly over her voluptuous curves. A pair of black Giuseppe Zanotti crystal heels accentuating her look. She in that instant looked like the most beautiful woman to Ryat. A smile threatened to spread across his face but he thought better of it while the C.O. was still in the room.

"Thankyou officer, I got him from here. I just have a few questions for him then you can have him back," said Grace as she stood, gesturing for Ryat to take the seat across from her.

"That's alright detective I know how this goes, you just take as long as you want with Mr. Tuff Guy here," replied the correctional officer with a sardonic expression on his face as he shoved Ryat into the chair then left the room, shutting the door behind him.

"Wow Ryat they must really not like you here but judging from all the trouble you've seemed to get yourself into lately, I'm not surprised. Why haven't you been contacted me Ryat? I probably could have helped you before you got yourself in

such a deep hole," said Grace as she sat down in her chair staring into his face.

"Man fuck these racist pigs, they just mad I got they salary on my books three times over and that's just commissary money, man I could pay for the rest of that fat inbred's life if I wanted too. But fuck them, to answer your question, I ain't been contacted you because I felt I owed you and your brother not to risk your job and reputation more than I already have behind my bullshit., plus I really thought I had this case beat but I couldn't even have imagined what went down and how it went down."

"Yeah I heard how your boy Potta flipped on you."

"Man that shit ain't even half of it, that's why I got you here."

Ryat then told her everything he needed her to do and why. Which she promised him she would carry out every letter of the plan thoroughly. This finally putting a smile on his face as they both commenced to looking into each other's eye's lustfully. Grace then got up from her seat letting her hair down while sashaying around the table until she stood in front of him.

Kneeling, she grabbed his penis from inside his County issued orange pants and began sucking and licking him into euphoria. He removed her detective badge from around her neck as she stood hiking her skirt up around her waist. Revealing that she wasn't wearing any panties. She turned with her back facing him and squatted into his lap as he guided his manhood into her. They then got into a harmonious rhythm, meeting each other's every motion. Until they both reached their peak and simultaneously climaxed hard, both feeling completed sated. They both then quickly got themselves together just before she summoned the C.O. to take Ryat back to his block.

*"You can take this asshole back to his block now, "s*aid Grace in a stern voice with the accompanying expression on her face the minute the C.O. stepped into the room.

"Gave you a hard time huh detective? No surprise there but don't you worry we'll take good care of Mr. Tuff Guy here, " responded the fat white tobacco chewing C.O. with a smirk on his face as he shoved Ryat out of the room.

One month and four days later, Ryat sat with a smile on his face as he read the front page of the local paper. It had a haggard looking mug shot of detective Burke plastered across it. Telling the story of how after a tip from a high-ranking officer inside the police department lead to the arrest of detective David Burke. After majority of the crack from the evidence room at police headquarters gradually disappeared, the tip lead to most of it being found in detective Burke's residence. A subsequent drug test performed on the detective showed him positive for high levels of crack. All of which corroborated the informant's story.

The high-ranking officer inside the police department tipped the internal affairs unit that detective Burke had been stealing seized crack from the evidence room for over two years. Using it for his own personal habit. Which lead to the detective being arrested and charged with a slew of felony's.

Meanwhile the residual effects of the detective's arrest caused for the reopening of many criminal cases. Men who were locked-up with Ryat had their sentences reduced or cases thrown out because of detective Burke being the lead detective on their case. These were men sitting in prison for narcotics there was no longer any evidence of courtesy of detective David Burke and the Courts agreed.

Ryat sat around smiling nonstop as he watched groups of these guys go home. Never knowing that it was because of his diabolical plan to take down the detective that they had regained their freedom.

The best news Ryat had gotten while waiting for sentencing was when Dollas informed him that the detective had a secret crack addiction. This dark secret of the detective helped Ryat fully formulate his plan of revenge. This information came after Ryat told Dollas of everything concerning the detective and his desire to destroy his life ever since he was a child in an ongoing scheme of revenge against his father. Ryat used the information that Dollas gave him for his benefit by having Grace take the seized crack from the evidence room on different occasions and give it to Boody. Who would then break into detective Burke's home on those different occasions and cleverly hide the narcotics inside the house unbeknownst to the detective. Grace then put the Internal Affairs Unit onto the detective, subsequently leading to his arrest.

All of which came as a complete shock to the detective. The taste of his own diabolical medicine triggered the beginning of his burgeoning psychosis. For the life of him, after doing so much dirt, he could not remember if he *really* stole the narcotics from the evidence room for his own personal use. Therefore against his attorney's wishes he instantly plead guilty to the crimes believing it would gain him favor with the judge. Yet the judge had no sympathy, immediately revoking his bail after his plea and directing that the detective be held in County lockup until his sentencing. The detective was committed to protective custody immediately after being processed into the prison. He was confined to his cell by himself for 23 hours a day with only an hour for recreation outside the cell. This isolation coupled with the detective's insidious mind exacerbated his psychosis, driving him completely mad. First the detective started off excessively talking to himself, he then became combative with himself as he ceaselessly hallucinated. Not knowing if he was coming or going. He soon took to eating shit sandwiches. Prompting doctors to put him on all sorts of psyche meds which only temporarily sedated him while causing permanent damage to his mental faculties. He would never have complete control of them ever again.

All of Which transpired within the 3 and a half months it took before Ryat and Mil were sentenced. They stood in front of the judge and was sentenced to the maximum of 20 to 40 years for the 3rd degree homicide followed by a consecutive 16 to 32 years for the attempted homicide. The judge made it his point to mention repeatedly thereafter that they would spend no less than 36 years, no more than 72 years in a State Correctional Facility.

Mil immediately became melancholic and introspective as his mind centered on the fact that the next time he could possibly see the streets again would be approximately at the age of 56. This caused him to suddenly think of all the things he hadn't done in his young life. As well as all he would miss as his beautiful little girl grew and developed into a woman. At that moment he would have gave anything to be able to go back and live his life differently.

Ryat stood staring at the judge with a smirk spread across his face, completely numb to what had just transpired. After being found guilty he had already pretty much figured this would transpire. Therefore he refused to let the judge, D.A., or detective Jenson see him sweat. Adding an extra lift on his smirk as he looked towards the detective thinking of his partner.

Ryat and Mil then only spent about two more weeks in County lockup before being shipped to the State Correctional Facility Camphill. They spent 6 months there going through the classification process until they were then separated and sent to two different institutions. Mil being sent to SCI Huntington as Ryat was sent to SCI Western.

Meanwhile Potta had been home for 4 months, spending most of his time with his girlfriend in the Hall Manor projects on the Southside. He knew he could never go back to the way his life was after snitching on Ryat and Mil. Therefore he stayed off the radar and resorted back to petty hustling to earn an income. Only hitting the streets at night. It was a little past one O'clock in the morning when his cellphone rang as he sat on the couch inside his girlfriend's row home in the middle of the projects. Recognizing the number on his cell phone screen as a payphone number, he quickly answered, figuring it to be one of his crack-fiend clientele.

"Yo what up?" answered Potta into his phone.

"Hey buddy, it's me, your guy Dan. you remember me? I met you on Thirteenth street a few nights ago," said the caller from the other end of the line whom sounded like a white man.

"Oh yeah yeah, I know who you are. So what's up, you need to see me?" responded Potta not really knowing who it was but knowing that he had

given his cell number to so many crack-fiends in an attempt to build up his clientele that it was most likely one of them.

"Yeah buddy I need to see you for a sixty. Do you want me to meet you at the same place behind the school where I met you at last time?"

"Oh Ok so that's where I met you at last time, yeah yeah alright, I'll meet you there with that in a few minutes."

"Alright buddy I'm pulling up to there as we speak," said Dan as Potta hung up his cellphone.

Separating the $60 worth of crack from his small package, Potta headed out the door to meet Dan. Little did he know the guy who disguised his voice as Dan was at the end of the project row waiting for him to exit his girlfriend's residence.

"Hey buddy!" Is what Potta heard just as he reached the end of the project row.

Startled and confused he quickly turned on his heels then broke into a run for his life in the other direction. Terrified after seeing the big gun and sinister smirk on the face of the man who said it. Yet Potta couldn't outrun the bullets that began to tear into his body as the guy fired with a deadly precision while calmly walking him down. Potta suddenly collapsed in between two cars on the far end of a parking lot that sat in the middle of the projects. The man then stood over him with a baleful scowl on his face as he pointed his big gun down on Potta.

"Ca...ca...come on man...this is Me! you killed me already, I-I...I 'm dead already," pleaded Potta in agony as he held his stomach and chest while looking up at his assailant.

Apathetically the man then simply focused the barrow of his .50 caliber Desert Eagle on Potta's neck where there was a tattoo of the initials D.B.D. The same tattoo that Hochee had also bore on his neck, which Ryat had on his forearm, Mil and Bryce had on their hands, Melvin had on his upper arm, and Boody had across his chest. The tattoo was their motto, meaning *Death Before Dishonor.* The gunman then blasted off two shots directly into Potta's tattoo, completely ravaging it, thereby decimating half of his neck. Instantly killing Potta a millisecond after the first shot.

Receiving the news of Potta's death affected Mil and Ryat in different ways as Mil hardly felt anything. Mostly apathy as he felt for the most part that Potta deserved everything he got. Whereas Ryat felt nothing but hurt all over again as that intangible pain seemed as if it were perpetual in his life. Though he was angry over his childhood friend's betrayal, it hurt him even more to read of his murder in his city's paper. The killer was mentioned as unidentified, Yet Ryat knew without a doubt who done it. Especially after reading what type of gun was used and the fact that it was a complete overkill.

It was as if Mil had matured into manhood the minute he was sentenced to the majority of the rest of his life in prison. Therefore his character did a complete 180 as he humbled himself while striving to better himself as a man. Mentally, physically, and spiritually day in and day out. Thereby he constantly read intellectual books. Availing himself in every academic vocation he could while ceaselessly studying law and working on his appeal.

Spending his remaining downtime in the yard working out, he never wasted an idle second. Knowing full well from his past that ignorance coupled with an idle mind creates destruction. Reason why though he was well respected, especially by those who knew of him from the streets, he made it his point to deal with very few, that few being intellectual mature men on a quest like him to gain knowledge of self. Thereby alleviating himself of all the ignorant idle conversations most of his pseudo-gangsta peers indulged themselves in constantly. Telling trivial stories of how much *"work"* they put in on the streets, how much money they made, how many whores the fucked, or of all the cars, clothes, and homes they had. These guys never ceased to amuse Mil with their hypocrisy.

Meanwhile Ryat spent his first few years getting shipped from institution to institution for smuggling drugs inside the prisons, trouncing a guard in one, and stabbing an inmate in another. After being kicked out of three state prisons, Ryat ended up doing two years in Long Term Segregation at SCI Fayette. Where after being released back into population he decided to mellow out. Taking some of the advice, Mil, Asaria, and Dollas gave him through the mail while in the hole. Therefore he stayed under the radar while finally commencing to read the books Dollas sent him. Reading books like Sun Tzu's *"Art of War"*, Napolean Hill's *"Think and Grow Rich"*, Carl Upchurch's *"Convicted in the Womb"*, George Jackson's *"Soledad Brother"*, etc., all of which helped him began to see his existence and life from a different perspective, Yet Ryat's decision to mellow out in his new environment was rnore strategic than a change of heart. The desire for retribution against his mother's killer still raged in his young heart.

Inside the institution he didn't associate with no one as he conjured up ways to exact his plan. He even refused to converse with his cellmate until one day after being in the cell with the older Muslim man for over a month, the man said something to Ryat that instantly caught his attention.

"You got to get that hate out your heart young brother. It's evident, you can see it in your eyes. And I'm telling you to get that hate out your

*heart because it only leads to suffering and
destruction, especially in here,"* said Ryat's cellmate
as he splashed water on his face while looking back
at Ryat through the mirror.

Ryat had no response as what his cellmate
said abruptly triggered memories of his late
grandmother. Knowing it was something she would
have told him, he became aloof and nostalgic as
memories of her pragmatic outlook on life
permeated his mind for the rest of the night.

Chapter 24

"Adversity is facing a man with self, if he is not nonchalant concerning his existence, he will genuinely understand his true self. An assumed impasse will either break or strengthen but in all reveal the true self in man. Adversity in the end will leave either or three type of man, the ignorant inept man, the self-perpetuating failure, or the insatiable wisdom seeking man on a journey to appropriate one's life."

-Author

OVER THE next several months Ryat began to build a bond with his older cellmate Mr. Abdul. Whom helped him gain insight as if Mr. Abdul was merely the conduit in which his late grandmother used to guide him into a new perspective on life. Which was almost scary to Ryat as he thought of how most of what his cellmate said sounded like it came straight from his late grandmother's life lessons manual. Ryat fully embraced Mr. Abdul, only making dissent with him when it came to religion. Whereas Ryat took a more deist outlook, Mr. Abdul tried to no avail to get him to subscribe to the tutelage of Islam. Mr. Abdul believed Ryat only needed to see for himself the way of a believer and it's benefits outside of the superficial light cast upon them. Therefore Mr. Abdul decided to familiarize Ryat with his inner circle and their teachings. Starting with introducing Ryat to a man of the faith he felt Ryat would be able to relate better too. Mr. Abdul had once also watched that man come into the prison system an angry volatile young man and be transformed into a humble charismatic Imam. Believing this man known as Shabir Muhammad would be influential in converting Ryat, Mr. Abdul made Ryat aware of his plans to introduce them. Which surprisingly enough to Mr. Abdul, Ryat was a little on the eager side to be formerly introduced to Shabir Muhammad. Unbeknownst to Mr. Abdul, Ryat had been furtively studying Shabir Muhammad and wanted nothing more than to get within arms-length of him, past all of the many followers that flocked around him daily.

It was later that week when Mr. Abdul introduced Ryat to Shabir Muhammad in the main yard where Shabir Muhammad sat at one of the rear tables playing another Muslim man in chess.

"As-Salaam-Alaikum," greeted Mr. Abdul as he and Ryat approached the two Muslim men playing chess.

"Wa-Alaikum-Salaam," crisply responded the two men.

"Shabir this is the young man I told you I wanted you to meet. He reminds me alot of the old you and it just so happens you both come from the

same place. His name is Ryat and he's pretty good at that game you're playing there too," said Mr. Abdul as Ryat got a good look at the darker skinned Shabir Muhammad sitting there with a salt & pepper beard like a lion's mane that came down to his chest.

Meanwhile Shabir also briefly stole a glance of the young brown skinned man whom he had heard so much about outside of what Mr. Abdul told him. He had heard how vicious the young man was on the same streets he had once reeked havoc upon. Shabir then asked the man he was playing chess with to give him a minute with the young man he believed to be suffering from megalomania as he once was. Shabir then asked Ryat to join him in a game of chess. Ryat obliged as Mr. Abdul and the other men made their way away from the table, giving Shabir and Ryat an intimate chance to get familiar. Whereas Ryat commenced to taking a seat across from Shabir Muhammad who had his head focused on the chess board, a malefic glint suddenly appeared in Ryat's eyes. He gripped the razor sharp 6 inch knife-like shank tucked at his waist. Poised to strike just as Shabir Muhammad raised his head to speak. Ryat in that fraction of a second seen something in his eyes that momentarily deterred him from sticking his shank in Shabir's neck like he had planned.

Vacillating between his negative and positive emotions for the man, Ryat hissed, *"nigga I just want to know why my mother had to die."*

Taken aback with shock and confusion, Shabir Muhammad looked away fram Ryat knowing he had never murdered any woman. He wondered tersely what the young man could be talking about until it hit him. The realization caused his heart to beat rapidly and his eyes to pop out as he slowly turned his head back towards Ryat. He silently prayed to God that what he felt to be his worst nightmare was not sitting before him as it's physical equivalent.

It had been 20 plus years since losing his best friend and pregnant girlfriend to a lifestyle he chose. Now just when he thought it couldn't get any worse, Tanell was staring into the face of he and the love of his life's love child. Whom was the exact likeness of Ashely with mannish features displaying the same nefarious glare in his eyes that Tanell knew was his own when hate ruled his heart. Completely addled and incredulous, Tanell could not believe that he had went through life all those years convinced that he and the love the of his life's progeny had also died that fateful day. Believing this to be a cruel joke, he became briefly neurotic as he looked towards the sky and began raucously cursing God in Arabic.

Aroused by Tanell' s abnormal behavior, a group of Muslim men converged around Ryat poised to attack in defense of their Islamic brother.

Ryat was already on his feet with his weapon drawn ready for action. Snapping from his short-lived neurotic rant. Tanell then began barking at his fellow Muslim brothers while showing a side of himself that most of them had never seen. He aggressively jumped in each of their faces with a rapacious look in his eyes while advising them that it would be best for them to just walk away and dare not harm a hair on Ryat. For which they immediately obliged, confused and leery of their brother's abnormal behavior.

Tanell then focusing his attention back on Ryat took a seat back down at the table with a defeated posture as he put his head between his hands. still disbelieving that he and Ashely's child now hovered over him with a weapon in hand and extreme hate in his heart. This being the same young man he had heard so many wicked stories about regarding his street endeavors. It took every ounce of Tanell to except as reality that his worst nightmare stood before him in the form of his own misguided son. Experiencing the same hell on earth he would have gave his life to prevent. Knowing of all the pain Ryat must have suffered throughout his life. Tanell could only feel a modicum of joy that he had survived the tragedy that befell his mother.

Meanwhile Ryat stood witnessing the man he felt responsible for his mother's death fall apart. Suddenly for the first time he felt a sense of forgiveness. As the bitterness he felt for his long lost father abated. Still the resentment he felt because of his mother' s tragedy caused for the loathe he held in his heart to remain.

"The last thing I ever wanted was for that to happen to your mother and this for you," said Tanell in a low melancholic audible.

"Nigga I ain't trying hear that shit. You shouldn't have sent your pregnant girlfriend out to hustle your bricks so you could get a lawyer. I mean what type of so-called gangsta does that anyway. Then maybe my mother would be alive," countered Ryat with rage laced in every word.

Addled, Tanell lifted his head towards Ryat with a confused look and responded, *"What? I never sent you mother to hustle for me."*

"Yeah whatever nigga, I already know how just before my mother was murdered she was supposed to be meeting somebody about selling them some bricks for you to get you a lawyer."

With a look of pure shock, Tanell turned his attention from Ryat back towards the ground. Shaking his head in disbelief as he realized what must have really happened that fateful morning when Ashely was fatally shot to death. He thought of how she must of went against his advising her not to meet the guy for the drug deal. Which suddenly enraged him as he thought of that guy, whom he didn't know, must have murdered Ashely. Though he knew that it was his old cellmate who recommended the guy to him so that's where he wanted to exact his rage. Tanell then looked Ryat in the eyes and told him everything.

Explaining how he had set up a deal through his old cellmate with another guy whom Ray was supposed to meet and sell the bricks to but then Ray had gotten locked-up. Therefore, Ashely suggested that she could make the deal happen to get him a lawyer.

Tanell now staring intensely into Ryat's eyes swore to Allah about how he had emphatically advised her that he did not want his pregnant girlfriend involved. Tanell then looked away not wanting to mention the obvious.

Ryat hearing this after years of built up hate against the man, wanted so bad to disbelieve him but without a doubt in his mind he knew that the man, from which he came was not telling a lie.

The most troubling part of his father's exposition was when he mentioned the name of the lawyer whom at the time was making his climb up the latter of success. The same lawyer his mother had lost her life trying to procure enough money to secure this lawyers services in hopes to save the love of her life. The sore irony being that this was the same auspicious attorney Ryat spared no expense hiring for his trial and whom currently represented him.

Ryat then took a seat at the table and like his father commenced to staring into the sky in silence while trying to make sense of everything. Then almost arbitrarily he stood from his seat at the table and calmly walked away. Without even the slightest glance back at the man he longed to have in his life throughout his childhood but had built up so much hate against throughout the years.

Meanwhile Tanell wanted nothing more than to go after his long-lost son and give him a hug, profess his love, and beg his forgiveness for the choices he made that he felt lead to Ryat being raised parentless. Yet Tanell understood that, it would be best if he gave Ryat his space. In hopes that he'd come around to where they could form some aspect of a bond. With that understanding Tanell simply looked towards the sky and mouthed the word *"why?"*.

Months on end went by as Ryat refused to be in same vicinity as Tanell until the day after one of his visits. Where prior to the visit, his aunt Anita told him about a surprise she had for him on his visit. Not knowing what it could be, he anxiously and curiously waited until that Saturday when he walked on the visiting room floor. He noticed his aunt waiting for him with a broad smile on her face while standing next to a healthy looking, clean-cut, burly, light-complected older man who happened to be his grandfather Carl. It had been almost two decades since he had seen his grandfather like that as he immediately realized what happened. With a broad smile now plastered across his face, Ryat embraced his grandfather in a tight hug, then his aunt. They all then sat down as Mr. Carl told Ryat all about his recovery from drug addiction. Which brought Ryat pure joy to hear how the man he loved more than any other had for the most part overcome his demons.

After a couple hours of conversing about Mr. Carl's recovery, family matters, and Anita's forthcoming marriage and her and Keith's 1 year old daughter Aneeka's birthday party, Ryat then decided to tell them about Tanell. Explaining to them everything from how they finally met to everything Tanell had told him regarding his mother's tragic death. He told them how he believed Tanell's version of what happened and how Tanell was genuinely shocked to find out that his mother tried to sell the drugs for him that fateful morning. How Tanell had believed all those years like everybody else that her death was a retaliation for the life he took. Yet Ryat also explained to them how he still couldn't get past his resentment for the man enough to even speak with him any further. Surprisingly enough to him, Anita and Mr. Carl also believed Tanell's version after Ryat explained it and even more surprising was them encouraging him to form some aspect of a relationship with the man from which he came. Telling him how they even felt bad for Tanell having to go through all those years believing his son had died in his mother's belly which they also expressed their regrets about.

Mr. Carl then with a sober mind for the first time in decades explained to Ryat how after his mother's death they needed someone to blame which easily made Tanell culpable. So they immediately in their ignorance directed their hate

towards him. Mr. Carl expressed how he now felt
bad after hearing how Tanell had even advised
Ashely about not involving herself in his
affairs. Knowing how much he loved her, Mr. Carl
then along with Anita further surprised Ryat by
telling him to ask Tanell for their forgiveness for
using him as some form of psychological weapon.
In exacting their hate on him by not even making
him aware of his own son's survival and birth.

 After the visit Ryat had a lot on his mind as
he sat in his cell until night yard. He then
immediately went out and found Tanell alone, as
he'd been a lot lately, reading Islamic literature
while standing under the light post at the farthest
end of the yard. Ryat walked up to him and after a
few awkward seconds, he began telling Tanell what
his aunt and grandfather had expressed during their
visit. Which brought on a sense of serenity for
Tanell to hear of Mr. Carl and Anita finally letting
go of their hate for him and even asking for his
forgiveness. Tanell told Ryat that the next time he
talked to them could he tell them that it was he who
should be asking for their forgiveness for the
choices he made that still lead up to what happened.

 Tanell and Ryat soon found themselves
engrossed in a deep conversation ranging from
Tanell and Ashely's life together to Ryat' s
childhood. The conversation soon got deeply
intimate as Ryat learned a great deal about his

mother outside of what his family had told him. It moved him to learn how much she and Tanell really loved one another.

Over the next few months they both learned a lot about one another, especially how ironically their fatherless upbringings were so closely related. Tanell learned of how much his non-presence in his son's life had led to so many traumatic experiences that made Ryat the vicious young boy he had heard so much about.

It wasn't long before Tanell suggested that they become cellmates. Ryat was initially reluctant but soon obliged as he was starting to enjoy the bond they were forming. Shortly after becoming cellmates, Tanell commenced to edifying Ryat in hopes that he would stop the cycle with his son.

"Let me ask you Ryat, why is it that you always refer to me and every other black man as nigga? And refer to every sistah as a bitch?" inquired Tanell one day as he laid across his bottom bunk while Ryat lay across his top bunk on his back with his arms spread eagle behind his head.

Twisting up his face, Ryat responded as if Tanell had asked one of the most stupid questions he had ever heard, *"because that's just how we talk in da hood, you know like that's my nigga or that's my bitch. It ain't like I'm disrespecting just because I use those words."*

"But you are disrespecting because no matter what context you use those words they were created to be derogatory. Do you even know what

you're saying? Like you may know that a bitch is a female dog but do you know that the term you use it in was created for and likened to a female who is promiscuous or one that yaps and complains to much because a female dog in heat will mate with any male dog that sniffs behind her or for the simple fact the female dog is a ceaseless barker."

"Damn that's deep, I never knew that or even thought about it."

"Right, like most ignorant young men. So, let me ask you how could you use such a word as a term of endearment in any sense. Like how could you say something like that's my bitch or just call any and every woman a bitch then in the same sense say that your mother and sister aren't bitches. Better yet to call another black male nigga or nigger no matter how you say it is worse because the word is a derivative of the word Negro which comes from the Latin root Necro, which means dead! So, when you call another black male nigga, you're calling him a dead man just like the white male seen you to justify their lack of humanity during slavery. They deemed you as mentally dead therefore inhumane. And the sad reality is that the average young ignorant black male is keeping their sinister perspective alive and self-perpetuating throughout each commencing generation which is destroying the black nation as a whole."

After that conversation, Ryat instead of being obstinate like his usual-self decided to embrace what his long-lost father was trying to embed in him. Therefore, he made up his mind to eradicate the words bitch and nigga from his lexicon. Like everything else insightful Tanell inculcated him with, it gradually became a part of his make-up.

Chapter 25

"When you fall, don't analyze where you have fallen; analyze where you stumbled."

-Hannibal Afrik

IT WAS the middle of winter when both Ryat and Mil got the news of Bryce's shoot-out with police which lead to two police officers along with Bryce in critical condition. This happened after a squadron of police raided the Super 8 hotel where Bryce was staying to arrest him for an outstanding murder warrant. The second the squadron bust down the hotel door Bryce opened fire with his .50 caliber Desert Eagle. Nailing two of the initial officers through the door before he was hit several times in the upper torso.

After spending three weeks in I.C.U. cuffed to a hospital bed, Bryce was taken from the hospital to the police station and charged ironically with the death of Lurelle Mullins Jr. and the attempted homicide of two police officers. He was then taken to an interrogation room and pressed for over four hours about his involvement in a number of homicides that his gun had been linked too. They badgered and threatened him to no end about the fact that he would be sentenced to die after being convicted of all the bodies they planned to pen on him off the gun found in his possession. Where after four hours of raucous denials and inviting the detectives to his penis, Bryce in a surprising turn of events sat down with his lawyer and the detectives.

They worked out a deal for life in prison if Bryce told them of all the grisly murders he committed with the gun. In a 6 hour-long taped interview Bryce admitted to 13 murders with the gun dating back ten years to the murder of Juan Malone. All of which he put extra emphasis on the fact that he committed the murders alone like the proof they had that he had acted alone in the Lurelle Mullins Jr. case. Wherefore one of the first crimes he took sole responsibility for was the murder of Bennett "Bo" Green and the attempted homicide of Eric "Rip" Bryant.

Receiving the news of Bryce's admission to the crimes in which they were committed for, Ryat and Mil's attorney's immediately put in a motion for Post-Conviction Relief under newly discovered evidence. Where after a year of waiting for the court's decision on their freedom and 6 years of imprisonment, Ryat and Mil's convictions were vacated. Therefore, they regained their freedom at approximately 12:01 a.m, on a Tuesday. Just before Ryat left his cell for the last time, Tanell seemed more elated than him as they finally shared a long hug.

It was then that Tanell used their last moment together to impart his last bit of jewels to his long-lost son before he left from behind those walls.

"Ryat please remember this for me and most importantly for your son. Remember that Manhood defined is a state of being, consciousness wherein a male willingly accepts his societal responsibilities. A man seeks self-knowledge/wisdom, then acts upon it; A man is humble; A man is prepared for multiple situations A man is trustworthy; A man is a critical and consequential thinker; A man is a consciously spiritual and intellectual being; A man is not materialistic but seeks financial stability; A man masters his emotions; A man has a conscious knowledge of right and wrong; A man is exemplary; A man is humane; A man is responsive/responsible to his own children and others; A man has a collective consciousness and accountability...

Ryat I need you to understand these principles. Understand that there's a big difference between a man and an existing male. Males are born every day but you don't become a man because you grow physically into the embodiment of one. One must consciously choose to became a man but most never realize this therefore they go through life as nothing more than existing males. Ryat you have to this choice or the cycle will just continue with your son. "

"No doubt...Understood;" replied Ryat as they broke away from their embrace staring into each other's eyes that welled with tears of joy and pain.

It was a cold morning as Ryat and Mil stood elated beyond words outside of their respective prisons. Ryat with a broad smile ran straight into the arms of Asaria who stuck by him throughout the entire ordeal. He then snatched up Lil Ray in a bear hug, who stood hesitant close by his mother with a shy smile on his face. Whereas Mil with a broad smile ran into the group hug of his mother, sister, and daughter. All who stood by him unconditionally and who were beyond joyous to see him a free man. Instead of the misguided young male he was when he went in. Missing was Mil' s first love Essie and the mother of his daughter who like most guys sentenced to years of imprisonment, she moved on with her life. Thereby finding another man to fill the empty void Mil left to whom she had more kids with during Mil's time away. Which like most guys in his predicament, Mil experienced the hurt but cloaked it with hate directed towards her. Yet with some time, unlike most guys in his predicament, he got over his anger towards her by putting it in its proper perspective. Reasoning that it wasn't she who left him but he who actually left her. A young single mother with a lot of living and growing to do on her own. Therefore, he realized that he couldn't mentally subjugate her because of his poor decision.

A week had gone by since regaining their freedom as Ryat and Mil spent most of their time with family getting reacquainted. One of the first things each of them did was contact Bryce professing their love and undying fidelity. Months soon went by as each of them did their best to work different jobs given to them by temp. agencies. All while they were both ceaselessly looking for permanent work. Ryat was quickly becoming unsettled with his new life. Being a creature of habit, he slowly ingratiated himself back into the game by first being around Boody during most of his off time.

Ryat instantly noticed while riding with Boody through the city streets all the things that had changed. The newly erected buildings, the new business', the renovated projects that now resembled Town Homes, the newer futuristic looking vehicles. Then there were what seemed to be an increase in abandoned homes with smoldered looks that probably took some innocent lives in the process. There were the older model abandon vehicles that lined most of the city streets. The younger generation of thugs who from their physiques looked to be strung out on crack but were mere products of the designer drug age. Whom were mostly the little brothers and nephews of Ryat's friends, enemies, and associates. All who simply filled their relative's spot once they went on to prison or died in those streets. Through all this Ryat noticed one constant, that the game remained the same. There was still drug dealers and drug buyers, users and abusers, debauch capitalist and those who are capitalized upon.

All the while Boody was pretty much running the streets with a deadly iron fist. Ryat quickly realized that Boody and his crew the *"YoungBullz"* were far too reckless and prone to violence in their affairs. He knew in order to never see the pen again like he planned he had to distance himself from Boody. Therefore, he contacted his old connect out in D.C. who were a little leery of him and how he got out of his predicament. Yet in a show of faith in him from their past dealings they agreed to sell him two bricks and front him two, Which Ryat seen as his opportunity to get back where he once was and make enough to live comfortably. Oddly enough he felt comfortable for the first time since returning home.

Meanwhile Mil was doing everything within his power to be an honest working man that provided for his daughter and family. Yet the drain of working for next to nothing was really starting to take a toll on him as he still hadn't found a permanent job. His financial struggles were really beginning to become a burden. Being as though before when he was home he was used to living a certain way where finances were the least of his worries. Now he was broke because of legal fees and being liberal with his family while on the inside.

Therefore, when Ryat made him aware of his plans, explaining how the hustle would only be short lived until they got enough money to live comfortably, Mil was reluctant. Yet the more Ryat pressed him, making his plans sound all the more tempting, and expressed emphatically how he couldn't get tack involved without him, MLtl then of his own volition after weighing the risk and rewards obliged Ryat. \vhere they then made plans to make the trip to D.C. in two weeks.

In the meantime, Ryat had other plans as he was being processed into the Lewisburg Federal Penitentiary. He waited impatiently for over a half hour before Roe came walking through the visiting room doors with a broad smile plastered across his face.

"Damn. it's good seeing you youngen. It's good to see, you know like Hov said, that at least one of us made it, " greeted Roe as he came within a foot of Ryat. But quickly changed his approach as his smile immediately faded after Ryat didn't stand to greet him and telling from his body language, Ryat obviously had a major problem with him.

Ryat wanting to act off impulse decided not to make the same mistake he did with his father out of ignorance. Therefore, he would get the facts before reacting, thereby giving Roe a chance to explain his side.

"So, you and my father were celly's about twenty-six years ago, and you set up a deal, where he was supposed to have his people meet with one of your people to sell him some bricks?" inquired Ryat as he glared into the eyes of Roe who sat across from him.

"Hold up, hold up, what the...what are you talking about youngen? I don't even know who your father is and what the fu-"

"Muthafucka you can't to play dumb! I'm talking bout Tanell being my father and that faggot you sent to make the deal murdered my mother while she was nine months pregnant with me!"

"Oh shit!" blurted Roe while holding Ryat's menacing stare as his addled expression quickly changed with realization.

"Hold up youngen, believe me when I tell you this first and foremost, I'm truly sorry for what happened to your mother. Just like I was when your father was my celly when it first happened. Listen you know I had nothing but genuine love for you all these years. I never knew that was your father or she was your mother and I would have never done no grimy shit like that. I was just trying to help your father in his situation at the time and as far as I was lead to believe, your mother was murdered in retaliation. And from what I know the deal never went down but now it all makes sense because that faggot muthafucka I sent to make the deal did just blew up out of nowhere at the time."

Ryat in his heart believed everything Roe told him, coupled with the fact that Roe showed genuine empathy and never broke eye contact. Which Ryat knew breaking eye contact indicates stress and possible deception.

"So, who was the faggot muthafucka you sent to make the deal?"

Two days later Ryat was in Atlanta for Black College Week. A place where a lot of out-of-towners were at the time for vacation and parties. Yet Ryat was there simply on a mission as he leaned impatiently against a rental car in the parking garage of a very prominent and luxurious hotel on Peachtree street. He watched as Kevin came walking from an elevator towards the rental car. His head down, twirling keys in his right hand while humming the melody to a new Ne-yo tune.

Startled at the sight of a man when he lifted his head as he came within a few feet of his rental car, Kevin exclaimed, *"Oh shit! What the fuck?!"*

Then after almost jumping out of his skin and a closer inspection of who it was leaning against his rental, Kevin said, *"damn is that you Ryat? What you doing down here? Where's Mil?"*

"Mil couldn't make it and maybe that's a good thing for you cause I'm pretty sure he wouldn't like how you spent the whole night cheating on his moms with that fine piece you had in your 'tel room."

"Aww man youngen tha-"

"Look I don't need no explanation, it's really none of my business. I'm not here to bust your chops or nothing. I'm actually here because I need a ride."

"Well where do you need a ride too and how did you know where I was at and that this was my car?" inquired Kevin, leery of Ryat and as always uneasy in his presence.

"You know I got my ways Kev," replied Ryat with an impish smirk as he glared at Kevin.

"But that's neither here nor there Kev and I don't really know the name of the place I need a ride to but I know where it's at so I can show you how to get there."

"Alright," responded Kevin, becoming leerier of Ryat by the second.

They then got into Kevin's Dodge Charger rental car and began their route to Ryat's destination. Besides Ryat giving Kevin directions, the conversation was held to a minimal. Suddenly, before Kevin realized it, he was pulling into an old desolate industrial zone.

"Damn yo Ryat, where you got me going cuz?" asked Kevin with a hint of paranoia in his tone as he looked towards Ryat.

With a nefarious look now showing on his face as Kevin stared at him apprehensively, Ryat with his right hand pulled a .357 magnum from his waist.

"Pussy shut the fuck up and pull into that spot over there," hissed Ryat as he gestured with his left hand for Kevin to pull into the garage door type opening of a warehouse like structure. All the while placing the barrel of his gun on the bridge of Kevin's nose.

"Oh and by the way Kev, does this type of gun look familiar?"

"Come on youngen this is me. I know you ain't bout to rob ME! Come on man I know you just came home and you trying get right but you ain't got to rob me. You know I'll look out," pleaded Kevin as he began to have a panic attack.

"Nah, you know what Kev, unlike you, I ain't here to rob you of your crumbs like you did my mother," said Ryat placidly with a wicked smile on his face as his eyes bore into Kevin who had just pulled to a stop inside the desolate warehouse. *"You know Kev, like when you murdered her like the lil bitch you are and left me for dead inside her."*

Now trembling, pale, and wide eyed with horror written all over his face. Kevin realized the inevitable that he feared all these years was coming to fruition. As it goes what is done in the dark shall come to light. The seed of Kevin's dirty little secret was coming back to reap or better yet as the Reaper.

"Please, please, listen yo I...I never meant for that to...to happen...I was young, dumb and angry. I...I never meant to do that to your mother...I ...I..." pleaded Kevin with tears now streaming down his face. *"See youngen I was just mad at your*

dad for getting my girl Nia pregnant so to get him back, when Roe set the deal up I had a hidden agenda to rob your dad's people of his last. But then your mom showed up to make the deal and before I knew it one thing lead to another. All I remember is thinking about your dad getting my girl pregnant so before I knew it, it just happened. You have to believe me Ryat, please, I regret it so much, please youngen, I...I-I don't want to die. Pleeease Ryat don't kill me I swear I'll turn myself in, I swear. You have to believe me, please don't kill me!"

Ryat then after hearing everything Kevin said, stared at him stone faced for a second poised to murder him. Then suddenly Ryat began experiencing a sort of convulsion as he began to violently shake with the gun in his hand still pointed at Kevin. His eyes also began rolling into the back of his head. Kevin seen this as an opening to save his life but afraid, knowing any act of offense would surely cost him his life, he decided against it. Meanwhile Ryat for that fraction of a second in time vicariously found himself there that fateful day witnessing his mother's grisly murder. He watched as his mother with pleading eyes and tears running down her face held firmly onto a bag just before Kevin cold bloodedly fired two shots directly into her chest.

As Ryat came back to his senses he considered Kevin's face. It displayed the same pleading look in his eyes and tears running down his face.

Ryat suddenly thought of how his mother wouldn't want this and of the last conversation he had with his father about manhood and ending the cycle. He then with a look of forgiveness in his eyes put his head down for a split second. Kevin who already had his head down between his legs sobbing, slowly lifted his tear ridden face with his arms still between his legs, focusing his attention back on Ryat. Who then looked right back up at Kevin with tears now running down his face.

"You know what Kev, it's not my job to judge you. Only God can do that and I've learned in order to release this hate from my heart I have to forgive you. So Kev I truly forgive you man," said a contrite melancholic sounding Ryat as he then again lowered his head while slowly shaking it from side to side.

"Aww man thanks Ryat, I swear I'll turn myself in. I'm so sorry man, thanks man," responded Kevin with relief written all over his face as he thanked God he wasn't gone have to do what moments ago, he planned to do to save his life.

"Yeah Kev and now I'ma give you a chance to find out if my mother forgives you," hissed Ryat in an almost inaudible whisper as he raised his now dry face towards Kevin with a sinister look back in his eyes.

"Huh?" breathed Kevin, wide eyed with trepidation just before Ryat raised his gun and blasted him twice in the face.

The first shot pierced his forehead as the inertia from it slammed his head against the drivers side window, instantly killing him.

Ryat then calmly got out of the car, walked. to one end of the warehouse like structure and found a group of 55 gallon drums clustered together. Locating the one he was looking for, he lifted the lid and dropped his gun in the vat of acid. He then calmly walked to the opposite end of the warehouse and jumped inside a car he had previously parked there. Pulling off into the afternoon sun with thoughts of the irony in the name his uncle gave him upon birth. Which the meaning of to him seemed perfect in representing his manifest destiny.

Chapter 26

*"Our destiny is largely in our own hands. If
we find, we shall have to seek. If we succeed in the
race for life it must be by our own energies, and our
own exertions. Others may clear the road, but we
must go forward or be left behind in the race for
life. If we remain poor and dependent, the wealth of
others will not avail us. If we are ignorant, the
intelligence of others will do but little for us. If we
are foolish, the wisdom of others will not guide us.
If we are wasteful of our time and money, the
economy of others will only make our destination
the more disgraceful."*

-Frederick Douglass

INSIDE THE municipal building on 11th
street in Philadelphia PA, sat Karen Smalls behind
the reception desk for the Social Service Agency
inside the building. She was engrossed in an e-mail
on her computer when she heard a small folder
sound hit her desk. Which she immediately focused
her attention towards. She instantly laid eyes on a
small children's book instead. The cover showed a
cartoon picture of a mother duck and her ducklings
on the front. The title read; *The Search for Mother*

Geete's Lost Duckling. Recognizing what she had just laid her eyes upon, Karen suddenly became breathless as her heart began to beat rapidly. She slowly lifted her head towards the figure standing before her.

To her initial surprise and shock stood before her the first born of her three children. A broad smile plastered across his face. This being the same child she gave up at birth to afford him a better life because she surmised at the time that she couldn't give it to him. That coupled with the fact that she did not want him growing up under his father's shadow who in the late 80's and early 90's was a vicious drug lord. That ran a very pernicious gang out of north Philly whom had no regard for human life in their daily motives.

"How you doing Momma? I've been searching for you my whole life," said Boody, purely elated as he watched his mother's shocked reaction at the sight of him.

"Oh my...Oh my God," responded Karen breathlessly, at a loss for words as she stared at the reason for her life's work in helping fractured family's. This being the son she regretted so much giving up and went out of her way 11 years ago to get back. Yet just when the courts ruled in her favor she got the news that her son had run away from the foster home where he was living. This news rendered her completely distraught for years as she began to think she would never see her long lost son again. She now couldn't even find the words to

express how much joy she felt in her heart as she took a good look at him from toe to head. As she stared at him, though she felt extreme love and joy she couldn't help but notice how he had grown into the exact physical image and embodiment of his father. Upon which she also took notice of the jewelry that decorated his wrist, fingers, and neck. The platinum Gucci link chain hanging from his neck displaying a diamond encrusted pendant that read "YBZ". She realized in that instant that not only was he the physical image and embodiment of his father but he was also a modern-day replica of a life she made her decision after his birth to protect him from. A life that had his father sitting on death row.

$¢

Nothing brought Tanell much joy these days except for the days when he received mail from his son. Though Ryat rarely corresponded with him, Asaria wrote him constantly which resulted in them developing a strong bond. As Tanell through Asaria's consistent letters got the blessing of vicariously witnessing his grandson's childhood and growth.

He walked in his cell that day after Jumu'ah service and an envelope with Asaria's name sat on the floor. Tanell picked it up and in no time was at the desk in his cell tearing the envelope open. The first thing that fell from inside the envelope was a picture of Ryat and little Ray standing side by side with identical smiles plastered across their faces. Smiles that Tanell recognized as his own. This instantly put a smile on his face. He then read Asaria's letter in which she told him about Lil Ray's first full year of school, about how Ryat had proposed to her just days prior and how they all planned to visit him within the coming weeks.

Tanell then with a loving smile still stretching the surface of his face, picked the picture back up, staring at his son and grandson as he ruminated on his life's journey thus far. He arrived at the perspective of how most people live in a world that knows the cost of everything but the value of nothing. He then thought of a quote that touched him deep in his soul at that point, from Mark Twain: *"Twenty years from now you will be more disappointed by the things you didn't do than by the ones you did do."*

Ryat was in route to pick up Mil for their trip to D.C. when his aunt Anita called him over to her house, stating it was an emergency. He immediately made his way there, fearing the worst, blowing past red lights in the process. Once there, he ran inside his aunt's house only to find nothing wrong. It was actually the opposite of what he expected as the first sight he saw once inside the house was his little cousin Aneeka. Anita and Keith's daughter, playing Barbie dolls with one of her friends in the middle of the living room floor. With her having her back towards him he decided to catch her by surprise. So he crept up behind her and in one swift motion lightly touched her and yelled, *"Boo!"*

Except for when the startled little girl turned around, it wasn't Aneeka. Aneeka was the one he thought was the friend whom now also looked towards him startled with doe eyes. Ryat then focusing his attention back on the little girl he had spooked, suddenly noticed that she looked to be about 10 years old, 3 years older than Aneeka. Yet as Ryat stared at the little girl he was suddenly left breathless as she looked like an exact identical miniature version of his late mother. He slowly turned his attention to the figure standing behind him who happened to be Tiffany, his first love.

"I'm sorry Ryat. I know I' m wrong for not letting you know all these years. At first I was just so mad at you and being young and ignorant didn't help either. I kept trying to reason with myself that I didn't want her apart of your lifestyle and before I knew it time flew by. I'm so sorry for the both of you...her name is Rayne, " said Tiffany with her

arms crossed as a single tear streamed from her right eye.

Ryat stood genuinely shocked and at a loss for words as he looked from Tiffany towards Anita who stood off behind Tiffany.

Rayne? He thought as his mind momentarily flashed back to one of the last intimate moments he and Tiffany shared together on the hotel balcony that night in the rain. He then focused his attention back on the beautiful little girl whom was an exact replica of his mother. Her addled innocent stare breaking him down as he dealt with a wealth of ambivalence.

"So Ryat you mean to tell me she kept that little girl from you all these years?" inquired Mil as they pulled away from his house in route to D.C.

"Yeah man, it's crazy. I was at a loss for words the whole tine. It was like in that instance I hated Tiff for that shit but at the same time I couldn't express it because I instantly fell in love with that little girl...man she's so beautiful...she looks just like my mother. I told Tiff I was going to get her when I get back. That way I can start the process of us getting to know each other. Plus, I

plan on introducing her to Lil Ray and Ria right away."

"Damn word, that's what's up. I can't wait to see the lil beauty. Oh, anyway yo, you heard they found Kev slumped down in Atlanta? They think it was a robbery that went bad because when they pulled his body from the car he was killed in, they say he was clutching a gun between his legs."

Ryat then doing his best to show a look of shock, found it not hard to do after hearing the irony in that Kevin was most-likely about to murder him. To prevent from having to turn himself in after he thought Ryat's forgiveness meant he would live.

"Nah I ain't even hear about that shit. How's ya folks taking it?"

"I mean my sister taking it kinda hard. My moms seem cool though. You already know how I see it, fuck it shit happens," said Mil with a look of pure apathy on his face just before he noticed the police headlights a little distance behind them.

"Oh shit! Yo Ryat you see this shit?"

"Yea yea, I see it," replied Ryat frantically as he stared at the two sets of police lights gaining on them as they were riding south down Cameron street.

Both of their minds immediately centered on the two guns and 42 thousand dollars in cash inside the car as well as the bulletproof vest each of them wore. They knew this was enough to send them both back to jail for a very long time. Therefore, they both resolved that they would rather die than go back to jail and suffer all sorts of mental torture. All while their prime years rolled by as feebleness set in. Ryat then put the petal to the metal with the police cars in hot pursuit as Mil firmly gripped his glock poised to shoot if need be. Altering their route, Ryat made a hard right from Cameron onto Maclay towards the Maclay street bridge.

As they made their way across the bridge, with their guns out ready to shoot their way out of a jam, the police cruisers had gained on them and were now neck and neck with the Ford station wagon they were in. Yet as Ryat and Mil were preparing to shoot, they suddenly noticed that the police cruisers were no longer neck and neck with them. The police were now ahead of them and looked to not have been chasing them at all. One of the police officers behind the wheel of one of the police cruisers looked towards them with an addled expression as he flew past them.

Ryat and Mil then breathed a sigh of relief as Ryat slowed the car down and looked towards Mil with pure relief written all over his face. Mil's face showed the same sense of tranquility while returning the silent stare. Neither of the two needed to say a thing as that moment made them appreciate how lucky and blessed each of them felt. 'They both then decided to put a halt to their trip and park after such a close call. They made their way to an alleyway adjacent to Emerald Park where they parked the station wagon and made their way to a bench inside the park.

"Man, that shit was crazy cuz, you seent that? I thought for sure we were goners and all I could think about was how it wasn't even worth it," said Mil, followed by a light chuckle then with a serious look on his face.

"Aye Ryat...I'm done man. That had to be a sign."

"Yeah man, that shit was crazy, All I could think about was lil Ray and my daughter who I just met. I wasn't going back to prison Mil. All I could think about was how much those kids need me man. And just to think that situation could have been the end of me."

"Yea I feel you Ryat, I'm wit you man. Like I told you all I could think about was how that potential money or whatever wasn't even worth it when you really weigh the risk and rewards of the situation. You know what Ryat, one of the most; insightful things I learned in prison was how integral a father's role is in a child's development. Like a father teaches a boy the benefits of being a real man and what a real man is. That way that boy don't grow up misguided like us. Having the wrong concept of what a real man is like. We thought the dude on the corner with all the money, cars, and fine females was the man. Whereas the father also is the one that teaches the little girl her true value. That way she knows her true self-worth and don't just let any man treat her less than her true worth. That way by knowing her true worth she won't go seeking attention from any and every man to fill the

void of the fatherly male attention she lacked during her formative years."

"Damn Mil, I definitely feel what you saying. It's crazy cause I remember Ria used to always tell me before I went to prison how much my son needed me. Saying how a father is a boy's first hero and a girl's first love. That shit used to really have me thinking when I was in prison. Then I found out that eighty percent of fatherless children come into contact with the criminal justice system at some point in their lives. That really had me thinking bout my own fatherless childhood and how much that may have played a role. Then it's crazy cause it's like I met my father in prison and all I could think about was how I didn't want that for lil Ray."

Ryat and Mil then sat in a pensive trance for a moment reflecting on their fatherless childhood's and how they wanted nothing more than to give their children the father that they never had.

"You want to know what's even more crazy and ironic now that I remember and we're pretty much talking bout it?" asked Mil, pausing for a second to fully absorb his surroundings. *"Man, Ryat this is the same bench we sat on about twelve years ago, when we was bucks, before we even thought about the game. Talking bout how out of me, you, Hochee, Bryce, Potta, Lati, and Melvin, all of our fathers was either in jail or dead except for Melvin. And look we all either been in jail, is in jail, or dead except for Melvin."*

"*Damn that's deep Mil. I never even thought about that.*"

"*Yeah Ryat man, the shit's deep man. That's why I'm telling you man straight up, I'm done with this so-called game that we risk our lives to lose at, and even if you do win, do you really? Cause at the cost it takes to win, when you look back with all your money, is it really worth it after all the lives lost in the process? I guess that's for one to weigh himself but I know for me…I got to be there for my kid's man.*"

"*No doubt Mil, I'm wit you man. I'm done with this shit too man. Like Ria keep telling me, lil Ray need me and now I find out I got a daughter that needs me,*" said Ryat as he and Mil both then spent the next 15 minutes staring off into space pensively.

"*Aye I'ma get up wit you later then. I'm bout to go head and spend some time wit my daughter cause more than ever right now I feel blessed,*" said Mil, breaking the silence.

"*No doubt, I guess I'ma go head and take this blessing to introduce my daughter to lil Ray and Ria.*"

"*Al'ight man. Brothers for life,*" said Mil as he and Ryat embraced after they stood to leave from the bench.

Ryat then triggered by Mil's statement, thought of the irony in it before casually responding with, "*Yeah ain't no doubt about that. Nothing trumps blood.*"

"Blood?...Yo what you talking bout cuz?" asked Mil with an addled expression on his face.

"I'm saying I know where I get my looks from, my mom. But you look just like OUR father," responded Ryat with an impish smile stretching the surface of his face.

"Wha-what?!"

"Yeah man Mil, just ask your mom. I'm pretty sure she can tell you better than I can. You'll like him though. Matter of fact you should go check him out after your mom tells you everything. I'm pretty sure he'd be surprised too."

"Yo what the Fuck you talking bout Ryat!" exclaimed Mil, addled and in shock.

"Mil just go ask your mom man. It's time she told you anyway. I'ma catch up wit you later," said Ryat as he was walking away.

45 minutes later, Ryat was walking up the steps to his house holding his daughter's hand when he noticed Ria pulling up in her car with lil Ray in the passenger seat.

"Yo where yall coming from dressed up like yall coming from a funeral?" asked Ryat as Asaria and lil Ray emerged from the car.

"That's because we ARE coming from a funeral, my father's funeral. You know Ryat, the one I've been telling you about ever since he passed eight days ago, but of course you don't remember Ryat because your too busy trying to get caught back up in a life that almost put you away until you were damn near sixty," hissed Asaria as she came

within a foot of Ryat, thrusting her father's obituary in his face with apparent indignation.

"Oh I'm so sorry beautiful. I didn't see you there. How are you doing?" greeted Asaria to Rayne with a smile now gracing her face.

"Fine," responded Rayne in a modest melodic tone as she innocently smiled back at Asaria.

Asaria then quickly turned her attention back towards Ryat, who was staring with ambivalence at her father's obituary. *"Ryat who's this beautiful little girl right here?"*

Ryat then looking as if he was on the edge of a nervous breakdown, looked away from the obituary towards Asaria and asked hesitantly, *"Aye...uh...Ria...Vi-Victor George is your father?"*

"Yeah, I been told you my father's name, didn't I Ryat?" replied Asaria with a look on her face as if Ryat had asked a stupid question and she didn't understand his seemingly sudden befuddlement.

Ryat in that instant became unconscious of everything around him as he looked from the obituary of the man who killed his uncle towards his son, his uncles namesake. Where he suddenly noticed that his son had the same eyes he stared into after Victor murdered the man who was basically a father to him. Yet instead of feeling any sense of negative emotions, Ryat for the first time since he was 9 years old suddenly felt a sense of serenity wash over him. Whereas the fire that was kindled inside him so many years prior, that then came to a simmer, then ablaze, resulting in an inferno that raged in his heart, was finally extinguished. By a deep love and empirical understanding in the true value of life.